Laurel Ridge

Seven Ways to Love

Diana Stout

Cover design by R.C. Matthews
Formatting by
Sharpened Pencils Productions LLC
Cairn Terriers photo by DepositPhotos 85311254

Paperback ISBN-13: 979-8-9870751-3-5

DEDICATION

For anyone who still believes.

Also by Diana Stout

Epic Fantasy

Grendel's Mother

Romance

Determined Hearts

Love's New Beginnings

Tomorrow's Wish for Love

Laurel Ridge Novella Series

Shattered Dreams #1

Burning Desire #2

Arrested Pleasures #3

Buried Hearts #4

Tangled Passions #5

Reserved Yearnings #6

Sweet Cravings #7

Literary / Short Story

Maggie's Story

Anthology / Collections

Lost and Found (contributor & editor, anthology)

Screenplays published as books

David & Goliath

Charlie's Christmas Carole

Nonfiction

The Super Simple Easy Basic Cookbook

Finding Your Fire & Keeping It Hot

CONTENTS

ACKNOWLEDGEMENTS

Without the support and encouragement of my writer friends, including members of The Keyboard Cafe—a daily Zoom write-in, this series would have never been completed.

A special thank you to beta readers Linda Bradley, Anne Stone, Diane Flannery, Linda Fletcher, and Lucy Kubash. And a special heartfelt thank you to Patty Gordon who beta read all seven stories.

And, I can't forget my cover artist, R.C. Matthews, who does amazing work and quickly, too. Thank you for getting me and understanding my visions.

Author's Note

Instead of chapters, I have *Day* headings. Why?

All seven novellas in this series take place within the same 15 days. Not every story starts on Day 1 or ends on Day 15, when the big celebratory party takes place and where all characters are present in the final seventh novella.

The seven couples move in and out of each other's stories, along with minor characters.

Laurel Ridge is a small-town community of classmates, best friends, ex-lovers, second chances, and a mystery involving a 1969 Volkswagen Beetle fished out of the community's Lake Whippoorwill on Day 1.

Seven couples, seven conflicts, seven romances.

To help you remember these characters, I've provided a character list and legend, plus provided the pairings of classmates, best friends, roommates, and so forth. This legend is located at the back of the book.

Laurel Ridge
Seven Ways to Love

Diana Stout

Shattered Dreams #1

Is it too late to rekindle the love they shared 12 years ago or will their dreams be shattered forever?

Day 1

Mason Baylock opened the diner door, wondering if tonight he'd finally get to talk to Shelley alone. He was frustrated at how she'd been avoiding him. At the same time, he was willing to wait her out.

The tinkling sound overhead reminded him to duck to avoid smacking his forehead on the little brass bell. A quick glance revealed the diner was empty. Good. He hoped it would stay that way. He'd been frequenting the diner often enough hoping for just this opportunity. Since Shelley refused to go out with him or give him her phone number, he had no choice but to become one of her customers.

In her sight, in her mind was his motto.

Connie, whose age Mason guessed to range anywhere between retirement and infinity, came through the swinging doors that led to the kitchen, while slipping her arm into a sweater. Seeing him, she grinned, giving him the usual greeting. "Howdy, Mason."

She hung her apron on a peg by the door, then

stopped at the mirror on the wall behind the register and fluffed her chin-length gray hair, for all the good it did. It always looked windblown. Each move was pure habit, and she never omitted one part of the routine, a ritual that Mason had first observed when he was no more than knee-high to his little red wagon.

"Going home, Connie?"

"Want to come along, Judge?"

Mason chuckled. It was a running joke with them, ever since his return half a year ago. The small community of Laurel Ridge where he'd been born and raised, located an hour north of Albany, Georgia, hadn't changed a bit. He lowered his voice purposefully, emphasizing his southern drawl, an accent that had returned rather quickly, knowing full well she expected a retort. Connie was the epitome of a flirt. "And do what?"

"Ah, a big strong guy like you? I'm sure we can find something creative to do."

Mason bent his six-foot-six frame to her five-feet one-inch height and kissed her on the cheek.

"You're good for the ego, even if you are a baby," she said.

"Baby?"

"You're barely thirty."

"Thirty-two."

"Like I said. Too young for me. Besides, you work too hard." She tilted her head toward the large window that dominated the diner and framed the courthouse across the street. "Saw you leave with your good buddy, Cutter. What'd he done now?"

"Got sentenced."

Connie looked horror struck. "No. Not Cutter."

Mason took her hand and patted it. "Get the gruesome thoughts out of your mind, Connie. He just ran into some problems with the game warden."

"Annie? That sweet little thing." She chuckled. "Nothing new there. He probably did it on purpose."

"Cutter doesn't know it, yet, but that sweet little thing has him sighted in her scope, and before he can blink, he's going to be bagged and tagged. And probably in that order. He thinks she adores him. She'll have him arrested before he even knows what happened. His bad boy behavior doesn't impress her a bit."

"Annie arrested him?"

"Not this time. It was another game warden."

Connie shook her head. "That boy thinks he's still fifteen and in high school."

"Yup. After Annie rejected him, he'd ask other girls out right after a relationship breakup. He bragged how they rarely said no."

"Bet that made him popular."

They both chuckled at her sarcasm. "Some of us tried to tell him differently, but you know that ego of his—wouldn't listen."

Connie burst out laughing. "Lord, I love a man who recognizes the way it really is."

"Isn't that what you've preached all these years, Connie? That y'all let us chase you until you let us catch you?"

"You're a credit to your sex, Judge. So how come a big stag like you hasn't claimed a doe for your own? You need to get out and display those antlers of yours." As he opened his mouth to respond, she turned toward the kitchen, and yelled. "Shelley! Customer! See ya' tomorrow."

From the kitchen came a muffled, "Bye."

She turned back to him. Performing the last of her ritual, she patted him on the arm. "Night, Judge."

The bell rang as she opened the door and again as the door closed behind her.

Mason eased into a booth in front of the window so he could observe his favorite time of day. Dusk. That golden moment between day and night.

The clunk of an empty mug set down in front of him brought his attention back inside. Turning his head, Mason found his sight line level to Shelley Willis' chest. She'd had the best figure of all the girls in their class. Still did some ten plus years later.

Quickly, he looked up. The last thing he wanted to do was embarrass Shelley. She looked tired. "Long day?" he asked.

*****

She wished he wasn't so observant. But then, that's what made him a good judge, so she'd heard. And what had made him such a good boyfriend—*Stop!* To be polite, she responded. "Yes." Inwardly, Shelley sighed. Even her toes ached. "The usual or something else?"

"How about a piece of apple pie à la mode?"

"Sure." Finished pouring Mason's coffee, Shelley

glanced out the window. "What in the world?"

The swirling amber light of a wrecker beaconed into the diner. Loaded on the flatbed was an old, but bright, canary yellow Volkswagen Bug shrouded in mud, weeds, and dripping water.

"Cutter was telling me about it," Mason said. "Apparently, he snagged it on his fishing line earlier."

"In the fishing contest? Cutter? Our Cutter who fishes from a tiny boat and swims like a three-year-old with flailing arms and legs?"

"The one and only," Mason said. "Told me he was only fishing for the prize money. Seems, he lost his hunting license for a year. Not that he ever hunted anything bigger than squirrels or rabbits. I doubt he has the patience to sit for hours waiting for a wild hog to show up. Doesn't want to do the real work."

"Was always wanting my notes in science class. Makes me wonder how he ever became an arborist. Whose car is it?"

"William's," Mason responded. "Had to have been all those hours spent in the forest—among the trees tracking those rabbits."

"What? Our can-do-no-wrong local librarian, William? The same perfect student who never got into trouble while we were in school?"

"Seems he drove it into the lake, some years back. Accidently, according to what I've heard through the courthouse grapevine. William never told anyone. Told his father he had sold it. Guess his father was furious—"

"I remember that! The car was a graduation gift

from his parents," Shelley said. "I remember him telling everyone he sold it because he didn't like the color. His father was so angry, he told William that he could buy the next car himself, with his own money. William became quite the walker after that. We always did wonder why."

"When did this happen? Him driving it into the lake?"

"That summer, a couple days after graduation, just after you..."

"Left?"

Shelley paused, feeling uncomfortable. "Yeah." She didn't like where the conversation was going. She moved toward the booth behind Mason, the one she hadn't cleared or cleaned earlier.

Fortunately, Mason changed the subject back to the car. "I doubt there's a mechanic around here that can fix what ails that car now. What a waste."

Shelley dropped her dishcloth on the table and started stacking the dirty plates. She glanced at Mason's coffee to see if she needed to refill his mug yet and noticed the newspaper he shook out in front of him. One headline in particular drew her attention: *Historic Home to be Auctioned.*

"No," she breathed.

He twisted around quickly. "Shelley?" His look was one of concern but also inquiring.

She pointed at the headline. "My house..."

Mason frowned. "Your house? This place belongs to the Browne family. Or rather the estate, now that ol' man Browne is dead. I heard the proceeds are going to Georgia University. Folks are saying more than likely that Eddie Taylor will get the property, that she's had her eye on it for years."

"That realtor is a bloodhound," Shelley spit out. "Her only goal is to line her own pockets. She'll demolish the house and put up a hotel, or worse yet, a motel that charges by the hour."

"You never did like her in high school, but you were best friends before that."

"I didn't like her new airs," she spit out. "She dumped me. Thought she was better than everyone else. Still does." She picked up some dishes from the table behind him, carried them behind the counter, dumping them into a bin under the counter.

"Now that you mention it, she did stop hanging with everyone that last year." He frowned. "Philandering spouses in area counties would love another motel here," he said, changing the subject. "Not to mention that we could use more tourists. Be good for the economy."

Shelley, returned to the table with a cloth to wipe it down. "But, what about the history of the house? Doesn't anyone care about that?"

"I didn't know you were interested in its history."

She shrugged her shoulders. "I love this town. It's old houses." She sighed in frustration but couldn't stop thinking about her dream. "I've always had plans for a day-care center on the ground floor, rooms on the second floor—with an elevator—for the elderly, plus a common kitchen and living area, a place that would be more reasonable than an expensive retirement home. I could convert the attic into a small apartment and live there myself. I picture them—the elderly—helping in the day-care. Children and old folks are meant to be together."

Damn. Talk about gushing! She'd just told him more in the last two minutes than she had in the last six months since his return. Information he didn't need to know. Hoping to sidetrack him, she decided to throw him a bone she knew he'd go after. "Plus, it'll let me get Gramps back home with me."

"You know Henry is better off where he is."

"Why? Because you said so? You separated us." Her outburst surprised even her. She thought she'd reconciled herself to Gramps no longer living with her. The truth was, she missed him. It wasn't the same just visiting him. There weren't enough hours in the day to see him every day, but see him every day she did. He was her last and only living relative. As an only child of parents who had no siblings, there were no cousins, aunts, or uncles. And, her parents had been killed in a car accident a few years ago.

"Honey, quit beating yourself up with that. You had no choice. Is that why you've been avoiding me since I've gotten back?" he asked.

She hated how he got right to the center of her issues with him. He'd always been like that. It was one of the reasons she'd fallen so hard for him, one of the reasons she'd tried to keep their conversations focused on food when he was here in the diner, and why she went out of her way to avoid him everywhere else.

"Well, it was one of the first cases on your docket," she admitted.

"I had no choice. He was a danger to himself and potentially to others. Granted, it never got more serious than his forgetting to wear pants that last time he decided to stroll down main street. It was just a matter of time before something more serious happened."

"Only because I can't be with him all day."

"And because there's no one else to look after him either."

"All right. You did what had to be done. For now. One way or another, I'm going to change that." Shelley sighed. "Though thanks to Eddie, it looks like it'll be later rather than sooner. I can't compete with her. My savings account is limited, so I guess that means my dream is gone. I could save forever and never be able to beat her bid. I don't get it. She could build a motel anywhere, so why go after a grand old house that can never be replaced?" Silently cursing, Shelley realized she'd said too much again.

After all she'd done to keep Mason from knowing anything about her life, she'd just gone and spilled her guts. Great.

Oh, what was the use anymore? Her plans were finished now.

Feeling defeated, with tears threatening to well up, Shelley spun around, dashed behind the counter, and dumped the dirty dishes. "One apple pie à la mode coming up."

She knew Mason was watching her intently. She

just hoped her actions were more efficient than what she was feeling, because she didn't feel efficient. She opened the glass case on the counter that bedded the cut pieces of pie and pulled out a plate. Bending over, she opened the door of the small freezer door situated under the counter. Only a small spoonful of vanilla ice cream remained. Marty. Though he was a great cook and an okay boss, he was lazy when it came to restocking. She left everything on the counter and shut the freezer door. "I'll be right back."

Going through the swinging door into the kitchen, Shelley went to the cooler and opened the door. She propped it open with the brick kept handy as a doorstop. Inside the cold, shelved space, she carefully moved past the five-foot tall ice sculpture, carved into the number *50*. Safely past it, she went to the shelf where the ice cream was stored. She moved the plastic bin that held some frozen hamburger patties and that sat in front of the ice cream to the side. She picked up a large, round carton of ice cream. Instantly, she realized she'd forgotten the towel to wrap around it, so she could carry it out without her skin getting cold. She dropped the carton back on the shelf. It tilted, fell over, then rolled off the shelf, and dropped heavily on her foot.

"Damn it," she exclaimed, hopping around on one foot. She bent over, grabbing the toe of her shoe, hoping pressure would ease the throbbing.

"Shelley? Are you all right? Do you need help?" Mason's hands suddenly on her hips startled her. She straightened, the top of her head jamming into his chin.

"Argh!" he yelped.

She spun around in time to see his foot catch the handle of a half-filled pickle bucket. He shook his foot free, but the bucket tipped and rolled toward the door, spilling pickles and brine along the way, and then, pushing away the brick.

"The door!" Shelley yelled.

Mason lunged for it. His feet slid around as if he were a new-born calf trying to stand up for the first time. His hands knocked a couple of bins loaded with frozen fish and hamburger patties off the shelf with the bins flipping. Anything and everything on the floor beside him and in front of him from the opened bag of potatoes, the near empty plastic bins, along with the fish and burgers were either slapped, snagged, or dug into.

"Look out!" Shelley screamed. "Not the—"

A crash, then hundreds of shards of ice spilled across the floor from wall to wall. The cooler door snapped shut plunging them into darkness.

"—ice sculpture." Her voice faded to a whisper.

For several seconds there was only silence.

"Don't worry about me," Mason said. "I'm fine."

"Oh, Mason. I'm sorry. Are you hurt?"

"No. But, I think I've got a sliver in my pride. Or maybe it's an icicle."

"He's going to kill me."

"Who?"

"Marty. That *icicle* was part of the ice sculpture for the Anderson's 50th wedding anniversary. Marty paid a hundred dollars for that sculpture. Now, it'll come out of my pocket."

"It's my fault. I'll pay for it."

"Marty's going to be furious."

"I said I'd pay for it."

"He promised their son, Clint, that there would be an ice sculpture. Clint ordered it. It was the most beautiful five-oh you ever saw."

"I can replace it."

"You can do that? You know how to sculpt ice?"

"No. But I can do a wood carving."

"Don't kid me at a time like this."

"I'm not. Let me do this. Wood lasts a lot longer than ice anyway. This way the Anderson's will have a lasting memory—one that will outlive them."

"Well..."

"Come on, Shelley. Besides, what other choice do you have?"

"None, really."

Silence swirled around them.

"If you're worried about Marty, let me handle him."

"Okay, but only on one condition. I get to pick the wood."

"Tree. I don't have anything in stock quite that big. We'll have to find a tree. Preferably a dead one, where the wood has dried out some. Can you come out to my place tomorrow? We could go now, but it's a little dark outside."

"Not to mention being dark in here." Shelley heard him moving around. "Where are you?"

"Smile so I can see you."

Shelley chuckled, unable to help herself. So like Mason to joke when there was a problem.

She heard him moving. "What are you doing?"

"Let's pretend we're blind, and we'll talk with our hands."

"We are blind. It's dark, remember? Besides, I can't see your hands."

"That's the point. We can use the braille method."

Silence filled the room. No way was she responding to *that* innuendo.

She pondered what they could do. "Mason, do you have your cell phone with you?"

"No," he replied. "It's on my table."

Shelley frowned. He sounded closer. "Where are you?"

"Here."

She jumped hearing his voice next to her. She hadn't even heard him move. Just like the old days.

She took a step back. Shelves dug into her back. She felt him move too. Toward her.

"Why are you running from me, Shelley?"

"I'm not."

"If the lights were on, we'd both see that your nose is getting longer. You've been running from me ever since I came back to Laurel Ridge. And, I want to know why."

"You're imagining things."

"I'm not. The only reason we're having a discussion here at all is because the door shut."

"We have discussions all the time."

"Yeah, like what I want to eat."

Shelley felt her cheeks get hot. She had every right to avoid him.

She wished he'd stopped talking. The more he talked, the more she wanted to melt into a puddle, despite the frigid air. That voice. She'd turned to mush the first time she heard him.

He had sat behind her in English class. She'd been late coming in and all her attention had been in getting to a seat before the teacher turned around from the blackboard.

The deep timbre of his voice, even then in twelfth grade, had sent shivers up and down her spine. She'd always wanted to meet him but they'd never shared any classes until now. Now, she was afraid to turn around in her seat, so she'd stayed behind when the bell rang and tried to guess which fellow the voice belonged to as they passed by her desk on their way out the door. She hoped the voice belonged to the lanky boy with the dark hair and blue eyes.

It had.

But now, since Mason had moved back to Laurel Ridge, it was all Shelley could do not to notice how the lankiness had turned to breadth and strength. She imagined those in the courtroom he presided over had no idea of the muscles that filled out the clothes he wore under his robe. He didn't look like a judge in her opinion. More like a lumberjack. How appropriate that he worked with wood.

His voice always had been her undoing. Especially in the dark. It was as if the years had melted away and they were out in the middle of nowhere again, far removed from anyone or anything. At their secret place in the country with no lights around them except the stars. Necking in the car. She could have sworn she was seeing stars now. She shivered.

She felt his breath on her neck. "Cold?" he asked. "I bet you didn't know that the best way to create heat is to rub two people together. Remember?"

She was trying hard to forget. "You mean sticks."

"You do it your way, I'll do it mine. Let me show you."

Before she could answer, his arms were wrapped around her. He tightened his hold, forcing her to stand on tiptoes, chest to chest, hip to hip. Heaven help her. It was just as she'd remembered.

Her hands on his arms, she pushed away, then sidestepped, moving away from him. It would be disastrous to remain in his arms. With her hands in front of her, she felt her way to what she thought was the door. It felt like the opposite wall, instead. She couldn't tell anymore. She was lost in the cooler just as she'd been lost in love in high school. Then, totally lost when he'd dumped her at a time when she was most vulnerable. And now, having lost Gramps to a nursing home and the house—her last dream—she felt more lost and alone than ever before.

Something was under her foot. She reached down and picked it up. A frozen hamburger. There'd been so much stuff flying around, she had no idea what was where, at the moment, and where she was.

Mason yelped.

"Don't move," Shelley warned.

"I can't. I'm surrounded by hard, flat, round things."

"Hamburgers."

"Where's the light?"

"There isn't one."

"Come on. All coolers have lights."

"You know Marty."

"It's not that you don't have a light fixture. You just don't have a light bulb."

"You got it."

"Remind me to reason with him. When's he due back?"

"Not until tomorrow morning. I was closing tonight."

"What?"

"We're stuck here for the night. We're going to suffocate."

"Like hell! We'll freeze to death before that!"

"I think I liked the idea of suffocating better."

"How could this happen?"

"I always have to prop the door open so it won't shut on me."

"I can't believe the door doesn't have a safety knob."

"It doesn't."

Shelley heard him moving around again. In an instant, she felt him nearby. The door opened. She blinked against the bright kitchen light.

"How did you do that?"

"This red knob." he said, touching the knob that was located toward the middle of the door but in line with the handle.

She moved out of the cooler, examining the knob. She'd noticed it before and always wondered what it was for.

He continued, pushing it in to show her. "You just push it in, like this." He did so with the heel of his hand. "It's a safety feature."

"How did you know that?"

"Worked as a cook while I was in college." He shrugged his shoulders. He let go of the door and it stopped, just short of closing completely. She saw a chunk of ice on the floor, keeping the door slightly ajar.

"Why would Connie tell me I had to keep the door propped open?"

"Was Marty always in the kitchen when you were back here?"

"Well, sure. He's the cook."

"But the grill is out front."

She looked at him blankly.

"After all these years, you're still naïve, too trusting."

Shelley bristled. "Am not."

"Then, how could you not know that Marty is a lech?"

"He's old enough to be my grandfather!"

"So? Older men like younger women. Connie's had you leave the door open so you wouldn't get caught in the cooler with him."

She frowned, mentally trying to put Marty into the lech category.

"You don't believe me, do you? He's male and you're female, with a figure women envy and men lust for."

He moved toward her and she stepped backward. He was looking at her differently. Reminding her of the times he'd back her into her locker and would steal a kiss from her, which she gave willingly, and where the teachers couldn't see them. Her heartbeat began to race. Her movement abruptly stopped when her back was flattened against the wall. He towered over her. Had he gotten taller?

His hands placed on the wall, on either side of her shoulders, boxed her neatly in the circle of his arms. Even though he wasn't touching her, he might as well be. One look at the muscles on his upper arms, Shelley knew there was no escaping. She so wanted to give in to her desires. She wanted to glare at him. She looked up.

Mason groaned. "Those eyes," he said softly. "Big, brown eyes." She was sunk. The words were almost a whisper. His thumb rubbed against her lower lip. She wanted to stay mad. She fought her emotions and resisted the urge to open her mouth and touch his finger with her tongue.

"How is it you never married, Shelley?" He moved closer. So close their clothing almost touched. So close that if she'd inserted a piece of paper between the tips of her breasts and his chest, it would hold for a second before falling. So close she could almost feel the heat and hardness behind his fly, the strength of this thighs. She wanted to put her hands on his tush and pull him that millimeter of an inch closer that would let her nestle his sex against hers if she stood on her tiptoes, to crush her breasts against his chest and to have him hold her tight. Oh, the memories!

But, she didn't...

Instead, she swallowed and forced herself to answer his question and ignore—if only for a second—the tingling sensation that started in her toes, gaining speed as it rushed through her abdomen and ended at the tips of her breasts, turning her nipples hard. "I... never found the right person." Even to her ears, her voice sounded weak.

"That's not how I remember it," he said softly. "Let me remind you what it was like before."

"Before you left town, you mean?"

He stepped back as if she had slapped him. "Not by choice. Dad's business moved him—moved us—and then, I went to college right after that."

Shelley wanted to argue that, but she didn't. She wanted to know why he hadn't even said goodbye. To ask now was courting disaster. She was too tired. She couldn't think rationally right now. She gritted her teeth to stop any response and just stared at him.

"You can run, Sweetheart, but you can't hide," he said. We had something good once before. We can have it again."

"Never."

Mason studied her. He took his time. It was as if he was memorizing her features. A bug under a microscope had never been studied this intensely. "One of these days I'm going to find out why you're so afraid of me."

"I'm not afraid of you. I just don't like you."

"I think you're fibbing. And, I know how to find out if you are."

Mason's arms went around her. Everything she'd just imagined he did. Crushing her to his length and kissing her thoroughly, the old touches, sensations, and responses returned. Her will was gone. She felt his sex nestled against her, her breasts tight against his chest. He ran a hand down her back, cupped her bottom, and lifted her up so that she rubbed against the tip of his manhood, then the length of it as he slowly let her back down. She heard a moan, not knowing if it came from her or from him.

His lips swept lightly across hers, then firmly as he slid his tongue into her mouth. She opened her mouth readily, much like a baby bird waiting for its mother to feed. Mason was her nourishment, always had been. She'd hadn't fully realized until just now how she'd been starving herself for the one thing that only Mason could provide. His touch. Oh, how she craved his touch. If only he would tell her that he loved her.

Mason ended the kiss. She wanted to protest, but she remained silent.

"Now, tell me you don't like me," he demanded.

"Our making out was never the problem." She'd be a fool to declare otherwise. They both knew from her response that she liked him, liked making out with him, but she didn't want him to believe all was forgiven and forgotten either. "I just don't like what you did."

"Are we back to your grandfather again?"

Not in Shelley's mind, but she saw it as a way to escape his questions. "Yes," she said. Let him think what he wanted for now. She couldn't do this, feeling raw and vulnerable. She just wanted to get away from him. Another kiss would be fatal.

Frustrated, Mason straightened, his arms falling to his side. "I don't believe you. You've already admitted the right thing was done for your grandfather."

"For now."

"For now," Mason echoed. "Why do you have to be so childish with this useless grudge of yours?"

They both heard the bell jingle. Another customer.

Shelley swallowed the lump in her throat. "Just let me get your dessert and do my job."

Mason stared down at her. Her heart thudded. She could barely stand to look at him, but she did, only to show she wasn't backing down.

"Forget the dessert," he growled, moving toward the front part of the diner. "I'll pick you up first thing tomorrow morning so we can find your piece of wood." His hand slammed against the swinging door. It banged against the wall and started swinging shut, going back and forth wildly at first. She heard the front door bell ring and the door slamming shut behind him. Her feet were rooted to the spot. She wasn't about to go chasing after him.

He was gone. The swinging door swiveled back and forth a few more times, slowing, until finally it stopped.

Shelley closed her eyes. A tear slid down her cheek. Angrily she brushed it away.

A useless grudge? Childish?

How could he forget their baby so easily? She couldn't. And she'd never forgive him for brushing it aside.

She opened the cooler door and shoved the chunk of ice back into the cooler with her foot. With a shoulder to the door, she shut it against the debris inside, knowing she'd be spending an extra hour or two cleaning up after she closed. The door latched. She wished she could shut a door as easily on the debris in her heart. Sooner or later, she knew she'd have to deal with that debris, too.

*****

"Hi, Gramps."

Later that night, when she first came into his room at the retirement home where the court—Mason more explicitly—had deemed him to go, Shelley noted her grandfather looked pre-occupied. Lost in thought. But now, having spotted her, he smiled genuinely at her.

"Hi," he said.

"Everything okay?"

"Couldn't be better."

"I miss you."

"Miss you too, Girlie-Girl. There's been lots of

hummers, hummingbirds out there."

Shelley stood behind his chair and looked out the window at the half-empty feeder that hung on the soffit. It was dark out, too late for birds to feed.

Thankfully, the staff here understood her late hours and let her in every night after her late shift so she could say goodnight to Gramps.

"Scrappy little creatures," he said.

"How have you really been?" she asked, settling on a corner of his bed.

"I have good days, some bad. Just like you, I imagine. You look like you're bursting at the seams. What's up?"

"Nothing much."

He waited patiently while she tried to dig her toe into the carpet.

"Mason Baylock was at the restaurant today," she finally said, hating the silence. "He broke the ice sculpture Marty had commissioned for the Anderson's party. Mason's going to replace it with a wood carving."

"Nice young man. Always did like him. Shame he moved away when he did. Thought the two of you would marry one day."

"Grandpa!"

"It's true and you know it. Don't know what your problem is now. He's back and available. What's the matter, girl? Got no starch in your petticoats anymore?"

She opened her mouth to speak, but he interrupted her.

"And don't Grandpa! me. I may be old, but I'm not blind. Anybody with a lick of common sense can see you're still in love with him and he with you. Connie tells me the way things are."

"I didn't know Connie's been seeing you."

"Regular, like clockwork. Speaking of which, it's getting past my bedtime. Hate to chase you out, but I get crotchety if I don't get my beauty sleep."

Shelley kissed him goodbye and left. During the short ride home, she dismissed Gramps' view on how she felt about Mason. Connie's view, too. How could either of them know how she felt? She had never revealed or said anything to either of them. They saw only what they wanted to see.

*****

Day 2

At the crack of dawn, Mason and Shelley had tramped through the forest around his cabin located just north of town. Now, she sat on the back porch steps watching him work with a chainsaw on the hickory stump she had picked out. From here, the view was magnificent. There were hills behind the house in the distance, the trees easy to imagine in fall—the evergreens staying green, the birch turning yellow, the oaks turning brown. It was too far south for a forest of maples with the brilliant red, yellow, and orange, but there was an occasional maple here and there.

Her gaze returned to Mason. With each cut he made, she was amazed to see the same sculpture that had been demolished come to life beneath his hands.

He'd been right. This carving would be a beautiful memorial for the Andersons.

Mason, at work, was beautiful to watch, too. Always had been. His looks were rugged, reminding her a lot of his surroundings. As easily as he fit into these surroundings, he looked equally at home in his courtroom. Authoritative, a force to be reckoned with when he wore his robes. A force to be reckoned with without the robe, too.

When Mason first arrived back in Laurel Ridge, the single women had lined up hoping to get his attention. Once they found he wasn't interested in dating, there'd been a flurry of traffic tickets written. Shelley heard the stories from the officers who habitually stopped by the diner during their coffee breaks. The women were flinging themselves upon the mercy of Mason's court, hoping to get more than just a fine—for all the good it did them. The much sought after judge remained dateless, but the city's coffers became richer. After a time, the women and the citations finally returned to normal.

Gazing at Mason, watching how his muscles moved as he danced around the stump with his buzzing chainsaw, she wondered at his real motive for moving back. She'd never heard.

She'd been filled with panic the first time he'd entered the diner, when she realized she'd have to wait on him. She hadn't known what to expect, but Mason had been nothing but a kind, generous tipping customer. Several months later, however, things started to change.

He had asked her out. She had refused. She had even thought about getting an unlisted number for fear he would start calling her at home but realized how stupid that thinking was. No doubt, he already knew where she lived; it was a small community, and he had government access to records if he wanted. Ever since then, once a week a least, he'd ask her out. She always turned him down. Lesser men would have given up long ago. Shelley never gave an excuse, and Mason never pressured her. One simple request. A simple refusal. Once a week every week for the past three months and two weeks.

Until yesterday.

She shivered. She had shivered all night remembering the toe-tingling, deep kiss he'd given her last night. Needless to say, her sheets had been tangled and her thoughts no clearer when she got up this morning.

Frustrated and knowing she couldn't sit here any longer watching him, she got up, dusting off her bottom.

He noticed and turned off his chainsaw. "I don't know about you, but I'm starved. Want some lunch?"

Figuring he meant in town, she said, "Sure." Once she was back in town, she'd make her excuses and stay in town. Mason could finish the carving without her.

"Great." He set down the saw and started up the steps, then stopped when she didn't follow. "Aren't you coming in? I made some egg salad last night. That or I've got some roast beef."

Now that she'd agreed to lunch, there wasn't any way she could back out. She followed him into the house. They entered a back room. Mason tugged his shirt out of his pants, unbuttoning it as he talked.

"The kitchen is in there." He pointed at a doorway to his left. "Help yourself."

She stood where she was and watched as he pulled the shirt off, muscles rippling across his back as he walked down the hall. Then, he disappeared from sight. The image lingered in her mind, and she didn't like to admit how much she had enjoyed the view. Too easily, she imagined his stomach still resembling a washboard, just as it had years ago.

She went into the kitchen, and with shaky hands opened the refrigerator, and retrieved the egg salad. By the time Mason returned, wearing a clean shirt and smelling of soap and mountain air, she couldn't remember having made the sandwiches that were stacked on a platter in front of her. Nor did it help her roller-coaster-like thoughts, seeing him barefoot and the top button of his jeans unfastened, which had been revealed as he reached above her head, grabbing a big bowl for the chips.

Mason got two glasses and filled each with milk, setting one in front of her. "So, what do you think of my house?"

"It's lovely." It was true. "What made you choose this house?" She was grateful for the oak tabletop that hid his unfastened jeans from her prying eyes. It was like waving the green flag at the beginning of the race. She didn't want anything started, but he was making it damn tough for her to keep from stepping on that gas pedal and propelling herself right into his arms.

"I've always wanted to come back. I love the countryside and this house was in sore need of restoration. I like how it fits into nature's landscape, like it belongs here."

"So why didn't you come back? Before this, I mean."

"A variety of reasons. After I finished school and had my law degree, I was offered a job as a prosecuting attorney that I couldn't refuse. I took it, mostly because it got me away from my father. He always expected me to join the corporation where he worked, become his protégé. Actually, he wanted a duplicate of himself. Trouble is, I could never live up to his standards. His image of what I should be: a business executive."

"Promotions came along, other jobs with opportunities to serve the people. Then, Dad got sick and died."

"I hadn't heard. I'm sorry." Though she was angry at his father for his role in her own loss, she was sorry that Mason had lost a parent.

"I couldn't leave Mother. She just wasn't strong enough after that."

"She never was. I remember how she always kowtowed to your father."

"There was one time when she didn't." He frowned. "She fought him fiercely for a day or so. After that, things were never the same. I never did find out what it was about."

"When was that?"

"Just before we moved away."

Was it possible that Mason's parents had fought about her? No, not the way they had stood united against her and her parents during that difficult time.

Mason continued. "I got the impression Mother didn't want to leave. She remarried a year after dad died, and then when Joe Benton—he was a year ahead of us in school—offered me a job with his law firm here, I knew this was what I'd been wanting all along. To come home. The timing was perfect."

"Now, you're Judge Baylock."

"Only when Judge Benton—Joe's dad—died suddenly of a heart attack, and I was appointed. Don't let the robes fool you. Oh sure, I look grand in my black robes, a real impressive figure. Authoritative. People are afraid of me. Hell, a black robe would improve anybody's wardrobe. When those robes come off, though, I'm just like anyone else."

"Are you sure you can have it done in time for the party tomorrow tonight?"

"You doubt my ability?"

Shelley took her plate and glass to the sink. "From here," she said, looking out the window, "it looks like a long way from a finished product."

He joined her at the sink, stacking his dishes with hers, his arm brushing hers slightly. "Not as far away from being done as you'd think. But, you're right. I'd better get back to work. Going to join me?"

"No," she said quickly. His touch had sent her

nerve endings into spasms. She had to stay away from him. "I'm going to...to wash up these dishes."

"No need for you to do that."

"I want to. I'll be out in a jiffy."

Shelley plugged the sink, squirted soap on the dishes, and turned on the tap. She plunged her hands into the hot water and looked out the window. Her hands stilled as she watched him work the wood with a chisel. Beneath his hands, the natural beauty of the wood was emerging. Shelley remembered a time when she'd felt just as beautiful because of Mason.

The dishes done, Shelley looked for the bathroom. She took a cursory glance in the mirror, then stopped. She had color in her cheeks and a sparkle to her eyes that hadn't been there in a long time. It had to be the fresh air she tried telling herself, knowing the real reason for the sparkle and color was just a few steps out the back door.

Leaving the bathroom, she saw an open door at the end of the hall. She paused, considering whether to satisfy her curiosity or not. Earlier Mason had offered to give her a tour of the house. She'd declined. But now...

She pushed the door opening it wider. It was the master bedroom. The bed was unmade, the pillow still holding the depression of his head. From the tangle of sheets, it appeared Mason had had a restless night, too. The room was done in browns and blues, reflecting a continuation of the outdoors through the huge Palladian windows. The view was breathtaking, providing a glimpse of the Lake Whippoorwill through the trees and the water shimmering like a jewel.

Interested in the rest of the house, Shelley took a quick tour. It was comfortable, with simple furnishings, yet luxurious. A house that was truly livable but could be easy to clean and enjoy. Mason had good taste, but then he always had.

She remembered the time her mother had been hospitalized with gall bladder surgery. Mason had brightened her room with a poster of a mountain waterfall and a huge bouquet of fresh flowers. Always thoughtful and thinking of others.

So how could things have gone so wrong between them?

Unable to remain in Mason's house any longer, Shelley escaped out the back door. She hesitated on the steps. Sitting here watching Mason work was more than she could handle at the moment, too.

She needed to walk. Rarely able to get away from work or the numerous chores that needed to be done when she wasn't working, she opted to take advantage of the landscape surrounding Mason's cottage home. To the right and in the distance, about a quarter of a mile, was another home. The State Senator's get-away. Between the two houses was the senator's pecan orchard. At heart, Jefferson was a farmer first, a senator second. She knew Mason and Jefferson had grown up together here and were still best of friends. Beyond that, there were no other signs of inhabitants in the area.

Quickly, as she walked away, the two homes

disappeared from view. Everywhere she looked, it was beautiful, everything a lush green. Spring had finally arrived in earnest. New green leaves on tall trees. Wildflowers everywhere she looked, especially white lilies of the valley and creeping phlox. Though she realized she'd been climbing ever since she'd headed north of Mason's cabin, she hadn't realized how far she'd gone until she turned around.

Shelley gasped. The scenery—the lake in front of her, along with a few of the town's rooftops, and the forests that circled the town—was picture postcard perfect. She sighed. It was all incredible, and it brought back memories. She'd never seen it in the daytime before. She knew there was a little-known service road behind her—the way she and Mason had traveled up here in his car. A lump formed in her throat. Tears welled up and threatened to spill. Their last time alone together had been here, the first time they had made love. After that night, for the following couple months, taking them through graduation, there was always someone nearby. Family. Friends. Classmates. It had been annoying that they couldn't find time to be alone, but it had been a busy, happy time. Until she realized she was pregnant. She hadn't been fearful at all, not until she met up with Mason's father.

"You remember it too, don't you?" Mason said from behind. He had followed her. Once again, he had crept up on her, where she hadn't even heard him.

Shelley swallowed the lump as best she could and

blinked rapidly several times. She turned.

A few more steps and he was beside her, in front of the tree she stood next to. He leaned back against the huge live oak.

She couldn't deny the scenery any more than she could deny that day, the last time she'd seen it.

She gazed out at the view. "It's been a long time since I've been here."

"You never came back up here?"

"No."

"Why not?"

"I didn't want to taint the memory," she whispered.

"Of us?"

"Yes."

"There's something you're not telling me."

She couldn't speak. She looked at the scenery, but instead of seeing the trees and the sky, she saw a hospital room instead.

"Shelley?"

She closed her eyes against the pain.

"Shelley?"

She opened her eyes again. Mason put a hand under her chin and turned her head until she was facing him. "Shelley. Tell me."

"You already know."

"I want to hear it. Tell me."

"This is where I received my first kiss."

"Our first kiss."

"Yes. Ours." She took a deep shaky breath. "You spoiled me for every other boy who followed. No one else had your gentle touch or could melt my heart with a glance."

He smiled broadly. "Honey, you've had the same effect on me for a long time." He moved, his arms coming up as if to pull her into a hug.

She shook her head no and pushed him away. Taking a few steps back toward his home, she turned back around. "How could you do it?"

"Do what?"

A chill ran up her spine. He didn't know. He honestly didn't know. All this time, she had blamed him.

Stunned and speechless, she wasn't ready to confide in him. What would he think of her? Of his dad? She didn't want to be the one to crush his world. He needed to know but how could she tell him? Were there any words she could utter that could make this sound right? Sound good?

"Nothing." She moved to go back to his cottage. "Let's go see how that block of wood is looking."

Mason snagged her arm, turning her around. "Even after all these years, I still know you. I know that set of your jaw. We're not going anywhere. This conversation is going to get finished here and now. I've been dancing around you for half a year. My endurance isn't limitless, Shelley." Not once had he raised his voice. He appeared calm while her insides were rolling and roiling, like waves on the lake during rough, stormy weather. And all the while, his gaze caressed her, as if he was looking for a way in so that he could help her help him.

It wounded her to see him so anguished. She had no choice. She had to tell him and what she was about to tell him would devastate him. She was too far in to back out now, nor would Mason let her.

"Apparently, your father didn't want you to know."

"Know what? Shelley, tell me. You're driving me crazy! What didn't my father want me to know?"

"About our baby."

His face paled. "Our *what*?"

"That last time we spent up here..."

"Spring vacation of our senior year. I remember."

She paused, willing her voice to stay steady. "I got pregnant."

Mason started to say something, then clamped his jaw shut. For several minutes the only sounds were those of squirrels chattering to each other in the treetops as they chased each other. How could they be so carefree and playing happily while she stood here feeling cold and miserable?

"There's more, isn't there?" he asked.

She nodded.

"When did you find out?" he asked.

"The day after graduation. I came to tell you, but your father intercepted me in the driveway. He never did like me, you know."

Shelley held up her hand to stop whatever it was he was going to say. "It's all right, Mason. I reconciled myself to that fact a long time ago. He wanted the best for you, and I wasn't it."

Mason jaw hardened. "What did he do, Shelley?"

"He told me I wasn't going to be part of your future."

"But why would he say that?"

"Because I made the mistake of blurting out I was pregnant. He told me that you wanted to break up with me. In my hurry to get away from there, I tripped, jamming a rock into my stomach."

She heard Mason catch his breath.

"I jumped up, saying I was all right when your dad asked if I was hurt, but I wasn't all right."

"Your mother said it was appendicitis."

"My mother? You came to the hospital?"

"Of course I did. That night. I called your house and your mother told me that you were in the hospital. But you were asleep, and the nurses wouldn't let me in. I was concerned. More so because you hadn't called me yourself. Why didn't you call me?"

"Your father already told me you were breaking up with me! He paid me a visit, too. The day after..." She nearly lost it then. She looked down, taking a deep breath, trying to calm her anxiety as she relived the emotions. And now, to learn that her mother had never told her of Mason's call. Resigned and subdued, she began again. "He visited the following day, after my fall, telling me he'd told you about the baby and that you didn't want anything to do with me."

"I don't believe you."

Stunned, Shelley's lungs stopped working. The man she'd loved thought she was lying. The worst part of it was, she still loved him. All this time, without him, she'd just been existing. Once Mason had left town years ago, she had never felt whole. He had taken her heart with him.

Now, she had nothing. Because he thought she was lying.

"My father was a lot of things, but for him to do something like that—not even tell me that you were pregnant—makes him a monster. What was his motive?" Mason ran a hand through his hair. He was pacing now.

All Shelley could do was watch him. She wanted to wrap her arms around him. Instead, she wrapped them around herself. Words froze in her throat. Nothing she could say would make him feel better. No words could make this wrong right.

The truth was ugly and now Mason would have to bear the responsibility of his family's actions. Actions that had been played out on his behalf, without his knowledge.

"He wasn't like that!" Mason cried out.

Shelley's heart wrenched in two. He still idolized his father, faults and all. Quietly and with a calm she didn't quite feel, she repeated herself. "He told me you didn't want to see me anymore, that you were breaking up with me." She paused, then added, "I couldn't believe you made him your messenger. According to him, you had. Seems he lied to both of us."

"Why? Why would he do this?" he asked.

"You said it yourself. He wanted you to be a

mirror image of himself. Doesn't it seem odd that you and your family moved away from here? Moved away before I was even out of the hospital?"

Mason froze. He stared at her. "I thought so at the time, but Dad said he'd been made an offer he couldn't refuse and that the move couldn't be delayed. It *was* business..." His words trailed off.

He jammed his hands into his pockets and stared out at the mountaintops. She knew from the tortured look on his face that he was oblivious to his surroundings. The news she'd given him had just changed his world, his perception of reality. Their reality.

Finally he spoke, evenly and with no emotion. "Let me take you home."

Dread, cold mind-numbing dread, filled her. Despite the sun, she shivered. He was dismissing her just as he dismissed the cases in his court. As far as he was concerned, there was no more discussion. With leaden feet, she followed him back to the house, retrieved her purse, and got into the car. The last thing she wanted was to be driven home, but she had no choice. It was too far to walk.

During the drive home, she managed to keep her eyes focused straight ahead, staring at the road but seeing nothing until they passed the house of her dreams. A sign announcing the upcoming auction was staked on the lawn.

Shelley's head twisted as she tried to read the words in large print as they passed. Unable to see anymore, she faced forward again.

"When is the auction?" Mason asked. "I couldn't read the sign."

"Two days." Two days and all hope of her dream would be gone. There wasn't another house like it in town. Not where she could have had a day-care center downstairs, run a boarding house for the elderly upstairs, and live there herself, too. She entertained a brief thought of going back to college, moving away from Laurel Ridge, but the thought left just as quickly as it had arrived. She didn't want to go to college any more than she wanted to move away. This had always been her home. Where could she possibly go without feeling any lonelier or lost than she did right now? Besides, she couldn't leave Gramps.

He stopped the car at the curb. She opened the door.

"Will you be at the party tomorrow?" he asked.

"Yes. The Andersons have been a driving force behind most everything good that has happened to this community. I want to pay my respects to them." She couldn't believe they were being this civil to one another, but what choice did they have?

Silence finally propelled her out of the car.

"Goodbye, Mason." She shut the door. She didn't want to hear him echo the words. Immediately, she turned and headed for her apartment. She couldn't stand to watch him drive away either. A second later, despite herself, she turned her head just in time to see his car turn the corner. Then, he was gone.

For a brief moment, she had hoped they could

have worked everything out. If only she could go back and change...

Change what? Change that she had lost the baby? Change that Mason and his family had moved away? Change that his father had lied about the truth?

Of course, she wished she could have changed everything, but there was nothing she could change, nothing she could do.

*****

Day 3

The next night at the Anderson's door, her finger inches from the door bell, Shelley hesitated. She wasn't in a party mood, but she couldn't go back home now. Not only were guests arriving behind her, but she knew people would question her tomorrow, asking why she hadn't come. She rang the bell and moments later drifted among the other guests. She grabbed a drink from a tray sitting on the kitchen counter and stepped through the sliding glass doors onto the bricked patio. The bulk of the guests were here, outside, enjoying the evening as the day's hotter weather was cooling down. And in the middle of the throng was a work of art that pulled everyone to admire it at close scrutiny. Mason's sculpture.

It was beautiful. Up close, she saw that he had polished the wood until it gleamed. Having seen him at work, she knew the attention to detail he had provided. It was easy to imagine his hands lovingly giving the work the finishing touches. The closer she got to it, the more it gleamed. It was only when she was up close that she saw the smaller statue sitting beside it. About a foot tall, it was the slenderized heads of a man and woman, their necks twisted around each other as they gazed into each other's eyes. The wood looked to be pecan, and it was unlike anything she had ever seen. The profiles reminded her of herself and Mason.

"Isn't it gorgeous?" Mrs. Anderson said. "I was speechless when Clint told me Mason had sculpted the five-oh. I had no idea he had such hidden talents. But this." She picked up the smaller carving. "This is priceless. I only wish I could thank him myself."

"Mason isn't here?"

"No," Mrs. Anderson said, replacing the piece back on the table. "He was here only long enough to drop these off. Said he had some business to take care. Said he'd be gone for a couple days." As much as she hadn't wanted to run into him, Shelley was disappointed that Mason wasn't here. This state of confusion was wearing her down.

An hour later, Shelley decided she'd had enough. Even though she hadn't seen Mason, she had overheard his name repeatedly. And each time she had heard his name, her heart felt like it was being wrenched all over again.

An exclamation of surprise and wonderment rose up from the crowd. She hadn't even noticed the hot air balloon that was being inflated away from the house in the backyard. She's been so self-absorbed. Now the balloon dominated the scenery.

The crowd moved closer. Clint was in the basket with the balloonist, a pretty brunette, and he beckoned wildly for his parents to join him. Once they were in the basket, the balloonist turned on the burner. Instantly, a jet of gas, a bright orange flame, shot straight up, heating the air inside the balloon. The guests applauded. Then, the balloon and basket of occupants began to rise up into the still blue, early evening sky. In another hour, it would be dark.

Shortly after the balloon left, so did Shelley.

*****

Day 4

The next day, as she walked to work as she did every day, Shelley passed the house of her dreams. Today, however, was different. Cars lined both sides of the road. People crossed the street oblivious to the traffic, all headed in the same direction—the front lawn of the property.

Shelley's steps slowed. The auctioneer was describing the house. She could have just as easily described it to the crowd herself. Two parlors, huge kitchen, pantry, formal dining room, a den, and a library with a half bath downstairs. Five bedrooms with a full bathroom upstairs.

A car honking jolted her from her thoughts. She walked on. There wasn't time for her to linger, for woolgathering. She had customers waiting for her at the diner. Today should be like any other day. The only problem was, it wasn't. Mason was gone, and in a short time so would be the house.

An hour later, the diner filled up. Most were faces Shelley had never seen. She overheard them talking about the auction. She wanted to ask who had bought it, but she refrained. It wouldn't do her any good to know, anyway.

After the lunch crowd thinned out, Connie arrived. It was her day for the late shift.

"Did you hear the news?" she asked. Connie grabbed her apron off the hook and tied it around her waist. Not waiting for an answer, she continued. "Some corporation bought the house. Didn't recognize the name."

"What do you think they want with it?"

"Heck if I know. I heard some people talking about how it was going to be turned into offices. Someone else said a parking lot."

Whatever it would become, Shelley knew it would never be a day-care center.

Connie frowned seeing Shelley's slumped shoulders. "What's the matter, Shelley? I don't think I've ever seen you this down."

There wasn't any reason to keep her dream a secret anymore, so she told Connie what her plans had been for the big old house. Shelley shrugged her shoulders. "I guess some plans just aren't meant to be."

Connie gave Shelley's arm a pat. "Don't you worry. Something will come along. Something always does. Oh, did I tell you? I saw the Judge at the auction. I wonder where he's been the last couple of days."

Shelley looked toward the courthouse. His car was in its usual spot. He was back in town. Whatever his business had been out of town, life would go on.

That would mean he'd be coming to the diner for dinner. Sooner or later she would have to face him.

Then again, maybe not. Maybe he was so disgusted with her, he would never step foot in the diner as long as she was working here.

The time Mason usually came for dinner came and went. Now that it was time for her to go home, Shelley realized she'd been on pins and needles all day, ever since Connie told her she'd seen Mason.

She hadn't eaten much all day and was too keyed up to eat now.

Finally home, she changed from her uniform into jeans, a sleeveless summer shirt, and tennis shoes. The only way she'd get this tension out of her system was to walk it off. She opened the door and gasped, her hand going up and covering her heart in surprise.

Mason stood on the stoop, his hand still in the air as he'd been prepared to knock.

"I'm sorry," he said. "I didn't mean to frighten you."

Shelley caught her breath. She hadn't expected to see him. "Come...come in," she said, opening the door wide.

Mason ducked as he came inside. Shelley closed the door, instantly regretting inviting him in. She should have joined him on the stoop, instead. Immediately, the room appeared to shrink in size. It was big enough to suit her needs, allowing her to save money toward her goal. Her previous goal, she amended. But the place was tiny with him here.

"Sit down. Please."

"No. I..." Mason paused. He started, and then stopped again. "Oh, hell, Shelley. This isn't coming out right...I never have trouble with words, but now..." He paced the length of the room, then turned around. She'd never seen him like this.

"Please, Mason. Sit down. You're making me nervous."

He sat, but just on the edge of the sofa. He looked uncomfortable. "Am I stopping you from going somewhere?"

"No. I was just going to take a walk."

Quickly, Mason sprung up. "Good idea. Let me walk with you."

Shelley hadn't planned on having company, and she wasn't sure she was up for his company, but he seemed to have something on his mind. "All right." She was curious. Plus, she had to admit—she had missed him.

As they walked, the silence was killing her. She wanted to ask questions, but she wasn't going to say anything until he did first. Until he spoke, there really wasn't anything to say. Instead of focusing on him, she focused on her steps and worked to keep up with his longer stride.

Minutes later, they had achieved a reasonably brisk pace.

Finally, Mason spoke. "I went to see my mother." Shelley's steps slowed. She frowned and glanced at him. His steps slowed to match hers. She noticed he was waiting for her reaction. She didn't give him one. While she wanted to hear more, she kept walking but focused her gaze on the road.

He continued. "I needed to know for myself if what you'd said had been true. It wasn't that I didn't believe you. The fact that we'd, that you were...that you'd been pregnant threw me for a loop."

Mason stopped and put out a hand, grabbing her arm. He moved so that he was in front of her, forcing her to stop, forcing her to look at him. "Shelley, I didn't mean to be so abrupt the other day. I just didn't know what to say at the time."

"What did your mother have to say?"

"She confirmed everything. Told me that Dad had paid your hospital bill, that he hadn't been offered a job but had gone seeking it himself, transferring to another location, which meant moving us. He really thought I would follow his example and become a corporate executive. She claims he was doing what he thought was best for me. She said she wanted to tell me about the baby, that she and Dad fought about it, but Dad forbade her say a word. Mom never crossed Dad a day in her life. It didn't occur to her to do differently, despite how strongly she felt that I should be told."

"So what happens now?"

"Marry me. Let me make everything right again."

Shelley could only stare at him.

"Just like that? Marry you? You find out I was pregnant twelve years ago, and you want me to marry you? I'm not one of your cases, Judge Baylock. Someone you can counsel and try to put the pieces back together again the way you want. The way you think it should be. It might have been different had you bothered to stay in touch with me all these years, but you didn't even say goodbye. As much as we loved each other, as much as you professed to love me, you didn't even call to say goodbye. You believed your father over me! That's what hurts the most. You didn't even try to see if what he told you was true."

"Because he told me that *you* didn't want to see *me*."

"He told me the same thing. That you didn't want to talk to me." Quietly, she added, "It seems we were both naïve. We both believed him."

The silence was long. She knew her words to be true. And then, she saw it. The look on his face that told her he knew they were true, too. She hated how he looked. Defeated. And lost.

Finally, he said, "Let me make it up to you."

"I don't want you to make anything up to me. It's not necessary. All I ever wanted..."

"What?" he asked. "What did you want?"

Jutting her chin out, she had nothing to lose in speaking the truth. "All I ever wanted was your love."

Mason opened his mouth.

"Don't," she said stopping him. "Don't say it now. It's too late. I can't marry you. It wouldn't work."

There was nothing more to say. It was over. Even Mason couldn't make this right now. She felt her chin quiver. Everything she'd ever wanted in a man stood before her, and he'd asked her to marry him. But, she couldn't marry him because he felt guilty. He was asking out of a sense of duty. Because they'd been linked in the past.

She wanted his love, not his pity.

She turned and walked away. A tear trickled down her cheek.

"Shelley!"

She ran.

*****

Day 7

The past few days had been miserable. Every waking moment she'd driven herself, scrubbing the apartment, then scrubbing every surface clean at the diner.

Finally, after Shelley had worked nine hours straight without a break, Connie took the sponge out of her hand and told her, no ordered her to go home.

Now, Shelley sat in her apartment, sprawled in the chair. Bone tired as she was, her mind raced with thoughts of Mason. Pushing herself out of the chair, Shelley paced. She didn't want to think of Mason.

The doorbell rang. She hesitated. If it was Mason, she didn't want to answer the door. But, if it wasn't...

Curiosity won out. She opened the door. The mayor and two city commissioners stood there.

Mayor Weston spoke. "Sorry to bother you at home, Shelley. May we come in?"

Shelley frowned but stepped aside. Shutting the door, she turned and offered them a seat.

"It's come to our attention that you had intentions of operating a day-care center in the old Browne estate," Commissioner Smith said.

Shelley blinked. “But how... I mean... how did you know that? Connie?” It had to have been Connie. With Connie around, there was no need for a newspaper.

The mayor continued. “You probably know the house was purchased by a corporation.”

“Yes,” she replied.

“Well, it seems the owner is a philanthropist who wants the building returned to the community but only under certain conditions.”

“I don't understand.”

“The building is yours providing you still want to establish the day-care center.”

“And the second story as a boarding house for the elderly?” she asked.

Commissioner Smith answered. “Yes. With an elevator and bathrooms for each bedroom, all to be installed or updated accordingly.”

“I don't get it,” Shelley said shaking her head. “What's the catch?”

“There is none,” Mayor Weston told her. “As we explained, the owner is a philanthropist, a former citizen who continues to stay in touch with the community. They only ask one thing.”

“And what's that?”

“That you let them handle the renovations, the costs, and major construction and improvements. But, they want your input for the overall plans and decorating. You'll be working closely with the contractor.”

“What's the catch?”

"Excuse me?"

"What's the hook. What does this company really want?"

"Nothing. Absolutely nothing. They just want to give back."

Immediately, Shelley wondered if Mason was behind this. She knew better than to push. She would have time to find out who was behind this corporation later. For now, she wasn't willing to let this wonderful gift, her dream, get away.

"What about rent?"

"Your rent, along with a salary and benefits, is partial compensation for managing and running the enterprise. You'll be paid a salary, too."

"I'm speechless."

"Then you'll accept?"

Shelley stood. She was too excited to sit now. "I would be stupid not to. It's everything I've ever dreamed of." Almost everything, she realized. She shook off the last thought, not willing to let thoughts of Mason detract from her excitement.

*****

Day 13

A week later, Shelley stood in the middle of what would be the toddlers' playroom. In her mind's eye, she imagined the walls brightly decorated with murals of zoo animals, the ceiling painted as clouds, a dozen children hard at play, with various assistants helping, but more importantly, the second story residents involved with the children, as well.

Once the news had gotten out about her plans,

her phone started ringing. By the end of the first day, the resident apartments were all taken. All except for the rooms where she and her grandfather would reside. He on the second floor, she on the third.

She was headed to the nursing home, now, to see Gramps. Once she had him under her roof, she'd truly have everything she ever wanted.

Almost.

Stop! To be honest, she and Mason had never talked of marriage as sweethearts, never talked about the future much at all, so how could he have been a part of a dream that didn't really exist?

Besides, ever since she'd turned Mason down, he had stopped coming to the diner. She didn't want to admit it at first, but she missed seeing him. At night, as she lay alone in her bed, she wondered if she'd done the right thing. But then, she'd punch her pillow, fluffing it up, telling herself she had. She couldn't have endured a marriage that started with pity.

Up until now, she'd been busy planning and getting the Whippoorwill House ready. But, no matter what she did or where she went, Mason was with her. He filled her thoughts. She remembered the way he smiled. The way he always greeted everyone else in the diner when he came in. The way he made others laugh. Though he might not realize it, she knew the community had warmed up to him and was welcoming him back into the fold. They respected him.

Though she wasn't working at the diner anymore

as of a couple days ago, she continued to eat a number of her meals there. Sitting in front of the large window, she would sometimes see him walking to or from the parking lot. Despite her happiness at her new job, she had a hollow spot in her heart that all the children and all the elderly folks in the world couldn't fill.

Minutes later, she entered her grandfather's room.

"How's the project?" he asked.

"Nearly finished," she claimed, smiling broadly. "I can't believe how fast everything is coming together. In another two weeks, Whippoorwill House will be open for business. That means you'll be able to come back and live with me."

He took her hand and placed it in his frail-looking but still stronger one. "Shelley, I know that's what you want, but it's not what I want."

"What?" Shelley was shocked.

He continued. "That idea of my coming back to live with you has always been your dream—not mine."

"But you're all I've got, Gramps."

"You're wrong, Lassie. And here I thought you were smarter than that. I'm happy here. I need more care than you think. I'm not like your other residents. I can't take care of myself anymore, and I don't want you to be burdened with it. You and that fellow of yours did the right thing by me. Instead of taking care of an old man, you need to be taking care of a husband."

"But you wouldn't be a bur—"

"Yes, I would. I know you. When you love someone, you give your all. That's how it should be. Besides, you wouldn't want to move me away from my sweetie, would you?"

"You've got a girlfriend?"

The old man peered around Shelley while putting a finger to his lips. "She doesn't know it yet, but I'm just about ready to sweep her off her feet."

Shelley laughed. He was telling the truth. He was happy here and it showed. He hadn't been this peppy in a long time.

"Let go of the past, Shelley. Stop wrapping it around you like a shroud."

Shelley walked to the window, hugging herself. "I don't do that."

Her grandfather chuckled and pointed at her. "Look at you. Look at what you're doing."

Shelley glanced down, and wiggled her toes in her shoes.

"Look how you're protecting yourself from what I'm saying, the way you've got yourself all wrapped up with your arms. I hit the bull's-eye, didn't I? Come give your ol' Gramps a hug. It's almost dinnertime. I can smell the Jell-O now."

Shelley looked at her grandfather. Everything he said was true. It hurt knowing that they'd never be living together again.

"It's hard recognizing that a door has just closed, isn't it?" he asked.

Shelley nodded. He held open his arms and she went into them and gave him a hug. He returned her squeeze. "But remember, when one door closes, another opens. Don't wait for it to open. Some doors you have to open yourself."

"Oh, Gramps."

"I know you well enough to know you shut a door on your young man recently. You need to forget the past. Just don't forget that every house has a front door and a back door. You're not stuck shut in that lonely box unless you want to be. Think about it." He turned her around to the door and propelled her forward. "Walk an old man to the dining room."

Minutes later, she stood on the sidewalk, hoping that one day she would be as wise as her only living relative.

Doors opening, doors closing. Only because she'd shared her dreams was it possible that her dream was in operation as she'd always envisioned. Connie and Mason, along with Gramps, were the only people she'd told. Every time she confronted Connie, asking what she knew about Whippoorwill House, Connie always said that her lips were sealed. Gramps, too. Shelley finally dropped the subject. It wasn't *her* house, but it was the next best thing. The benefits were still the same.

She'd been wrong to slam the door on her relationship with Mason. They were bound to see each other time and again. It was a small community. Eventually, Mason would marry and would have children who could end up at her day-care center.

If Shelley were honest with herself, she knew without a doubt that Mason was behind the house and had Connie conspiring with him. And, if Shelley continued being honest, she was wrong about herself, too. Pride made for a sad, lonely companion. Gramps was right.

She needed to put herself out there. To make things right. If nothing else, she wanted to be friends with Mason. If she lost Mason because of her foolish pride, she had no one to blame but herself.

Hoping to catch Mason before he went home for the day, Shelley went to the courthouse.

Slipping into the still active courtroom, Shelley slid into the last bench.

"Your honor—" an attorney argued.

Mason struck his gavel. "The sentence has been given, Mr. Gundrige. I've made my decision. Court dismissed."

The gavel sounded again. Mason stood, then paused, seeing her. He turned, moved toward the side door to his office, said something to the deputy who stood at the door, and left the room. The door shut behind him. In a minute, the courtroom was clear.

The deputy was the last to leave, exiting through the same door Mason had gone through.

Shelley let out a sigh. Mason had seen her and left.

Tired and disgusted with herself for even thinking she could set things right, she rose from her seat. She'd blown it but good. He never wanted to see her again.

A door opened.

Shelley looked up.

Mason stood across the room, his hand still on the knob. The black robe was gone, and he was dressed in jeans and a gray polo shirt.

She smiled, nervously.

"What are you doing here, Shelley?"

She walked up to the rail that separated the spectators from those actively involved in the proceedings. To hell with her nerves. If she didn't say it all now, she never would.

"I'm here to throw myself upon the mercy of the court." She passed through the gate, then went to the table where the defendants usually sat with their attorneys. "Please Your Honor, I have no one else to speak for me."

A corner of Mason's mouth twitched. Other than that, there was no reaction.

"Proceed," he said in his court-is-now-in-session voice. He moved until he stood in front of his bench, then leaned back against it, crossing one foot in front of the other, his arms folded in front of him. "I'm listening."

Damn, he wasn't going to make this easy. But then, could she blame him?

"I've been a fool."

"The court needs details."

"I was a fool to take the word of a second party, doubting the first party when I hadn't even spoken to the first party. It was a horrible misunderstanding and I'm to blame. I should have tried harder. I realize that now, but I was young. It's in the past, and I want to keep it there."

"You're right. Though in my courtroom, I have to deal with the past, judge from it, because often the past is all I have to base an opinion on. To predict what the future will be."

He straightened and moved closer, filling the space in front her. Appearing like an unmovable object. She saw a devilish gleam in his eyes. "So how do you plead?"

"Guilty, your Honor. Extremely guilty."

"You realize you're going to have to be punished. A life sentence hardly seems enough. I'll have to add hard labor on top of that. A least twice. A boy and a girl. Maybe more if I deem you haven't been punished enough."

"Yes, your Honor."

"I don't know." He paused. "Based on your past, I could be making a risky judgement. Have you anything else to add to your case?"

"Only that I love you. Always have and always will. You were the first and I want you to be the last. And that I want to thank you for giving me my dream."

"How did you know?"

"Guess you'll have to order a full scale investigation to find out." She grinned.

"If that's a challenge, then I accept. I suggest we retire to my office while I review the evidence."

"Oh, your Honor. How you talk."

"There's something else I do even better than talk."

Mason grabbed her, pulling her into his embrace, kissing her soundly.

"I'll say," she said when they finally parted.

"I love you," he said. "And just so you know, you're not the only guilty party here. I was young and naïve, too."

She pulled his head down to give him another kiss. When they broke apart, he said, "Case dismissed."

Burning Desire #2

Once a bubbly teenager, Eddie (Edwina) Taylor spurned everyone, hiding a painful secret. A decade later, when firefighter Aaron Rhett Sinclair Renoux—a man who hates liars—investigates a fire in her grandmother's farmhouse, she's fears he has the potential to blow up her world completely.

Day 4

Aaron Rhett Sinclair Renoux, known as Rhett, stood at the fringes of the large crowd. Unlike the eager bidders who held numbered paddles and stood in the hot Georgia summer sun near the auctioneer, he stood in the shade and observed. His experience with auctions and one of this magnitude told him the bidders would have had to pre-register and provide approved funding. He'd just finished his workout and was on his way to the county animal shelter when he'd seen the auction that he'd forgotten about. Not a bidder this time but as someone who restored houses, flipping most of them, he was curious who would end up with one of the big historical Victorian homes in town that was still a one-family home…or had been. Now, it was in desperate need of a restoration. He would have bid on it himself had he learned about it sooner than the other day.

Arms crossed, legs apart in a comfortable but solid stance, he watched the proceedings. In the beginning, there had been a dozen bidders, but in the last ten minutes, only three were left. It was the third bidder who attracted his attention.

She was a local realtor, whose office was a block down and across the street from the fire department where he worked, but other than her name—Edwina Taylor—which he'd read on the front door of the office building and whom his co-workers called Eddie, he didn't know much about her. Anytime he and his fellow firefighters sat in a semi-circle in folding chairs just inside the station's bay, enjoying the weather and waiting for an alarm, they'd talk about fishing, the community, and the townspeople. Particularly those who drove or walked by. Since moving here five years ago, he'd learned a lot about the community and most of its people. There'd been little discussion about Eddie, though.

Up until now, he'd only seen her in passing. Here, he found himself staring, wanting to know more about her. Like what was her favorite flavor of ice cream? Did she like sports? Did she have any interesting hobbies? So many questions he wanted to ask.

He judged her to be five-three, about his age—thirty. Certainly, she couldn't be much older than that. Fresh looking. Little makeup. Not skinny, not voluptuous either. Fit, but, not from a gym. He wondered what she did in her spare time that kept her fit. He liked how the sun highlighted her auburn hair, sometimes revealing the red, sometimes an occasional strand of almost blonde. What would her hair look like up close? To touch? She looked like money but without the glitter and brand names.

Her simple, sleeveless, flower-print dress reminded him of a garden. The dress hugged her breasts, emphasized her small waist, and then flared out at the hips, the hem just at her knees. A leg man, he appreciated the glimpse of upper leg any time the wind lifted her skirt. Unlike many of the other women here today who wore flimsy sandals or skyscraper high heels, she wore sensible flats. Other than a watch and what looked like diamond studs, she wore no other jewelry. The entire outfit gave her the appearance of freedom, like she belonged in a cool forest or tree-shaded park rather than this wilting hot sun. She stood out from all the other women and he wasn't sure why. Yes, she dressed differently, but there was something more.

Her concentration on the auctioneer was intense and intrigued him. How she bit her lip when her two opponents outbid her, the brief hesitation when raising her paddle to counter their bids, but then shooting her hand up in the air, her arm ramrod straight. She may have thought she was hiding her disappointment when outbid, but she was taking each defeat personally. He wondered why.

A couple of the other firefighters had gone to school with her. What little he did know came from them when they talked how she'd been fun, a cheerleader, involved in sports, and other activities until her parents had died in a car accident just after her junior year.

Then suddenly, she became a recluse, never dating but always busy. One had suggested that she'd gone off and had a secret baby somewhere. Another said it was like she went crazy, never talking to anyone, backing out of all school activities. When Rhett had asked if any of them had dated her, they responded, "She hates men." "You'd be wasting your time with her."

Their comments made him more curious. She wasn't a typical woman, not now or even back then. Those differences made her all the more attractive. Somehow, he was going to get to know her.

Tires squealed.

He turned his head.

*****

Eddie stood in the hot sun watching her dream slip through her fingers. Seconds ago, she had raised the auction paddle, knowing it would be the last time. The old historic house, last owned by the Browne family, was being auctioned. She had hoped to buy it and flip it quickly. While she did care about the historic quality of the home considering her long ancestry ties to the community, her financial condition didn't allow her that luxury now. She'd been dancing with the devil the last five bids, watching her potential profit margin shrink, but to bid anymore would ruin her. What funds she had left would barely cover basic minimum expenses for a month…if she were lucky.

Tires squealed.

She turned her head.

A tall, lean, broad-shouldered man raced toward the street. She gasped seeing a young boy in the middle of the street, clutching a big ball between his hands.

A car, just a few lengths away, headed straight for the boy.

A woman screamed.

The man reached the child.

Grabbed him with both hands.

Then dove toward the other side of the road, tucking the child tightly against his own stomach and chest.

They disappeared from view as the car came to a screeching halt, blocking them from sight.

People began running, herself included. She stopped at the curb, seeing the man rise. Quickly, he was surrounded by others.

He held the child tightly against him but let go when someone else took the child.

He was taller than most of those around him. One man checked him over, while another carried the child to the fire truck and first responders who had already been there, having stopped moments earlier at the auction. The fire station was only a few blocks away. Another siren, sounding in the distance, headed toward them.

She saw the man shake his head and mouth the words, *I'm okay*.

An ambulance pulled up. Someone opened the

back doors before the driver and the second paramedic exited the cab. The responder with the child stepped into the ambulance and a woman—she presumed to be the child's mother—followed. She could see a paramedic inside checking the child's vitals. Amazingly, the child looked unharmed. Just scared.

Her attention returned to the first man, the rescuer. Tall, with dark hair. He looked familiar but she couldn't place him. She frowned. Where had she seen him before?

He wasn't a life-long local. With Laurel Ridge a small community of only five thousand, she'd grown up with many of its residents. Additionally, as one of only three realtors, she always got to meet new arrivals, either as a client or as clients of the other two realtors whenever she was the realtor selling the house. This man she'd never met. Not officially anyway.

The child and mother exited the ambulance. A couple of men pulled the man over to the ambulance. When he turned his back toward her, she gasped. His T-shirt was torn. She could only imagine the scrapes on his skin. Others began pulling his shirt off. They were being careful, pulling the material away from his back. Once again, he shook his head, saying he was okay, but the paramedic inspected his back, dabbing it with what Eddie figured was antiseptic. The man's muscles flexed under the medic's touch. The medic finished and the man turned around.

Even from this distance, his washboard abdomen

was impressive. Obviously, he worked out. When someone motioned for him to get into the back of the ambulance, he raised his hands, shaking his head, saying *no.*

One of the firefighters walked up to the injured man and handed him a dark blue T-shirt, which he put on. *Laurel Ridge Firefighter* stretched across his chest. The shirt was a duplicate of the first responders' shirts. She remembered. He was a firefighter. She'd seen him before at the station washing trucks or sitting in one of the folding chairs on the sidewalk, in the shade, enjoying a breeze with his peers.

He shook hands with the two medics, who then shut the ambulance's back doors and got into the vehicle, driving off.

He turned, his gaze scanning the crowd until he saw her. His gaze held hers, rooting her to edge of the curb. Unable to move, she couldn't stop looking at him either.

Behind her, Eddie heard the auctioneer speaking again, asking if there were any final bids. Snapped out of her trance, she turned, and took steps back toward the auction. The auctioneer's gavel hit the podium ending the sale.

The auction was over. Nothing to do now but return the paddle.

As she made her way toward the table, she could feel the man's gaze on her back. The warmth of her cheeks had nothing to do with the hot sun.

She didn't want to be noticed.

Eddie glanced at the winning buyer who'd been bidding against her but didn't recognize him. Judging from the briefcase he carried and the suit he wore, he had to be an out-of-town attorney or a corporate representative. He stopped and spoke to Mason Baylock, a former classmate of hers who had returned to Laurel Ridge six months ago, joining Joe Benton's law firm, and was now a circuit judge. Gossips revealed Mason was pursuing his high school sweetheart, Shelley Willis, by eating at the diner nearly every night during her shift.

The two men shook hands. Nothing unusual for him to be chatting with another attorney, but attorneys here in Laurel Ridge didn't dress formal unless they were in court.

She looked back at the house again and sighed. Only someone with deep pockets would be able to restore this large house to its former glory.

The house was grand and situated on prime real estate where just blocks away the area was fast being rezoned as commercial. Already, several large homes like it nearby had been turned into offices or small businesses.

For a small town, commercial improvements kept the town alive and functional. It would be sad to see the old home gone, but Eddie could only imagine the hundred-year-old pipes and electrical wiring that would need replacing. In fact, she suspected that the place needed to be gutted, brought up to code, and insulated properly before any other beautification remodeling and restoration could begin. Had it been hers, she could have made money taking out the antiquated bathroom and kitchen materials, reselling them before selling the house to outsiders. Rarely did anyone want one-hundred-year-old tubs, knobs, and faucets. Most of her buyers wanted granite and stainless steel in the kitchen and the most up-to-date utilities in the bathrooms.

The crowd began dispersing. Eddie finally reached the auctioneer's table and handed in her paddle.

Hungry, she decided to forgo the usual peanut butter sandwich at her desk. Even though she was counting pennies, she decided to splurge a little and go to the diner a few doors down from her office and across the street from the courthouse.

Minutes later, she opened the diner door, the bell above her head jingling. Mid-afternoon, she expected to see only a few patrons sipping ice tea or lemonade. Instead, the place was packed as if it was lunch or dinnertime. Some were strangers, out-of-towners who'd just come from the auction and were now seeking an air-conditioned haven from the heat and humidity, sitting among the usual locals, many of whom she'd seen at the auction.

A couple got up from a booth near the back. She made her way there, meeting Connie, the diner's head waitress, who had an empty tub in hand for the dirty dishes. She began filling the tub while talking. Eddie couldn't remember a time when Connie hadn't worked here. In the space of a minute, Connie told her who had bought the house—an out of towner, a historian with deep pockets, signaling the attorney Eddie had seen earlier, in a booth across the room. Connie excelled at talking to and with strangers.

"Hang on just a minute, Eddie," she said, indicating the tabletop. "I'll be right back to wipe it down."

A minute later and finally seated, Eddie gave Connie her drink order. She propped her chin in her hand and stared out the window. She didn't want to think about her circumstances. She was so tired of trying to make all the pieces fit.

That sale with a quick flip could have given her a year's cushion. Something she needed desperately. She'd been making good headway on her father's debts up until two years ago. Now, she was stymied, stuck on this financial and economic plateau. She was tired of the market working against her. Tired of trying her best and pretending that she was doing well.

She sighed, clasped her hands in front of her, and looked around the room. Various families and couples sat in most of the booths and tables talking and eating. Here and there the occasional single woman sat alone—all of them familiar faces and most of them widows on small fixed incomes who weren't interested in selling homes paid for long ago. She couldn't blame them. If she could afford the maintenance of a house already paid for, she doubted she would move either.

Several men sat at the counter, some eating alone, a few at the end of the counter engaged in boisterous conversation. The man who had rescued the child was there, too. He appeared to be the butt of some jokes. His eyes twinkled as he laughed and his smile was wide and sincere. Perfect white teeth offset his tan. Muscles in his arms and shoulders flexed as he moved and laughed. A good-looking man. In high school, he was just the type she would have dated. Until her senior year that is. The year she stopped dating. When life had changed completely. The rumors that had swirled around her that she was secretly married, pregnant, or crazy had all been outrageous. Fortunately, no one had guessed the truth.

As Connie delivered her drink, Eddie looked up to see Shelley Willis seating William Stuart, a former classmate now library director, in the booth in front of hers. He sat facing her. Shelley walked away without a glance toward Eddie. Every time Shelley snubbed her, she felt bad. Once, they had been best friends. Before Eddie's world had been turned upside down. She frowned. Come to think of it, she couldn't remember spending a lot of time with Shelley in high school. Why not?

Hearing Connie call her name, Eddie looked up. "Sorry. You caught me not paying attention."

"Oh, you were paying attention to something all right," Connie said, tilting her head toward the noisy men. "Something worth noticing, I'd say. Whatchya having?" she asked.

Eddie ordered a hamburger and fries.

Connie started to move away, hesitated, and then

leaned in toward Eddie. "She still cares. More than you think. Both of y'alls let pride get in the way. A shame that." She turned and left.

Eddie stared after her, surprised yet not surprised. Eddie knew she was referring to Shelley. Connie was unlike anyone she knew. Never married, she cared about everyone equally and deeply. She remembered customers' names and their favorite meals easily. More than once, Connie had given Eddie unasked-for advice and always when Eddie needed it most. Was this one of those times?

Eddie glanced at William. He looked as if he was waiting for a response.

"I'm sorry," she said. "Did you say something?"

"I did, but you were miles away."

"Actually, not that far away."

"Sorry you didn't get the house. You gave it a good try."

"You were there? I didn't see you."

Connie arrived at William's table to take his order.

Laughter at the end of the counter drew Eddie's attention. The firefighter looked her way, then patted the shoulder of the guy next to him, moving away from the group, heading her way. She couldn't tear her gaze away from him. His gait was long and he walked with confidence. Was he really coming this way? Why? The bathrooms were on the other side of the building.

Connie blocked her view for a long second, then Connie walked around the firefighter, laughing at something William said to her.

The man grasped William's shoulder. William greeted the man warmly, calling him Flame. *Flame*? That was an odd name. Especially, since there was nothing flame-like about him, other than being a firefighter.

Immediately, Flame slid into the seat opposite William's, his back to Eddie. His dark hair, not quite long enough to cover the edge of the shirt, curled at the ends. She wondered if the humidity made it curl.

An image of her fingers in his hair popped into her mind. Immediately, goosebumps crawled up and down her arms. She pushed the thought out of her head, happy at Connie's distraction of placing her burger and fries before her.

She picked up the sandwich and bit into it hungrily. Incredible. Marty, the cook, never failed to make a great burger, one worthy of several napkins. The mark of a good sandwich. Truth be told, every meal she'd ever had in here always exceeded her expectations.

She heard her name. She looked up and saw Flame turned around in his seat, both he and William looking at her. She grabbed her napkin and wiped her mouth, chewing quickly. She swallowed. "I'm sorry." She grabbed her glass of water and took a quick sip.

"Your burger had your full interest," William said.

She laughed. "Yes, it did."

William continued. "I was telling Rhett—"

That was his name! Rhett Renoux.

"—that with all of your connections, you might

know of a restorer."

She frowned. William had taken an old foundry and turned it into a beautiful library, with two gorgeous condos above. He lived in one of them.

"But, William, you rebuilt and restored the library and condos yourself."

Rhett responded. "We need one for the car. William is helping me restore my house, but we don't know of anyone who can restore the car—you know, the yellow Volkswagen that was pulled out of the lake earlier this week."

She looked at William, incredulous that she hadn't made the connection. "*That* was *your* car? That's right. I forgot all about it. I vaguely remember you saying you sold it because it was yellow." The event had captured the seniors' attention because he'd sold it the day after their big graduation party that took place a week before graduation, getting it as an early graduation gift. But then, their attention was quickly diverted to the next big event—Mason and Shelley's big breakup the day after graduation. She never did know any of the details of either event. That entire year she'd been too busy coping with the mess her parents had left her with, so she'd only heard snippets of those two big events.

William shrugged his shoulders and grinned sheepishly. "Unfortunately, yes. That's what I told everyone back then. Hard to say anything else at the time considering I knew it was at the bottom of the lake. Thankfully, I wasn't revealed as its owner when the newspaper wrote about it earlier this week.

Though, I doubt my identity will be a secret anymore."

Rhett laughed. "He gave a TV news interview this morning."

"What choice did I have?" William responded. "I'd rather everyone hear the truth from me than interview old classmates and provide credence to any one of the rumors that were going around back then."

"Where is it now?" she asked.

William pointed a finger at Rhett.

"Was in my garage," Rhett said. "It's on its way to Clint's house as we speak. He's the new owner."

"You sold it? Why?" she asked. "I would think it would be a collector's item."

"Not in the shape it's in. Besides, I don't care to keep it," William said.

"You're sounding mysterious."

William laughed. "Not in the least."

She knew differently. That laugh guaranteed he was hiding something. Something was off, but she couldn't put a finger on what exactly.

Behind the library, William had built an attached garage, big enough for both condo residents and with an elevator that allowed them access to their homes without access into the library. No one could tell that the garage hadn't been part of the original foundry. But, the garage only allowed each resident just one car. William loved his Corvette too much to park it outside in the elements, even though he drove it year-round. It made sense that he'd park the disabled car elsewhere.

"I can't promise anything," she said, "Maybe one of the contractors I've worked with will know of someone."

"If you find anyone," Williams said, "let Rhett or Clint know since it's Clint's car now. He'll be the one restoring it. Rhett's just a middleman helping me find a restorer.

Rhett leaned toward her and whispered. "William couldn't *wait* to get rid of it." Rhett's gaze captured hers. His eyes were darker than his hair, almost black and mesmerizing this close. He sat back in his seat, adding, "Regardless of anything he says."

William laughed. To Eddie, he said, "Hopefully, you'll have better luck than we've had. Thanks for helping."

"No problem," she replied. She needed a diversion from her own situation right now. She was happy to help.

"Talk to you soon," Rhett said, then turned so he was facing William again.

Rhett had conversed with her as if they'd known each other forever. Wasn't that the Southern way? That no one was a stranger? And yet…how long had Rhett lived here in Laurel Ridge without either of them exchanging a word? Saying hello to the entire group of men at the fire house didn't count.

She picked up a couple fries and bit off the ends, contemplating the man who had his back to her. He made her nervous in a tingly kind of way, but she couldn't figure out why. He had an aura of self-confidence and strength, yet something gentle she couldn't name. Was that because she'd seen him rescue a child?

Just as she finished her meal, Rhett got up and left. She got up, collected her purse, the bill, said goodbye to William as she passed his booth, and went to the end of the short line at the register to pay.

Waiting her turn, she watched through the diner's big windows as Rhett walked toward the fire station. So entranced, she didn't notice that Connie, at the register, had called her name twice already. Connie touched her arm.

"Oh, sorry," Eddie said, realizing she was apologizing yet again, that she'd been distracted. She paid for the meal, smiled at Connie's teasing, who was telling her it was about time a man caught her attention. Eddie poo-pooed Connie's remarks, annoyed that Connie smiled in return.

Eddie walked back to her office, enjoying the slight breeze. The temperature had dropped a bit, too. A storm on the way?

As she walked past the fire department, she glanced at the open bays. Both ladder trucks were there with no one around. Even though she had tried to laugh away Connie's comments, was it possible that for the first time in a long time, someone *had* caught her attention? She dismissed the thought. A good-looking man with the name of Rhett would capture any woman's attention for a few moments. Nothing more.

At her building, she grabbed the front door's handle. Lettering on the door told of the five offices located here. Opening the door, she entered the hallway, moved past the wall mailboxes and the staircase on the right that led to the apartments above, and walked past the first two offices on the left. Hers was the third, with two more beyond. All the offices were small and on the same side of the hall with their own doors to lock. The main walls of the complex, on the right and left, were brick from floor to ceiling, walls shared by businesses on either side of this building. All the offices had glass fronts and were divided with plastered walls that didn't quite reach the ceiling for heating and cooling purposes.

She liked having her office in the middle. Out of sight from the front windows and the winter temps and hot summer sun, but not so far in the back that she felt forgotten. The only time she really suffered was when there was no power with no air moving, especially in the summer. During those few occasions, she'd go home and return to work after the power had been restored. As a sole proprietor with no assistant, it was easy to work at home if needed.

Had been, she corrected herself. No working from home these days. Not after recently selling the only home she'd ever known. Her parents' house.

She sat at her desk, staring at the computer screen, contemplating her situation. Her financial spreadsheet hadn't changed a bit this week.

No answers were forthcoming.

With no customers buying, she couldn't show new properties, and the proceeds from the last closing were nearly spent. The immediate bills were stacking up again. She didn't want to think about the deep overwhelming fear that threatened to swamp her every time she thought about no one wanting to sell or buy in the next couple weeks.

She picked up the phone. Needing a distraction and with nothing else to do, she started looking for a car restorer.

*****

When William had told him at lunchtime that Shelley had once been friends with Eddie, Rhett decided Mason would be a source for accurate information, plus he'd be more open than Shelley. He doubted Shelley would volunteer much of anything. William had provided some details but Mason would know more considering his position in the community.

"You're a welcome interruption," Mason said, motioning Rhett into his courthouse office, shutting the door. "My day's been boring with paperwork and files. What brings you here?"

Normally, Rhett and Mason met for lunch at the diner once a week. They'd become fast friends ever since their first meeting a few weeks after Mason's return, when he'd joined Joe Benton's law firm. Soon after, he had been appointed Circuit Judge when Joe's dad, who had held the position for two decades had died of a sudden heart attack. It was at the post-funeral gathering that Rhett had met the rest of Mason's friends who were also classmates—Cutter Logan, Annie Martin, Clint Anderson, William Stuart, Joe Benton, Jefferson Jackson, and Shelley Willis.

Eddie, another classmate, had left immediately after the funeral, so he didn't get a chance to meet her then. It was at that gathering when he'd become part of the group.

Soon after, Mason had hired Rhett as a contractor to restore his cottage because he lacked the time to do it himself. After the work was done, he, Mason, and William talked about forming a company to restore homes and other buildings in the community. Rhett had revealed he had money to invest. Mason advised him to keep quiet about it, otherwise he'd find himself the victim of some Laurel Ridge mothers who would be matchmaking him to their daughters.

In a few days, they'd be signing corporate papers that would include Joe and Clint.

"Tell me about Eddie," he asked Mason. "What do you know about her? I know you were in her class."

"Shelley and I both were," Mason replied.

"Oh, congratulations on getting the house at the auction," Rhett said, accepting the cold can of soda Mason retrieved from the tiny refrigerator hidden behind a credenza door. Mason had hired an attorney to bid on the house for him. He didn't want anyone in town knowing that he was the actual owner, letting only Rhett & William in on the secret.

"I bought it with the intention of surprising Shelley with it, but now I doubt she'll accept it as a gift. She's rebuffed me at every turn, until the other day."

Since arriving back in town again, Mason had been trying to get back with his high school sweetheart—Shelley—and he'd been failing miserably. Mason had told him that Shelley's dream was to turn the house into a day-care center and a home for seniors who didn't need much assistance, renting out the upstairs bedrooms, getting the two age groups together.

Mason continued. "She's got a lot of pride...like all of us."

"It'll make a great first project for our new company," Rhett said. "I'd bet she'd accept a management position for the building if it came from the corporation. Wait a minute. What happened the other day?"

"We got locked in the freezer long enough for me to ask questions where she couldn't run away."

"And?" Rhett asked.

Mason leaned back in his chair with a sigh, a smile, and then a look of frustration. "We kissed."

"And?"

"Her lips said yes and she didn't try to stop me, but the words she uttered later contradicted the passion we both felt. I thought she was just in denial. The next day, I learned she'd been pregnant back then and had lost the baby after having run away from my father, falling in the process. She didn't know how my father knew about the baby--guessed it more like. He'd told me she came to the house to break up with me and I believed him! I never knew about the baby. All these years, I believed him. I went to see Mom the other day, and she confirmed everything."

Anytime Rhett was in the diner with Mason, it

was easy to see how smitten his friend was with Shelley, the way his gaze followed her around the diner. Mason had confided that his main reason for returning to Laurel Ridge was to connect with Shelley again. He hadn't been able to forget her. Now that he was here, he didn't want to move away regardless of where their relationship went. He liked the community's slower pace to the fast-moving Atlanta.

Mason continued. "I can't stand this waiting, not talking."

"Then go to her place tonight and talk to her."

Mason nodded. "You're right. I need to. Enough about me. So, one of our local gals has finally piqued your interest?" He grinned at Rhett.

"Looks that way, doesn't it?" Rhett hated anyone knowing he was curious, but this was the fastest way to get information, and he knew Mason would keep their conversation private.

"What do you want to know?" Mason asked. "Eddie and Shelley were best friends up until they started high school."

"What happened?"

Mason hesitated. "I don't know. Shelley never said back then. They just stopped being friends." He paused for a few seconds, then continued. "Up until our senior year, Eddie was a cheerleader, involved in student government, an honor student, lots of clubs and organizations. She was the life of any party. Everyone loved her. Bubbly, talkative, every boy's dream of a date. She dated casually, wasn't serious with anyone. She liked to instigate group dates, saying that serious romances were for after high school. When we finished our junior year, we were all set to nominate her as homecoming queen in the fall."

"And, she wasn't? You didn't?"

"Well, she was, but she turned it down, so it went to the next highest vote getter."

Rhett frowned. "Doesn't sound like a typical high schooler. What happened?"

"Her parents died just after our junior year. There was no other family, just her. She petitioned the courts to allow her to stay in her parents' home as a minor and they let her since she was a month away from turning eighteen. Connie volunteered to supervise. You know Connie, mother to all with no children of her own. Eddie changed totally. She became withdrawn, disappeared from all events. No one knew what she was doing. Immediately after graduation, she became a realtor and has been working hard at it ever since. Successful at it, too."

"Did she start dating after high school?"

"No. At least, not that I heard of anyway. And, you know this community—"

"A regular gossip mill?"

Mason laughed. "It is that. Used to be I hated it, but now…it does have its benefits. As for Eddie…" He looked at Rhett with renewed interest. "I'm glad you're interested."

Rhett grinned a little. "Maybe…" He frowned. "Yes… No… Yes."

"Decisive, aren't you?"

"I'll admit, I've been curious since the first time I

saw her walk past the station. I'm intrigued."

Mason laughed. "And, that's how it always starts."

Hurriedly, Rhett added, "I don't want a full-blown relationship, but she's…okay, yes, I'm interested. I'm more than curious."

Mason laughed aloud. "This should be interesting. The Uncommitted meeting up with the Non-Dater."

"Uncommitted?"

"You don't know? You're seen as Laurel Ridge's mysterious playboy. Seems you've been around the block a few times, with a reputation of first dates."

"I'm not ready to settle down."

"Hence, The Uncommitted."

Rhett laughed. He couldn't argue the tag. The only things he was committed to were his career and the houses he restored. No one had interested him enough for him to want a second, let alone a third date.

Minutes later, Rhett left Mason's office as Mason's phone began ringing. They agreed to have lunch later in the week.

As Rhett walked toward the firehouse, he thought back over their conversation. *Been around the block a few times.* He never talked about his dates. Usually, he tried to date out of town, but if people were talking, then it had to be the girls who were sharing information. He sure hadn't and wouldn't. Never had.

Mysterious? He laughed at that one. Just because he didn't blab about his past? In the five years since he had moved here, no one had asked the questions he would have happily answered. Only William and Mason knew much about him and even they only knew a little. Everyone talked about everyone else but rarely listened to each other. At least, that had been his experience. Besides, it was far easier to ask the questions than to answer them. He enjoyed getting to know people. If they didn't get to know him to the same degree, well, that wasn't his fault. All they had to do was ask. He'd be forthcoming.

Playboy? No. Never. He respected women too much to take advantage of them. His mother would have slapped him silly if he had. He liked to think she and his father would have been proud of their son had they seen him growing up.

And, the bit about Mason laughing at his not being ready to settle down? *Was he ready?* He shook his head. The fact that he had to ask himself the question told him he wasn't. No one could convince him otherwise. Curiosity wasn't the same as being ready.

*****

Taking her peanut butter sandwich outside, Eddie walked around the old farmhouse, re-examining it. The original front wall was stone and included one of two fireplaces. As additions had been made, wood siding had been used, all painted a robin's egg blue. A huge wrap-around-porch encased the house, making it appear even larger than it was. On hot summer days, though, the porch had been a welcome relief for her grandmother as she canned and quilted out on the porch.

Eddie acknowledged she needed to put the house on the market and to quit stalling. While it was historic, it needed more work than she could afford. The porch plus the wide hall that ran from front to back splitting the lower floor in two, allowing fresh air to cool the house naturally when the two side-by-side doors at both ends of the hall were wide open, were its best features.

Her grandparents had built onto the original small house, turning it into the farmhouse that it was now. Located a couple miles from town, the nearest neighbor was Connie. A dense copse between the two houses kept each secluded, and Eddie liked it that way. Once upon a time, they were the only two houses out here. Not anymore.

Her parents had inherited it upon her grandmother's death when Eddie had been in grade school. And then, she had inherited the property when her parents died, but it had been tied into a trust that she couldn't touch until she was twenty-five. The bank who served as the trust's receiver always kept it rented to pay for the basic expenses, but they had never made the upgrade repairs that should have been done over the years. Once she reached twenty-five, it was easier just to keep renting it out. While she'd wanted to make upgrades, she never had enough money to do it. She needed the rental money.

Selling it wouldn't provide the real income she needed, but it would cut her losses for this place since losing her tenant recently. The insurance, electricity, having the lawn cut… Granted, the place was a bit of an eyesore in an up-and-coming neighborhood based on the for-sale farmland across the street that would no doubt become an urban community. The town had finally stretched out toward the farmhouse.

She needed to let go of her memories and just sell it.

Finished with her sandwich, Eddie entered the house through the mudroom entrance that led to the kitchen. At her grandmother's request, her grandfather had changed the floorplan, splitting the huge country kitchen into two rooms: a smaller kitchen and a mudroom that included a washer and dryer. This way, the farm shoes and boots didn't track into the rest of the house. Heaven help anyone who tracked dirt into it. Entering the mudroom from outside, immediately to the right—the outside wall—were hooks on the wall for coats and a bench for muddy shoes and boots underneath. The opposite interior wall, with the kitchen on the other side, contained the washer and dryer. The wall to the left of the entrance was storage: closets and cupboards for out of season coats, seasonal equipment, and canning equipment that had been used out on the porch, like peelers and bushel baskets.

As she strolled through the empty downstairs rooms, her steps sounded hollow. *Like my heart feels,* she thought.

Standing in the door frame of the formal parlor, she felt goosebumps. From memory, she saw faint images of her grandmother, parents, and a Christmas tree in the corner of the parlor, a fire blazing in the fireplace, the old heavy sofa unlike today's furniture, and other remembered pieces of heavy, wood furniture. Just as quickly the images became shadows. The emptiness of the room clutched at her heart. She gasped at the sudden sadness and walked out the front door to the wrap-around porch.

She loved this house. How could she think about selling it?

Up until now, she'd been successful in masking the real circumstances of her existence, but now she was at the end of that financial road, feeling worn out, defeated, and without a new creative idea of any kind. A year ago, she had put her parents' house up for sale. Its closing had been a little over a month ago.

At that same time, the farmhouse renter had left so she figured she could clean the farmhouse up quickly and sell it right away, too. After all, she really didn't need a house this big, but the more time she'd spent this last month cleaning and doing a little painting, the more she'd grown to love it all over again.

Now, she didn't want to sell it.

Unfortunately, with the economy forcing her hand, she'd written up the listing last week. She still needed to polish the ad, take some photos, post it online, and stick the For Sale sign in the yard, but she kept hesitating. Waiting. But, for what? A miracle?

Back inside, she moved into the dining room, admiring the sparkle of the old chandelier that had come back to life after washing the crystals one by one and rehanging them. So many good memories from when she was a child visiting her grandparents.

She got her sleeping bag out of the closet under the stairway and set it on the floor in the den, a room facing the road. Fortunately, the heavy drapes kept any inside light from leaking out. As far as anyone knew, the farmhouse was empty. She didn't want anyone knowing she slept here. She didn't want to answer the questions, and she didn't want people talking about her.

Grabbing the last of her grandma's crystal—the candlesticks and by far her most favorite pieces of her grandma's dishes—Eddie stuck new candles into the holders, just like she used to do at Christmas time when she was little. The Christmas dinners were magical—a sea of color, textures, wonderful smells, and even better, the tastes.

These candlesticks were the only crystal she had kept. She didn't need or want closets full of heirlooms she'd never use. She'd be renting an apartment once this place sold.

She set the crystal on the fireplace mantle.

Even though she'd kept the electricity on because of the refrigerator, she hadn't brought in any lamps, which this room required as there was no overhead light. The candles served as her only light.

Because the farmhouse was supposed to be empty, she parked the car in the carriage house, always keeping its door shut. She was grateful that there weren't any windows in the relatively small building. No one would ever know that her car was parked in there.

Back in the kitchen, she looked out the window and the fields of corn that grew behind the farmhouse. She sighed deeply, thinking back over the afternoon. Usually able to find the people she needed in her research, this time she'd drawn a blank trying to find a restorer for Clint's car.

She sighed again. Tomorrow was another day.

Whippoorwill Lake was behind the corn, less than half a mile away. Once the corn was cut, she'd have a clear view of the lake.

The sun was sinking, but there was still lots of light left in the day.

From the kitchen, she entered the hall, going out the hallway's back door rather than through the mudroom and onto the wrap-around porch, welcoming the evening breeze. She fled from the farmhouse, breathing in the fresh air. No wallowing in memories right now. A walk would clear the cobwebs.

She clattered down the steps and walked down the service dirt road that led to Whippoorwill Lake. Few people used this road and it would allow her the privacy she needed and craved right now.

A quarter mile down the road, she began to relax. Crows, red-winged blackbirds, and other birds flew among the corn, sitting on the tasseled tops communicating and singing. Eddie admired their freedom, their lack of desperation. She knew their lives were led by instinctive needs: to mate, to eat, to stay safe, and that their lives were relatively short in comparison.

She wondered if they ever had thoughts of want other than their immediate need or desire.

Isn't that what she'd been doing these past twelve years? Reacting rather than planning or wanting?

What did she want?

Truthfully, she never thought much about her future since losing her parents, becoming a realtor, and paying down their debt. She enjoyed her job—career actually—more than she would have thought. Each new house put on the market and each new buyer became challenges. She was a matchmaker and good at it. Enough people had told her so. The last ten years had been a decade of financial highs and lows but never this low.

Up until now, she hadn't been interested in dating; she'd been too busy. Old-fashioned enough to believe she needed to be asked out, once she became standoffish and distant in high school, the invitations stopped. Once she withdrew and wasn't arranging the group dates, those stopped as well. At the time, it had been self-preservation and she often wondered if maybe she hadn't isolated herself too far from everyone.

She stopped and stared ahead for a minute. Had her promise to pay her parents' debt become like this road, with a seemingly dead end? While she knew this road eventually ended at Whippoorwill Lake, where did her road end?

Other than paying off that debt, she had no plan,

no goal. Worse, she wasn't even sure she wanted to continue walking this debt-ladened road anymore. What would happen if she quit? Gave up? Told her father's company that she wanted to renege on paying back the money her father had embezzled? Would they think badly of her? What if she gave up being a realtor?

No, she couldn't give up on her career. There wasn't any other job she wanted to try.

She sighed and started walking again. She wished she had answers. How many more years must she be shackled to her parents' lies?

Once the sun dropped below the horizon of corn, Eddie turned around and headed back. It was getting dark quickly, and she didn't relish being caught out here without a flashlight.

Just as the last sliver of light faded from the sky, she reached the yard. Inside, she lit the candles and unrolled her sleeping bag. That's when she realized that she'd left her overnight bag in the car. While she stashed and kept the sleeping bag and pillows in the closet, she kept her personal bag of toiletries in the trunk of her car with her clothes.

And, on the walk out to the carriage house, she remembered her phone was at the office, recharging. Not a good day for remembering, she surmised.

Returning from the carriage house a few minutes later, the bag on her shoulder, she stepped back into the house. She frowned. What was that smell?

SMOKE!

She ran to the den.

Drapes at one window were on fire!

Flames rose quickly, licking the ceiling, with other curtains catching fire.

No phone!

Help. She had to get help.

Running to the car, she threw the bag still in her hand into the backseat, and backed out of the carriage house, not bothering to shut its doors. She drove toward town. Connie's driveway was empty.

She continued down the road, passing a couple cars.

Turning into the first driveway that had a car, she put her car into park and jumped out.

Sirens sounded in the distance. She hesitated. Were they coming out here?

Already?

How was that possible?

Two firetrucks raced past the driveway. She jumped in the car, backed out, and followed the trucks.

Sure enough, they pulled into her grandparents' driveway. Someone driving past must have called it in.

She parked alongside the road, out of the way, and got out.

Crossing the street, she stood on the grass next to a large tree near the road and out of the way. Volunteer vehicles with swirling amber lights pulled into the driveway behind the firetrucks and onto the lawn.

Men spilled across the yard, some pulling hoses,

dragging them to the farmhouse. Some with axes went around to the back, disappearing from view.

She saw Rhett with one of the hoses, holding it ready, yelling for someone to turn on the water.

Stunned, Eddie just stood there.

An upstairs bedroom window, the one above the den, reflected flames. The candles! But, how could they have started the fire? They'd been nowhere near the windows. How could she have been so stupid to leave the room with the candles lit?

Flames shot through the roof.

How was the fire racing through the farmhouse so fast? The house was old, but was it so dry that it acted like kindling?

She wrapped her arms around herself. Tears slid down her face. Everything she owned that wasn't in the car was gone. Everything. Her last hope of being able to rebound from her parents' debt was now bright orange and red from the fire in front of her.

The roof over the bedroom collapsed. She heard shouts as the men warned each other.

An explosion sounded, and flames shot out of the den windows, glass shattering onto the lawn.

Eddie gasped, her hand going to her mouth.

She couldn't bear to watch anymore. She turned and went back to her car. There was nothing she could do. She headed toward town.

She found herself parked in front of the diner, not remembering driving there. The diner's lights beamed out onto the sidewalk. The only lights in any of the downtown buildings. As usual.

How late was it?

She looked at her watch. The lights in the diner dimmed. Closing time. Was it eleven already?

She lay her forehead on the steering wheel.

A tap on the window next to her. She jumped, startled.

Connie. The car still running, Eddie pressed the button to lower the window.

"Come into the diner."

"You're closed."

"Doesn't matter. Turn the car off and come in." Connie moved away, walking in front of the car toward the diner, heading for the front door.

Eddie knew better than to argue. She rolled up the window and turned off the ignition, pulling out the keys. She followed Connie into the diner, shutting the front door.

"Lock it, will you?" Connie said, from behind the register.

Eddie did. She turned and stood there, not knowing what to do. Connie had taken off her apron and was hanging it on the wall peg behind the register.

"Come back here and sit," she said, indicating a booth farthest away from the windows, moving that way herself.

Eddie followed and slid into the booth opposite Connie.

Eddie let out a huge breath of air, realizing she'd been holding it. She felt her shoulders drop. Exhaustion, mixed with a deep sadness, filled her.

"You're coming home with me tonight," Connie began.

Eddie looked up, surprised. Connie had that look that Eddie had seen lots of times. A look of both empathy and of knowing. How did she do it?

Connie continued. "I heard about the fire on the CB," she said pointing toward the kitchen. "So, you certainly can't stay there anymore."

Eddie opened her mouth, but to say what?

Connie kept going. "I know you've been staying out there nights for several weeks. Don't deny it. You have nowhere to go and I'm not letting you live in your car. You're coming home with me."

Eddie closed her mouth and considered her options. Connie was right. She couldn't live in her car. Not in the summer heat. She didn't have enough money to start renting an apartment. And, right now, she didn't have the energy to consider other options.

"Yes, Ma'am."

"Good. I'm glad you can still see reason. Don't you think you've carried the weight of your parents on your shoulders long enough?"

She stared at Connie. "Ho…how…how'd you find—?"

"Don't you know by now that everyone tells me everything? You kids," she said, shaking her head. "Come on, let's get going. You're tired. I'm tired. We could both use some sleep. Tomorrow's my day off. We can talk then."

*****

Day 5

The next morning, Eddie woke to the smell of bacon. Even before she opened her eyes, she could tell the room was bright with sunshine. The windows faced east and the walls were painted a bright yellow that equaled the sun. Even on a cloudy day, she imagined the room retained its cheery color.

Images of last night's events replayed in her mind like a bad movie. Standing in the shower, she wanted to stay in the warm mist that cocooned her body and relaxed her muscles at the same time.

Dressed, she entered the kitchen and saw Connie at the stove, scrambling eggs. "Morning, Connie."

"Morning, Sunshine. How'd you sleep?"

"Not good at first."

"Considering everything, I'm not surprised."

"I finally fell asleep about five." Eddie pulled out a chair and sat down. The table already set, Connie dumped eggs on Eddie's plate and then her own.

Eddie sighed. "I wish the fire was nothing more than a bad dream. The house is gone. I have nothing left."

"You have me and lots of other people who care about you. And, the house isn't gone. Rhett stopped by this morning and said despite everything, most of the house is okay. I called the station last night, letting them know where you were staying. In the meantime, eat."

Connie plopped the empty pan in the sink, then moved to the refrigerator, opening it. "Orange or apple juice?"

"Apple, please."

Connie poured two glasses, while Eddie reached for some bacon, then toast. Connie moved to the table, set the juice glasses down, then sat across from Eddie, grabbing her share of the bacon and toast.

"You can do this, Eddie. You're stronger than you realize."

"Doesn't feel like it."

They began eating.

Eddie paused. "Where do I even begin?"

"Rhett said you'll need to contact your insurance company right away. That you'll need to get the fire report from them when you file."

"Fire report?" Oh gawd, the candles. Her stomach rolled over, knowing that she would be found having caused the fire.

"He offered to help with the insurance forms, too."

"What time is it?"

"Nine."

"Seriously?"

"You were more exhausted than you know. Stress does that."

"I remember." After her parents died, there'd been days she didn't even dress or brush her teeth. Just crawled back into the sheets and slept time away.

It was as if Connie knew what she was thinking when she replied, "We all go through it, plus I see it in customers all the time. When you feel tired, rest. It's the best thing you can do for yourself. And, you're going to stay here until you can move back into the farmhouse. I'll enjoy the company."

Suddenly, Eddie felt more overwhelmed and scared about her future than she had last night. She let her fork rest on her plate, rested both hands in her lap, and sat back in the chair. The weight of it all pressed down on her, just like when her parents had died. No, this was worse. It was like losing them all over again, because the farmhouse was her last connection to them. She had so little left now. She wrung her hands.

Connie reached over and patted her arm. "Everything will get done in its time. Try not to worry, and I'm here anytime you want to talk or need me."

Eddie squeezed Connie's hand. "Thank you." The problem was Connie didn't know how she was losing everything. Absolutely everything.

Connie got up and picked up both plates, taking them to the sink.

Eddie wanted to spill her guts, tell Connie everything, but she couldn't. She couldn't bear to have Connie thinking badly of her.

"Let me help you," Eddie said.

"No, go on down to the firehouse and get that paperwork started. We can talk about a plan, your immediate future later tonight."

Eddie looked at Connie with renewed interest. "I'm beginning to suspect you know a lot more than even I think."

Connie winked at her. "Time will tell. Now get out of here before Rhett comes looking for you again."

Eddie got up from the table, tucking in her chair.

"Oh, wait," Connie said, pulling open a drawer. She reached in, grabbed something, then handed it to Eddie. A key.

"Yours to come and go as you please."

Eddie moved around the table and gave Connie a hug and a kiss on the cheek. "Thanks. For everything. I have no idea how I'll ever be able to repay you."

"No need. I'm here for you. As are many others. I have no doubt that sometime in the future, you'll be paying it forward."

*****

Eddie parked her car in front of the fire department.

Even though it was early in the day, the fire trucks' bay doors were already open. With no one in sight, she walked into the building.

"Hello?"

Hank Thompson, a school teacher and volunteer fireman, came out of a door that led to the private quarters.

"Hi Eddie. Sorry about your grandmother's house. I was there last night."

"Thanks, Hank. I didn't see you. After the explosion…I just couldn't watch. How bad is it?"

"The explosion was the combustion of the fire, nothing more, and fortunately was contained mostly to that one first-floor room and the room above it. Not as bad as you'd think. The damage didn't spread to the rest of the house."

"It's known for sure it started downstairs?" Eddie wanted to disappear. It had to have been the candles.

"That's what Flame says. And, he's the expert."

"How so? I thought Reggie was the expert." Reggie had been with the fire department all his life and was the captain.

"He's getting ready to retire. Flame's the one with the education, plus he worked with the FBI for a while."

Eddie licked her lips. *FBI?* "He…he was was looking for me earlier."

"Just go on through to the back," he said. "They're hashing out the menu for the week. See ya' around."

Eddie said goodbye, wishing she was dealing with someone she knew, like Hank. Not knowing Rhett unsettled her.

When she entered the heart of the firehouse, where the men ate and slept, all conversation stopped and all heads turned toward her. Immediately, Rhett jumped up from the table and told the men that he'd see them later.

Quickly, she found herself heading to the farmhouse.

Now, Rhett was behind her. Seeing him in her rearview mirror, her nervousness continued. She parked the car in the driveway and waited for him to pull up behind her. She stared at the house. A large black scar from the den's windows all the way to the roof or rather where the roof had been told of last night's horror.

He joined her at the side of her car.

She sighed and rubbed the middle of her forehead with the first two fingers of her left hand. A nervous habit. It was a wonder she had any forehead left. How much did he know about her? How much should she reveal?

"Let's go through the back door," Rhett suggested. "The damage is all in the front."

They walked side by side. This close to her, he was even taller than she had first thought. Strangely, she felt comforted.

No sooner had the thought entered her head when she stumbled. Rhett grabbed her upper arm and steadied her.

"Thanks." He continued holding her arm until they were at the back door. The minute his touch was gone, her arm felt cold. Naked. When *was* the last time a man had touched her?

"Oh, I meant to tell you," he said, while she unlocked the door. "Clint found a restorer."

"I'd totally forgotten about it, what with the fire. Didn't have any luck anyway."

"Apparently, Clint started looking even before the car was in his garage—er, rather the workshop behind his house. Got lucky. Some hot shot expert from Atlanta. Should be arriving at his place this morning."

Rhett grabbed the screen door, opening it wide. She inserted her key, turned it, pushing open the old wooden door that was in sore need of paint. She wouldn't apologize for the home's condition, though she wished it looked better than it did right now.

They entered the mudroom first, moving into the kitchen. She laid her purse on the counter and turned to him as he spoke.

"You said this was your grandmother's house?" He opened the folder he'd laid on the counter, pulling out a few sheets of paper, closing the folder again.

"Yes, she was born here. Told me that her grandmother was raised here, too. Back then, this was the only farmhouse for miles. And, it was much smaller than this."

He pushed the papers toward her. "If you could fill out this basic information and get it back to the station later?"

She nodded.

He looked around. "Certainly is a grand old house now."

She tucked the paper into her purse. "I fear it's seen better days."

"No doubt, but there's no reason why it couldn't be restored, refurbished."

"I wish I could."

"If money was no problem, would you do it?"

Startled, she glanced at him. What did he know about her finances? Wait...she was being paranoid. He didn't know anything. He was asking as a general question, making conversation. Having no money for extensive updates was usually a problem for a lot of homeowners. "I'd love to but the house is so big." She paused, thinking about all the various rooms. "At one time, I entertained moving my store front here, but that wouldn't be good for business. Too far from town. I doubt it could work as a bed and breakfast for the same reason."

"Actually, it's not that far out. Have you ever considered just keeping it as a home?"

"Not really. There's no air conditioning and the cost to heat it is outrageous. Good thing our winters are short and not that cold."

"Those costs could be reduced to almost nothing by using geothermal and other renewable energies. I suspect heating costs were high because there's little to no insulation, let alone modern insulation."

She looked at him with interest, curious where this was going. "I guess I never thought about a restoration that included modern technology. Wouldn't that be expensive to install?"

"Not if the contractor knows what he's doing. Plus, you recoup the money spent after a short timeframe from the expenses you're no longer paying."

"Why do I get the feeling that you would be that kind of contractor?"

He grinned. "Because I have experience?" Then his expression changed. "In the meantime, though, I've got some questions and need you to look at the damage."

They moved through the dining room. Eddie was relieved to see the room undamaged, the chandelier still hanging from the ceiling. Next door, the parlor, with the den behind it, was relatively okay other than the farthest wall across the room, which was blackened.

Rhett noticed her gaze. "The wall on the other side was burned. We put the fire out before it could burn all the way through. The drywall on both sides and the studs will have to be replaced."

Eddie nodded. She followed him to the next room, the den where she'd been sleeping, and gasped.

They stood just inside the doorway.

All the walls and ceiling were blackened, the top of the wall opposite her and facing the road was exposed to the outside wall. Taking a couple steps into the room, she heard the squish of water in the carpet. Looking down, she saw water pool around her shoes. Surprisingly, most of the floor was hardly burned, though the carpet was ruined.

"The worst damage is in here." Rhett led the way into the den. She followed. She wanted to cry, seeing a hole in the floor by the wall that faced the road and the holes above, where the ceiling used to be, where the second-floor ceiling and the attic roof used to be. He held out his arm to stop her from moving forward.

"The floor is weaker than it looks."

Glancing back at the road wall, she could see stones that were part of the foundation and outside wall. The studs were heavily charred, any insulation gone.

"Even though there's no rain predicted for the next few days, you'll want to get some protective covering over that hole, otherwise you'll have all kinds of critters in here."

Looking up again, Eddie sighed.

"Overwhelming, isn't it?" he said, reading her thoughts.

"I'll say." She chewed her lip, looking around. She

blew out a long breath of air.

"I felt I'd bitten off more than I could handle when I bought my first house, restoring it. I learned a lot though." He shrugged. "Made some mistakes, for sure, but I learned that eventually everything could be fixed. A little bit of time—"

"And money—"

He laughed. "True."

He pointed to the outside wall, pointing to one of the studs. "See how this stud is more burned than the ones next to it on either side?"

"Yes, I can see the difference. What does that mean?"

"The fire started there on that one stud. It's where the wiring was tacked to the wood. Heat from the wiring smoldered for a long time before the fire broke out."

Eddie frowned. How was that possible? Did that mean the candles didn't start the fire? She looked for the candlesticks. Where were they? She glanced at the fireplace. Soot covered the stones. At the base, on the floor, was one. Tipped over. She gasped.

Moving toward it, she picked it up. A corner was chipped.

"Is it yours?"

"My grandmother's. There were two of them."

She looked around. Rhett moved around her and bent over. Rising, he had the second one in his hand. He examined it. "Looks like fresh wax on it. As if there was a candle in it recently."

She opened her mouth to respond to tell him, but

he continued.

"Considering the house is empty, you should know we think someone was staying here. We found a pillow and a blanket in the closet under the staircase. And, what little food there is in the kitchen, along with a jug of water. Where would these candlesticks have been?"

"In…in a kitchen cabinet…originally." She had found them deep in a kitchen cabinet, along with Gram's best china that Eddie had already sold, along with all the rest of antique glassware she'd found. She was thankful the candlesticks had survived the fire.

She looked to the wall where he said the fire had started "I'm confused. If the fire started in that wall, the stone wall, why did it burn more intensely on these other walls?"

"It's about the material. That outer wall," he said pointing to where the fire started, "is stone. Naturally, the dry wall and old insulation burned, along with the other materials in the room. Once the fire reached the ceiling, it started working on the connecting walls. Faulty wiring started the fire. Old tube and knob wiring from when the house was first built. It's throughout the house and needs to be replaced. You're lucky the house didn't burn before this."

Rhett kept the candlestick, turning toward the doorway. "Let's go back to the kitchen."

She followed. He took the other candlestick from her and set both on the counter. "No doubt you want to take these with you."

She nodded, staring at them. "They're pretty

much all I have left of Gram and this house..." She looked around.

"I've got an idea. It's a wild one," he said.

"I'm always open to new ideas." That much was true. She might not always follow up, but at this point what did she have to lose by listening?

"I'm a restorer, you're the property owner. I have some money that needs to be put to good use. What if I front the restoration and repairs and when you sell this place, I get reimbursed, paid for my services. I'm sure we could work out reasonable terms."

"Wow. That's quite an idea." It was. Her immediate reaction in liking it was a surprise, too. Normally, she liked to think about new ideas, but this one...well, it could be the godsend she'd been looking for.

He grinned and shrugged. "I like to think I have some good ones occasionally. Granted, it doesn't happen often, but occasionally I get lucky. What do you say?"

"I'm willing to discuss it."

"Over dinner tonight?"

"Oh, I don't—"

"Not as a date. Just two potential business partners talking terms and ideas."

What did she have to lose? Nothing.

At the moment, she had everything to gain. She sure didn't have any other prospects in the immediate future on getting the farmhouse fixed, and the roof needed immediate attention.

As if he was reading her thoughts, he said, "I'll go

get my tarps and a couple guys and we'll get that hole covered this afternoon." He grabbed the crystal candlesticks and picked up his folder. "You'll want to contact your insurance agent today. And, you'll want to contact the sheriff regarding any trespassers."

Eddie blinked, turned, and grabbed her purse. She needed to get her poker face in place before tonight. He had a way of changing the subject so fast that she was sure her face could be giving away her thoughts. While she felt guilty not admitting that the pillow and blanket were hers right away, at the same time, he never gave her a chance to tell him differently, as he moved quickly from one subject to another. Plus, he made her nervous, overall, yet at the same time, she wasn't feeling anxious. She headed for the back door.

He followed her as they left the house. "I'm excited thinking about bringing this place back to its former glory. If I had my way, we'd be talking over lunch, but I want to get that hole covered first."

"Wish I had your enthusiasm."

"Don't worry, you will. You're still in stun mode."

At her car, he opened the back door and put the crystal on the floor.

"Do you need a key?" she asked.

"No, not to cover the roof, but if we do partner up, I'll need one."

She opened her door and tossed in her purse. "Thanks for your help. I'll see you tonight then."

"I'll pick you up. Just tell me—"

"No. No, you're doing enough already. And, I

could be coming from the office. How about the pizza place downtown? Or maybe you'd rather—"

"No, that place is perfect," he said.

They set a time and quickly enough, Eddie found herself following him back into town.

She needed to be careful. She could get comfortable having a shoulder to lean on. She didn't want to reveal too much too soon, but if they became partners in restoring Gram's farmhouse… No, she didn't want to think too far ahead or get her hopes too high.

*****

Eddie opened the door to the restaurant, grateful for the blast of cool air, glad that she had thought to bring a lightweight sweater with her. As much as she enjoyed the respite from the heat and humidity, it would fast feel like a meat locker in here, like it did in most stores at the height of summer—and she'd be glad for the sweater.

Stepping in, her eyes adjusted to the dark interior. She didn't see Rhett.

The door opened behind her.

"You beat me."

Eddie turned her head. Rhett stood directly behind her. Placing a hand on her lower back, he steered her toward an open booth in the back, away from the boisterous crowds of young people and families.

A few minutes later, they had drinks before them, their pizza ordered. Rhett picked up his beer, holding it up and toward her. "To new beginnings and a possible partnership."

Eddie picked up her glass and clinked it to his. "To new beginnings."

"And partnerships."

"Possibly." She clinked her glass to his again.

Rhett smiled broadly at her. Two slight dimples appeared on either side of his mouth. Her heart skipped a beat. She smiled in return. He was GQ handsome when he smiled, and she'd always been a sucker for dimples.

"So, where do we start?" he asked.

"With what?"

"Getting to know each other."

"You start." No way did she want to begin. The less he knew about her the better.

"Okay, what do you want to know?" he asked.

One way or another, he appeared determined to engage her fully into a get-to-know-you conversation. "What do you do for fun?" she asked. Focus on him. Everyone loved talking about themselves if given a chance. Not her, though.

"Restore houses and cars. If Clint hadn't bought that Bug, I would have."

"But, you're a fireman."

"Firemen can't have hobbies?"

She laughed. "Touché."

He shrugged. "I have a lot of interests. What can I say?"

"Did you always want to be a fireman?"

"No." He paused, then continued. "I restored homes alongside my dad. My parents were huge fans of preserving history, bringing life back to homes whose glory days were in the eighties."

Eddie frowned. "Nineteen-eighties?"

"Eighteen-eighties."

"Ah, right. Isn't it a costly endeavor?"

"Not for them, it wasn't. They had an arsenal of craftsmen at their disposal. It was their business. When Mom died, I spent more time with Dad. I learned a lot from these old-time masters, plus I watch a lot of HGTV."

Eddie laughed.

He smiled at her laugh. "You know the channel."

"I do. One of my favorites. That and old movies." How did he do that? As much as she was reluctant to share her life with anyone, she felt strangely at ease with him and hadn't thought twice about blurting out the information.

"Which ones? I like the old mysteries and classics myself. Especially those starring Gregory Peck. *Big Country* is my all-time favorite."

"One of my favorites, too. So, how did you get the nickname Flame?"

"Got it as a kid, actually. I liked playing with matches when I was little, until the day I set fire to our backyard."

"Oh, no!"

"Nothing disastrous, though I *was* grounded forever. At least, it felt like forever. I was five and made to work with the local forest rangers that summer planting a lot of trees. Actually, we all went and planted trees that summer. I loved climbing up into the towers, getting that bird's-eye view of the forest. Learned a lot about the Rangers' job that summer. Made me more respectful of fires. It was the beginning of huge dose of curiosity, which led me to becoming a firefighter."

"Your parents, no doubt, were proud of you."

"Dad certainly was. Mom would have been, too. Our house burned when I was nine—"

Eddie gasped. "Surely, you didn't—"

"No, I had nothing to do with it. It was an old house. Mice had gotten in the walls and chewed through the insulation on some wires. Mom and my only sibling—a brother—died in the fire. Dad was burned trying to rescue them."

"I'm so sorry. That's *why* you became a fireman."

He nodded.

"So, how did you come to work for the fire department here?"

"I heard there was an opening from one of my father's friends—the chief, actually. I thought I'd give it a try."

"I heard you worked for the FBI."

"I did. For a year. My interest in firefighting led to fire forensics, which I pursued in college and then received an internship with the bureau. Interesting work. But, I didn't like living in Atlanta. Having grown up in New Orleans, it just didn't feel like the Old South and I love these old Southern homes. How long have you been a realtor?"

"Twelve years now."

"You got your license as a teenager."

That information was no secret since hanging her shingle at eighteen, opening shop at her present location. "I did, just after graduation. I studied for my license exams while a senior in high school. I lost my parents in an auto accident that summer." Vehicular suicide actually, but that part she kept confident. She never believed the police who reported it was unavoidable accident to weather, not with her parents' anguish of dealing with his embezzlement less than a week earlier.

"Becoming a realtor drew my interest—something that didn't require college—and I needed something to occupy my time and mind, not wanting to dwell on their loss." She paused reflecting. "Spending time with other kids was too painful. It reminded me too much of the life I'd lost. Plus, I needed a quick way to earn money, too. There wasn't much insurance, surprisingly. College became out of the question." Not to mention her father's embezzlement she'd been determined to pay back.

"So, what do you do when not working? Besides old movies, that is?"

She exhaled, feeling her shoulders drop. Why had she been so nervous about his questions? He wasn't doubting her. He was just trying to get to know her. Being friendly, that's all. "Well, since I'm all about helping others buy and sell homes, I tie that activity into helping the local pound find homes for their many dogs and cats. And, when I have time, I get involved with Habitat for Humanity." Years ago, she'd gotten involved with Habitat for Humanity needing an outlet for her mental frustration, which she found eased with physical exertion. Nothing like hammering nails or wielding a paint brush, attacking a wall with fresh paint to get the worry or stress out of her system for a while. Plus, she learned how to make repairs in her parents' home, allowing her to save money.

As for the animals, there had been a few occasions where people had moved, leaving their pets behind for someone else to deal with them.

"That's interesting. I'm a volunteer at both myself. I haven't seen you there."

"I've not been as active as I once was," she responded. In the first year, she been at Homes for Humanity most of her free time. As time healed her wounds, she didn't require the same kind of workout.

He continued. "I enjoy fostering dogs from time to time. Allows me to tame and train them, get them ready for a new owner. To have a pet of sorts for a short duration, and I get to bring the animal to work at the station house, provided I crate it while we're gone, attending a fire. It lets the animal get used to other people, other noises, etc. Though, it's been more than a year since my last foster."

Their pizza arrived and conversation stopped as their server handed them plates and refilled their glasses. Pizza slices dished up, Eddie picked up her slice and bit into it. Immediately, she reached for her water glass. Definitely hot! Even so, the pizza was delicious.

Between bites, Rhett outlined his idea for a

working partnership.

At first, she felt he was being benevolent, but the more he outlined his plan, the more she was convinced that he'd given the idea a great deal of thought.

"The insurance should cover the cost of materials and if the two of us work together, doing much of the labor, it'll keep the costs down. While we could repair the damaged rooms first, if we order everything for the entire house at the same time, it's another way to keep costs down."

"Not fix the damaged rooms first?"

"Actually, it would be better to deconstruct anything and everything in the house all at the same time. Fill and get rid of the dumpster right away. Then, have the electricians and plumbers come in. Then, paint, trim, etc. I'd suggest saving the bathrooms and kitchen for last, tying those materials to other houses when we order appliances and cabinets. Again, cut the costs with quantity orders."

For now, he'd supply the finances. After they restored the farmhouse, she'd be the one to find houses that they could easily flip. Her equity, for now, would be earned in time spent researching, finding the homes, and then physically helping with the renovations. Net proceeds would be invested for the next house and its restoration.

By the time the pizza was gone, Eddie was convinced. If she ever wanted to see her grandmother's ancestry home restored while still in her possession, at least in the near future, her best hope was to team up with Rhett.

"But three houses as a trial?" she asked. "What if we discover the partnership won't work while working on this house?"

"Then we dissolve it, no questions asked. We'd have to finish it together, but I promise to make it as painless as possible. We'd figure out a way to get it done without bumping into each other excessively."

She looked at him, her head spinning and her heart tugging at her to say yes. Finally, she said, "Okay, three houses as a trial. An easy out for either of us if it doesn't work. Do we write it up?"

"Yes, a simple contract. And, if it works, we can write up a more complex contract for the partnership."

She'd be stupid to throw away this opportunity with both hands. Rhett was the one being strung out, as it would be his finances and his signature on various documents and contracts for services. Basically, he was trusting her.

They were trusting each other. And yet, he knew so little about her. Was it possible he had secrets like she did? The weight of hiding behind the truth was wearing her down.

"Look," she said. "If you don't want to go through with this partnership, I understand. It's a huge risk and you don't really know me."

"I know enough. I'm in," he responded.

He smiled and her heart fluttered and goosebumps covered her arms.

She nodded. "Okay, I'm in, too. You said you're

restoring the house you're living in?" she asked.

"Yes, I prefer to live in them, especially as I sell them when I'm done and can provide special tips and details to prospective buyers. I've not found my forever home yet. This one is another temporary situation. What about the farmhouse? Do you have plans to live there?"

She bit her lip. "At one time, I thought I could." Was it possible that she *could* keep it?

Less than an hour later, they had a timeline and a plan hashed out for repairs and restoration, and considering all the changes to be made, he admitted it would be better not to live there. Usually, the work would be stretched over a month. They were trying to get it done in a week's time, if possible. "I'll need that soft bed at night rather than a sleeping bag on the floor."

She startled. "I have to tell you. There's been no transient in the house. The pillow and sleeping bag—they're mine, and—"

"And here I thought I was the only one who lived with my work!" He believed her to be living in the house because she'd been working on it?

The waitress placed the bill on the table and she reached for it. Rhett snatched it before she could grab it.

"My treat," he said. "You can get the next one."

She watched him sign the receipt, contemplating the entire dinner, how she had agreed to his partnership idea. As a business owner, she knew a good thing when presented. She was equally amazed that he wanted to take on this new project when he was so deeply involved in other projects: flipping houses, helping William restore his car, his job as a firefighter, volunteer work. When did he sleep?

He walked her to her car, opening the door. She took a step forward, then stopped, digging in her purse, wrapping her fingers around the key. She put her hand out and extended the key to him. He took it from her, his fingers enveloping hers, and a sensation that made her entire hand tingle. Surprised at the warmth of his hand, she quickly released the key. Looking up, she could see that he felt it, too.

"To the farmhouse. I have an extra one at the office."

"Right." He started to say something else, but paused, changing his mind. "Tomorrow then."

She nodded, turned, and slid into the car. "Tomorrow."

He shut the door, stepped back, and waved.

As she drove out of the parking lot, she couldn't help but watch him in the rearview mirror, surprised to see him still standing there, watching her drive away.

*****

Day 6

Glad she had chosen to work on the house, Eddie put her *out of office* sign on her door that provided her cell phone number to clients or anyone looking for her. If called, she could be back in her office in ten or fifteen minutes.

She pulled her car into the farmhouse driveway,

parking behind Rhett's truck. Right away, she noticed the blue tarp covering the damaged roof. A big blue dumpster sat near the front door. A plank was already in place connecting the trash bin and the porch, creating a safe walkway.

Entering the house, she put her purse down on the counter and followed the sound of a hammer to the den. She found Rhett tearing up burned floor boards. The walls were already stripped of any damaged drywall.

"You must have gotten here at the crack of dawn. I never thought to ask last night about a schedule to work around our jobs."

"I'm on vacation for two weeks."

She held up her cell phone. "And, I can do business via this. It's slow going right now anyway, so I doubt there will be many calls. I'm ready to start. Where do you want me?"

*****

Rhett gulped. Seeing her standing there looking as fresh as the morning sunrise, he wanted to say, *underneath me, in my bed*. Instead, he swallowed the silent words and said, "You'll find gloves and a mask in the kitchen. If you want to get a crowbar and start demo'ing that wall over there but from the other side so we can get it down to its studs, that would be great."

She gave him a thumbs up, turned, and disappeared. He hung his head both to stretch it and in despair. How was he going to keep his cool with that cute figure flaunted in front of him? If he had liked her figure in a dress, he liked even better her figure-hugging dungarees, tennis shoes, and a sleeveless shirt tied at the waist. Setting her up in the other room would help…for a while.

When she stood in the doorway a few minutes later with her hair in a ponytail, a mask covering her face, gloves, and a crowbar in her hands, with it looking half as big as her and more like a weapon than a tool, he wanted to groan. Who would have thought she could be this sexy in working clothes? She waved and disappeared. A few seconds later, he heard her attacking the wall beside him. He turned his back on it and focused on the floor, determined to get the damaged boards out before lunch.

After he finished clearing out the burned wood in the first room, dumping it all in the bin outside the front door, he moved to the room upstairs, doing the same thing. He wasn't sure how long he'd been working when he noticed Eddie in the doorway.

"I'm hungry. We worked right through lunch and breakfast was a long time ago. Wanna burger?" She took off one glove, then the other, and swiped her finger across her forehead, brushing her hair away. In doing so, she marked her forehead with soot.

"Sounds good." He took steps toward her, taking off his own gloves, pulling a handkerchief out of his pocket and grabbing his water bottle. He tipped the bottle, wetting the material. Standing in front of her, he moved the material toward her face.

Startled, she grabbed his wrist and leaned back. "What?"

"You've marked yourself with soot."

"Oh." She let go and stood straight again, looking up at him.

Trying not to look at her eyes directly, he wiped her forehead gently, taking his time. Lilacs. She smelled like lilacs. He inhaled deeply and made the mistake of looking at her eyes.

His hand paused.

Time stood still.

"Did you get it all?" she whispered.

He blinked. Stepped back. Lowered his arm. "Yeah…I did." He cleared his throat. "Ready?"

"For…?"

"Dinner." Just then his stomach growled. She grinned. He grinned back.

Following her down the stairs, watching her hips sway with her every step, he realized he was in dangerous territory. He'd been attracted to many women, but never like this. *Just keep it cool.* Yeah, right. *No, seriously, just concentrate on the work.* How? *Don't even think about her. She's not thinking about you.* How do you know?

*****

Eddie felt her cheeks redden knowing Rhett was watching her from behind. *He almost kissed you!* No, he didn't. *Liar.* We're just partners, cleaning up Grandma's house. *So, you say.* Go away.

*****

Twenty minutes later, sitting opposite one another in the diner, enjoying burgers and fries, they talked about potential colors and materials. Then,

Rhett found himself smiling, enamored watching Eddie's face light up as she answered his questions about the farmhouse when she was little, about her grandparents and the various holidays celebrated there.

When she talked about the fields and the landscape, he could easily imagine how it looked. Increasingly, he found himself watching her mouth as she spoke, imagining himself kissing her.

"So, how have you managed to escape marriage?" she asked.

"Honestly? I couldn't settle. I've seen too many people not willing to wait, so they settled. I want the real thing. Like the relationship my parents had."

"That my grandparents had," she added.

At that point, they both picked up their burgers, thoughts unsaid. A few minutes later, they were back to talking about restoration plans again. He wondered if the discussion had touched a nerve with her as much as it had with him.

He really did want that same kind of relationship that his parents had had, something that had been missing in his relationships. What was it about her that attracted him so much? That made him think she could be the one? *Wait! Where had that come from?*

Rhett picked up the tab.

"It's my turn," Eddie argued.

"Not when it's a business expense."

"Oh.

"I have a spreadsheet for each of the houses I've restored. I'll be doing the same for our partnership."

"I guess I hadn't thought that far ahead."

"Are you okay with my doing it? Would you prefer to do it? It's a process that evolved over time. It's simple and effective, not requiring a lot of time. Wasn't simple at first, but it is now."

"One less thing for me to worry about with you tracking the finances. I don't think I could handle working on another set of books right now. Though, I'd love to see your system. I might be something I could use as a realtor."

"No problem. I'm happy to share it," he said, then added. "Anytime you want to see the spreadsheet, just holler. I don't want to hide anything from you."

She hesitated, started to say something, then changed her mind, giving him a half smile. "We ready to go?"

Inwardly, he paused. Their previous meal, they'd stayed half an hour more to talk about the farmhouse and future projects. Suddenly, she seemed eager to leave. Why?

*****

Once she was in her car, Eddie realized she shouldn't have been in such a hurry to leave. He'd caught her by surprise saying he didn't want to hide anything. Her own guilt was tripping her up. She wanted to reveal everything, but the timing didn't feel right. He'd frowned slightly and acted surprised, but then covered it up when she got up to leave. She should have told him the truth about her finances and that she'd been sleeping in the house from the very first. Why couldn't she just come out and tell him?

Fear that he wouldn't like her anymore?

*****

Day 7

Rhett sat on the back stoop waiting for Eddie to arrive. He found himself rethinking if he should have offered a partnership to someone he knew so little about. *What was he thinking?* Not with the right head, obviously. Yes, he was attracted to her. Yes, he was smitten. He enjoyed spending time with her, watching how she had a slight dimple on the right side of her mouth when she laughed. Tilting her head back a little, exposing her neck that for him made her appear vulnerable. Many times, he'd wondered what it'd be like to kiss that neck. Would her skin be as it appeared? Smooth as silk? Or would he be disappointed?

He heard a vehicle turn into the driveway. Jumping up, he tugged on his jeans, wishing they weren't quite so tight. He needed to control his thoughts better if they were going to be working together.

A car door slammed and seconds later, Eddie rounded the corner of the house. He tried not to smile but couldn't help himself. Without a fussy hairdo and any jewelry, she looked fresh and inviting, like a cool glass of lemonade on a hot thirsty day. All he wanted to do was sip and enjoy the drink.

"Sorry I'm late. I lost track of time." She frowned. "Why are you sitting out here? You could have gone in."

"Just enjoying the quiet, watching the wildlife,

waiting for you." Key in hand, she came up the porch.

Inside, she put her bag on the kitchen counter.

"Good news," he announced. "The Chief got the official report back this morning from the Fire Marshall. I was right. The fire started because of faulty wiring, exactly where I showed you." She looked relieved.

"By the way," he continued. "Since you know a lot of folks in town, do you know of anyone who would like to manage apartments? My chief's friend, the owner—an out-of-towner—has a manager/liaison who's leaving at the end of the month. Both the manager and maintenance get a two-bedroom apartment rent-free along with the part-time pay with no benefits—"

"Hence the free apartment—"

"The manager collects the rent, make deposits, show apartments to potential renters and when someone does want to rent, give their name to his management office in Columbus. They do all the paper work there." He gave Eddie his Chief's card, along with the owner's card. "If you know of anyone, he'd appreciate you giving them his number." Why was she looking at the card for so long?

Finally, she slipped the card into her bag, then reached for gloves sitting on the counter. "I'm ready to pull carpet."

*****

Mid-afternoon, Eddie looked around the room, knowing the other rooms looked like this one. She was amazed at how quickly they'd been able to remove all the carpet throughout the house, finding oak floors. The entire time she'd been thinking of that management job. A place to live when she sold the farm house, guaranteed income along with her not-so-steady realtor earnings.

By the end of the day, they had torn everything out throughout the house that needed to be dumped and hauled away. Watching the walls come down, she was appalled at the old and damaged wiring that was everywhere. She *had* been lucky that the house hadn't burned before this.

As they worked, they talked about houses, and Rhett shared his experience in flipping them, his knowledge of wood, tiles, roofing, plumbing, electrical, and more. He admitted that while he could do some of the work, he depended on the electricians and plumbers to make those systems solid and safe. She liked how easily he could comment on his failings, as he called them. She didn't see them as failings at all. She wished she could judge herself as easily as he did himself. Why was she so hard on herself?

*****

Eddie entered Connie's house and joined her in the kitchen.

Connie looked up seeing her. "Long day?"

Eddie nodded.

"Have you eaten?"

"No—"

"Meatloaf and mashed potatoes coming up. Everything's already cooked. Just needs heating up"

Eddie laughed. "You're not serving me. I can get it myself. You sit down."

Connie laughed, too. "Deal. I must be getting old if sitting down sounds like a good idea."

"You're not old."

Minutes later, Eddie set their loaded two plates on the table.

"So, how's the farmhouse coming along?"

"With the demolition done, we got the new framing installed, thanks to Rhett's firefighter friends helping. The electricians came and will finish up tomorrow along with the plumbers."

"You and Rhett are making fast work of the place."

"We are." Eddie paused. "I think it's time for me to move out. Find my own place."

"How did you come to that decision? Especially now?"

"I can't stay here forever."

"Whoever said anything about forever?"

"I don't want to intrude."

"You're not intruding. I enjoy our visits. It's not like we're always here at the same time."

"I know, but still…"

Connie frowned, got up, and grabbed two beers out of the fridge.

Eddie fidgeted with her fork, stirring the mashed potatoes around before scooping some up. Connie watched, then finally said, "Open up your beer before I do it for you." After Eddie did and swallowed, Connie spoke. "What are you afraid of?" she asked.

Startled, Eddie sat back. "Afraid?"

"Yes, afraid."

Eddie stared at her plate, letting out a sigh. There was no way she'd ever be able to hide anything from Connie. "Lots of things."

"Like what?"

"Rhett."

Connie's eyebrows went up. Then, her eyes twinkled and she laughed. "Honey, a good-looking specimen like Rhett does lots of things to people, particularly the women around here, but being afraid of him has never been one of them."

Eddie looked down. Connie didn't get it.

"You have feelings for him."

Eddie glanced up. She did get it. Concern and care were on Connie's face now. She genuinely wanted to know what was going on.

Putting the fork down, Eddie pushed the plate away. Suddenly, she wasn't hungry anymore. "I do. On one hand, when he looks at me, it's like he can see everything and yet knows nothing."

"And, the other hand?"

Eddie shrugged. "I'm wondering if I'm imagining things. Yesterday, we were fairly close to each other, and I thought he was going to kiss me. But then, he didn't. I still don't know what to think. I must have imagined it."

"Oh, Honey." Connie paused for a few seconds. Her brows came together again, and she cocked her head, asking, "Have you ever been in love before?"

Startled once again, Eddie thought back. "I…I…I

don't know."

"Don't over think it would be my advice. If he really wanted to kiss you, he would have. But then, what do I know? You're getting advice from a spinster."

"Surely, you dated in your day."

Connie laughed. "Yes, I did." Her beer empty, she rose and put the bottle in the recycle bin. Back at the table, she reached for Eddie's plate. "Done?"

Eddie nodded. Connie took the plate, scrapped it, and placed it into the dishwasher. She went to the fridge and got two more beers, putting one in front of Eddie.

"But, I don't—"

"Tonight, you do." Sitting down, Connie opened hers, and extended her arm out with the beer in her hand. "Here's to better days."

Eddie mimicked Connie's motions, clinking her beer against Connie's. "I'll go along with that." She took a gulp and chased it with a second. "I'm due."

"Everyone isn't your enemy, you know."

Eddie stared at Connie. "I have a feeling you know more than I think."

"Ever since your parents died, you've been holding people at arm's length. They respected your space at first. Then later, with any and every approach rebuffed, people learned to walk around you rather than toward you. You must have gotten that big chip that's on your shoulder from your father."

Eddie opened her mouth to protest, then stopped.

Connie was right. She did have a chip on her shoulder.

The last decade played on the screen in Eddie's mind, the seasons and years flashing forward. Where she was always alone, unless with a client, showing or selling. Her shoulders slumped feeling the weight of her loneliness now.

"What can I do?"

"Stop running."

"But, I'm not."

"Yes, you are. Running and hiding. That bit tonight about moving out…running. What are you running from? Because you're certainly not running toward anything."

Eddie shrugged her shoulders.

"Did you respect your parents?"

"No…Yes…No," she said finally. "I used to but then when I found out— "

"That they had lied?"

"You did know. How? Why must everyone know everybody else's business. It's not right."

"It's called being a community, Honey. People care about each other. They rally around in bad times and gossip during the good. They get bored. They don't want to talk about their own lives, so they talk about everyone else's."

"I hate it."

"Then move away."

"I can't. I have no money. I was going to sell Grandma's farm but now I don't want to. It's home. I want to keep it." There. She'd finally said it. Aloud.

And, in front of someone else. "I don't want to move away. I love Laurel Ridge."

"If it makes you feel any better, no one else knows about your parents. Not unless your mom confided in them as she did me. You never knew we were friends, did you?"

Eddie shook her head.

"From a long time ago. Our lives took different paths, but we talked from time to time. She came to the diner one night at closing and stayed, talking. She was horribly upset, having learned what your father had done. He'd kept it from her, too."

"When did she find out?"

"Less than a week before they died."

"Image was everything to Mom."

"Your dad, too."

"Yeah." Memories flooded back of all the times when one or the other would say, *What will others think?*

"Image means a lot for you, too. More than you acknowledge," Connie said.

"No…" She paused, reflecting. "Oh..." She sighed with realization. "I've become my mother, haven't I? Where image *is* everything."

Connie nodded.

"I've been in such a jam. I've even considered filing bankruptcy."

"It's not your job to pay off your parents' debt."

"Why do I feel like it is? No, don't answer that. I know. Pride. Wanting to return their honor." She frowned. "I don't remember you and Mom being friends. When were you?"

"In grade school."

"What happened?"

"She discovered I didn't live in the best of neighborhoods."

Eddie sighed. "I remember thinking so many times how she was such a snob. And, I've gone and done the same thing. All these years... Hiding the truth. The way I left Shelley behind. I've been so obsessed with what my parents did... Then, I became ashamed of my own circumstances." She leaned forward, covering her face with her hands. "What have I done?"

"Nothing that can't be undone."

"But—"

"Just be honest."

Eddie lowered her hands. "You make it sound so easy."

"It's not, but you can do it. It'll mean letting go and facing your fears out in the open. You're stronger than you know. Smart, too. Something my mother told me that I'll share with you--whenever you find yourself worrying about what others might think, if it doesn't concern them, it doesn't matter what they think. Do what's best *for you*. Who cares what they think? Now, come help me with dishes."

*****

Day 10

Three days later, late into the evening, she and Rhett finished painting the last room and were cleaning up the paint brushes and pans out in the yard. Every day, she'd been wanting to talk to him but there's always been someone around or he was there when she wasn't and vice versa. When she finally had him alone yesterday, she'd gotten a call from a new client who wanted to meet right then, so she left frustrated that what she wanted to tell him would have to wait."

"Hard to believe we've accomplished so much in such a short time." Eddie said.

"Once everything was torn out that first day and the electricians and plumbers were able to do their thing—"

"Along with the roof and walls repaired—" she added.

"It was easy to put up the drywall, mud them—"

"I wouldn't say easy," she said laughing. "If not for your firefighter friends helping with the drywall…their muscle made all the difference."

"But, you're no slacker."

"And, our experience with Homes with Humanity certainly helped," she said shaking the excess water from her brush. "How did you get involved with it?" These last couple days, they'd worked separately and late into the evening. No dinners, no lunches either, at least not where they could talk. Now, she was hungry to talk with him and have that opportunity to tell him about her past, but she was exhausted, too tired to have that conversation. He looked like he was tired, too. Her guilt had continued gnawing at her these past few days.

Who was she kidding? She was scared to death to

start the discussion.

"I wanted to help others after Hurricane Katrina. I was still in school then. Both Dad and I worked with them for several years. And then later, when my girlfriend and I broke up—I had discovered she had lied to me—I needed to be busy, so I went back to helping them, which then gave me the idea of flipping houses. Been doing that ever since."

"Working around your firefighting career?" As much as she wanted to ask him what kind of lie had his girlfriend had told, Eddie was hesitant to ask. *Because of your own hiding the truth?*

"Yes. I've not made the commitment to flipping full time yet. Not sure what it would take for me to do so."

The paint brushes clean, the paint cans sealed, and everything else put away for the night, they walked out to their vehicles.

Approaching her car first, Rhett reached for her door handle but didn't open it. She had moved in expecting it to be open. Instead, she found herself standing next to him, closer than she'd ever been before. She looked up only to find him studying her. Differently. He was staring at her mouth. Surprised, she blinked and opened her mouth to say something. But what? He bent his head toward her. She closed her eyes, his lips covering hers, his late-afternoon facial hair rubbing against her skin. Breathing in his cologne and musty scent, along with paint, she melted against him. And then, suddenly, he withdrew. She opened her eyes, her face cooled by the night air. She blinked, looking up at him.

He opened her door. "Goodnight," he said, leaving her still standing. She turned, hearing the gravel crunch under his steps, watching as he moved toward his truck. Just before he reached his door, she slid into her car and shut the door.

Her gaze went to the rearview mirror. He got in. Not wanting to get caught staring, she started her car, though she kept glancing up at the mirror. He was already backing up. She put her car into reverse, waiting for him to go. Out in the street, he gave a wave.

She waved back, then lowered her arm slowly. What the heck just happened? It was useless to deny her attraction to him. In fact, the more she got to know him, the more she wanted to know. She enjoyed his company. So much so that she couldn't imagine him not in her life or how it had felt before working with him.

Pulling into Connie's driveway, she acknowledged that compared to her own life, his had to have been more difficult having lost both his mother and brother at a young age.

They still had two more houses to fix after this one as part of their trial partnership. He wasn't going anywhere. And, neither was she. And yet, either one of them could back out without an explanation. She frowned, grimacing at the idea he could once he learned of her lies.

*****

Day 11

"You look like a man with a dilemma," William told Rhett after giving their breakfast order to Connie.

"Conflicted."

"Eddie?"

Rhett nodded and sighed. "I kissed her last night."

"And, this is bad, how?"

"I hadn't planned it. It just happened."

William laughed. "It usually does."

"What am I going to do?"

"Wait," William said. "I'm confused. You said you were interested in her."

"Curious," he corrected. "Where's Mason?"

"Said he's got something going. Isn't telling yet. I suspect it has to do with one former girlfriend waitress and the Brown house he purchased at auction" William held up his hand and whispered, "Shhh."

Rhett frowned. Immediately, Connie was at their table delivering their breakfast plates.

"Anything else I can get you boys?" she asked.

"Looks good," Rhett replied. The second she left, Rhett leaned toward William and said, "Too many secrets being kept lately. The sooner we sign papers for our new company, the happier I'll be."

"Mason says—along with the regular gossip mill—that you and Eddie have become a couple."

Rhett stared at William. "Just because we've spent the better part of this past week together fixing up her house?"

"That and the fact you kissed her last night."

"*THAT'S* being gossiped about, *ALREADY*?"

Rhett croaked.

William laughed. "The truth of it? No. The believing it's happened before this? Yes. You know how people talk. What are you so afraid of?"

"That I'll end up alone." *Geesh, where had that come from?*

William laughed again, shaking his head. "Dude, you *are* alone. Wait a minute—are you saying being alone, as in unmarried—has been a problem? That you're ready for a real relationship?"

"Okay, I'll admit it. I want a wife and a family. Just like the rest of you do, even though we've never really proclaimed that aloud."

The discussion moved to Joe's blind date with Clint's mechanic—JoJo Wheeler—who was restoring the Volkswagen. But all the while they talked about the car, Rhett was thinking about Eddie, wondering, and remembering the kiss from last night. Her response told him she cared, but how much?

*****

Eddie and Rhett had been working on the floors for a couple hours. It was slow going at first as Eddie learned how to lay the wooden floor, tapping each plank into place, and using material from different packages. Once Rhett was satisfied that she could do this on her own, he started moving the rest of the flooring into other rooms where it would be needed.

Eddie found her movements meditative, finding a rhythm that suited her. Slower than Rhett's movements, she was okay with that. She was learning a new skill. If she was going to partner up with Rhett in future homes, she wanted to be more valuable, more skillful. She loved her work as a realtor but was finding that she enjoyed working with her hands, too. It provided a peacefulness, a satisfaction that being a realtor didn't provide. Couldn't provide.

Eddie sighed and sat back on her heels looking at her handiwork. She'd done half a dozen rows so far. As she looked at her accomplishment, she realized she was putting her own touch, her own design into Granny's house. Isn't that what remodeling was about, making it your own?

She hadn't thought about the farm that way before. It had always belonged to someone else. Why was she struggling so hard to accept that it *was* hers? Because she'd made no changes before this. Could the fire be deemed as a positive event, after all?

She reached for new panels and worked methodically once again, considering how and when she would come clean with Rhett. Talk about facing her fears. She didn't want him thinking badly of her or that *he* might want out of the partnership.

She looked up hearing Rhett nearby. He entered the room. "You're speeding right along." He grabbed a mallet and joined her. "Hopefully, we can have this done before it's totally dark outside."

Eddie glanced out through the new wide window that had been installed yesterday, along with its framing and finishings. The sun was low on the horizon. She glanced back at Rhett. He'd already finished her row and was starting the next. No way was she going to let him out pace her, though she had to admit that he probably would.

Half an hour later, just as dusk began to settle into the room, they were done. She stood up, stretching her back muscles, and looked around in satisfaction. What a difference this light oak flooring made from the old, dark carpet that had been in the room for as long as she could remember. With the light walls that melded with the green outside the windows, bringing the outdoors in, the room felt far more expansive than before. She could visualize some big, soft easy chairs and a comfortable couch. The chimney's stone had been scrubbed clean of soot, and in the winter this room would be warm and comfortable.

"I'm always amazed how different colors, different textures can change a room," Rhett said, mimicking her own thoughts. "Satisfied with the colors?"

"Yes!" She hadn't been this excited about a house in a long time. Not for what the house could do for her, but this time for the house itself. Like it had its own character, its own personality. "I can see why you enjoy this," she said.

*****

Rhett had another meeting, so their dinner had been quick, far quicker than she would have liked. She'd planned to tell him everything at dinner. Now, she lingered over the dessert she'd ordered after he left, wishing they could have had that discussion.

Shelley was clearing dishes from a table on the other side of the restaurant. When was the last time they had giggled as best friends?

Shelley looked her way. Immediately, Shelley shifted her gaze so she was looking out the window instead. Eddie grimaced, knowing the fault was hers for their distance. Working with Rhett, she'd become aware of how lonely her life had become. She missed that girl she once was, the one who had socialized fully.

She sighed. Connie was right. She'd been hiding her feelings, her thoughts, even her physical presence from others far too long. Well, if she couldn't fix things with Rhett tonight, she could at least fix them with Shelley.

Eddie looked around. The diner was empty other than the two of them. Shelley had swapped her full bin of dirty dishes for an empty one and was headed toward Eddie, probably to the table next to her. Shelley put the bin on a chair.

"Shelley, do you have a minute to talk?"

Shelley looked up, surprised. She looked behind her, moving the dishrag from hand to hand. Shelley was nervous, and Eddie didn't blame her a bit. Was Shelley disappointed that there were no new customers to distract her?

"Please?" Eddie added.

Shelley's shoulders dropped and then she shrugged. "Sure."

Eddie extended her hand to the empty bench across from her. "Are you able to sit down?"

"For a minute."

Eddie smiled. "Great."

Shelley sat down and stared at Eddie.

Shelley wasn't going to make this easy, nor should she. "I want to apologize," Eddie began. Shelley's eyes widened in surprise. "I miss being your friend."

"You sure didn't miss our friendship when we were in high school."

Eddie frowned. "When did we stop being friends?"

"The summer we were going into high school."

An awkward silence. Eddie thought back. "Is that the summer I went to Europe with my parents?"

Shelley nodded.

"I never wrote to you, did I?"

Shelley shook her head.

"Oh, Shelley, I'm so sorry. We—I was so busy, what with Dad involved with his new business, Mom and I—"

"That isn't what bothered me. It's okay you didn't write while you were gone. I probably wouldn't have either in your place. What I didn't like was how you snubbed me when we were back in school again."

"Snubbed you?"

"You never sought me out."

Eddie opened her mouth to speak, but Shelley interrupted before she could utter a word.

"You snubbed everyone you'd been close friends with. It was like we weren't good enough for you. In middle school, you were never involved with anything and then suddenly you were in every organization and everyone's friend except me and those like me."

"Those like you?"

"You know, those of us who lived in the not-so-elite neighborhoods."

"That's not true," Eddie said.

"Isn't it?" Shelley didn't look away.

Eddie thought back to that time. She'd been so excited about the places and things she'd seen that she had gravitated to those kids who had traveled, too. She'd been so occupied with all the organizations and the tougher school work that she *had* turned her back on everything she had once known. Her style of clothes, interests, and friends… Connie was right. She'd become just like her parents. Caring too much about what others thought. And, she'd been doing it her entire adult life.

"You're right," Eddie admitted. "I turned my back on you. Why didn't you say anything? Confront me?"

Shelley shrugged her shoulders. "I don't know. I should have, I guess."

Eddie reached out, touching Shelley's arm. "I'm so sorry." She paused. "Is it possible for us to become friends again?"

Shelley looked down. Different emotions flit across Shelley's face, though none remained long enough that Eddie could put a name to them. Shelley folded her hands and unfolded them several times. She looked up, her gaze searching Eddie's.

Shelley sighed, grinned slightly, and said, "I'd like that."

Eddie smiled in return. They made plans to have

lunch in a few days. It felt good to have her old friend as a new friend. As she watched Shelley return to her work, disappearing into the kitchen, Eddie knew that to make her life full again, she'd need to have lots of these conversations with lots of people. She doubted any of the conversations would be easy. And, she doubted everyone would be as forgiving as Shelley had been.

Connie came out of the kitchen and set a tray of clean mugs by the coffee pots. Wiping her hands on the towel that hung at her hip, she walked toward Eddie and sat down across from her.

"Shelley just told me the news."

"It's a start."

"A good start." Connie patted Eddie's hand and rose, taking the bill. Rhett had forgotten to take it. "Dinner's on me tonight."

"I can't let you do that. The thing is Shelley doesn't know the whole story, yet." She rose from her seat and faced Connie. "I don't know how to tell her without her feeling sorry for me."

"One step at a time. Trust me. No one is going to feel sorry for you. If anything, they'll admire how strong you are despite it all. Stop listening to those inner demons of yours and stop giving into your fear. You've let it dominate your life long enough." Before Eddie could respond, Connie turned and said over her shoulder, "I'll be late coming home tonight, so I'll see you in morning."

Eddie left the diner, walking around the building to where her car was parked. As she unlocked the car door, then slid behind the wheel, pondering Connie's words.

By the time, she pulled into Connie's driveway, there was no undoing the truth. Connie was right. Fear *had* dominated her life from the minute she learned her parents were dead. Fear she'd be kicked out of the house and would become a foster child. Fear that she wouldn't be able to stay in the house and pay the bills. Fear she'd never find a job quickly enough or pay well enough to allow her to pay her parents' debt. Fear that everyone would find out. Fear that she'd be labeled as a cheat like her father. Fear that…

"Arrrrghhhhh," she cried out. "I created my own self-prison! Out of fear!"

She gathered her things and got out of car, crossed the driveway, and entered Connie's house, shutting the door firmly behind her. Tomorrow was a new day and everything was going to change. She wasn't going to live in that same fear anymore. First thing tomorrow, Rhett would learn the truth. All of it.

*****

Day 12

When she pulled into the farmhouse drive, Rhett was already there and at work, no doubt, as today was going to be a big day, where they'd be working on finishing touches of hardware, lights, and cleaning up.

Instead, she found him in the kitchen, almost as if waiting for her. An open file folder lay on the countertop. Hearing her, he looked up, shutting the folder at the same time.

She frowned. Why the mystery? Was there something she wasn't supposed to see?

"Good morning," she said, smiling. Reaching the counter, she laid down her bag.

He didn't smile back. In fact, he had a bit of a frown. Then, it disappeared. "Good morning," he answered.

She decided to skip through the rest of the pleasantries and went straight to issue. "Is there a problem?"

"You tell me." He opened the folder and turned it around so she could see it. It was her application. Only now a line had been highlighted in yellow. The address. She had listed the farmhouse.

She bit her lip. "I was going to tell you."

"It's not like we haven't spent time together. How long were you living here?"

"Almost a month."

His shoulders sagged. As if she'd let the air out of his balloon.

"I feel like I've been duped," he said.

She had no choice but to tell him everything now. "I had no place to go after closing on my parents' house. They wanted immediate occupancy, and I didn't have the funds to rent an apartment. It was that or pay past due bills. I chose the latter." She turned and walked over to the sink, then turned around again, her hands behind her, grasping the edge of the counter. "I'm not the success everyone thinks I am. Haven't been for the past few years. When my parents committed suicide, I was ashamed what Dad had done and vowed to repay every cent he had embezzled."

Rhett frowned. "Wait. What? Suicide? Embezzled?"

She turned, staring out the window but seeing nothing. "Only Connie knows the truth. No one else has a clue. It's why I became such a recluse. I was embarrassed, ashamed of what they had done."

"So, you moved out here—"

"It was just temporary. I wanted to tell you but were afraid you'd judge me."

She heard papers being shuffled.

She turned.

He was closing the folder, the frown back on his face.

"Just like you're doing, now, " she continued." Her stomach rolled and tightened. Why had she so stupidly kept everything a secret? She knew why. So many times she'd been told not to talk about family's secrets to anyone. "You want me to be fully transparent with you, but how transparent have you really been? Several times when I've asked about certain areas of your life—particularly your past relationships—you've avoided that subject like the clichéd plague. If I'm expected to come clean, so should you. Hello, Pot. Kettle here. I've got news for you. I'm not a cat or dog to be rescued." She grabbed her bag and turned, walking to the door. "When I return, don't be here. This partnership is over. I'll find a way to pay you back for—" She held back a sob. "—

everything."

She slammed the door behind her, running to the car so he wouldn't hear her crying. The dam to her emotions that she'd been holding back all these years had finally given way. No way would he ever want to work with her after this.

If her life was a mess before, it was a massive train wreck now.

*****

Rhett heard her car start, tires crunching on the gravel, the vehicle driving away. What just happened? He didn't mean to piss her off. He just wanted the truth. Even now, he still didn't believe that he knew everything. And, she'd been right about him avoiding the truth, too. He was going to say that, but she ran off before he could.

Obviously, she felt terrible, but had he made any attempt to make her feel good about telling him the truth?

No. He'd been caught off guard. He loved her work ethic, respected her honor in wanting to do the right thing even to her own detriment. He wanted to help. She'd been homeless for a month and no one knew. Except for Connie.

Her saying her parents had committed suicide didn't make sense. He hadn't heard anything of the sort down at the fire station or from his buddies. Any time they talked about Eddie, it was about her good looks, her success of selling houses, or their warning him to stay away from her. And, as far as her parents' accident went...it had been just that: a terrible accident.

Yet, listening to Eddie, it sounded like her sales weren't the great success the guys claimed. If she was so successful, what was she doing with the money? Something didn't make sense, and he wanted to know everything. The truth.

He grabbed his keys off the counter. Only one person in town would know what was really going on. Connie.

*****

She'd driven around out in the country for half an hour—angry, sad, disgusted at herself, afraid, then angry again—crying the entire time.

Tears filling her eyes, she turned into the farmhouse driveway glad to see it empty.

POP!

Startled, the steering wheel dragged to the right. She tried to control the steering wheel and brake quickly. A front tire had blown.

With a lurch, the car jumped forward, crashing into a corner of the porch, the porch roof tilting down and digging into the hood, blocking her view. She'd punched the gas instead of the brake.

She swore loudly. Putting the car into *park,* she jumped out berating herself. How could she have been so stupid? She went to look. The car was about a foot into the foundation. The bumper was crushed, the hood damaged, scrunched up like aluminum foil plus pinned under the roof. Steam rose from the sides of the hood. And, the front tire was flat, the initial instigating event.

Could her life get any worse? She grabbed her purse out of the car. The phone was dead. Her charger was inside.

In the kitchen, she went to the counter where she'd been charging the phone only to find the charger gone. That's right, she'd taken it upstairs while finishing a few paint touchups in one of the bedrooms.

She ran upstairs, retrieved the charger, and ran toward the staircase. Tripping on her own feet, she started falling into the open space of the stairs. Frantic, she grabbed at the hand rail, missing it.

Her sports training from years ago, kicked in. Knowing she had to just roll with the fall or that she'd do more harm trying to stop the fall, she tucked her arms in. Too late. Hitting the hard wooden stairs, she heard and felt a snap in her right arm followed by extreme pain. She tried to protect her left hand and arm with the right one, relaxing as much as she could. The bottom was a long way down.

*****

The noise hurt.

Someone was talking too loudly.

The light was too bright.

Her head ached. She tried to raise her right arm but couldn't. She raised the left to her head and felt something taped to her forehead.

She groaned. Her right arm felt heavy.

"Eddie. It's me, Rhett. Can you open your eyes? Nurse!"

Eddie grimaced. "Don't yell," she whispered.

Someone came close to her. A female voice. "Can you open your eyes?"

Eddie opened them to just slits. It hurt too much. Someone pulled up one eyelid, flashed a light, then did the same to the other. She put her hand above her eyes, shielding them from the light and opened her eyes a bit more. The nurse was leaving the room.

She was in a bed. She looked down her body and saw her right arm was in a cast. She was in the hospital. Rhett stood at the foot of the bed.

"Thank god, you're okay."

"I wouldn't say that," she croaked. He moved to her side, putting a hand on her sheet-covered leg. "What happened?"

"I found you the bottom of the stairs. You gave me, all of us quite a scare."

"Oh. Yeah. Right." Now, she remembered. "How long have I—"

"Just a couple hours. They're going to keep you overnight. You've got a slight concussion—"

"And, a broken arm. Broken car...porch." She frowned, her eyes shutting. She couldn't open them again. What had she been saying?

She welcomed the ability to drift away.

*****

Day 13

It'd been late in the day, just minutes ago, when Connie had picked her up at the hospital. They were on their way to Connie's when she stopped and parked in front of the diner.

"Why are we stopping here?" Eddie had been

released during the supper hour and it was later than that now. Her stomach growled having missed the meal.

"I left my favorite sweater. Hey, why don't you come in. I made your special pie early today."

"Chocolate cream?"

"Silk."

Eddie sighed. As tired as she was, Connie's silk chocolate cream pie would be just the thing for her sweet tooth. Maybe it could help her forget everything for a few delicious moments. "Okay, but you'll have to help me out of the car. I don't have the energy. My muscles aren't cooperating like they should either."

Connie laughed. "Not a problem, Dear. I suspect given a day or two, you'll be feeling almost new again."

When Connie opened the door, Eddie swung around, reaching out to accept Connie's help getting out of the car. Eddie grimaced as pain shot through her head. Remnants of the headache. Luckily, the concussion hadn't been serious.

Slowly, as not to make any sudden movements, she made her way to the diner's door, letting Connie open the door for her. She stepped across the threshold.

"Surprise!" People popped up from behind the counter and were pouring into the room through the kitchen.

She startled. William. Mason with Shelley. Classmates, other business owners, former customers.

Friends of her parents. So many people. The Laurel Ridge community. Then, the bank president stepped forward.

"You may not know it, but people around here like to take care of their own. You've had your share of bad luck recently and people reached out asking how they could help. I'm happy to present you with a check for fifty thousand dollars to help cover your hospital bill and other expenses." He held the check out to her.

Reluctantly, she took it and stared at it, the text blurry. A tear dropped onto the check. She'd not been the kind of friend that deserved this. She had conducted business but shied away from the community for too many years. "I can't accept this. It's too much."

Before she could say anything else, everyone burst into applause.

Connie was at her elbow. "Honey, people like to help. You'd be offending them if you don't accept it."

Eddie looked around. It was like everyone was holding their breath. Waiting. Connie was right. They did want to help.

How could she deny them that?

Eddie took a step forward, taking time to look at the entire room, seeing the community but more importantly seeing the individuals.

"Thank you for this. I…" She bit her lip. No, she had to tell them. She took a deep breath, then let it out. "As many of you know, I lost my parents just before my senior year. What you don't know is that

Dad had embezzled from the company he worked with."

A gasp arose from the crowd and stunned faces replaced the smiles.

"And then a week later, their suicide—"

"That's not true," Joe Benton said.

She frowned. "What?"

Rhett stepped forward from the crowd. How had she not seen him before?

"They didn't commit suicide. With Joe's help and a buddy who's in forensics, particularly old cases, we learned their accident was just that—an accident."

Joe spoke again. "With Jefferson's help, we talked with your dad's company." He handed her another check.

She couldn't take her eyes off the amount. Four times what the other check was worth.

When she looked up, she could hardly see through the tears that were accumulating and threatened to spill over. "I don't understand—"

"It's all the money you've paid them. They never wanted it to begin with. It wasn't your fault or your responsibility. Apparently when you wouldn't listen to them, they decided to wait you out. Just so you know, they expected you to stop paying after about a year. They had no idea that you'd be this stubborn."

She laughed and then sighed. "I was that, wasn't I?" She looked around the room again. "How can I ever thank you?"

Shelley, tucked under Mason's arm, said, "You can't. It's all about taking care of family—this family," she said, sweeping her arm out to the group, "And paying it forward." She looked up at Mason lovingly, who gave her a resounding kiss.

This time, Eddie couldn't stop the tears that ran down her cheek. "Thank you everyone. Thank you."

She gave Joe a hug and to those closest to her. By the time most everyone had left, she was exhausted. She moved to one of the tables and sat down. Connie set a piece of pie in front of her. She took a bite, closing her eyes, relishing the rich taste. She heard steps and someone sitting next to her.

She opened her eyes.

Rhett.

She hadn't seen him the rest of the evening, thinking he'd left. If she had learned anything from the past few days' events, it was that she needed to be honest with everyone. Including Rhett.

And, if she was truthful with herself, she was in love with him. He deserved total honesty.

"I'm sorry I locked you out," she said, "that I didn't trust you enough with the truth. I only hurt myself in the end."

"I'm sorry, too. You were right about me. I wasn't being honest either. I lied to myself saying I didn't want a relationship when all the time I really did want one. I didn't give you a chance and then judged you by my own lies. I was wrong in never giving my last girlfriend a chance to explain. I was in the process of doing the same thing to you. I want a family someday, but more importantly, I want to be with a woman who wants to be with me for the right reasons." He looked at her, his face softening. "And, that woman is you. I *want* you as my partner."

She smiled. "I'm glad. I enjoyed working with you on the house. And, yes, I'd love to be your partner. Do we need Joe to write up the papers?"

"No, we need Mason."

"Mason? But, he's a judge."

"Exactly."

She frowned. "But—"

"I want you to be my partner for life." He slid out of his chair and got on one knee in front of her, pulling a ring box out of his pocket, and opening it, presenting it to her.

She gasped and looked up from the ring box to his face. "It looks like Grandma's vintage diamond daisy ring! I was so disappointed not finding it in her belongings or in Mom's. How did you—"

"I saw pictures of her with it. And, I saw one with you holding her hand admiring the ring."

"What? What pictures?"

"Connie has them."

She looked at Connie, who nodded her head. Eddie's vision blurred as tears filled her eyes again. She had no idea that Connie had pictures of her grandmother. It made sense since Connie and her mother had been best friends. She turned to Rhett again. "But, we've only been together a week."

"Love doesn't recognize a timeline," he responded. "When it's right, it's right. All the time in the world doesn't change that."

"But—"

"And, we have a lifetime to learn more. But, we can have a long engagement if you'd like, for as long as you'd like."

She stared at him, her heart saying yes—an inner voice she had ignored and squashed for far too long—while her head was saying, *caution*. She smiled. "Yes." It was time for her to stop listening to her head and listen to her heart instead.

He stood, pulling her up, wrapping his arms around her, lowering his head. They kissed.

Breathless, she pulled her head back, looking up at him and asked, "How soon before the farmhouse is finished?"

"Livable finished or finished finished?"

"Honeymoon finished."

He grinned. "Two days?"

Eddie grabbed his shoulder with her good hand and peered around him. "Connie?"

"Yeah?"

"Want to be my maid of honor in two days?"

Eddie never heard her answer. Rhett was kissing her soundly again.

Connie went into the kitchen. Smiling.

Arrested Pleasures #3

Can Cutter, the bad boy womanizer of Laurel Ridge, ever win the heart of game warden Annie Martin, who'd rather see him in handcuffs?

Night Before

Annie Martin sat on the floor of her parents' empty bedroom with a box of papers she'd just found far back on the closet shelf that she had missed when emptying their house the week before.

It was the only house her parents had lived in as a married couple, both born and raised in Laurel Ridge, the county seat of Ridge County in southwest Georgia. And, where she had been born.

Or, so she had thought.

Now, she wasn't so sure.

Laurel Ridge was home, always had been. She didn't want to learn that she'd been born elsewhere.

Or worse, that her parents weren't her real parents as suggested by the paper in her hand.

The house was empty save for these papers. Tomorrow, as executor of her parents' estate, she'd be signing the house over to the new owners. She had expected the house to take a couple months to sell. Instead, it had sold in two days and they wanted possession in two weeks. Annie had scrambled to deal with the furniture and all of their collections, selling much of it. Earlier while she'd been at work, the movers had come in and had transferred the last few pieces of furniture she wanted to keep and the scores of boxes of papers and other valuables she'd handle later to her house, stashing everything in her living room for now.

Earlier, before going home after work, she'd taken one last, thorough look around in all the cupboards and closets to make sure nothing had been forgotten or overlooked.

That's how she'd found this box, secreted deep in the corner of her parents' closet.

Three and a half weeks ago, her parents had died tragically in an auto accident at dusk when an eighteen-year-old who was texting and driving had crossed the median, slamming into her parents' car. They had all died immediately.

As tragic as the accident was, both of her parents had been dealing with life-altering health issues because of their advanced ages. They'd had her fairly late in life. According to the paper in her hand, she wasn't sure what they'd been to her.

Staring at it, Annie wondered how much of her life had been an accident. The paper declared her parents as legal guardians. She was six months old when she came under their care. What did that mean? Had they adopted her? Was she related to them in some other way?

How could she have never known? How many people in town knew and had kept their secret with them? Or, was everyone else in the dark, as well? Had her parents gone on an extended trip, pretending to be pregnant, coming back with a baby?

No, she couldn't believe they'd lie like that. And yet, she was holding the biggest lie of all in her hand.

How many times had people said she looked like her dad? Was that a lie? How could she possibly look like her father if she'd been adopted? Unless he had cheated and it was her mom who was accepting her into the family?

She shook her head, rejecting that possibility. They had been devoted to each other. Neither would have cheated.

Thoughts swirled, only to circle back to the same initial thoughts. Who could she go to? How could she learn the truth behind this guardianship? Seated on the floor with crossed legs, like a child ready to hear a story at the library, she continued staring at the paper.

It was a story all right.

She dropped the paper and put an elbow on each folded knee and leaned forward, her head in her hands.

Thoughts swirled again. None of it made sense. And, there was nothing tangible to grab onto, other than this stinking piece of paper that she now wished she'd never found.

What if the family moving in had found it?

She sighed, wanting to cry. She sighed again, instead.

She couldn't cry. Wouldn't. Couldn't remember

the last time she had. Not even after having been pulled through the mud, burning her hands on the rope, during a long and intense tug-of-war competition on field day in the third grade with the entire school watching the play-offs between the two third-grade classes. Her face covered with mud, she wiped at her eyes and mouth, swiping her dirty hands on her mud-caked clothes, and said, "Can we have a rematch?"

That was when the boys started letting her hang out with them. That summer, when she fell from the apple tree in the woods behind Jefferson's house with a broken arm, she hadn't cried then either. When Jefferson had walked with her back to her house so her parents could take her to the hospital, he'd told her it'd be okay if she cried. That it had to hurt. He had confided he cried when he'd broken his arm, admitting the other guys never knew.

"It does hurt," she had said. "I'll keep your secret." He had grinned at her, put a hand around her shoulders and opened the house door for her. They'd been best friends ever since.

Wherever the boys were those next years until they left grade school and most of middle school, she was there with them. Fishing, climbing, baseball, board games, camping. They welcomed her as one of the boys.

But then, puberty struck and she noticed they looked at her a little differently. Her mirror told her what they were really looking at. Her budding breasts.

She ignored their looks, pretending nothing had changed. She knew things would change, though. She saw it happen to Jefferson and Joe who were a class ahead of them. Once they entered high school, they hung out with the gang less, spending more time around girls, playing school sports, or other school activities.

The fishing though. They all verbally acknowledged her as the expert. She knew what bait to use, where and when, and how to hook the worms correctly. She'd just been happy that they wanted her along, even if it was to bait their hooks or untangle their lines.

It was late. She'd already been through the box twice. She was tired. Her eyes felt scratchy. Mostly from spending much of the day on the lake, her first day back from a three-week leave that should have been vacation time. Instead, she'd spent it burying her parents and getting this house ready to sell.

As a game warden, she loved her job, but today had been difficult. Everywhere she went had been reminders of her dad. He'd been a game warden, too. The lake was one place he didn't patrol, but even so, she remembered the many times she had begged him to go fishing with her. He always said he preferred hunting to fishing, telling her the lake was her special place. The one place they'd never shared. While he had taught her how to fish, they never went fishing together after that first year. She usually fished by herself.

He'd been right after all—the lake was her special

place.

As much as she hated discovering the box's contents, she'd been lucky finding it. The fact it had been so well hidden from view spoke volumes of her mother not wanting it found. Hopefully, she wouldn't find any more secrets. She wasn't sure she could deal with any more surprises.

*****

Day 1

Angry, Cutter Logan punched open the side door to the county's courthouse. Immediately, the bright sun had him looking down and reaching for his sunglasses. Barely noon, the heat and stifling humidity promised another sweltering day. Not to mention nothing going his way so far today. First, stupidly hooking a car instead of a fish, and now this hideous court sentence. Dark clouds and a thunderous rain to match his mood would suit him just fine. It wasn't like he could enjoy the sunshine for a year to his way of thinking. Hunting was everything to him. Now what?

"Hey B-Boy! What's your hurry?"

Hearing his high school nickname—Beta Boy shortened—Cutter stopped and turned to look behind him. Even after all these years, his buddies wouldn't let him forget how he'd announced during one football practice that he was an Alpha. They had just laughed and called him Beta Boy just to get his goat. Over time, he'd learned to go along with the joke.

Judge Mason Baylock exited the courthouse. He might be a judge now, but they'd grown up together, graduated in the same class, and saw each other frequently now that Mason had moved back to town six months earlier, becoming a circuit judge.

"Mason. What's new?"

"That's my question for you. I saw your name on the docket this morning. What'd you do this time?"

Cutter really didn't want to talk about it, but he knew Mason would detain him until he got an answer. It's what made him an excellent judge and a good man. "I was ready to pay a fine for being stupid. Lost my hunting license for a year, instead."

"Ouch, that's got to hurt your business."

"Yeah. Big time. Not sure what I'm going to do now."

"You could always turn to fishing full time."

Cutter snorted. As much as he enjoyed fishing, he preferred doing it from shore rather than from a boat. But, to make money at it, he needed to be out on the water. He hadn't invested in fishing equipment over the years. Now, he wished he had. "I'd be better off mowing lawns."

"Heard you hooked a car this morning, in the first hour of the first day of Whippoorwill's fishing contest."

"Can you believe it? William's car. Didn't catch a thing after that and then I had to quit because of this morning's sentencing. Doubt I can win the contest now. No one will let me count the car as a catch."

Mason chuckled. "Sorry, man. Wasn't that the car William told us he'd sold back in high school?"

"Yup. Same one. Supposedly sold it because he

didn't like the color. Can you imagine? Hey, you still chasing after Shelley?"

"Headed to the diner later on tonight. Want to join me?"

"What? And interrupt that fine cast of a line you're trying to angle her with?" Before Mason could ask him another question, Cutter slapped Mason on the back in a friendly goodbye, adding, "Gotta run. Got a hot date."

Yeah, he had a hot date all right, with a cool refreshing pool of water. After everything that had been happening so far today, he needed to cool down and cool off.

*****

Annie Martin entered the Department of Natural Resources office located on the outskirts of town and noticed Sarah wasn't at her desk. Sarah was the heart and soul of the place, and Annie depended on the clerk who'd been at the job for forty years. Annie didn't want to think about what they'd all do when Sarah would retire in another year. It was bad enough when she took an extended weekend, which is why she was gone today and which Annie had forgotten. Karen, who was much younger and a fairly new employee who manned the phones and assisted Sarah, handed her the day's log of calls.

Headed to her own office while scanning the sheet, she stopped at the mini kitchenette, hidden out of sight, and grabbed a cup of coffee. She heard the front door open and close and a male voice call out. "Anyone home?"

"In here," she said, walking out of the kitchenette and into her office.

She walked around her desk and sat down just as Daryl's six-foot-eight frame filled her door. At fifty and her boss, he looked as fit as he did a decade ago when he had hired her. For the time being, he was overseeing the county next door, what with Georgia's need for officers in half a dozen counties statewide. Basically, it was her responsibility to oversee Ridge County.

He sat in one of the two chairs on the other side of her desk. "Just got back from court. Cutter lost his hunting license."

"As well he should have, considering he and his party shot over the legal limit, not to mention killing game out of season. Took them long enough to bring the case to trial."

"There was no trial. Cutter pled guilty before a jury could be picked. Sentencing was delayed until this morning. The judge had an emergency at the end of last week."

"Mason?"

"No," he said.

"Knowing Mason," she said, "he would have recused himself since he and Cutter are friends."

"Anything important on my blotter or yours?" he asked.

"Not that I can see," she said, scanning the sheet again. She handed it to him. A quick glance, he tossed it back on her desk.

"How are you spending your second day back?

Welcome back, by the way. Going to ride the trails?"

"Might as well. Rain's predicted for tomorrow. Would rather deal with the heat and dust than to be sliding in the clay." She rose and picked up the keys from the corner of her desk, tossing them in the air.

"Unlike your dad. Don't know how many times—"

"—he always got stuck on them," Annie injected.

"And, had to dig himself out," Daryl finished. He paused. "Sorry."

"Don't be. I know you miss him, too." She laughed. "At least, I don't come back covered in red clay."

Daryl chuckled. "He despised you for that, you know."

She nodded at the memories, the laughter that always erupted when he'd enter the office covered in muddy red. Just for a moment, she considered asking Daryl if he knew anything about her adoption, but then she stopped herself. *Dad wasn't one for talking about his personal life.* He was great at telling stories from out in the field, but never anything personal. She wondered how much anyone knew about her parents' personal life.

"Enjoy." Daryl got up and followed her out of her office, heading for his vehicle as she climbed into hers.

"Will do." Pulling out, Annie waved.

Despite the heat, it felt good to be outside again. Even before her parents' deaths, being in the office had become claustrophobic and she didn't know why.

Though, maybe, it had nothing to do with the office and everything to do with having turned thirty this year.

Their death and now this adoption issue just made everything more intense.

She had lost more than her parents in that accident. She had expected to feel grief. Just not this yawning abyss of mistrust that settled on her last night, creating this extreme doubt where she was questioning everything, including her own life.

She'd always wondered why her parents didn't have any pictures of her as a newborn. They had claimed they had no camera back then. And, with no other relatives, there hadn't been anyone else taking pictures either.

The sparse clues on the back of the few pictures she'd found last night led nowhere. And then, she'd found adoption papers at the bottom of that box, stuck to the back of other papers. They'd been more than just her guardians. They had officially become her parents. Her world crashed reading that document. But, why weren't her biological parents listed anywhere? That lack of information was puzzling.

Thirty years old and for the first time in her life, she felt lost.

*****

Half an hour later, driving on one of the backwoods' trails that eventually led to a few mobile homes, Annie found a pickup parked alongside the trail. A pickup she'd never seen before. Only after she got out of her truck, did she see a somewhat hidden trail that went off into the woods. A path she'd not seen before, and here she thought she knew them all.

It looked more like a deer path than anything else and even then, not well used. She recognized the area, though, and knew deep in the woods there was a waterfall, where the water wasn't stagnant and stayed pretty cold even on the hottest of summer days—like today—so it had to be fed by a natural spring in the slight stream that formed somewhere before the fall and then drained under the rocks just after the pool. Her dad had shown her the pool, saying it was a great place to go skinny dipping on a hot day. Their trek that day had come from the opposite direction on another well-hidden path. Though now, Annie had to wonder how many people knew about this location.

Getting close to the fall, she circled around so that she was climbing the hill to view the stream and where she could look down on the pool. No one appeared to be here.

Then, she heard male laughter. Someone was in the pool below, at the base of the falls where she couldn't see.

She squatted down to peer over the rocks. A man swam toward the opposite edge of the pool, away from her. She opened her mouth to yell, but then he started clambering out of the pool naked. She clamped her mouth shut. She didn't want him turning around.

Strangely, he looked familiar. Not that she'd seen many naked men in her lifetime, but this man held her attention—besides his being naked—and she didn't know why. It was the way he carried himself. With confidence. Total comfort being in nature. As if he was one with nature. The only person she knew like that was—

No. It couldn't be.

Just then, he turned his head and looked her way.

She ducked. Damn! He'd seen her. She just knew it. The last person she wanted knowing she'd been watching.

Cutter.

She knew that cocky grin as well as she knew her own face in the mirror.

She stayed hunkered down until her thighs were screaming in pain. Slowly, she peeked over the edge.

He was gone. But where? She didn't see a pile of clothes anywhere. Had he dressed and left?

She rose slowly, looking over the falls to make sure.

Not seeing him, she sighed with relief. He would never pretend he hadn't seen her there. Already, she dreaded the confrontation to come.

She was back on her earlier path, returning to her vehicle, when she heard a motor start. *Please let it be him leaving.*

The vehicle drove away.

Coming out of the brush and seeing only her vehicle, she sighed in relief. No doubt he'd find a way to talk about her spying on him, which hadn't been her intent at all, but neither did she want him turning around, naked as the day he was born. Knowing him, he would have loved the opportunity to reveal—well, just everything.

She rolled her eyes at the thought of their future conversation. She'd do as she'd always done — let him think what he wanted.

*****

Later, stepping into the diner, Annie took a quick look around. Per his usual habit whenever they'd meet, she saw Jefferson Jackson, a state senator, back in the corner. He was pretty much alone on that side of the diner, just the way he liked it. Whenever he was home on recess, he'd eat lunch here in the middle of the afternoon when the diner wasn't crazy with customers. If he had meetings with anyone locally, he'd usually conduct them here rather than in his office in the courthouse. Said that he preferred the less formal setting, that everyone tended to be more open here.

Annie slid into the bench opposite him.

"Officer," he said.

"Senator," she responded.

They both laughed at their usual greeting. It felt good talking with her trusted classmate and best friend again. They'd been neighbors growing up, and now, they each owned a cabin outside of town, though hers was a snug cottage, while his resembled a huge hunting lodge. And even though it was his home, he lived half the time in an Atlanta condo he said he hated—all glass and metal. Too modern for his taste, but he had no desire to change it. He figured if he got voted out, it would sell better in the current modern style than any other style.

Connie set a coffee mug in front of her automatically. Annie looked up and smiled. "Nothing else for me, thanks, Connie."

Connie left.

"Hard to believe we're all in our thirties now," Annie said.

"Agreed. I often think back to myself as that skinny freshman obsessed with debate, wondering how it'd fit into my life."

"Little did you know. Still getting used to the job?"

"I thought being a lawyer was tough." He shook his head. "I had no idea. It's only been a few months and I'm still learning something new every day. Don't know what I'd do if not for my experienced staff. I knew politics was complicated, but so much more than any of us were ever taught or thought we knew. And, from day one, there's been someone's trying to buy me off. I've come to despise lobbyists. Enough about me. What's new with you?"

Annie took a sip of coffee, set down her mug, wrapping her hands around it. She looked up at Jefferson, wanting to see his expression. "Last night, I discovered I was adopted."

He frowned. "You didn't know?"

She stared at him, stunned. "You knew?"

Jefferson sighed. "I knew, but only in the past few years. Your parents came to me, asking me who would be a good attorney to write up their will to make sure you would rightfully inherit. Somehow, they'd gotten the idea that because you were adopted, you couldn't inherit. Someone spreading bad information, obviously. I told them they were wrong and recommended Joe. I had to reassure them that I wouldn't betray their confiding in me—they were worried I'd say something to you. I told them they should tell you. Don't be too hard on them. They wanted to do the right thing."

"By never telling me? Do you know what a shock this is to find out now? And with them gone? I can't ask them anything! And Joe knew, too?"

She felt like her entire insides had dropped, her stomach rolling. She couldn't hide her feelings anymore. Not right now. Not from him. If she had felt abandoned finding that box, she felt that abandonment even more sharply now.

Her best friend had known.

He reached out, cupping his hand over hers. "Look, you can ask me anything. Joe, too. We'll help you anyway we can."

"Have you two talked about it?"

"No. That would have been unethical. Joe has never said a word. I haven't either."

She pulled back, sticking her hands in her pockets, leaning back in her chair. "At this point, I'm not sure what to do."

"What do you know?"

"Not much."

"What do you want to do?"

"I'm not sure. Would it be a mistake to look for my real parents?"

"Not if you want answers, though you might not like what you find."

"What do you mean?"

"All kinds of possibilities. That your biological mother doesn't know who the father is, that you might have been conceived through rape or abuse. That you were related to your parents through one of their brothers or sisters—"

"There is no other family. Both were an only child"

"—that maybe your biological parents married later. That her parents were ashamed of the stigma—"

"In this day and age?"

"Sure, it still happens in certain families, certain cultures. You might find that your biological parents are of a different culture or religion, immigrants, for instance. There are so many unknown factors."

She considered his comments. "I can't stop thinking about it all. I want to know, need to know, if for no other reason than for medical purposes. But, I'm so overwhelmed by it all. If I don't find out, it'll gnaw at me. Isn't it good to know your background for health reasons?"

"It's one argument."

"I don't even know where to start."

"I know someone who knows how to find people."

"Who?"

"Cutter."

Annie looked at him with skepticism. "But—"

"He's got some serious computer skills and—"

"No, not Cutter—"

"Seriously. He's good at digging out information with no one knowing the wiser. I've used him before to help me track down heirs."

"How did I not know this?"

Jefferson smiled. "Easy. You don't spend quality time with him. Or, ask me the serious questions—until now."

"That's not true. I've asked you lots of serious questions over the years."

"I remember the ones about boys."

"And, that's not serious when you're a teenage girl?"

Jefferson laughed. "Okay, you got me there."

"And, we lunch together several times a month when you're around," she added.

"And, talk about what?"

"Your work. My work..." She paused. "You're right. We rarely go down deep. Dull, ordinary surface stuff. Work and the outdoors." She frowned, realizing. "Matter of fact, Cutter's always asking me questions, rarely answering mine, now that I think about it."

Jefferson laughed again, then tilted his head toward the door, looking in that direction. "Speak of the devil."

Annie twisted her head around. Sure enough, Cutter was in the diner, heading their way.

Jefferson slid out of his seat, stood, and grasped Cutter's outstretched hand, pulling him into a hug where they clapped each other on the back loudly.

"Long time no see," Jefferson exclaimed. "Though,

I hear you're still getting into trouble. That's got to be tough, losing your hunting license for any length of time."

"As always, bad news travels fast. What am I saying? In this community, all news travels fast. Hear you're doing the same up in Atlanta. Getting into trouble, trying to keep the politicians honest. How'd that meeting go?"

"Successfully, thanks to you, with the information you found. Speaking of help, Annie could use some."

Cutter looked down at her. Then grinned. "Really?"

"Not that kind," both Annie and Jefferson said at the same time.

"I've got to get going," Jefferson said.

Annie stood and gave Jefferson a hug. "Thanks for listening."

"Any time." In her ear, as he hugged her, he said, "Let me know how it goes."

Cutter sat where Jefferson had been just seconds ago. Annie took her seat again. Connie approached with a fresh cup of coffee for Cutter in one hand and the pot in the other to refill Annie's mug.

After Connie left, Cutter held up his mug. "Truth or Dare."

As much as she didn't want to, Annie clicked her mug to his. If she refused, he'd be questioning her anyway. At least with their version of Truth or Dare, she could avoid any question she didn't like. At the same time, she had good reason to question his Dares. She always suspected he had an ulterior motive, and he usually did. Sipping er coffee, she watched him over the rim of her mug watching her. How many times had she baked his favorite chocolate chip cookies or made a double batch of her twice baked macaroni and cheese as a result of not wanting to answer a question, taking the Dare instead? Thankfully, his Dare requests were usually food related. Most of the time. He never requested anything too personal or inappropriate. So far.

It was a game he insisted on playing with her long before she made the mistake of going out on a date with him, and he continued playing it afterward, basically every time he saw her in the years since. Now, she'd think something was seriously wrong if he didn't want to play. Truth of the matter was, the losses got her baking, and she enjoyed keeping half of the spoils for her own tastebud pleasure.

"So, what's going on, Pee Wee?" he asked.

"Don't call me that."

"Okay, Short Stuff."

She gave him her look. The one that said she was done with his short nicknames for her. "Don't make me call you B-Boy."

He laughed. "Okay, okay, I get it. You can't help that you're so short, but seriously, Teeny just fits you so well."

"Just like you can't help that you're really a beta."

"Alpha."

Annie laughed. She couldn't help herself. At least the conversation followed the usual path. "Says you."

His grin widened.

She hated how he could make her laugh, even when she didn't want to. And, being called Teeny…no one but Cutter called her that and had ever since their first meeting when they were kids. Anyone else who tried using that name with her got punched. By her.

"So, what help was Jefferson talking about?"

"I don't—"

"Ah, ah, ah. Truth or Dare."

She rolled her eyes, tilted her head so she was staring at her mug and cursing under her breath.

"What was that?" he asked, purposely being cocky. "Did you really—while in uniform? Tsk, tsk."

She dropped her shoulders and blew out a breath. She couldn't do this. Not yet. Not now. Not with him. "Cutter—"

"You don't want to talk about it."

It was a statement, not a question. It never ceased to amaze her how he could read her mind. How many times had she denied what she was thinking because he had guessed correctly?

He'd been the first to offer his condolences and to give her a big hug when her parents had died. When he hugged her, she had just relaxed against him. Easily and instinctively. Too easily, actually.

As much as she hated to deny it, she was glad to see him today. Though, she could have been happy having seen less of him earlier…walking out of the water, his bum perfectly rounded, a strong back, and long muscled legs—

"Earth to Annie."

"Sorry, what?"

"Let me walk you to your truck. You're working today, right?'

She got up. He mimicked her movement. "You don't have to do that."

"Not a problem. We're both leaving anyway."

They left money on the table for the coffee and tip, and she turned, walking toward the door, knowing that Cutter followed behind her.

At the door, he reached around her for the handle, pulling the door open. Outside, they walked toward her truck, neither saying a word.

She grabbed the door's handle. He came around, standing in her way. "Give me a kiss."

She sputtered with laughter. *That* was the last thing she expected him to say. And yet, how many times in any year since that one disastrous date they'd had in high school had he been making this same request? So many times that it had become a standing joke.

She looked at him, biting her lip to keep from laughing some more. Cutter was giving her that lost puppy-dog look he displayed when begging.

"No," she said.

"That's what you always say!"

"And I'll keep saying it until you stop asking."

"I'll stop asking once you give me one."

"No."

"Aw, come on, Little Bits, don't be such a party pooper."

"Never did like parties."

"A party for two is always a delightful party."

"Delightful?" She laughed. "Says you."

"Always, even when it doesn't go well."

"Speak for yourself."

"Give me another chance."

"You had your chance."

"That wasn't a chance. It was a series of mistakes."

"That you started by being late."

"I couldn't help it. I ran out of gas."

"Which you should have planned ahead and filled your tank."

"Okay, point taken. But—"

"Then we were so late to the movie, we didn't go and ended up at the diner for sundaes, and mine ended up in my lap."

"An accident."

"That you caused because you were ogling Shelley's boobs when she walked by, knocking over your water that splashed all over me, with your glass pushing my split into my lap!"

"I was a teenage boy!"

"And the raspberry syrup stained my shirt—my favorite—which I had to throw away."

"You didn't keep it as a memory keepsake?"

"What are you, an ad man? Worst first date ever."

"But, not our last. At least, not until you forgive me. You will, you know."

"Not happening."

"That's cruel."

She laughed again.

"Goodnight, Cutter," she said, pushing him out of

her way, opening the door, shutting it before he could say anything more. Starting the truck, she wiggled her fingers *goodbye* at him, and backed up. Going forward, she glanced at her side mirror, seeing him still rooted to the spot, with an even more exaggerated crest-fallen expression.

For the first time ever, he had failed to ask his Dare question. She wondered if he'd even realized it.

Pulling out of the parking lot, she raised her hand and waved again, this time not looking in the mirror.

Was it a mistake not asking for his help?

No, she didn't want him knowing her personal business. She'd be forced to spend even more time with him if he did.

She'd always had her guard up, but now, asking for help with her adoption quest, that would mean letting her guard down. He'd take advantage of it. It's how their Truth and Dare game got started and which she sometimes regretted. He had a disarming way of drawing her into his silly games. Just like in high school, only it was now a decade later. Apparently, he hadn't matured all that much, having lost his hunting license. Pure foolishness.

No, this was the way to go. Keep their lives separate—as much as was possible considering their small community where everyone knew everything about everyone else. And, since she had control of this quest of hers, no way was she letting him into that circle. Even if Jefferson did recommend him.

*****

Day 2

The minute Cutter saw the swirling overhead lights on the vehicle behind him, he heaved a sigh. He had promised Jefferson to pick up the new truck Jefferson had purchased and drive it to his house. Jefferson was then going to drive Cutter back to town.

Unfortunately, Cutter had gotten so engrossed with the buttons and fancy screen on the dashboard that he'd lost track of the posted speed limit. It didn't help that he was lead-footed, too.

He braked and pulled over. Looking in the rearview mirror, he saw Annie get out. He grinned. *Oh, this is going to be fun.*

Watching her approach his window, he could tell the minute she saw him in his side mirror and regretted pulling him over. Her step slowed slightly and the look on her face relaxed because she knew the occupant, but then steeled in the way he'd seen her do whenever she didn't want to answer him. He loved how he could read her like a book, even though she denied it profusely.

She was at his window. "Howdy, Officer," he said. He wanted to grin but knew better.

"Cutter."

"Jefferson's new truck."

"It's a beauty."

"Aren't you going to ask for my license and registration?"

Her mouth twisted to one side as she chewed on the question and the side of her mouth. She sighed. "Let's just rack this up to a friendly warning. Slow down."

"No, I insist. By the book."

"Cutter, really, I—"

Cutter opened the door and jumped out, shutting it, holding his hands up in the air. "Aren't you going to frisk me? Ask me if I'm packing?"

"Are you?"

"Always?"

"You really want me to search you, don't you?"

"I'm hoping."

A couple cars passed by, the drivers waving. Cutter waved back, smiling, his hands still in the air. He glanced at her. She wasn't grinning. He sobered up.

"Why does it always have to be like this with you?"

"How do you know if I'm not carrying the deadliest of weapons?"

She gave him that stern stare. He laughed.

"You have a dirty mind, Officer. I meant as in guns, knives—"

"Why does everything have to be ha-ha with you?"

He lowered his hands. "It's not a ha-ha unless I'm naked. Can I do it naked? Oh, wait, you saw me naked. Yesterday. I was packing then, too, Pee Wee, I mean Officer Martin."

She glared at him. "Turn around," she demanded. "Hands on the truck."

"Do I have to keep my clothes on?"

"Stop it, just stop. I don't have the energy."

He frowned and looked around. She was looking at the ground, her shoulders slumped over a bit. He turned around, facing her. "What's really going on, Teeny?"

She glared at him again.

Wow, something was really wrong. Usually, she'd start laughing at his calling her Teeny. Not this time.

"Okay, Truth or Dare," he said.

Uh-oh. He didn't like that look in her eye. The look that always left him breathless, giddy, and wary all at the same time. Was she about to be serious, making him want to be a better person or would she suddenly become silly, leaving him in stitches at the absurdity of her deductive reasoning—at least absurd to him—but which hit the bullseye every time? She was such a distraction, and yet, he always wanted more. It didn't matter that she was stingy with her thoughts, her deep-down feelings. She kept so much private, and he wanted to peel away the layers.

"You hate fishing," she said.

"No, I don't." *Damn. Where had this come from?* It wasn't like her to segue off topic like this. That was his role. He wanted to talk about his speeding, instead.

"Truth?"

Oh, crap. She was trapping him better than he'd ever trapped her. "Well... okay, I'd rather be hunting than fishing."

"Because..."

"Hunting is safer."

"Using a gun is safer than using a line?"

"That's not what I meant."

"Hunting is safer because you're traipsing around in the woods with other hunters than sitting in a boat or standing on a shore?"

"That's not what I meant, either."

"What do you mean, then? Truth."

"I'll take Dare."

"Nope. Truth."

He paused, staring at her. She wasn't going to let this go. Most of the time, when he segued away from her questions, she'd follow him down his paths. Not this time.

"Okay. Truth." Another pause. "I hate the water."

Annie laughed. "That's ridiculous. I've seen you in water. I saw you the other day."

"Ah-ha, so you *did* see me!"

"You're trying to divert. You were in water!"

“Naked.” He hated that she was going to be the first to learn of his well-kept secret. More ammunition for her not to like him.

Annie frowned. "I've seen you in water lots of times."

"But never swimming. Wading. Or in a boat.”

She frowned. “You can't be afraid of drowning. You were swimming yesterday.”

“Naked.”

“What does wearing clothes have to do with it?”

“Everything.” She wasn't going to give up. He sighed. “Boy Scout camp—the only summer I ever attended. I got thrown out of a boat with my clothes on. I felt like I was drowning. The clothes were so heavy."

"That doesn't make any sense."

"It does to me."

She frowned not understanding.

"Someone had to reach down and rescue me. It was humiliating."

"When have you not minded not being humiliated? The guys tease you all the time about everything, B-Boy."

"Not with this, they don't."

"All the more reason why you should wear a life jacket."

"I hate 'em. They're confining."

"Just like everything else in your life."

"What's that supposed to mean?"

"You like to be in control. Of everything and everyone. Even if it's against the law."

"Ridiculous. Okay, so I like being in control. So do you."

"Isn't that how you lost your hunting license? Because you had to be in control?"

He had no retort. He was always in control when he took others out on hunts. He was their guide and responsible for them. Only this time, he had screwed up.

"Just saying," she said.

They stared at each other, neither backing down.

Damn, she was feisty. That's what he loved most about her. She didn't let him get away with anything. He wanted to be a better person because of her, but here she was thinking the worst about him. He knew better than to try to change her mind. Clichéd stubborn as a mule, always in her must-do-it-by-the-book mentality.

He didn't remember her being like that in high school. But then again, they didn't spend much time together in school unless they were seated next to each other, which didn't happen often since so many teachers assigned seats alphabetically. He'd always wondered why, asking a teacher one time, and got the response that it was easier to figure out who was absent for roll call. Made sense, but he preferred sitting in the back watching the girls, and where he didn't get called on unless he was sleeping or goofing off.

He stepped toward her, shortening the distance between them. He towered over her, but she didn't budge. She looked up at him, pure determination on her face.

"You're so hot," he said. "Sexy as hell."

Her lips twitched, then she busted out laughing, bowing her head so she was looking down at the ground, still laughing.

He knew she thought her uniform was about as sexy as a mud puddle, but to him, it didn't matter what she wore.

He welcomed her hat touching his chest, wondering if she knew they were touching. He leaned forward just slightly.

Instantly, her head tilted back again. Yup, she knew.

"I want to kiss you."

Her eyes went back and forth as she gazed at him, searching his face for clues—his eyes, his mouth, even his eyebrows.

He gave her nothing.

She stepped back, her head down enough so that her face was hidden by her hat.

"Take your hat off."

"Is that what you say to all the girls?"

"Just you. Only you."

Her head jerked back again, staring at him with surprise.

Internally, secretly, he grinned broadly. If she only knew how much she revealed just now. He could feel his lips twitching. "You're the only one who wears a hat."

Too quickly, she said. "No. No way." She raised her hand as if she was going to swat at him as she'd done in the past from time to time, but she stopped herself. Probably because she was in uniform. Just once, he wished she wouldn't be so stiff, so formal while in uniform.

He laughed. "One day, Bitsy, one day, you *will kiss* me, and you'll like it."

"Says you."

"Yup, says me."

He got in the truck and turned on the motor, moving forward onto the pavement. Once on the road, he waved.

*****

Watching him walk away as he got into the truck,

Annie saw him as she'd seen him the other day at the pond. Naked. A tight bottom, long legs, a long torso, and a strong back. She blinked several times to wipe away the image as it morphed into him walking away in his nicely fit jeans and tucked-in shirt. So few men wore button-down shirts these days. She loved them. Way sexier than T-shirts.

And then, he was gone.

There was something about those buttons. And, his confidence. His buttons always teased at her and his level of confidence frustrated her. It was such an act most of the time. Because of his buffoonery, she could never tell when he was serious.

Getting into her truck, she acknowledged that for just a few seconds she had considered asking him for help, as Jefferson had suggested. But then, the conversation had taken a different turn—as it always did.

Last night, she had spent hours on the internet, frustrated that she'd found nothing about her biological parents. She had so little to go on. She really didn't want to resort to asking him for help.

*****

Day 3

Annie pushed open the agency's door and saw Sarah at her desk. Immediately, Annie felt her shoulders drop. Sarah's presence made everything less stressful. Annie wasn't sure what Sarah's secret was, though she was convinced it had to do with Sarah's aura and chakras, a healing practice Sarah pursued in her free time and weekends. Sarah's long gray hair was up in her usual loose topknot secured with an unsharpened number-two lead pencil.

"You're back!" Annie exclaimed.

"You thought I wouldn't be?"

"Well, no, but—"

"I know, you're just happy to see me, because I'm the oil that lubricates this place and makes everything work smoothly." Sarah handed her a stack of papers.

Annie laughed. "Yes," she admitted, looking at the stack. "What's this?"

"Reports of lost licenses. Daryl told me he wanted you to follow up on them. I saw you breaking bread with Cutter Logan yesterday. Nice to see that you're not judging him for losing his license."

"Most certainly am. Doesn't mean I hate the guy, but what a stupid thing to do. He knows better."

"You haven't heard, then? He took the blame for the ones who actually did the shooting."

"Wait a minute, you're telling me Cutter's completely innocent?"

"Yes. He admitted he had failed to tell them of their limit. He blames himself."

"How do you know this? No, don't tell me. Wait a minute, you got this from your husband?"

"Yeah, he and Jim Jr. forget I was there at the dinner table, too. It's like I'm invisible or something as they start talking shop."

"Sounds like two attorneys." Both Sarah's husband, Jim, and their son were attorneys in Joe's office. Jim senior was going to retire the same time as Sarah so that the two of them could travel.

"Jim wanted Cutter to plead not guilty, but Cutter didn't want a trial."

"Wait, should you be telling me this? Isn't that client/attorney privilege or something?"

"Not if the attorney—my husband—is telling the story to me. If it was privileged, he wouldn't be telling me."

Annie frowned. "Why would Cutter do that? Pleading guilty always means losing your license for a time. Everyone knows that."

"From what they said last night, Cutter was willing to gamble he'd get a slap on the wrist and maybe a couple of months of service. Was even willing to risk jail time."

"But—"

"He didn't count on past offenses coming back to bite."

"Jim said it'd be three weeks before a trial could start—"

"And, Cutter doesn't like to be kept waiting," Annie said.

"Odd, considering he's a hunter. I've known that boy to sit in a tree stand all day, waiting for that prize trophy to appear."

"The only thing he's ever waited for—the perfect shot. He loves the outdoors, hates sitting around *inside*. Always has. It's why he hated school so much."

"Can't say I blame him," Sarah chuckled.

Annie took the stack of reports and phone messages into her office to deal with the urgent ones right away before heading out for her usual drive around the county. More often than not, any stops she made were just inspections. Nothing serious.

She sighed, dropping the stack of papers. Who was Cutter really? She was so confused by this latest news that he wasn't at fault and yet had taken responsibility. It didn't make sense. Why would he do that? Nothing was making sense anymore.

She felt like Alice and had fallen down a rabbit hole herself where up was down and down was up. Where was the truth anymore? Could she ever feel safe and whole again?

She picked up the messages again, thumbing through them, then set them down, realizing she wasn't comprehending what she was reading.

Even though she wanted to know what made Cutter take responsibility like that, she wasn't about to spend more time with him just to satisfy her curiosity. Besides, what was that adage about curiosity killing the cat? No, she wouldn't do it. He would just confuse her more.

Who was she kidding? Her entire job was about being curious. Checking on hunters and fisherman to find whether they had the proper license, were using proper equipment, and catching only legal-sized fish or in-season game.

And now, she was curious about her biological parents. Not knowing was gnawing on her badly. She hated to admit it, but she needed help.

She had called Jefferson last night and once again, Jefferson offered Cutter's ability to locate people few others could find. After talking with Jefferson, she had called Joe, who also gave Cutter high praises for his ability to worm information out of the slimmest of all leads. Another part of Cutter she'd known nothing about.

She felt defeated, like she'd been driving for hours only to find herself on a dead-end road.

There was only one thing she could do.

*****

Cutter stood at the back of his truck, the tailgate down, his tackle box open, cleaning it out and restocking it, expecting to try his luck again in the fishing contest. No way could he win the overall prize, but he might have a chance at a daily prize, *if* he got started early enough tomorrow and stuck with it the entire day. Now that the court thing was behind him, he could focus elsewhere, not letting anything deter him away from his goal.

Hearing tires on his driveway, he looked up. *Except her*. His stomach flipped.

To hide his excitement at seeing her, he continued working on untangling the line, glancing at Annie as she got out of her truck, walking toward him. Halfway to him, she stuck her hands in her pockets. He grinned, focusing on the line. She wanted something. Anytime she stuck her hands in her pockets, she was surrendering—his term, not hers—needing his help. He was always willing to help. Anything she needed. How could she not know that?

Once she got to the tailgate, she stopped. He put everything down and turned toward her. "What's up Small Stuff?"

"Is that the line you used to snag the car?"

He laughed. "No. That entire reel became evidence. Was thinking I could save a few dollars using this. If I can untangle it, that is."

He waited. Interesting that she wasn't responding like she usually did when he used one of his nicknames for her. She wasn't here to talk about his fishing line, either. Something big was going on.

She confirmed that thought by rocking back on her heels, looking down, her hands still in her pockets. Finally, she stood still, pulling out her hands, placing them on the tailgate, looking up. He wanted to remove that resigned, worried look from her face. He wanted to see her smiling again. Instead, her frown deepened. A frown he'd never seen before.

She sighed heavily. "I need your help. Jefferson and Joe have both told me you often help them find information. That you know people who know people. That you know how to find people."

Annie took a deep breath. The last thing she wanted to do was talk about her situation, but she needed help. She couldn't do it alone, and she was at a point that she needed to know. It was no longer about wanting to know—it was about need. She needed some kind of closure. She couldn't get it from her parents or any of the documents they left before. She needed something, anything. She'd didn't want to be angry at her parents but knew if her thinking kept circling around, she'd explode. She didn't want to be angry with them for keeping her birth a secret.

She had no choice but to trust Cutter. "I found out

several weeks after my parents' deaths that I was adopted. I found a paper buried deep in their private papers." She paused and peeked a glance at him. He was frowning, concern written all over his face.

"A paper, as in only one?" he asked.

"Yes, why?"

"Usually, there are multiple papers, even photographs. That tells me that maybe they overlooked this paper, maybe having destroyed all the others, never wanting you to find any of them."

"Possibly. It *was* buried in the bottom of a box that had been buried deep on a closet shelf, but it doesn't look like an official adoption paper. A court document, maybe because it has a notary seal?"

"Which, if it is, anyone could find it as a recorded court document. That makes it public. Did they have a safe-deposit box?"

"No."

"Are you wanting to find your biological parents?"

"I'm not sure. Yes. No. I mean…"

"Do you want to find them without them knowing about you?"

"Yes."

"What do you want to know?"

Annie ran a fingers over her lip, moving her finger back and forth, thinking. There were so many questions. Did she want them to know where she was, who she was? Did they already know? She lowered her hand. "I'm not sure. Can you guarantee me they won't know about me until I want them to?"

"Yes, at least not through my inquiries, but that will limit how I conduct my search."

"Like not talking with anyone who might know them?"

He nodded. "Are you sure you want me to do this?"

"I don't know."

"What are you afraid of?"

"That this could get out of control. That they turn out to be people I don't want to associate with, that they'll bring drama into my life. I don't do well with drama." She released a huge breath of air. She'd just revealed herself.

Not even Jackson knew that about her. She hated drama with people close to her. Why she gave in to Cutter's Truth or Dare game all the time. He could be relentless with his asks. Strangers, though, were different. It was probably why she was so good at her job. Able to ratchet the drama down in tense situations.

"Is that why you avoid me?"

She looked up at him, startled. *Was it*? "Yes." She thought for a few seconds. "No. You don't have drama—well, yes, you do. You're usually at the center of any drama, though, aren't you? "

"What went so wrong with us, Mitsey? Truth."

Annie looked away, thinking. Then, looking at him, wanting to see any facial changes in his reaction, she told him the truth. "You scare me."

She waited for him to laugh. He didn't. In fact, he didn't react at all other than his eyebrows coming together. He was watching her face as much as she was watching his, looking for little revealing clues. He had explained to her once that all people—animals included—revealed their next actions through little clues. With people, it was their facial expressions. With animals, it was in their muscle twitches or foot movements, like stomping.

They both were extraordinarily good at reading others.

She hated how he had learned how to do that—to read her so well over the years, but her decade as a game warden had served her well. She had learned how to conceal her true feelings. To not react. To wait. To analyze internally before speaking. A minute ago, she wasn't thinking in having told him he scared her and that she didn’t like drama, but now she was analyzing it all. She shouldn't have told him. Now, she was second-guessing herself and hated that she was.

Is that why she had stayed friends with him all these years? Because he could make her laugh so easily? That they didn’t have a deep relationship? And yet, besides her best friend Jefferson—a man with huge authority—and her continued friendship with Cutter, there was no one else. Not really. Was her friendship with Cutter deeper than she realized?

"I'll help you," he said.

She breathed a sigh of relief. "Thank you."

Not wanting to talk anymore right now, she turned and walked toward her truck. She needed some space.

She heard him say, "Meet me for breakfast tomorrow. Bring the paper and anything else you have."

She raised her hand and waved in response, got into her truck, and left without looking back at him. She knew she'd fall apart if she looked back. Asking him for help made her feel even more vulnerable than being around him. Somehow, between now and tomorrow morning, she needed to find her backbone again.

As she drove away, she wondered how he could begin the search. The only piece of paper she had didn't reveal much information. She'd already checked online. How could he find anything more than she already had found—or not found?

*****

Day 4

Seated in the diner with their order placed, Annie pushed the paper toward Cutter. He picked it up and read it. Basically, the document stated that her parents were now legal guardians. No additional names, other than the judge and the notary. Not much to go on. It looked like a court document number up in a corner, but what court? Where?

Even though she was doing her best to keep her expression blank, he could tell she was as nervous as a cat surrounded by a dozen strange dogs. She was out of her comfort zone and didn't like it. She never did when it was personal.

He wanted so much to protect her, but knew he couldn't. All he could do was be there for her, to comfort her when she discovered who her biological parents were if needed, or to rejoice with her should it go well. For her sake, he hoped it would be the latter.

"Do you have a birth certificate?"

"No. Not that I could find."

"This is a start, even though it doesn't look like much," he said, putting the paper on the bench beside him, moving it off the tabletop.

She looked even more disappointed. He wanted to reassure her but knew she wouldn't receive any platitude well. Never had. He paused, wanting to be careful with his words. "Are you nervous?"

"Wouldn't you be? Yes!" She almost sounded relieved to have said it.

"Whatever the results are, I'm here for you. You won't have to go through this alone."

Her mouth turned up a little. "Thank you." And then, she asked him about his business, specifically what was he going to do since he couldn't lead any hunting groups for a year. It was obvious she was changing the subject, so he followed her lead.

"I don't know yet."

"No Plan B?"

"Got any ideas?" he asked.

During the entire meal, they talked about everything and nothing. They laughed as they compiled a list of new businesses he could create. Then, they talked about their friends, recent marriages and divorces, sports, the fishing contest.

Finished with their meal, they walked to their cars out in the back parking lot, going through a mini park with bricks, a light pole, and a bench that took advantage of the shortcut small space between the two buildings.

"Go out with me," he said.

She stopped and looked up at him. "Did you just ask me out on a date? A real date? A formal date?"

"No. Yes. Whatever. Yes. Look, you trust me enough to find your parents. Can't you trust me enough for an actual date? *Pleaseeeeee?*" He hated how he sounded like he was begging, but if begging worked, he wasn't above doing so.

She did that twisting of the mouth thing, which told him she was weighing the pros and cons.

Quickly, he added, "I don't want you to feel like you have to. Just because I'm helping you." He wasn't above putting a little guilt on that shameful pile of pleading.

Now, she was chewing on her bottom lip. Uh-oh. Had he gone too far?

"You'll plan it?"

"Whatever you want."

"Okay. Surprise me." And with that, she turned and walked to her truck.

He stood there stunned and speechless. Did he just hear her right? What made her change her mind suddenly?

She got into her truck, all without a backward glance, and drove off.

He ran a hand through his hair. He was getting his wish, and now he was terrified. He didn't want to screw it up. He'd be lost if he couldn't win her over.

For the last decade, he had watched her date other guys, some from their class, some younger, some older, even some he'd never seen or met before. She hadn't dated often, but more often that was to his liking.

Where was she finding them? Better question was, how were they finding her? Granted, she traveled the county most every day and met lots of new people as she did her job. Is that where she met these guys, out in the bushes? On the lakes? No, that was wrong. She wasn't like that. She took her job seriously.

He leaned against the hood of his car, crossed his arms, and stared off into the distance. She had finally said *yes*. This date had better be the best he could plan. If not, she'd dump him so fast, his head would spin.

He remembered seeing her break up with one of her dates a while back. The guy had been bulky like a wrestler and she had brought him to his knees. Literally. He had to have touched her wrong, because she had his thumb twisted in a way that had him crying out in pain. That's what had turned all heads in her direction in the diner that night.

The entire restaurant had gone totally silent.

She had leaned in and said in a low voice meant just for the man on his knees, but which was heard by most everyone there. "Don't ever touch me like that again. In fact, don't ever contact me again. Ever." She'd grabbed her purse from the table and stormed out of the diner, the bell above the door announcing her departure.

Then, all heads turned back toward him, and he glanced around, realizing he was the center of attention. "For such a tiny thing, she sure is powerful." Lots of laughter and nodding heads. The townspeople knew full well the power of her wrath.

It was the last thing Cutter wanted to experience. Ever. Not after witnessing that take-down firsthand.

*****

Day 5

"Wow. I'm impressed," Annie said.

Cutter continued shaking out the red-checkered tablecloth that was serving as a blanket for the noon picnic he'd put together, complete with a large basket loaded with food and a huge bottle of the best lemonade in town, all thanks to Connie's help and recommendations earlier this morning. Following her directions, he'd gone to several stores to collect everything, then home for assembly before meeting Annie here.

She had insisted that she drive her own vehicle when he called her last night. Probably just in case she wanted to leave when she was bored with him or when she was done, having had enough of his nonsense. She had a habit of walking away when she was really done.

Knowing her love of wildflowers, he'd chosen this field out in the middle of nowhere. No doubt a field she'd never seen, but one he'd visited many times during deer season. Deer loved this opening where the tall grasses and wildflowers grew. He had spread out the tablecloth under a huge live oak that provided shade at the edge of the clearing. He was hoping her love of wildflowers would win her over.

They munched on the veggies and dip, ate the sandwiches, and demolished the slices of chocolate silk pie—another one of her favorites and Connie's specialty.

"I half expected you to be picking some flowers to take home," he said.

"I'm content just to look at them. I hate taking anything from its natural setting. But, I'm not above buying flowers from the grocery store now and then. These are pretty to look at."

He made a mental note of that statement.

Until now, the conversation had stayed in safe territory. He knew by wading into this topic, he was chancing getting caught in rough waters. While never one to play it safe, he knew he was jeopardizing everything by bringing up the past, but he had to do it anyway. "So back in high school—"

She cut him off immediately, not letting him finish. "It was a mistake, that first date."

"How so?" He'd always believed he had blundered a little, but it wasn't the disaster she always made it out to be.

"You think it was good?"

"Well, yeah. I'm a guy. I was with the girl of my dreams."

"Wet dreams, you mean."

"Those, too."

She rolled her eyes.

"Hey, I'm not going to deny it. I was a teenager! But, you have to admit, I was a perfect gentleman."

"You had no choice. You knew my dad would kill you if you weren't."

"Well, there was that. I sure would have liked his respect, even when we weren't an item."

"We never were."

"Says you," he said.

"How could he respect you? You were always in trouble!"

"I was never in trouble."

"Being sent to the principal's office—"

"Rarely was my fault."

"Are you saying you got caught with your hand in the cookie jar but that you weren't eating the cookies?"

"If you like that metaphor, sure! I was passing the cookies out. Never did care much for them myself—"

"Yes, I know of your preference for chocolate cake. But, you had the propensity of always being in trouble."

He shrugged. "It's a gift. I have that kind of face. Besides, your dad didn't like me 'cause he didn't like my motorcycle."

"That wasn't personal. He didn't like anyone's motorcycle. Called them death machines."

"Not if you know how to ride 'em. It's about watching out for everyone else. It's the other drivers you can't trust. But, that's not the point. You aren't saying why you wouldn't go out with me again after that."

Several emotions flitted across Annie's face, almost as if she was having trouble deciding on which excuse to pick.

He added. "It was a great date."

"It was a disaster! We've talked about it before. Why do you want to keep rehashing history that we can't change?"

"You're right. Let's talk politics then."

"No," she said.

"Why not?"

"Because I don't like how you debate. You run me around in circles and rarely with facts." She pointed across the field, rising to her feet. "What's that?"

Cutter stood and peered across the field. Standing there for a minute, he crossed his arms, spreading his feet, planting himself squarely. Finally, he said, "Looks like a black bear."

"Great," she said, watching, too. "I'd heard they'd been migrating westward these last few years. Guess they've arrived. More complaints will be coming from campers and people having their trash cans flung around."

He stood watching until the bear disappeared deep into the woods. He turned his head and found her watching him. "What?"

"Look at the way you stand." Annie mimicked him, crossing her arms across her chest, spreading her legs apart, thrusting her hips out.

Cutter howled. "I don't stand like that."

"Yes, you do, and you're doing it right now! The crossed arms and leaning back tells me that your heart is closed off but you're leading with your—what do you call it?— most sacred tools, which says, *I'm open for business.*"

Cutter howled again.

Should he one, deny and call her bluff with a Dare, their rule for not wanting to tell the truth, or two, laugh it off, saying it was true even though he knew it wasn't true? He knew his being agreeable without really agreeing was a trait that annoyed her beyond measure. Being agreeable had always served him well with everyone else throughout his life. Just not with her.

"Truth," she said.

Damn, she just upped the stakes. He hated when she did that.

He unfolded his arms, put his feet closer together so he stood straighter, and looked down at her. "Dare."

Her lips curled in frustration. Inwardly, he grinned. She really wanted the truth. She'd have to pay for it.

"No."

He ignored her *no.* "I want a kis—" She was already shaking her head, no. "—mit double fudge chocolate cake with that special chocolate chip frosting."

Her lips twitched in amusement. "You're not distracting me this time. Truth."

He sighed.

She grinned.

"This stance helps my leg from hurting." That

much *was* true. The part he didn't tell her was that he *was* open for business, but only with her. He wasn't interested in anyone else, no matter what the rumors that floated around him said. Admittedly, he was no saint, not when he was younger. He'd tried a few relationships now and then, but they never worked out. They didn't measure up.

Packing up the remnants of their lunch, Cutter grabbed the tablecloth and shook it out. "Meet me for dinner tonight." He started balling up the material.

She grabbed the cloth and started folding it.

He continued. "I'll have some information for you by then. I've got some feelers out and expect to have phone calls returned this afternoon."

As soon as he said that, he was sorry he had. Her expression changed. She'd already forgotten the good time they'd just had and was already thinking ahead. He knew that worrying look.

"It'll be okay," he said. "I'll be by your side the entire way. You won't be alone."

She nodded.

*****

Annie entered the diner knowing she was late. Having wrestled with a stray dog in a muddy field just hours ago, she'd had no choice but to go home and shower first.

Connie came out of the kitchen and passed the register, her hands filled with ladened plates. She nodded her head toward the other direction. "Cutter's around the corner, in the back," she said. "I'll be there in a minute."

"No hurry," Annie replied, going to the back.

She scooted into her seat. Cutter was frowning at his cell phone that lay on the table. "Anything interesting?" she asked.

He looked up, sliding the phone into his pants pocket. "No. Just checking the weather for tomorrow's trip."

"What trip?"

"Ours, if you're interested."

Connie arrived with water and took their orders.

"Where to?" Annie asked, the minute Connie left.

Cutter named a hospital in a small town about one hundred miles away. "I searched all the names on the guardianship paper and it led to this town."

Annie just stared at him.

"Frankly, I find it all odd," he continued. "At least, we can start with the hospital. Want to go? I'd rather go see the place in person than to get a run-around with someone on the phone."

Annie thought for a second, then nodded. She knew if she didn't go, she'd be second-guessing herself until she learned something. Better to go with him and know right away than to wait until he returned home. At this point, she just wanted to put the whole thing behind her.

But, could she? Even if she discovered who her parents were?

For the rest of the evening, both with Cutter and then later when she was home alone, she was distracted, her concentration nonexistent. Even Cutter had suggested they cut the evening short because of it.

She sighed again, turning off the lights and headed for the bedroom, knowing any thoughts right now were just circular. Tomorrow, she might have some answers. She could only hope.

*****

Day 6

Walking out of the town's library the next day, Annie felt defeated. The only thing they had learned was that, yes, she'd been born here in this community. The hospital had verified that, then directed them to the courthouse, where they got a copy of her birth certificate. From there, they went to the library to use their computers to see if they could track down her parents who were listed on the birth certificate.

"Don't give up," Cutter said. He took her hand as they walked across the street to a large park.

Normally, she would have let go of his hand after a minute, but this time, she held on. Throughout this whole thing, he was fast becoming her rock.

"I don't get it. How can two people who are named on that birth certificate just disappear? It's as if they never existed."

In front of a copse stood a gazebo. She stopped and stared.

"What?" he asked.

"I don't know. That gazebo looks familiar and I don't know why."

"Could it be recent pictures you've seen?"

"No, I don't think so…but, I've seen it before." A few tears rolled down her cheeks, and then before she knew it, she was sobbing.

Cutter faced her, wrapping his arms around her, letting her cry, rubbing her back, just holding her tight.

Finally, the tears abated. She brushed her cheeks with her hands, pulling a tissue out of her pocket, wiping her nose. "I'm sorry."

"Don't be. You didn't cry about your parents, did you?"

She shook her head. "No. I don't cry."

"Ever?"

"Not that I can remember."

"Delayed reaction. My mom was like that, too. Tough as nails during a crisis. Would break down afterward, sometimes weeks later. It's understandable. You've gone through a lot in the last few weeks." He frowned. "You know, I don't think I've ever seen you cry before. Remember that time when you got between a bully with a bat on the edge of the playground and a turtle he was going to demolish?"

She nodded, climbing up the gazebo steps. "We were ten years old. There wasn't anyone else around at the time."

"I was. I was always in bushes. Watching bugs. Watching kids."

She laughed, taking a seat. "Now I know how you were always so dirty coming in from recess."

He sat down next to her, stretching his leg out, crossing them at the ankles. "Teacher was always asking, too. That bully was twice your size. What'd you say to him?"

"More like what I did. Being short has its advantages when slugging someone."

Cutter frowned, then laughed in acknowledgment. "You didn't?"

"I did. He raised the bat; I raised my fists, making first contact. All he could do was sputter."

"And fall to the ground?"

She looked up to the gazebo ceiling as if in thought. "Gee, I don't remember."

He laughed. "Such a liar. That boy avoided you like the proverbial plague after that."

She shrugged.

"So, where to next?" he asked. "Any place else you want to go while we're here."

She chewed on her lip, thinking. "Yeah… The cemetery."

"We don't know that—"

"No, we don't. Just a feeling."

*****

Fifteen minutes later, they exited Cutter's truck from where he parked under a large shade tree in the town's cemetery located at the edge of town.

Cutter hung back, following her, letting her lead the way. He noticed a few names, but then started noticing the dates. He stood staring at one set of graves. Small children and a parent all from the same family and all dying within days of each other. A tragedy. The date was October 1918. Spanish flu. The remaining parent lived for another twenty years.

He looked up. Annie stood in front of a

headstone, staring at it.

Walking over to her side, he stared down at the stone. Her parents. The day they got married was listed along with their birth and death dates.

"They got married. I wonder if they had any children."

"They had you."

"They got married *after* they had me, and died on the same day they got married."

"Let's go back to the library."

"Why?"

"Newspaper announcements. Archives."

*****

An hour later, they sat in front of a computer screen, looking at a young couple, standing in front of the gazebo. An engagement photo, the newspaper claimed, stating they had died that night when, during a horrible thunderstorm, a tree had landed on their car as they drove down a country road.

"I've seen that picture before."

"But you said it wasn't among your parents' pictures."

"Not the ones I looked at recently."

*****

After visiting the cemetery, hunger drove them to search out a restaurant. By the time they emerged from the restaurant, it was dark.

On the way home, Cutter turned down a side road and drove just a short distance before stopping.

"What are we doing here?" she asked.

"I have something to show you."

She wanted to protest but didn't want to expend the energy. Out of the truck, she noticed how pitch-black it was out. She shut the door and looked up. He had parked on a dirt, side road, alongside a huge clearing, so they were away from the two-lane highway.

The sky was cloudless and perfect, the Milky Way clearly cutting through the night sky, the dark new moon not hampering the view of starlight. A comet shot across the sky. Then a second one.

"Did you make a wish?" Cutter asked.

"No."

"There'll be more."

"I should get my wish list out," she said.

Cutter chuckled. "You and me both."

They stood there a few more minutes, admiring the view. Once they were both slapping at the mosquitoes, they admitted defeat and got back into the cab. The trip home was spent in silence. Usually, Cutter led their conversations. She wondered if he was as lost in thought as she was.

When he pulled into her driveway, she opened her door quickly, then paused. Turning around, she leaned toward him, giving him a hug. Just as he was reaching to return the hug, she kissed him on the cheek, and pulled away.

"Thank you for today." Then, she was out of the cab, shutting the door behind her.

Once inside the house, Annie went straight to her parents' few boxes of possessions she still needed to go through, looking for the scrapbooks. In particular, for the oldest one that she used to look at a lot when she was little, where she could see her baby pictures. Pictures *after* she'd been adopted. There were none of her as an infant.

This time, she went to the pictures before her birth and she found the picture she'd been looking for. The one she'd seen probably only a few times in her life.

A couple stood in front of the gazebo, her arm linked through his, his hand on hers. A duplicate of the picture she and Cutter had seen on a computer screen earlier. The couple both had dark hair, his short and hers chin-length but curly. While both smiled, they were shy smiles, not a smile with teeth showing or laughing. A definite pose someone had asked them for. It must have been winter since they both wore long pants and what looked like wool jackets.

Annie pulled the photo out of the scrapbook and flipped it over. Definitive proof of what she'd been looking for. She'd had it all this time and never knew it. She remembered one time seeing the picture, asking her mom who they were. Her mother had said, *just some cousins I haven't seen in a long time.*

On the back of the picture, it read: Annie's parents.

Could her biological parents still have kin in the area?

Annie shook her head. At this point, she didn't want to know. She didn't want to invest the time and heartache that could occur in that search.

Now that she knew who they were, she was okay with her life, contented that she'd had a happy childhood. A good life. She loved her career and knew as she sat holding their picture that even if she never married, she'd be okay. Unlike other girls, marriage had never been a forethought. Or even an afterthought. Instead, her focus had always been about being outside, in a rowboat fishing, climbing trees, or searching for bugs and birds, and her career. She loved her job.

She smiled, looking at her biological parents. She was okay not knowing everything about their part of her life. An extremely small part. Her adopted parents had been her parents and always would be.

She made a mental note that she needed to tell Cutter not to do any further searching in the online ancestry programs. He had asked her earlier if she wanted to do a DNA test. At the time, she had said she didn't know.

Now she knew, she wasn't going to do it. Maybe she did have relatives out there, but right now she was okay not knowing who they were.

Maybe in the future, she'd have him help her update her true lineage, but for now, she didn't want her birth parents' relatives—if there were any—to know of her existence.

She wanted her life back—the way it was before she'd found that box. Or rather, instead of getting it back, to put that part of her life behind her, and move into her future instead.

Putting the picture back into the scrapbook into

its original page, she closed the book, crossed the room, and stood it upright on the bookshelf next to the family bible that had been passed down through her father's family.

Going to the doorway, she reached for the light switch. She glanced at the bookshelf, at the books, and turned off the light.

It'd been a long day. Earlier, at lunch, long before they had learned anything, Cutter had asked if she'd go to the county fair with him tomorrow. A second date. She wished she hadn't said yes. And yet, she couldn't cancel. Not with the way he'd been supporting her, helping her.

Maybe after a good night's sleep, she'd feel differently than she did in this moment. Going to the fair every year and meeting up with Cutter was just as much a habit as was carving pumpkins for Halloween. That summer after graduation, they'd met up accidentally and stayed together for the entire evening. The following year, they agreed to meet up at the fair, and that's how that tradition evolved.

Always a fun event, there was no reason for this year's fair to be any different… well, except she was going as his date instead of as a friend. No, she was still his friend. If he wanted to make it a date, so be it. In her mind, however, nothing had changed.

*****

Day 7

Cutter arrived at her door just minutes after she'd changed out of her work clothes and into a pair of shorts and a cotton sleeveless top. Starting to sweep her hair into the bun at her nape as she did for work, she changed her mind and opted for a pony tail instead.

In past years, she and Cutter would meet and walk around, looking at the animal exhibits together, getting fair foods and sharing them, sometimes joining up with other classmates and friends, but this was the first time they'd gone together, not having made plans to meet other friends.

At the fair, Annie had to remind herself that it was a date, even though it didn't feel like it. She leaned over the fence of a pigpen in the barn and scratched the pig behind the ears.

Cutter had been doing his usual teasing, going through his list of short names for her until finally, she cried, "Stop!"

"Okay, but only with a Truth or Dare."

She hesitated.

"Choose Dare," he prodded.

She nodded, then hesitated. How did he do that?

Trying to create a bit of distance, she moved through the barn door at the back, the closest exit. An empty field was just across the road behind the barns. It was dark out here in this spot, as the pole's light was filtered through the tree in front of it. There was no one around.

He pulled on her arm, stopping her. She turned, facing him. If she said no, he'd call her a coward and heckle her for days. If she said yes, she could be heading for a bucketful of trouble. She took a deep breath and expelled it. "Dare."

Even though his face was shadowed, she could see his grin.

Oh, gawd, what had she done? She closed her eyes, chastising herself for getting suckered in, being backed into a corner that she knew was there but had ignored.

Opening her eyes, Cutter was still grinning. He was enjoying this. He inched forward. She stood her ground, determined not to turn, and run. *Focus. Think of him as a bear. Don't look him in the eye and don't run.*

She looked at his chest. Wrong move. She looked down. Worse! He was so close she was looking at the bulge of his jeans—

She looked back up at his chest. Then, she looked up for a nanosecond.

He was still grinning. Just standing there. Grinning.

She closed her eyes again, swallowed heavily, a sigh escaping. Was that a chuckle? Her shoulders dropped in defeat. Self-defeat.

Like it or not, she needed to face the inevitable. She tilted her head back and opened her eyes.

*****

Selfishly, Cutter admitted he was enjoying her discomfort. It wasn't often that anyone could get the better of Game Warden, Officer of the State, Annie Martin. And, he was doing it with one word: *Dare*.

It was the only way he could get her to engage with him and he enjoyed making her laugh. Confront her head on. All the other guys were thrown off with her long stare they called intrusive and cold. He called it curiosity. She was figuring them out while she stared. He called it calculating, too, because in that thinking, she was figuring out how to react or what to do. She calculated a lot. It's what made her a good game warden.

She was deep like that. Wanting to know. Wanting to understand. And, he wanted to travel that journey with her.

If only she would let him.

Any time they'd spent together in the past, their separation was always painful. He didn't care what he had to do to be by her side. She could arrest him and he wouldn't care. Being handcuffed by her was actually an exciting thought.

Down boy.

He couldn't stop smiling. She was with him, playing with him, or playing at him. He didn't care. He was just happy she was this close. To be this close, though, and not able to touch her was torture. Pure torture. Excruciatingly painful sweet torture. Torture below and sweet to his mind above.

"Wait a minute. You never answered my earlier Truth question," she said, her eyes popping open.

"What Truth was that? I've forgotten." He really had forgotten. She had him tied up in so many knots... Was it possible that she was tied up in as many knots as he was? He could only wish.

"Open body, closed heart?" she asked. "Truth."

"You're going back to your question from the other day? I did answer. My leg. But, you don't believe it, do you?"

She shook her head no.

"It's true. A doctor told me it was a hip thing. One leg is slightly shorter, so when standing, I discovered a tripod stance evens things out. The arms crossed? Let's just say I never know what to do with my hands."

She laughed.

"There's only one person I want to open my heart to, someone I'm willing to entrust it to," he said.

Her mouth opened a little in surprise.

"And now, the Dare. This."

He uncrossed his arms, stepped forward again and leaned toward her, closing the distance slowly, allowing her the opportunity to escape, to turn and run, to change her mind, but she didn't move.

Her gaze fastened on his mouth. Her eyes widen, he heard the catch in her breath, felt it whisper across his mouth like a feather, and then her eyelids drifted closed.

His lips skimmed hers. His eyes drifted closed. He pressed harder. Just slightly. His heart skipped a beat as she leaned into him and pressed back. And then, her mouth opened just a bit more. He slid one arm around her shoulders and back to hold her, his other hand cupping her face. She tilted her head, allowing his hand to fully cup her face.

He was kissing her. And, by everything that was magic, she was kissing him back.

*****

She couldn't help herself. She was mesmerized. As if following a pied piper. She knew all along what his Dare request was going to be and she had gone along with it.

Stunned that his lips could be so soft yet firm with welcoming intent, she leaned into him. One arm wrapped around her, lifting her up so that she stood on tiptoes, her breasts crushed to his stomach.

He cupped her face and she tilted her head, opening and offering herself up to him.

Her hands slid up his chest, hard muscles beneath her fingers, muscles which tightened and became harder still. She slid her hands and arms up until they were entwined around his neck and where she could pull him down, getting closer.

He groaned. Or had she?

The kiss that started so slow, soft, and tender had become erotic, their mouths searching, seeking, and finding, then searching some more.

When his tongue teased at the corners of her mouth, she could hear her own breath catch. His tongue slid into hers and she teased him back with her own.

He moaned again, his arms tightening his hold.

Not in her wildest dreams could she have imagined a kiss like this.

Suddenly, finally, one of them pulled back just the tiniest bit. Who?

She leaned in, wanting more. She asked. He answered. Then, he was kissing her neck, her cheek, her mouth again, then her other cheek and the other side of her neck. His hips pressed against her, and then his mouth found hers again.

How long had she needed this?

She'd been kissed before but these sensations, it was as if tiny fireworks were going off all over her body. Dormant sensations now alive. Sensations she swore no one would garner from her unless she gave her heart willingly.

Stark realization struck.

She moved her head back, opening her eyes. Lowering her arms, she pushed away, just enough to catch her breath. His arms were still wrapped around her and he wasn't letting go.

She bent her head so the top of her head rested on his chest. Her hands on his chest, she felt his racing heartbeat. Just as fast as hers. And, he was breathing hard. As if he'd just run a marathon.

At the moment, all she wanted to do was kiss him again.

Everything she'd ever read about or heard was true. Her toes had curled, she had been floating, the world around her had faded away and then disappeared completely.

Looking up at him, she was lost in the gray color of his eyes. Just mere millimeters away from his face, she'd never seen his eyes this close, this open, this mesmerizing. She could stare at them all day.

And then, they were kissing again. At first soft, slightly pressing. And then, his arms wrapped around her completely and she was pressed up against him again, her arms hugging him just as tightly.

Several long moments passed as they kissed

deeply, their mouths moving, searching, teasing.

When they separated this time, they both were breathing hard.

His hands moved to her neck, then cupped her jawline and cheek on both sides. *Holy mackerel.* What had she been missing all these years?

Cutter's gaze scanned her face. He kissed her lightly on the mouth, nose, and forehead. Then. With his hands on her forearms, he pushed her back a bit. "If I was Superman, you'd be my kryptonite."

She smiled. Always the flatterer, but she knew this statement was sincere and came from his heart.

If she were honest with herself, she felt the same way. All these years of telling him no, and here with just one kiss… Her body was a mass of goosebumps.

She'd lost control of all thought during that kiss. In those few minutes, her body had clamored for more, erasing any other thought. Did she have no control whatsoever over her body?

Cutter couldn't take his gaze off of her. So many different emotions were behind that smile, flittering across her face: ecstasy, enchantment, wonder…

All these years, he knew if he kissed her, there'd be explosions and were there ever! Right now, his pants fit so tight, he figured the zipper would break and then she'd see exactly how he felt. Everyone would. All he wanted to do was wrap his arms around her again and press his length against her, but he didn't dare. He didn't want to scare her. He didn't want her running. He wanted to win her, to woo her.

He wanted her to come to him, willingly. He

wanted it to be her idea, not his. All the teasing he'd subjected her to had been to win her, but now… It just didn't feel right. But how could it not if he loved her?

He enjoyed teasing her. Seeing her blush, laugh, and yes, even become annoyed with him from time to time. He liked the fire in her eyes. All those reactions told him that she was feeling something for him.

She mumbled, "That was a disaster."

With his finger under her chin, he tilted her head up so that she was looking at him again.

"Honey," he said, "That was no disaster. That was perfection. Pure, sweet, honest perfection."

She gulped. He was right, and she wanted to kick herself for having said that aloud. No disaster except for what it was doing to her libido. "You're right. But one kiss doesn't make a relationship."

He leaned toward her again and said, "What happens with another kiss?"

She gasped with no time to think before his lips were on hers again. At first, brushing hers softly, which she followed measure for measure. Then, the intensity ramped up until she wanted to crawl inside him.

Suddenly, he broke away. His gaze caressed her face, taking in her eyes, her lips, looking for any clue, every sign that she felt the same as he did.

He ran a hand through his hair. "I'm giddy and nervous as hell. I'm afraid of making the wrong move, saying the wrong thing—"

She put a finger to his lips. "Stop. Just be yourself."

"That's what I'm afraid of most. Tell me what you want and I'll become whatever you want me to be."

She shook her head and pulled away.

He tried to keep her in his arms but could feel her resistance as she moved backward again. He let go and slid his hands into his pants pockets to keep from reaching out.

She shook her head. "I've said it before, but I have to say it again. You scare the hell out of me. I don't know what to do."

"Don't do anything. Just be. Go with the flow."

"Is that how you live your life?"

"Yes and no."

"Yes and no? That's no answer"

"But, it's the truth." He shrugged. "At least, it has been."

She stepped back. Stared at him for a long moment, where he saw doubt taking hold again. "Night, Cutter."

"We came together."

"I'm going to go to the game office—booth rather. Daryl's supposed to be here. I want to say hi."

Cutter almost said, *I'll join you* but read something in her stance and on her face that made him rethink saying it. "Okay," he finally said. "I enjoyed tonight."

She started turning away, then hesitated, stopped, and looked at him. "I did too."

He watched her walk away, disappearing into the shadows, before entering another barn, finally disappearing from sight.

He'd been hoping she'd turned back around and at least look at him and wave. But, she didn't. Was she trying to put him out of her mind?

He hoped not.

*****

Day 8

After work, Annie went to her favorite fishing location on Whippoorwill Lake. With just a few feet of shore that was mostly stone and lots of brush where she could sit on a large rock and be fairly hidden from view from those out on the lake, she felt isolated and alone, which suited her fine. Especially today.

She'd spent a hot day in her truck as the air conditioner had stopped working about noon, and that was after a restless night of little sleep. She yawned big yearning for those lost hours. She should go home and take a nap, but she needed the respite she knew she'd get from the lake's restful sounds: water lapping at the rocks, the birds, nearby frogs, and crickets.

With the fishing contest coming to a close, there were a number of boats out on the lake. Most she recognized. There was one boat, though, that more resembled a canoe than rowboat and its owner was standing up. Fool. Suddenly, he sat down, the boat rocking a bit. *It'd serve him right to fall in.* The owner turned his head toward her. Cutter.

Where had he dug up that pile of wood that he was using as a boat? It looked old, really, really old.

If she were on duty on the lake, she'd be alongside him in a minute, checking his license but mostly for his life jacket. Knowing him, he probably had one, but it wouldn't be within reach. How stupid. Especially after telling her about how he couldn't swim with clothes on. If he was to tumble into the water... What was he thinking?

His attention returned to his line in the water. She couldn't help but notice that he was reeling in his line, then turning on the motor, swinging the boat around, and returning to the slips. Several other fishermen were calling it a day, too.

With sunset still an hour away, she considered casting her line that was in her trunk but slapping at the mosquitoes that were now biting, she decided it was time to go home.

*****

Day 9

The minute Annie walked into the office, she could tell something was wrong. Long faces, no noisy greeting, just a couple of quiet hellos.

Forty-five minutes later, she was tossing her personal belongings into a cardboard box.

"This sucks."

Annie looked up. Sarah stood in her doorway, leaning against the frame as if in needing the support.

Annie sighed. "I know, but I get it. State tax and license revenues are down. It's not like other offices haven't been downsized."

"Still sucks."

"Agreement."

Sarah watched Annie for a minute. "Can I get you anything?"

"A new job?" Annie asked.

Sarah shook her head.

Annie frowned. "You're not losing your job, are you?"

Sarah shook her head again. "I just get to retire earlier than I had wanted. That way Karen gets to stay, at least as long as the office doesn't close. "

"I hope for her sake that it stays open."

"At least we're both getting a nice severance package and insurance for several months," Sarah said.

"Yes, I'm thankful for that, plus what I've inherited from Mom and Dad will give me time to find another job, another career, but I have no idea what I'm going to do next. Not a clue."

"You don't want to move and remain a game warden somewhere else?"

"No, this is home."

*****

Half an hour later, after saying goodbye and giving long hugs to other officers who came in to say goodbye—after Sarah had secretly put out the call to those nearby—Annie left the office and drove home.

She'd barely set her belongings on the dining room table and taken off her hat when she heard a knock on the door.

Opening it, Cutter stood there.

Saying nothing, she turned and walked back toward the kitchen. She heard the door close, knowing he was following her.

"I'm so sorry—"

Her back to him, she held up her hand. She turned around. His face looked as pained as she felt.

"I can't talk about it right now. I need to be alone."

She looked at Cutter, knowing he wanted to help but knowing no one could help her at the moment. She really did need to be alone. He had to know what that meant.

Cutter opened his mouth as if to say something, but then didn't.

He stepped forward, gave her a kiss on the cheek, and said, "Call me if you need anything."

She could tell he needed a response. She nodded her head.

He turned and walked away. She heard the front door close.

She sank to the floor, her back sliding against the refrigerator, her legs folding up under her, huge sobs escaping.

Of all the things she had lost lately—her parents, her lineage, and now her job—it was her job that had kept her from falling apart.

Right now, in this moment, she felt as if she had nothing.

*****

Cutter left but not wanting to. He respected her space but hated seeing her in pain. He wanted to help her. To see her smiling again.

He had spent the day fishing, catching nothing. Coming off the lake, he realized his failure at fishing in this contest was summing up his life.

The only bright spots lately were in the kisses

he'd shared with Annie last night and the relationship he thought they'd been building.

But now? Coming off the lake and hearing the gossip that the local duty office for the Fish & Wildlife agency was closing, with jobs being lost, his first thought had been about Annie. He had raced to her house, only to be ejected.

Usually, he could fix anything…well, except for that stinking court order. But, with Annie, it was like taking two steps forward and two and a half backward.

He was at the lake now, standing in her secret spot. A spot he knew she thought was all hers. He slapped at the mosquitos, wondering if Annie saw him as a pesky bug.

He hated how his self-confidence was taking a beating.

*****

An hour later, he met with Mason and Jefferson for dinner.

"How's it going?" Mason asked.

"I'm going to lose her," he stated.

"You never had her in the first place," Jefferson said, then added, "Ever. One date isn't a relationship."

Cutter groaned, put his hands on either side of his forehead, elbows on the table, shaking his head. Then he sat up, one hand fisted, it coming down on the table. "No! We've had two dates this week. And, we kissed. It was amazing. I refuse to give up."

"Then tell her how you really feel," Mason said.

"We're honest with each other," he argued. "All

the time."

"To a point," Jefferson said. "You need to be vulnerable. Expose yourself."

"Not that way," Mason injected quickly.

"You can do this," Jefferson said. "You've always been helpful and protective—"

"Sometimes protective where it's not wanted—" Mason injected.

"—but that doesn't mean you stop," Jefferson continued. "It means you have to reveal your heart."

Mason agreed.

Cutter nodded, acknowledging their advice.

A few more rounds of bolstering each other up in the ways of the heart and sharing their own struggles in the ways of love, Jefferson and Mason left.

Cutter stayed behind. He was in no hurry to leave the air-conditioned diner. The humidity outside had been a killer today, zapping his energy.

He had no idea how long he'd been staring at his cup of coffee. A stream of dark, hot liquid was being poured into his cup. A slice of his favorite pie was put before him. He looked up. Connie.

She slid into the seat across from him. He looked around the diner. Empty. No escaping her mothering today.

"Couldn't help but overhear snatches of your conversation with the boys," she said.

"I imagine you hear a lot of good stuff," he replied.

"You look like you've lost your best friend and want to cry," she said.

"Real men don't cry."

"Who told you that trite bit of mythology?"

"Dad."

"He lied."

Cutter frowned, "But— "

She leaned closer, as if she didn't want anyone to hear. "I've got news for you. He knew he was lying telling you that." She leaned back and waited.

Cutter frowned, then frowned deeper. *Say what*? It didn't make sense.

"He cried," she repeated.

Cutter's eyes widened. *Unbelievable. No way.* "When?"

"The night you were born."

Cutter frowned again. Now, he was fully confused.

"You never knew, did you?"

"Knew what?"

"Your mom nearly died giving birth to you. She wasn't a big woman, and you were a whopping nine pounds."

Cutter nodded. His dad had repeated that number often enough. Nine pounds and two ounces, actually.

"They performed a cesarean to save you both. It was late when he stopped here coming straight from the hospital." She looked away, thinking back. "He was tired, and it was a crappy night out. The diner was empty. He was crying from exhaustion, fear, and exhilaration. He adored your mom. She was his everything. And, he was so happy to have a son but still terrified that he had almost lost her."

"But why wouldn't he tell me that?"

"Because of a stupid man code that men have to be tough all the time. He was simply following his dad's philosophy and probably a few generations back before him. She never really recovered, your mom."

"She died when I was two. I barely remember her."

Connie nodded. "I never saw a man so destroyed. The joy gone. Though he was always proud of you."

Cutter nodded. He always knew his dad loved him, though the words were never said. "Dad wasn't much of a talker."

"No, not after your mom died. Once upon a time, he'd been the life of any party. Very much like you. Your mom was a tough one, too. Fierce, independent, and your dad was lost without her. Eat your pie."

Obediently, Cutter picked up his fork and took a bite.

Connie said, "You know, for someone who talks a lot, much of the time, you don't say much. If you think you're gonna lose her, you will. Your buddies are right. You can't lose something you never had. Tell her how you feel. Without flowers, without fanfare. Not through your Truth or Dare—"

"But—"

"No buts."

Customers entered the diner. She started sliding out of the booth. "Looks like it's back to work."

Cutter grabbed her hand. "I know I haven't said it

enough over the years. Thank you."

She patted his hand and smiled. "You say it every time you come through that door." She winked and was gone.

They were right. All three of them. Jefferson, Mason, and Connie. He never had Annie to begin with. As much as he had tried over the last decade to get her to say yes to dating him, two dates didn't make a relationship. If he really believed that, he was delusional.

He finished the pie and gulped down the last of the coffee, leaving a huge tip. It was time to meet his worst fear head-on: acknowledging the fact that he might never win Annie. There was only one way to find out.

*****

He knocked on Annie's door. He knew she was still up because the downstairs was all lit up. The door opened. Her hair disheveled, his heart broke at her pain.

He held up his hand in self-defense and started talking before she could say anything. "I know it's late, but I had to stop—"

"Yes, stop. Just stop."

"I want to help."

"You can't."

"If I can get you anything, do anything—"

"I want my old world back."

Cutter stared at her. Finally, he said, "Which one? Where you were in ignorant bliss? Living with lies you didn't know about?"

"That'll do for a start."

He shook his head. "You know you'd be miserable."

"I need to be alone."

"Don't throw us away just because the rest of your world feels like crap right now."

"How do you do it?" she asked. "Seriously? How do you recover from your world being turned upside down?"

"Like I should know?"

"Well, you've sure had your share of negative events the past few years. Never looks like you're affected."

"I've learned not to take them personally."

"But, they *are* personal! They're personal to me!"

"Honey, was any of this done to you, with the intent to harm you, to purposely hurt you? Specifically?"

"No," she admitted.

"Then, it wasn't personal. Accidents happen. Mistakes get made. Our world changes. Life is chaotic. Nature is chaotic within structure, and it's all about nature, every time, at its core. Look how we're always trying to control nature, attempting to make it pretty."

The corners of her mouth lifted slightly.

It was their running argument about why he never mowed his lawn and she did, even though they both lived outside of the city limits. She had potted plants. He had an acre of wildflowers and wild grasses. She needed control.

"Don't throw us away without thinking this through," he said.

"That's the problem. Right now, I can't think. I don't want to think. I want to escape. Go out on one of your junkets, a trip into the woods, to get away from everyone and everything."

"Everyone?"

"Yes, everyone. Including you. Can you set it up for me?"

The last thing he wanted was for her to leave him and go off into the woods without him, but what choice did he have? It was that, or she'd find a way to do it on her own. He'd help her. "When do you want to leave?"

"Tomorrow. Just something overnight. Someplace remote. Someplace safe. Someplace where everything is set up already and isn't fancy. Know of a place? Can you make it happen? Or, is it a problem?"

"Not a problem." For her, anything. Even if it was a problem. The worst problem was that he wouldn't be with her.

He reached into his pocket and pulled out his keys. He slid one key off the ring and handed it to her.

"What's this?"

"The key to my cabin."

She frowned. "You have a cabin? Where?"

"Three hours north of here. In the mountains. No one knows about it. Well, except you, now." He shrugged. "It's my escape from—"

"Everything."

He nodded. "I'll draw you a map."

She gave him a piece of paper and a pen. Quickly, he drew the map and handed it to her.

She looked at it, then laid it on the table. "Thank you. I'll be back day after tomorrow. Late."

He nodded. "Before you go, I have to tell you… I love you. I've loved you since the first time I saw you. I've loved you while hating every and any other guy who was free to touch you, to kiss you, to hold you. I'm so jealous of them, I can't stand myself. I hate feeling this way. I'm lost without you. And, I've never opened myself up like this to anyone. Ever."

"Not even a judge?"

"I tell anyone in authority as much as they need to know so they can get their job done, which has usually been to punish me. When I pled guilty a few days ago, I figured I get a fine. I never thought I'd lose my license, which cost me a lot more than just my job. It cost me my reputation, too. But even in that, I don't care about as long as I don't lose you. I can't tell you any more than I already have. I love you."

They stared at each other for a moment.

"I appreciate hearing your truth. Thanks for the key, and—"

"You're welcome," he said. "Good night."

He turned and left, closing the door quietly behind him. As he walked down the path, he knew she wasn't about to tell him what he wanted to hear just now. He might have given her access to his cabin, but she'd never give him access to her heart. There was just too much history where she'd seen him flub up.

He needed to live with that truth and accept it.

He'd have to learn to live with the pain of losing her and hope one day, the pain would be nothing more than a fond memory.

*****

Annie stared at the door. A lump formed in her throat. She hurt for him. But she couldn't talk. She wanted to say the words, but they stuck in her throat. Was it because she'd never said them before? Because she was so scared that her own fear was getting in her way?

There was so much she wanted to say, yet couldn't.

Deep in her own heart, she knew how much he cared for her, but she'd always push the thoughts aside, not wanting to deal with them. She didn't want to lose him as her friend.

Even though they both loved nature and working in it, he had always said he wanted to live off the grid, wanting an adventurous life where each day differed from the one before. She could live off the grid, but she didn't want to be removed from people. They were as important to her as nature itself.

She sighed, picking up the map. She had a bag to pack, some groceries to gather for a two-day stay.

For the first time today, she felt better, even if just a smidgen, and even though nothing had changed except for Cutter's revelation. If anything, his confession just complicated things.

*****

Day 11

Annie returned home after dinner, feeling relaxed. Cutter's cabin had been tiny but cozy, stocked with a microwave and hot plate, minimum dishes, and some commonly needed condiments. She was glad she'd taken her food and a few dishes, just in case. The view had been incredible, the cabin set up high on a hill, overlooking a small lake where she could watch the fishermen but not close enough where she could fish. Not that she had wanted to. Just sitting out on the small front porch watching nature was all she'd been capable of doing.

Now that she was back, she wanted to get out on the lake. With a couple hours of daylight left, she refrigerated the cold foods she'd brought back home and left everything else to unpack later.

Out on the lake, she cast her line, then took notice of those nearby. She frowned, seeing someone standing in a canoe. Suddenly, the boat began listing to one side. *Fool! Doesn't he know*—Cutter!! The boat rocked, tossing him into the water. With no life jacket.

Immediately, Annie threw her rod into the water, tossing out a special buoy to mark it, turned on the engine, and swung the boat around, avoiding the rod and line. The buoy would mark the area, alerting any other boaters to be cautious. Hopefully, she'd be able to recover it all in just a matter of minutes.

Racing toward his boat, she watched his head disappear and bob back to the surface twice.

He was going down again when she grabbed the back of his shirt and pulled. His head surfaced and he gasped for air.

She pulled harder, twisting him around so he could grab the rim of her boat. As he started to lift a leg into the boat, she kept her hold on him, but leaned toward the opposite side to balance the weight. The last thing she wanted was for him to fall back into the water.

With one of his legs in, she pulled him until he rolled into the boat. He lay there coughing, then pushed up into a sitting position, grabbing a seat to hoist himself onto it.

He gave a final cough. "What? No scolding?"

"Other than saying that was stupid, standing up like that, you mean?"

He tried to laugh, but it came out like a choking sound.

"You don't get it, do you? You could have died!" At the side of the canoe, she grabbed the guide rope and handed it to him, so she could motor back to her rod, letting him drag his boat behind them. "What were you thinking?"

"I needed to get to the other end."

"Where's your other boat, the rowboat?"

"Docked and sinking. Totally worthless."

"How many people told you that?"

"Not enough, apparently." He sighed.

"Don't make me throw you back in."

"You'd couldn't. You're such a mosquito."

"They can be deadly, you know."

Frustrated at him, she turned away, focusing on the buoy just ahead.

At the buoy, she turned off the motor, and leaned out, grabbing first the buoy, then her rod. Reeling the line in, she straightened, then stepped back, tripping over his foot.

As she started falling, he grabbed her, sending them both backward, sprawled across the bottom of her boat, with her squarely on top of him.

"Are you okay?" she asked. "Did you hit your head?" She tried to move off of him, but he held her firmly in place.

"Stop moving!" he said. She stilled. "No, I'm not okay, and no, I didn't hit my head."

"What hurts?"

"My heart."

Annie lifted her torso up and looked down at him.

"I love you," he said. "Please say you'll give me a chance? That's all I want. A chance. I'm not proposing. At least not yet, but just so you know, I plan on doing it in the future, sometime when you least expect it."

Annie stared at him. Finally, she said, "I almost lost you. I had no choice but to rescue you."

Cutter kissed her, and she relaxed against him, kissing him back. He groaned.

"Shhhh," she whispered. "Noise travels over water, you know. Oh geesh," she added, "You're not a screamer, are you? I only ask because I love you."

He screamed.

She laughed, kissing him. Minutes later, she added, "I never realized until now when seeing you go under, that I've always loved you. I was scared of you because I was scared of my feelings. You and Jefferson are family. I couldn't lose you, too. In rescuing you, I've rescued my own heart."

*****

Day 15

Annie stood with her back to the door and put her hands on her hips. Amazingly, in just three days, she and Cutter had become partners in opening a bait shop. He'd already been thinking about it, had the property in mind, but hadn't pulled the plug. With her not having a job as a game warden—a job she had expected to have her entire life—she never would have considered owning a storefront.

With Cutter as a physical partner and with Mason & Jefferson's financial backing as one of their new company's restoration projects, she and Cutter had bought the old store on Whippoorwill Lake. It'd been empty for the last year, though never put on the market. Cutter had talked with the owners—the children of the former owner, recently deceased after a long illness—and secured the sale before it ever went on the market.

They'd spent the last couple of days cleaning it up.

She had just finished the last coat of paint in the showroom.

Cutter walked out of the office with a paint roller in his hand. "All done in there."

"Here, too," she said.

She had cleaned up the glass case earlier,

expecting to stock it with license applications, lures, reels, and other supplies later. The empty plastic advertising racks would hold booklets and pamphlets of rules and regulations. She'd worked out a deal with the Fish and Wildlife agency where she could oversee minimal services to county residents so, at least, they didn't have to travel to other counties. And, Sarah had agreed to volunteer a few hours a week to deal with any paperwork until Karen could come on board as a full-time employee. It turned out that the agency's office was going to close after all, but not for another month.

At the moment, she was unpacking a long box of fishing equipment. "I need help with these poles."

"I've got a pole I can show you."

"Have I seen it before?"

"Yes. Seems like you liked it, too."

She let go of all the poles in her hand. They clattered to the floor, loudly.

She went to where he stood, planting herself squarely in front of him. "So, where is it?"

"Here? Now?" he croaked.

"You got a better idea?"

He grabbed her, wrapping his arms around her, lifting her off her feet, and kissing her soundly. "Here, with the shades pulled?"

"Truth?"

"Truth," he said, kissing her again.

"How about a lunch break at my place?"

"Are you on the menu?

"I call that a Dare."

Buried Hearts #4

Will the long-buried emotions of archeology professor Clint Anderson stop him from taking a chance with balloonist Gabriella (Gabby) King where in one balloon ride, he loses his heart? Will Gabby with her psychic abilities and who's on the road attending national festivals and fairs ever be able to put down roots in one location?

Day 3

"We need your parents in the basket now or I take off without them."

Clint Anderson stood next to the balloonist in her basket wondering if he'd heard right. Her voice was husky, not at all what he had expected from such a tiny woman. She was shorter than his friend, Annie Martin. Another of their friends, Cutter Logan, called Annie by all kinds of different shortie nicknames, but he wouldn't dare do that to this woman. She'd probably silence him forever with her no-nonsense attitude.

Other than his parents, he couldn't remember the last time someone had been that direct and to the point with him. As a university professor, usually he was the one handing out the directives. Nor could he believe it had come from this dark-haired woman who barely came to his Adam's apple, with a figure so slight he found it hard to believe she'd been ballooning for fifteen years per her online website. *How old was she?*

"If we leave without them, you won't like the review you get on your website."

"Doesn't bother me," she responded, shrugging her shoulders. "I'm overbooked as it is. I could use some time off. I haven't had a vacation in two years. And, just so you know, I don't play games. I can sniff out those who are passive-aggressive. I can play that game way better than they can. Nor do I put up with any narcissistic nonsense."

He wondered how she'd get along with his mother. There wasn't anyone more narcissist in her age group than she was. He'd called her out on it after taking his first class in college that dealt with personalities. *That* discussion didn't go well. Later, he realized he'd made the typical classic mistakes most made when dealing with a narcissus. He was an academic, used to reason and logic. There was nothing logical about his mother. His father knew it and played up to her awful proposals and ideas, always able to move her away from her own lunacy and with humor to boot.

He stared at the balloonist for barely a second, then frantically scanned the crowd looking for his parents. The backyard was expansive. The lavish party and its big crowd was celebrating their fiftieth wedding anniversary.

Thankfully, with the grassy tiers close to the

house and people on various tiers, he could see everyone more easily.

Finally spotting them, he shouted and beckoned with his arm. "Mom, Dad, hurry up! Get over here!"

Late to the party he was throwing for them, he'd arrived just moments ago. Seeing the balloon already raised in the backyard, he knew the balloonist was ready to take off. So, he had gotten into the basket quickly.

His parents looked at him, waved, and started talking again in their circle. "Hurry up! Or, Ms. King is going to leave without you!" He knew he was waving at them like a crazy man.

"Gabby," she said.

He turned his head toward her. "What?"

"Not Ms. King, that's my mother. I'm Gabriella, Gabby for short."

Once again, Clint tore his gaze away from Gabby and looked toward his parents. They were headed this way.

"We're coming," his dad mouthed.

While the elderly couple couldn't exactly run, Clint was surprised at the speed they walked. They'd been holding out on him. If he didn't know better, they'd become power walkers in their elder years. Probably because they'd had to keep up with him, since he'd been born late in their lives and remained their only child. More than likely, it was their tendency to be late arriving to everything. With their love of cruises, he had a sudden imagine of them running down the gangway of a huge ship, demanding the crew wait for them. He laughed at the image in his head.

A glance at Gabby revealed a frown directed at him. It probably did look silly, him laughing at his parents hurrying. Ungrateful son, she probably was thinking. Quickly, he turned back to his approaching parents.

Two of his best friends from high school—Jefferson Jackson, a state senator, and Joe Benton, a lawyer—helped guide his mother up the steps and over the edge of the basket. Clinton helped her down into the basket. Another friend, Rhett Renoux, assisted his father, who kept trying to brush Rhett's arm away. Unfortunately for his father, he couldn't get rid of the firefighter's assistance that easily. Clint winked at Rhett in thankful acknowledgement.

"I saw that," his father said.

"I'm sure you did," Clint responded. "You don't miss a thing."

"Darn right."

Jefferson and Joe removed the temporary steps provided by the balloonist and all three men stepped back.

A loud gush of fire and gas had the three of them in the basket ducking, moving away from the sound. Clint noticed Gabby grinning at them, excitement in her eyes.

"Everyone ducks at first," she said. "You'll get used to it."

An exclamation of surprise and wonderment rose from the crowd as the hot air balloon rose from the ground.

"Look how fast we're going up!" his father exclaimed.

"Too bad we can't get Clint married off just as fast," his mother chirped.

"I have no desire to get married, fast or otherwise, Mother."

"That's because your expectations are too high," she said.

Clint heard Gabby chuckle. "Ignore them," he told her. "It's an old and ongoing conversation."

"And, I'm getting older by the minute," his mother said. "I want some grandchildren before I'm too old to enjoy them! No one is going to want a man who plays in the dirt."

Gabby leaned toward Clint and said quietly, "I get the same argument from my parents. It's a club they all belong to." Hearing that huskiness in his ear, there was no doubt. He was smitten. He liked her bold confidence. As bold as the multiple bright colors she wore in her clothes.

Then, she moved back and spoke normally not caring whether his parents heard. "You played in the dirt, too?"

"He still does," his mother said, giving him *the* stare.

Thankfully, Gabby hadn't heard her. She was busy firing off the burner.

His parents turned away and were enthusiastically pointing at the landscape as they recognized various landmarks.

Clint admired Gabby's trim figure, the way her long dark-haired ponytail bounced with her movements and how deftly she controlled the balloon.

He looked out at the horizon admiring the view, but his gaze kept returning to her. He was intrigued. Yes, it'd been her voice that first grabbed his attention, but there was more to this little package that was drawing his gaze to her repeatedly.

Suddenly, Gabby was next to him, pulling him down so that she could whisper in his ear, "What's with the dirt dig?"

He straightened up, grimacing, twisting his mouth to the side. *She'd heard.*

"I'm an archeologist," he said.

She laughed. "I go high and you go low. Down below."

"Cute," he replied. He couldn't help but grin. *She was sharp, too.* "What about you? Do you balloon full time?"

"Nope, just part-time. For parties, on weekends. During the week, I'm a psychic, a medium." She watched his face closely.

He was careful not to laugh, but he knew without using a mirror that one eyebrow had gone up.

She was staring at it. She squinted as if examining him.

"I read the dead through their belongings, what they leave behind," he said.

Her expression relaxed again, her eyes twinkling. "I talk to them."

Even though he knew he didn't stand a chance, he couldn't help himself but try anyway. "Say, would you be interested in having a late dinner with me, after the party?"

She hesitated. She was thinking it over. He could see it in her eyes, which hadn't stopped staring at him.

Finally, she said, "Actually, I can't. I've got a festival the day after tomorrow and then another one right after that one."

"A balloon festival? Where?"

"No, a paranormal festival first, then a balloon festival. Just north of Atlanta for the paranormal, then up in Nashville. But first, I need to stop at home to do some laundry and repack. I've been on the road for a week now, doing events in Florida."

"That's right. My assistant said you were from Atlanta."

Just then a gust of wind lifted the basket up, startling Clint and his parents, forcing them to grab the basket.

"Don't worry," Gabby said. "That's normal. Nothing to worry about. But, due to how late we got started," she said, giving them a look that made him feel guilty for being late, "we do need to land in about fifteen minutes. It'll be dark soon."

"And that's dangerous how?" his father asked.

"Not dangerous per se. Dusk and dawn are the best times to launch. That's when the air is most stable, usually without the winds. When the air hasn't been heated up by the sun yet. At night, after the sun has set, the air starts cooling down."

"Do you fly in the winter?"

"Me? No. The air's too cold for me, but some do if the conditions are right."

Minutes later all conversation stopped as Gabby announced they were going down. She had been watching for her truck below, the tracking vehicle that would be picking them up. Though in this case, there were two vehicles. Her truck with the trailer for her basket and the second car, a big sedan for the Andersons. While she'd be packing up the hot air balloon, they'd be returning to the party.

That suited her just fine. She wasn't a big party person despite the many celebrations she attended because of either the balloon events or her psychic skills.

They cleared a dense forest and down below was a field clear of wires. Rare in this area of the country to find a field not growing sweet corn, a pecan orchard, or slash pines. She'd landed in one such field where the pines had been cut recently. Bouncing across a few stumps, the basket had taken the brunt of that descent, forcing her to use this older, smaller basket while the larger, damaged one was being repaired. Fortunately, she'd learned to do her own mending, but it took time weaving wicker that needed to be steamed so it'd bend properly.

"Hang on," she told them.

They drifted down. She steered into the middle of a hay field. Only when they touched down, did she discover that the ground was damper than she would have liked. Probably due to the major thunderstorm that had gone through earlier in the day.

Minutes later, with the Andersons out of the basket and the balloon now on its side, laying on the grass, the two vehicles arrived. Clint's friend, Rhett, had volunteered to drive her truck and follow them after they went up.

Having unhooked the balloon from the basket, Gabby climbed out, watching as the Andersons walked toward the sedan that had stayed at the fringe of the field. Both Clint and his dad were on either side of Mrs. Anderson, both with a hand on an elbow, assisting her. At the car, all three turned and waved.

Gabby waved back. Rhett joined her.

"I should tell you, the truck started hard."

"Took several tries?"

"Yes."

"Damn. I knew I should have brought the part with me."

"Part? You know what's wrong?"

"Probably the starter. It's been touchy lately. Hopefully, it'll be fine the rest of tonight. Let's get this thing loaded up before it gets totally dark on us."

The parachute and lines folded properly, they loaded the basket onto the trailer and put the parachute in the basket. By the time they hit the road, with no problem in starting the truck, the last rays of light were gone.

*****

Back at Clint's house, Gabby noticed the crowd had thinned. There were a few clusters of people here and there, but the band that had been playing earlier was packing up. She looked at her watch. Nearly dawn already. It didn't feel that late.

She wanted to find Clint to say goodbye and collect her fee. She finally saw him. He was in the middle of what appeared to be an animated conversation with lots of laughter. She really didn't want to interrupt them, but she didn't want to stay around either. She walked up to the group and touched Clint's arm.

He turned and brightened seeing her. He put a hand on her back and brought her into the circle. "Guys, this is Gabriella—"

"Gabby," she interrupted.

"—Gabby King. The balloonist. A skilled aviator and I speak from experience."

Jefferson said to Clint, "Probably the first time you've been up in the air since your first plane ride with me!" Laughter followed.

Clint turned to her and said, "I'm not a fan of flying." He pointed, saying, "That's Jefferson Jackson, one of our state senators. He's a pilot, too. Took me up for my first and last tiny plane ride."

Gabby looked at Clint in total surprise. "Seriously? I wouldn't have known that. You looked quite comfortable up there. But you know, that wasn't flying. It was floating."

"Obviously, it was the company," a man on her other side said. He stuck out his hand. "Hi. I'm William Stuart—"

"Books. You work with books."

"Clint told you that."

"No, I didn't," Clint responded. To Gabby, he said, "He's our library director." To William, he said, "She's a medium."

"Some would say psychic," she replied, "but I'm a medium, too."

"There's a difference?" a woman asked. "I'm Annie Martin."

"She's a game warden," Clint said. "And, you've already met Rhett."

Gabby shook Annie's hand, then tilted her head. "I'm sorry about your recent loss."

Everyone looked at Gabby and then at each other, an eerie silence settling.

"Thank you," Annie said. "I lost both of my parents—"

"To a tragic accident," Gabby finished. She knew the look, the questions that were about to be asked. To everyone, Gabby said, "I pick up on your vibrations, which includes thoughts, events, and such. I'm also an intuitive. Seems less intrusive than psychic. And no, Clint didn't tell me anything about any of you. Other than I'd be taking his parents up in the balloon."

William spoke. "Say, the library is looking for a presenter in two days. The one I had cancelled. I'd like to hear more about your abilities. I'm sure others would, too."

Gabby smiled. "I wish I could, but I'll be heading north. Two festivals back-to-back." She turned to Clint. "I need to hit the road. Thank you so much for your invitation. Your parents are a cute couple."

"Let me get you your check," he said, guiding Gabby toward the house. "I'll be right back," he called back to the group he was leaving behind.

Up at the house, Clint pulled open the patio slider door. Gabby stepped over the threshold, welcoming the cooler air. Clint followed, shutting the door, shutting out the noisy chatter outside.

Gabby glanced around at the expansive room, admired the clean lines of the kitchen, and the light grey and white decor. Simple but elegant. Clint went to a drawer and pulled out a check, handing it to her. Folding it, she slipped it into her pocket. "Thank you."

"No, thank you. My parents may not have shown it, but they were thrilled."

Gabby smiled. "Their expressions showed that easily. I'm glad to have been part of their anniversary."

"Are you sure I can't invite you to stay a bit longer?"

"I wish I could." She turned to go back outside.

"Let me walk you out." Clint opened the door for her. She stepped outside, immediately bathed in the still sticky humid air. Clint followed her, shutting the door. Together, they stepped off the patio, across a bit of lawn and were on the driveway that with a short walk led to the big secondary garage at the back of the yard, where Rhett had parked her truck and trailer.

Clint looked disappointed. "Sorry that you can't stay," he said. Obviously, he wasn't happy that she was leaving. She recognized that walking her to her truck was his opportunity to chat further with her. He wasn't ready to say goodbye yet.

He added, "I'm interested in learning more about your intuitive abilities. As an academic, I don't get this kind of opportunity—. So, if I find myself up in Atlanta, could I give you a call?"

"Sure, I'd like that." She opened the truck's door. She would have enjoyed the opportunity to get to know him better, too. "Tell your assistant that once I get home, I'll send her some book titles."

Clint's jaw dropped.

Gabby laughed. "No hocus pocus there. She had asked me for some book recommendations when I last talked to her."

Clint laughed. "Have a safe journey. Thanks again for the ride."

Gabby smiled, climbed into the cab, shut the door, and turned the key.

Nothing happened. *Don't do this to me, Sweetheart.* She turned the key again. This time there was a click and then silence. *Great.*

Clint opened her door. "Is the battery dead?"

"No. It's the starter. I've been having trouble with it. Guess it finally died on me."

"Looks like you're stuck here for the night, after all. You're more than welcome to stay in my guest house."

"That would be great. Thanks. I'm sorry for the intrusion."

"Not an intrusion, at all." He smiled. She knew he

was happy that she was being delayed, not that he would admit it.

"I hate to be an imposition. Is it possible to get a burger somewhere?"

"You didn't like the party food?"

"You mean the finger foods and then cake? I was too late for any dinner that was served earlier. I need something a bit more substantial, like a burger since I didn't stop to eat earlier."

"Sure, and I know just the place. If you can wait a few minutes, while I say goodbye to a few guests," he said turning, already taking a step toward the remaining guests.

"No, no, I don't want you leaving your own party."

"Nothing new for these folks. It's why I hire a party planner. Besides, most everyone will be leaving before too long, anyway." He laughed and led her around the truck to the far end of the big garage, forgetting about his guests. All the bay doors were closed. He disappeared into the garage through a door.

Gabby contemplated whether to tell him she had changed her mind, even though she really hadn't. A burger sounded especially good right now considering she'd not stopped to eat on the road for lunch or dinner because she'd been running late getting here. That had been her life lately, running here and there, no chance to rest and take stock.

A bay door to her right opened, interrupting her thoughts. A small convertible sat inside. He went and opened the passenger door, beckoning for her.

Sliding into the seat, she said, "I would have never pictured you with a car like this."

He grinned, shutting her door. "Glad I could surprise you."

"A sedan. A big one. That's how I saw you," she said, as he walked around the front.

He opened his door, slid in, shut the door, and pushed the start button. "Being predictable isn't any fun. The last thing I want to be is someone's fuddy-duddy professor."

Gabby laughed. It's exactly how she'd been picturing him, ever since their first meeting just a few hours earlier.

As they drove past his guests, then the main house, she realized his everyday garage was attached to the house. "Wait a minute. The sedan is parked up here. It's your everyday car."

"Guilty as charged."

She had to admit, he wasn't a fuddy-duddy by any means. He was in great shape. And his smile was engaging. She'd seen how easily he'd jumped into her basket and then, without real effort, helped his parents into it. She peeked a glance at him only to find him looking at her. She laughed again. Too bad she wasn't going to be around for a couple days. This could be interesting.

*****

Walking into the diner situated across from the town's courthouse that occupied the block, like many Southern courthouses did in small communities,

Gabby noticed there was only one other couple in the restaurant. She turned in the opposite direction and took a booth in the corner.

"Being this late," Clint said, sliding into the opposite seat, "I didn't expect to see many people here."

"Because the sidewalks roll up early?"

"We're predictable that way."

"Small towns are."

A waitress placed two waters on the table. Clint smiled at her and said, "Connie, I'd like you meet Gabriella King—"

"Gabby," she interrupted, sticking out her hand. Connie shook hands with her.

Clint continued. "—Our balloonist. I didn't see you at the party."

Connie pulled out her tablet to take their order. "Did a double today. Martha, a new girl, was sick, so I covered for her." She put her pencil to paper. "And, you're just in time. Last order of the day. Ready?"

"Be careful of that oil spill back in the kitchen," Gabby said.

Connie looked at Gabby with surprise. "Wha—How did you know?"

Clint laughed. "She's been doing that all night long. She's psychic."

"I am, but not this time. I saw the sheen on the floor when you came through the kitchen as we came in the door."

"It just happened," Connie said. "Taking care of it right after this."

When Gabby asked what was good, Clint said everything but recommended the burger. Orders taken, Connie disappeared into the kitchen.

"I think she wanted to ask me some questions," Gabby said.

"That would be Connie. She talks with everyone. I don't ever remember her not being here. She's a mainstay. This place wouldn't run as smooth if she wasn't here. Let's talk about you instead. But first," he said raising his glass. "To friendship and new relationships."

Gabby smiled, clinking her glass to his. "Friendship." Suddenly, goosebumps ran up and down her arms and back. She wanted to add *new relationships* but didn't dare. She wasn't ready. Flustered and needing a distraction, she said, "Let me call my roommate real quick." A couple minutes later, she hung up, placing her phone face down on the table, and said, "Done. Charli will be here tomorrow afternoon with my starter."

"Charlie?"

She saw both the disappointment and curiosity in his eyes. If only she could make him more curious but not at the expense of disappointment.

"You've got a boyfriend," Clint stated.

"No, Charli with an *i* is one of my two best friends. The other is my roommate and both happened to be there at the apartment."

"We could have purchased the part here in town tomorrow."

"Maybe, but with my luck, they'd have to order it

anyway. Besides, I already have it in my possession. Getting one locally could be quicker but I've had this one too long and can't return it now."

"No nonsense thinking. You were already anticipating a problem."

She nodded. "Just forgot to put it in the truck so that I'd have it. Besides, I thought Charli was coming down this way tomorrow and she is. So, just how small is Laurel Ridge?"

"About five thousand."

"What was it like growing up here?"

"Small enough that too many people knew your business before you did. Still do."

The whole time, he talked about his friends, telling little antidotes about them all. Soon, he had her laughing at their antics. Having met some of them earlier, she was able to put names to faces easily.

Additionally, they talked about music and movies, found that they both liked musicals and shared a love of Jane Austen remakes.

"I'm surprised," she said.

"At what? That I like Jane Austen movies?"

She nodded.

He leaned forward, looked to the right, then to the left—

She frowned. Why was he looking to see if they were alone? They'd been alone since entering the diner.

—and spoke in a voice she could barely hear. "Don't tell anyone. I enjoy chick flicks."

Gabby nearly choked on her sweet tea. Moving

her napkin to her mouth, she covered up her awkwardness of swallowing, then burst out laughing. "I suspect your friends already know this about you."

"They do. Have you always lived in Atlanta?"

"Pretty much. I've been toying with the idea of moving away, but—" *What are you doing? Stop revealing every thought!* What magic did this man have over her that she was spilling her guts? Lately, she had no idea what she really wanted, let alone give voice to it.

"No idea where you want to go?"

She frowned. *Did he just read her mind?*

Clint laughed. "It's a common plight with my students. They talk about wanting to move away from home but never have a strong idea about where to go next."

"The jobs lead them."

Clint nodded.

Connie set down two plates of burgers and fries. "Can I get you anything else?"

"Not at the moment," Clint said.

To Connie, Gabby said, "When you get home, you'll want to soak your foot in some Epsom salts right away. You don't want that blister to get infected. A good thing you got the thorn out."

Connie's eyes widened. "Wow. You're good."

"Rose bushes, right?" Gabby asked.

Connie nodded. "You're really good." She cocked her head. "The real deal. I know a lot of folks around here who could use your services. I bet if you opened up a storefront here, you'd have a decent clientele right away." She laughed. "Besides, I have lots of friends, and—"

"You know everyone in town. All their secrets, too. You're good at keeping them. People trust you because of it."

Clint nodded. "She's everyone's mom, sister—"

"Grandmother, aunt," Connie added. "Just holler if you need anything else." She turned and left.

Gabby finally took a bite of her hamburger, noticing that Clint's was already half gone. As hungry as she was, when reading people, she tended to forget the time or what she was doing. Connie had a strong, rich aura around her. One that Gabby had noticed immediately. She could see why the townspeople were drawn to her and trusted her.

Swallowing, Gabby took a sip of water, then said, "So, tell me, how come you haven't had much luck in dating."

Clint nearly spit out his water. Gabby smiled, taking another bite.

She ate while Clint talked, telling her when younger, he dated around, but nothing serious. Then, after college, he got busy renovating the factory into the library, and the condos above.

She had a sense that he wasn't telling her the complete truth when he said there'd been nothing serious, that he hadn't had much luck in dating once he came home.

"You thought your mother was too involved in your decisions, that she scared away anyone you were really interested in."

He stared at her.

She continued. "Was she a narcissist back then?"

Clint frowned, thinking about it. Finally, he said, "I never thought about it, but you know what?" He laughed. "If she's one now, I bet she was then, too. I mean, you heard her tonight. It was all about her. She tries to guilt me about not giving her grandkids. She can be difficult at times. Dad just goes along with her. Says it's just easier."

She nodded. "Do you want kids?"

"Doesn't everyone?"

"No, not everyone."

"You?"

"No one ever asked me that before. I haven't been around many couples with kids. Most of my friends are single, like me."

"You're an only child," he ventured.

Gabby laughed. "You're guessing."

He smiled. "Internet. I looked you up."

She laughed. "Yes, only child. Probably just as well, too. We moved a lot. Both of my parents were in the army. I actually enjoyed the moves. New friends, new cultures. It was always an adventure for me. My friends thought I was nuts."

"No boyfriends?"

Gabby glanced at him, then quickly dropped her gaze to her burger, pretending to rearrange, realign the bread with the meat. He was falling in love with her. It happened frequently and she didn't know why. Was she that different from other women?

Most of the time she was able to escape before

anything happened, before she could take the temperature of her own feelings. Though, this time, she was getting caught up in whatever this was. Her having to spend the night was going to put a wrinkle in the usual getaway this time. Finally, she confessed. "Just about the time I got to know someone, we'd be moving shortly after. Short romances, if anything."

"So, you've never been to a prom?

"Nope. You?"

"If going in a group, with no one special date counts, then yes. A bunch of us—you've met most of them tonight—traveled in a pack. There were a couple connections, like Shelley and Mason—"

"And, Cutter & Annie?"

"They dated once in high school and he's been chasing her ever since."

"Think she'll catch him?"

"What, don't you mean him catching her?"

"No, she's the one who'll realize her perfect match was in front of her all along."

"Interesting."

"Don't tell either of them I said that."

"What about relationships as an adult? You can't blame your parents and their moving for the last decade."

"No, but I can blame my schedule. I'm on the road a lot." She raised her glass and drank half of its contents, watching him the entire time. Putting her glass down, she said, "You've been wanting to ask but refrained. Waiting for the right time. You're wanting to know more about my childhood."

"Everything is in its own time," he answered

She nodded. She appreciated that in him. Everyone else she'd ever met rushed her, wanting her to reveal everything. To talk, to unload, to divulge. It wasn't her nature. Or rather, it wasn't in the nature she had trained herself to become. Normally, when she felt uncomfortable, she'd talk surface topics just to fill the empty space, but this man was different. He was okay with the silence.

"Dot was her name," she began. *Why was she suddenly filling the silence?* "We were always moving, what with my parents always getting reassigned, both having military careers. We usually stayed in military apartments on base, for the convenience. Neither liked owning a lot of furniture and stuff, so moving was easy. Possessions were few for all of us. Even today.

This particular time, we'd just moved in, and I discovered whoever had lived there before had left the dog behind. Stuffed into a closet where she couldn't get out. In my bedroom closet, actually, and she wasn't making a sound. She started shaking when I opened the door. Someone hadn't treated her right, but when I started talking to her and knelt down to her level, her tail started wagging and the expression in her eyes changed. She was happy to see not just someone but to see me."

She paused, remembering everything like it was yesterday when she had opened that door, finding that white blur in the corner. She'd only been ten at the time and the dog became her buddy, following her everywhere. Slept with her, was at the front door when she came home from school, waiting. Would lay at her feet as she sat eating or at her desk doing homework. They'd lay on the floor watching TV together.

"I named her Dot because she was white with one smudge of black on her side, resembling a circle. It felt like she'd always been with me. She was exactly what I needed at the time—a new home, new school, trying to fit in but not allowing myself to make new friends because I knew I'd be saying goodbye in a year because my parents' assignment was shorter than usual." She shrugged. "It was just easier, having a friend by my side." She raised her glass and took a big swallow, wishing she could swallow the feelings that were swamping her.

All these years, she'd managed to push those feelings down, deep down, buried where they couldn't see light of day. And, here she was digging them all up again. Fitting that she was revealing herself to an archeologist.

"And, then, we were moving again. I overheard my parents talking. Saying that the next place wouldn't allow pets. I knew then that I'd have to give up Dot, but they weren't sure how to tell me." She scrunched up her mouth and swallowed hard. *What the heck was going on?* She'd never fallen apart like this in the past when talking about Dot. "I made it easy for them. I started pushing Dot away." She looked up at the ceiling, barely able to say the words. "I gave up on her so she wouldn't miss me when I had to give her away."

Clint grabbed her hand and squeezed. A tear slipped from the corner of her left eye. She brushed it away with her free hand, not wanting him to let go.

"Purposefully, I'd forget to feed her, shut her out of my room at times. I pretended like she was a nuisance." She sighed. "It worked." A week later, Mom said I wasn't being fair to Dot, that she needed a home where someone wanted her. I agreed. "She was gone that night. Dad found a family that had been looking for a small adult dog. We never talked about her again."

Clint pulled a couple of napkins from the dispenser and handed them to her. She wiped at her cheeks, surprised how wet they were.

He got up and went to pay the bill. She met him at the door. Quickly, he escorted her outside, then pulled her into his arms, hugging her tight. She hugged him back, clinging to him. And then, she found herself sobbing into his chest, into his shirt. He hugged her even tighter.

"I loved her sooo much," she sobbed.

His hand on her hair, he stroked her head. "I know."

Normally, whenever she heard someone telling her that, she knew it was just words. But with Clint, it was different. He knew because he'd had a similar experience.

Tucking her under his arm, he led her to the car.

"What was his name?" she asked.

"Buster. The sweetest pit bull. A pussy cat really. I

hated having to leave him behind while I went to college. When I came back, he lived only another year." He paused and then said, "Have you ever thought of getting another dog?"

"Yes, but I have no roots these days. It wouldn't be fair to them."

Clint nodded. "Maybe one day."

Gabby didn't remember the drive back to his house. Suddenly, they were in the big garage, the door shutting behind them.

"Wanna come in for a nightcap?" he asked.

Instinctively, she opened her mouth to say no. But then, rethought it. She actually felt better, cleansed in a strange kind of way. There'd never been anyone she trusted to reveal her deepest secret or any of her fears before. Not even to Charli and JoJo, her closest female friends.

That surprised her. Saying she had fears. That she had opened up to a man she'd known less than twenty-four hours. Was that the reason she had revealed so much of herself? Knowing that she'd probably never see him again? But, hadn't that been true of other men? Why Clint? "Sure, why not. It's not like I'm leaving early tomorrow, or today rather given how late it is."

"Or early," he countered, grinning.

She walked beside him, up to the house, noticing all of the guests were gone, and even the tables and decorations had disappeared too. One would never know that a party had been held here just hours earlier.

It was going to be a short night of sleep. Not that she slept well on the road anyway. She knew she'd be rehashing tonight's conversation several times before falling asleep.

Truth be known, she had always pushed her future into the future, never wanting to plan ahead, just living in the present, going from gig to gig. The only planning she was willing to do were for events like last night's balloon ride, where she could provide pleasure to others.

He opened the slider door and she followed him inside and into the kitchen where he grabbed a bottle of wine, opened it, and poured out two glasses, handing her one.

Watching Clint sip his wine, she was grateful that her family's travels had taught her how to be unafraid of new places, new foods, new cultures. So why did she fear new relationships?

Suddenly, she felt her fear had nothing to do with her short-term stays but rather something else. She was in new territory here and didn't like not knowing how to proceed.

Growing up, anytime a boy started talking about going steady, she'd change the subject. Looking back, why had she done that? Truthfully, she'd done it to herself, not allowing herself to develop feelings for a boy. She didn't want to feel that crushing loss again, like she had in losing Dot.

She found it ironic that for a huge part of her living, she was reading for young girls and women about their future and *the* man they hoped to meet.

He pulled out a chair for her to sit down at the table.

She sat, sipping her wine. Clint turned his chair to face her and sat. "Feeling better?"

She smiled knowing her response was genuine and said, "Yes."

"I'm glad." He smiled. "Tell me about these readings you do. I overheard you talking about them earlier. I know about the Tarot because of Italian history, where the first decks were created. But seriously, do you believe in them?"

"As much as I believe in anything else. Just like you believe in the things you find in your digs."

"But those are historic tools, dishes, jewelry. Inanimate objects, things we can touch and feel."

"And, those objects are represented in the cards as money, cups, wands or rods, and swords. Besides, no object or even person represents just one thing. There are multiple meanings in everything."

"Can you really tell someone's future?"

"The cards tell what's occurring in the moment, in the future if nothing were to change. But, change is as common as breathing air. The cards are a tool. They provide insight, a reading of person or a situation. Just as a dowsing rod is a tool to read water. Or as a barometer is a tool to read atmospheric pressure."

"But, those are tools that turn the invisible visible. Can you read someone without the cards."

Gabby hesitated. She knew her abilities to read other people was attributed to a number of things, things she couldn't easily explain. But, Clint was genuinely interested as an academic, someone who sought out facts that could lead to new theories and opinions. While science had been proving things which couldn't be seen in outer space—like dark matter—and on the microcosmic arena, science was only beginning to delve into the paranormal with the same interest. She'd been reading a bit about quantum connections. Would there ever be enough interest to scientifically prove the invisible that was visible to her and others like her?

"Yes," she answered.

"How old were you—?"

"When I knew?"

He nodded.

"Nineteen. Living on my own for the first time ever. Before, I'd had roommates, but this time, I was alone having lost my roommates—to boyfriends, college, new jobs. I was sitting there contemplating whether I wanted another roommate or not. I was enjoying the silence, sensing something was different when Mom called. She told me she had lost a favorite earring. Without thinking, I told her where it was—snagged on the last sweater she had worn, which was hanging up in her closet. My knowing astonished both of us, especially my blurting it out like that. She had set the phone down and went and looked. Sure enough, it was exactly where I said. She demanded to know how I knew that, could tell her that. I remember saying that I had seen it in my mind. Other than that, I couldn't tell her anything. I didn't know myself. I had small occurrences growing up but never put it all together until then."

"Incredible."

"I have visions. They appear out of nowhere, or so it seems."

"You're picking up on vibrations, tapping into—"

"Energy."

Clint nodded. "I feel it sometimes just before we make a significant find. It's magical and unexplainable. I've never spoken of it before."

"A lot of people don't believe in the mystical, don't know what we're talking about. Oh, I can tell that they're curious because they've experienced something they can't explain but are scared by it all, so they deny their abilities flat out."

He laughed. "I have colleagues who don't buy into it."

"Because for them, it's all about empirical evidence?"

"Exactly. Would—"

"I read you? Wanting to discover your future so you can satisfy your parents?"

He snorted and laughed. "That'll never happen. Not in my lifetime. Mom just likes to be contrary."

"She wants to be right."

"Remind me to never try to surprise you."

"You already have, with dinner, this conversation." She paused, cocking her head, looking at him. "You'll end up married much to her delight."

"How—"

"I see you at the altar, surrounded by friends—"

"What does she look like? Can you see her?"

"No."

"What about you? Will you get married?"

"I never get that sense about myself. Besides, I'm a realist. People marry for selfish reasons. Money. Security. Status. Power—"

"So, what's my reason for getting married?" he asked.

"Love."

"Not lust? Isn't that what attracts us to each other?"

A statement and phrase she always touted, too.

He continued. "You're right. I want to be one of those who marries for love. Otherwise, count me out. Mother will just have to be unhappy."

Gabby nodded. "The truly lucky ones find each other. I've seen too many couples who say they're happy but aren't. One or both want something different. They get bored or are angry in the moment and go have an encounter they later regret, or have long-term affairs. The women come to me asking questions, wanting readings. They're hungry for something more but can't name it specifically, other than they want more time with their spouse. Family time, they call it. It's all so sad because these people looking for love are looking in all the wrong places. They don't appear to realize that everything they need is within themselves, so they go looking for it in others. Take your parents for example. They seem happy enough—"

"They tolerate each other. It's better than being alone, so they've each said. Separately to me. They each have their own friends and activities. It's easy."

"And, I don't want that," she said. Her parents had been like his—tolerating each other—until finally they drifted away from each other and got a divorce a year ago.

"Neither do I," Clint said.

She looked at him, sensing he did want more, and that he was interested in her. Curious more like it. He was cute in a bookish kind of way. No doubt his female students all fell in love with him. "So, we're two individuals, content with our lives." Yet wanting that contentment enhanced, she added silently.

He held up his near empty glass. She reached for hers, raising it.

"To finding real love," he said.

"Real love," she repeated, clinking her glass to his.

They stared at each other as they finished their drinks. Then, smiled at each other.

"You want me to read you."

He raised an eyebrow. "That wasn't a question."

She laughed. "Does it need to be?"

He grinned. "I guess not."

She reached into her pocket and pulled out a deck.

"Whoa! Do you always carry a deck around like that?"

"Usually. If not on me, in my bag," she said, while shuffling.

An hour later, Gabby walked down the backyard terraces to the guest house, knowing that Clint watched her.

He'd been amused when the reading confirmed he'd be married soon. When he had asked who, she couldn't tell him. She wondered who it would be, too. The cards had said a new acquaintance. His gaze had changed for a few seconds, just long enough that she could tell when the curtain came down to cover up whatever it was he was feeling.

She frowned remembering that moment again. His eyes had a warm look of interest as if trying to look within her heart. She felt goosebumps again just as she had then. Even she had wondered in that moment if she was the new acquaintance, but that wasn't possible. Not with her schedule, not where she lived, not with their careers poles apart.

Reaching the cottage door, she grabbed the knob and paused. She looked back at the house. He still stood there, a dark silhouette against the kitchen lights at the slider door. She lifted an arm and waved. He waved back. She smiled and crossed the threshold.

She really liked him. For the first time in a long time, she was reluctant to leave. But, leave she would because that's what she knew to do. It's what she did and always had done.

Was still doing it well.

Too well.

Blame the schedule, she thought. It demanded and dictated her time.

Liar.

*****

Minutes later, from the second story hallway and

with the hall light on behind him, knowing anyone looking could see him, Clint stood at the large arched window and looked out at the backyard and the guest house that sat in the back-left corner of the yard. From this vantage point, and the fact that the back yard terraced down into the main yard, he could easily see the front of the cottage. The first-floor lights went out and the upstairs hall light came on. Having stood here before, watching his parents as they entered the house and moved through it, he knew exactly which lights were being turned on when.

The master bedroom light came on. A minute later, he saw her silhouette appear in the window. She was taking her hair down, releasing it from the pony tail she'd worn all evening. He could only imagine, considering how long the pony tail had been, that her hair darn near reached her waist.

Her movements stopped. He could feel her gaze upon him. Normally, he'd move away when he felt he'd been caught watching, but he was mesmerized this time. He couldn't stop thinking about her. Why was he so smitten with her? She was nothing like him. He suspected no matter how many times he asked her out, he'd be turned down.

He was nothing like her, not her type. And, if he were to be honest, she was nothing like the women he'd been attracted to in the past. So, what was it about her that had him so interested?

He started to turn away, then stopped. She stood at the window like he did. Was she watching him, too?

Raising his hand, he waved. She waved back. He inhaled sharply, then smiled. *Was it possible?*

He turned, whistling, as he got ready for bed.

*****

Day 4

The next morning, Gabby woke and shut the window. Last night after turning out the light, she had cracked the window open a tiny bit even though the air-conditioner was on. She needed to hear the night sounds and then the early morning twittering of the birds in the nearby bushes and trees. She didn't like sleeping with all the windows closed. She was a woman of nature and normally woke early enough to enjoy the morning's first light.

This morning, however, she had beaten the sun. Probably because she was anxious to get on the road, but that wasn't happening, not until Charli got here with the part and that wouldn't be until this evening or late afternoon, if she was lucky. It all depended on when Charli left Atlanta and its traffic.

Still dark outside, the dark lingered just long enough to create fingers of fog that rose from the dew-drenched lawn. The sky was a tad lighter in the east.

By the time she had showered and dressed, light filled the sky. But, it was still early. She went to the kitchen to make coffee. Only she couldn't. There weren't enough coffee grounds to brew a pot and she didn't find her favorite spice up in the cupboard. She glanced up at the big house.

Last night, Clint had told her he'd keep the slider

door unlocked just in case she needed anything. She decided to take advantage of his hospitality.

By the time she'd made coffee and toast, the sun was on the horizon. Already the temperature had risen by several degrees and would continue rising throughout the morning.

Finished with her coffee and not seeing any sign of Clint yet, she put her plate and cup in the sink, rinsing both first.

Stepping outside, the humidity wrapped itself around her. She knew her hair was curling into its predictable waves and curls as it dried. She was reluctant to tie it up, though she would once it was dry in another half hour or so. In this heat, the last thing she needed was a layer of thick hair on her back.

She decided to go ahead and remove the starter even though Charli wouldn't be here until later. Last night, when talking with JoJo, her roommate, Charli had been there. The three of them were best friends and often met up for meals when they were in town at the same time.

Charli Davidson was a photojournalist and JoJo Wheeler, known for her mechanical skills with older cars, were both on the road same as her. She knew JoJo was coming to Laurel Ridge tomorrow to start work on the Volkswagen bug that had been pulled out of a lake but had no idea it was Clint's car until she had glimpsed it at the other end of the huge dark garage last night. At the time, she decided to say nothing.

Obviously, Clint had no idea that JoJo was her roommate. He had said a mechanic was coming, calling her by her given name: Josephine.

At any rate, Charli had said she wanted to travel down to the area on her motorcycle and find some lesser-known tourists spots to highlight in her YouTube travel blog. Because Charli had a meeting with her boss first, she wouldn't be arriving until later in the day.

Not the first time Gabby had been delayed because of parts. Wouldn't be the last. Though, she wondered if maybe she should start planning to replace the truck. It did have some years on it and if she was going to continue traveling around the way she'd been in the past...

That was the hard part. Trying to figure out what she wanted to do next. Open a store front? Cut back on the balloon festivals she attended? Get a regular job with benefits she could count on? Was there such a thing these days? All three of them talked about reducing the traveling, but to do what? JoJo opening a shop? Charli finding a desk job?

She shook her head. No, she couldn't see it. All three of them loved their freedom, the autonomy of travel the jobs gave them.

Opening two of the bay doors, she went to the back and immediately opened two more, so that the air could flow. Last thing she wanted to do later was come into a hot, stuffy garage.

Last night while she and Clint went to the diner, someone or more likely a couple of his friends had unhitched the trailer and pushed the truck into the garage, where she could work on it under the cover of shade from the hot sun. Even though she didn't expect the repair to take much time, if she could cut some of that time down now, it would help.

In the daylight, looking down at the other end of the garage, she could see the car that JoJo would be working on.

She'd have to ask Clint about it later.

*****

Clint entered the kitchen prepared to call the cottage and invite Gabby up for breakfast. At the sink was evidence of a cup and spoon, soaking. A glance at the coffee pot told him someone had already had a cup or two. The pot was only half full. The last thing he did every night was to fill the coffeemaker, then switch it to automatic so it'd start brewing first thing in the morning while he showered.

Pouring a cup, he took a sip. Frowning, he lowered the cup and sniffed at its contents. The taste was different, but he couldn't determine how. Whatever it was, he couldn't smell it, but he liked it.

Carrying his cup, he strolled to the garage.

She was standing on a stepstool, leaning into the motor, working the tools.

She looked up seeing him. "Good morning. I hope the coffee is okay. I wasn't sure if you'd like my addition to the pot or not."

"I like it. What did you add?"

"Cayenne pepper. Gives it some zing."

She lay down the tools and clapped her hands

together, shaking off the dust, then picked up the rag, and wiped her hands before climbing down.

She pointed to the bright yellow VW bug at the end of the garage. She strolled over to it, not surprised when he followed her. "What's going on with this car?" With all the doors opened, she walked around it, peering inside. "It smells a little damp."

Clint stopped nearby, sipping his coffee, looking at it. "It was fished out of Whippoorwill Lake the other day—the first day of the annual fishing contest. The original owner didn't want to keep it, so I bought it. I'm a hopeless romantic. What can I say?"

Something twinkling caught her eye. On the floor of the car, almost under the driver's seat. She bent and stuck her torso into the car and reached for it. Whatever it was, it was stuck under the mat. It took both hands to roll the mat a little. A bracelet. She lifted the mat more and tugged at the bracelet. It was caught on something. Finally, disengaging where it was snagged, she withdrew and straightened. Opening her palm, the bracelet sparkled back at her. Expensive.

Clint moved to her side. She handed the bracelet to him, which he held in his palm. "Owned by a woman," she said.

He fingered it with his other hand. "Obviously, given how dainty it is."

"But not given by her husband."

Clint looked at her sharply. "How do you know that?"

"The vibrations it gives off. It was special to her."

She frowned, paused, then added. "She had a lover. Are there any markings on it?"

Clint stared at her, his brows together, and handed it back to her.

"You can still sense its vibrations even though it's been underwater for a decade?

She nodded, turning it this way and that way, scanning its back. "Energy doesn't disappear. It would have to move away or transform into something else completely. There's something here but I can't read it."

Clint walked over to a set of cabinets against the wall in one corner. She followed him. He opened the door of one and immediately withdrew a magnifying glass.

"Quite a tidy collection of tools you have in there," she said, indicating the shelves. An assortment of hammers, glass and plastic containers, brushes, picks that looked they could have come with a nut cracker, and more.

He shrugged his shoulders. "Organization makes it easy to find things."

"I get the sense all of your cupboards and drawers are just as organized."

He grinned helplessly.

"Even your refrigerator shelves."

He laughed. "Guilty." He handed her the magnifying glass.

She held it and looked at the bracelet. There it was. An inscription. "Thanks for the memories. There's some scratched initials." She looked up and at him. "Mean anything to you?"

"Not a clue." He scrunched his mouth to one side in thought. "It might mean something to William, though—our librarian. I bought the car from him. Want to go visit him?"

"Nothing but time on my hands at the moment. Not until Charli gets here."

"I'll drive," Clint said.

"Probably a good thing since I can't," she chuckled at his forgetting her truck was laid up. "Besides, you'd have a heart attack seeing the mess in my truck." She laughed seeing the look he gave her as if he didn't quite believe her. "Want to look?"

She laughed more when he hesitated and then said *not right now.* She wondered if he'd be turned off at her usual lack of organization. If he was that would be too bad. Despite his being kind of cute, it would be a deal breaker. Her organizational method suited her just fine.

Though, she had to admit, there was something about him that made him wildly attractive and yet she couldn't identify what it was. She had the entire day to find out.

*****

With Clint's house at the edge of town, in just a matter of minutes, they were at the library.

Inside the building, the air-conditioning was already a welcomed relief. As they approached William's office, he looked up, saw them, and waved.

Immediately, she remembered William from the party. He'd spent much of the evening with Rhett.

She'd heard snippets of their conversation of remodeling and flipping houses. On the drive here, Clint had told her how William had remodeled a neglected, old factory into this library, which included two condos on the second story, and where William lived in one of them.

When William had laughed last night, that's when he'd caught her attention. His laugh was contagious but not in a robust way. It had startled her because he had appeared too serious to have that kind of a laugh. She had found herself grinning any time she heard him laugh.

As the two men greeted each other, given their ease of familiarity and teasing, it was easily apparent that they were long-time friends.

William turned to her. "It's nice to finally see Clint with a woman."

Gabby looked at Clint, who was already holding up a hand, as if to push William's words back, even if he was laughing.

"You've got a vindictive streak," Clint said.

"And you already know, he likes to play in the dirt, right?" William teased. He winked at her.

Gabby laughed. "Yes, I know. Because I'm a woman outside of your normal circle of co-workers and classmates, you believe he's vulnerable."

"And, he's not?"

"No more than you are?"

" Touché," William said.

"Nothing gets past her," Clint added. "About the car you sold me—"

"No returns," William said quickly. "Sold as is."

Clint laughed. "No problem in that regard. We're trying to locate the owner of this." He pulled the bracelet out of his pocket and handed it to William. "Do you recognize it?"

"No. Can't say I've ever seen it."

"There was another owner before you," Gabby said. "They were the first owners."

William and Clint looked at her in surprise.

"That's amazing," William said. "You've made me a believer. What other skills do you have? Can you talk to the dead?"

"Yes, or rather they talk to me. So, that makes me a medium."

"But, what about the previous owner?" Clint asked William.

William dragged his glaze away from Gabby and looked at Clint with raised eyebrows.

It was almost as if they were speaking in code, the way their eyes and expressions changed slightly, and they weren't messaging about the car. *She* was their topic. Clint's mouth revealed just a hint of a grin, then William provided a slight nod and an equal grin.

Finally, he answered the question. "Dad bought the car from the Jackson's. It was Jefferson's mom who drove it the most."

"She was a pretty woman, much admired, a business woman?" Gabby asked.

William nodded. "She and her husband owned the jewelry store in town. She was fantastic in designing one-of-a-kind pieces. He did the bookkeeping, along with taking care of the long-standing family business—the pecan orchard that Jefferson owns and manages now." William frowned then. "If memory serves me right, they got divorced not too long after we all graduated. Though Jefferson and Joe had already been in college a year as they had graduated a year ahead of the rest of us. I remember Jefferson being closed-mouth when they got divorced. He wouldn't talk about it, at all. Not even when we asked questions."

Clint nodded at William's memory. "That's right. We were all surprised when they divorced. No one had any idea that there was trouble in the Jackson household."

William frowned. He turned to Clint. "Didn't they sell the store, then?"

"They did," Clint answered. "Jefferson never wanted to talk about that either. I got the impression he didn't know a whole lot, and what he did know he wasn't sharing. He was really angry at his father after that."

"Think he'd be open to talking to us?" Gabby asked.

"Jefferson?" William asked.

"Don't see why not," Clint answered. "It's been a decade. If not, he'll tell you no. He's a straight shooter that way."

"A characteristic most senators don't have these days," William said. "Wait a minute," he said looking at Gabby. "I thought you were leaving last night."

"Waiting for a part to repair my truck. I'll be

leaving later today."

*****

As Clint steered the car onto a dirt path, immediately they were shaded by pecan trees. The orchard was large. Gabby couldn't see anything beyond the trees, not in front of her or on either side. It was as if they had escaped into a magical world, one of emerald green and tranquility. Stepping out of the car, the air was easily ten degrees cooler.

Up ahead, Jefferson stood with a redhead. Both had turned their heads, hearing them drive up, then started walking toward them. Gabby vaguely remembered her from last night, though she'd didn't remember meeting the redhead directly.

A few steps and the redhead paused, taking off her shoes—high heels.

Moving forward the length of about two more trees into the orchard, Clint and Gabby met the other couple.

Jefferson stuck out his hand, and the two men shook hands, then hugged, greeting each other warmly, like long-lost brothers, slapping each other on the back. "Missed you at the usual kitchen talk, last night, Buddy."

Clint responded. "Gabby wanted some real food, not that expensive fluff I was serving. "You remember Gabby from last night," Clint said, stepping back so that she was forefront but still not too far from his side.

“Indeed, I do,” Jefferson said. “I was hoping for a chance to talk with you. I hear you have some special powers."

Gabby shook Jefferson's hand, then paused. She tried to keep her expression the same, but she picked up something that was troubling him. Did it have to do with the woman beside him? "Not so special really. Powers we all have, but which I've recognized and utilized. Want to learn how?"

Everyone laughed. Almost nervously. And yet, Gabby could feel genuine interest as well.

"And this," Jefferson said, a hand on the redhead's elbow, "is Madison Butler. She's a lobbyist, here on business."

Madison frowned slightly, glancing at him, then returned her gaze back to Gabby, smiling broadly, the frown gone. "Nice to see you again."

"We shouldn't be bothering you," Clint said. "Since you're here on business."

"No, no, it's quite all right," Madison said.

"No bother at all," Jefferson said at the same time.

Madison and Jefferson looked at each other in surprise, both having basically spoken at the same time. Gabby sensed there was a spark there, one that both were squashing down as much as they possibly could, both hoping that the other wasn't noticing.

Inwardly, she grinned. These two had no idea what was coming. And, they both were going to fight it hard.

"Good," Clint said, sliding his hand into his pants pocket. "We're here looking for information on this bracelet." He pulled the bracelet out of his pocket and handed it to Jefferson.

Gabby watched as Jefferson paled. He was stunned seeing the bracelet in the palm of his hand.

"It was your mother's," she said.

He nodded. Looking at Clint, he said, " How did you get it?

"You're upset," Gabby said.

Jefferson stared at her. "Shocked, more like it."

"It triggered a memory."

Again, he nodded.

She put a hand on his arm. "I'm sorry for your discomfit, your loss."

Clint looked confused. "Loss? I didn't know that someone died . . . other than your brother, that is."

Jefferson explained to Gabby. "My only sibling, a brother, died in a diving accident. He was nine. I was twelve. Mom took it the hardest. She was there when it happened. He dove, hitting his head on a rock."

"I'm sorry for your loss of Jay-Jay."

Jefferson stared at her. "Only Mom called him Jay-Jay. And only in private, at home." He looked at the bracelet again. "But you're not talking about Jay-Jay. You're talking about the death of a relationship."

Gabby nodded.

She watched as he closed his fingers around the bracelet. He was deep into that memory now.

Jefferson sighed, dropped his shoulders, and looked up, staring into the trees.

"I was home. My first year of college had just finished. Normally, I wasn't home that time of day. Mom and Dad had never shouted at each other until the end of my senior year. I never paid much attention as they had always squabbled through the years about this or that. Mostly about their jewelry business. The fights were typical of what I've seen of other kids' parents, but that one weekend was totally different. I came downstairs just in time to see Dad throwing this," he held up the bracelet, "at Mom, shouting at her. It hit her and bounced, landing at my feet. I picked it up and handed it to her. At the time, I remembered her as always wearing it. She stuck it in her pocket. I never saw it again. He left that night, returned the next day to pack his personal belongings, and moved out to California, never returning to Georgia until he retired, moving to Jekyll Island. Mom complained that he had sold her car—the Volkswagen—out from under her almost a week later. It was in his name, I learned, but she always drove it, feeling like it was her car and that she should have gotten it in the divorce. Said at the time that he was getting back at her. I blamed Dad, and Mom would never say anything. I didn't want to ask. I could tell she hated him. She was okay with my blaming him. And then, the divorce. It all happened so fast."

He paused. Opening his palm, he picked up the bracelet with the other hand, then used both hands to spin it around so that the inside was exposed. "There's something engraved here."

"Thanks for the memories and some initials," Gabby said.

"And, hearts," Clint added. "We couldn't make the initials out. One set has been scratched quite a bit.

Almost as if to remove the letters. Do you recognize them? The initials?"

"Mom's are the scratched ones. I don't recognize the other set. It's not Dad's. He looked at Gabby. "What message are you getting?"

Gabby hesitated.

"It's okay," Jefferson said, resolved. "I want to know."

"That it wasn't your dad who gave it to her."

"You're suggesting an affair," Jefferson guessed. It wasn't a question.

Gabby nodded.

"Looking back at how everything went down with Dad leaving, the divorce and everything, an affair makes sense."

Clint spoke. "What are you going to do?"

"I doubt Mom will talk about it. She clammed up totally when it came to Dad." Jefferson sighed. "Still won't talk about him. I guess I'll call Dad. I want to know the truth."

Gabby nodded again. "That would be my plan if I were in your shoes."

"Excuse me, while I give him a call to set up a meeting." Jefferson turned and walked away, digging into his pocket for his cell phone, leaving the three of them to chat without him.

Clint and Madison made small talk, mostly about the party last night. While listening, Gabby watched Jefferson. She didn't sense any pain or even anger. Just acceptance. His body language didn't reveal anything.

Jefferson hung up and rejoined them.

She and Clint said their goodbyes, with Clint explaining they were on their way to his dig.

"Showing off, again?" Jefferson teased.

"Always."

"I want to see it," Gabby exclaimed. "I've never been to a working dig before."

Jefferson and Madison waved as Clint backed the car out of the orchard. She waved back, wondering if their visit would affect Jefferson's and Madison's ability to get to know each other while Madison was here.

"Those two are going to have a lot of speed bumps to drive over on their way to the alter," she said.

Clint braked at the end of the orchard's path and stared at her. "Those two? No way. They're like oil and water together."

"Which only requires a good shaking before being poured onto a salad," she said, "with a few other ingredients. Makes for a tasty dish."

Clint laughed, shaking his head.

*****

An hour later, they were at an Indian mound where Clint and his students had been granted permission to excavate. As Gabby and he approached the mound, he explained how they were preserving its outer shell. Only when they walked around to the back of the mound, which was close to a tree line, did she see a wooden entry extending outward from the mound. The structure reminded her of a house vestibule.

Inside, she found the second door framed into the hill itself. She was surprised to discover that the mound was being excavated from the inside and shored up much like a coal mine would be as they stepped inside.

"All the dirt taken out will be returned when we're finished," Clint said as if reading her thoughts.

"Returned in such a way that the mound won't collapse over time?"

"Definitely. We'll leave the framing inside here up, though, just to further secure its shape."

She shuddered feeling much sadness associated with the mound, then felt a presence nearby. Looking that way, she saw a faint outline. She reached out but then drew her arm in quickly.

No, she didn't have much time to spend here. This place was magical and had much to reveal, but it would be Clint and his team who would be unearthing the information. The physical remnants of the souls she was sensing would be dealt with but not the paranormal presence she was sensing. She wondered if this individual was guarding their work and watching the removal of the artifacts.

His artifacts. The Indian's. She looked his way again. His image was stronger. He smiled at her. She smiled back and nodded.

She found it difficult to concentrate on what Clint was saying, knowing the native was watching and listening. She peeked another glance at him. He stood like a statue, his arms folded, his legs wide in a solid stance. Protective, yet accepting.

Once they were back outside, Gabby breathed in the fresh air. Clint had no clue what she had experienced. Should she tell him? To what end? She'd be gone later tonight, never to see him again.

For a short moment, she wondered what it would be like to work with him in the mound. He archiving the physical, she archiving the paranormal, whatever the native would have shared. Their work could be groundbreaking research.

While the dig itself was interesting, she preferred the open space to the dark, musty smell of that tight, dark space, despite wanting to remain and communicate with the Indian. She could have learned so much. But, no, this dig was Clint's to discover.

Suddenly, a Scottish terrier ran around her, barking excitedly. She froze, her heart in her throat. It was all white except for a black circle on its side. It couldn't be. Impossible. She shook her head. No. This dog just resembled—

She couldn't shake the feeling that this was Dot—the dog she had loved more than life itself.

Clint bent down, petting the dog enthusiastically. "Hi there, Carter. Where's your owner?" The dog ran off.

Her gazed followed the animal. It circled a woman before running back to Clint. Gabby swallowed. It even ran like Dot had. Tears threatened to fill her eyes. She couldn't allow that to happen. She turned and tried to take an interest in the people moving before her, coming in and out of the mound.

"Are you okay?"

Gabby turned her head, seeing Clint at her side. She nodded, hating that he was seeing her tear up.

"You look pale. Like you've seen a ghost."

She opened her mouth and inhaled deeply, looked upward, and breathed out, dropping her shoulders in an effort to relax.

"I have," she finally said. "Dot."

Frowning, he looked back toward the dog, awareness changing his expression.

He searched her face, then grabbed her hand, pulling her toward him. He turned and started walking to his car. "Come on. We're going home."

"No, it's okay—"

He stopped, turned to face her. She looked down. He put a crooked finger under her chin, tilting her head up so she had no choice but to look at him. "I'm calling your bluff."

She wanted to look away but couldn't. His gaze was straight forward, like an eagle's. Direct and non-flinching. He wasn't going to be satisfied with her brushing it aside.

Immediately, she saw a picture of him in an office, talking with a student who was confessing everything about an unfinished paper. Immediately, she knew he was a man of boundaries but was fair at the same time.

She nodded.

Not letting go of her hand, he led the way to his car, opened her door, a hand on her back as she slid inside, shut the door, and walked around to his side.

She stared ahead reliving that period of her life yet again. And, here she had thought she was done with the past last night.

Inside, Clint started the car and turned on the radio. Not loud, but just enough to fill the silence.

She reached over and turned it off. "Do you have any leftover party balloons?"

He glanced at her. "I believe so. Why?"

"I need to let it go."

All the way to his house, she waited for him to ask the question, but he didn't. Instead, he pulled into the garage, they went into the kitchen where he disappeared into the pantry and returned, handing her a balloon. "Will this work?"

She nodded.

"Want it blown up?"

"I need to do it."

He frowned.

"As I'm blowing, I'm putting all my thoughts and feelings surrounding Dot into it."

Done, she went to the slider door and stepped outside. He followed her.

Looking up at the sky, she said, "I'm giving you up into the universe, Dot, hoping you had a good life and forgave me." She let go of the balloon. Immediately, the light breeze claimed and lifted it, moving it up and away from them.

"I know you want to say it," she said. "That the balloon isn't good for environment."

"They're not."

"And, I agree."

"That's why you'll be happy to know that I only purchase biodegradable balloons."

He put an arm around her, and she put her arm around his waist, both of them watching the balloon until it disappeared into the higher atmosphere.

For the first time in a long time, she had felt she hadn't been in control, but in releasing that balloon, she had felt a total sense of relief. Of letting go.

Hearing a motor, they released their hold on each other and walked to the edge of the patio. The car drove by and stopped at the big garage.

Rhett and Cutter got out.

They looked around, saw them, and waved.

Clint waved back. "Looks like we've got company. Shall we?"

Gabby nodded. Time to get back to work. Looking at her watch, she hoped Charli would be arriving soon.

*****

Sitting in her truck cab looking at her events calendar, she heard male laughter erupting from her right. Turning her head, Clint, Rhett, and Cutter were huddled around the back of the bug, the back hood propped up, the engine exposed. She smiled at their laughter. Someone was getting ribbed but good.

Putting the calendar down, she slid out of the truck, moved around to the front, and climbed the footstool at the grill to finish what she'd started last night in checking the fluids. Everything was ready to go once the part was installed.

Hearing a motor, she peeked around the hood

and saw that William had arrived.

Aggravated that the ends her pony tail were dragging across the motor, she grabbed the base of the ponytail, and wrapped it around its base. Grabbing a skinny screwdriver, she stuck it into the wrap. It held.

William got out of his car, took a step, and stopped. He was looking toward the road. Gabby followed his gaze with her own.

A motorcycle came down the drive, parking next to William's car.

Charli! Dressed in her usual leather chaps and jacket, Charli took off her helmet and shook out her hair. She looked at William and asked, " I'm not sure I've got the right place. Is Gabby King here?"

Climbing down the footstool, Gabby stopped. William looked absolutely gob smacked. He nodded.

She watched him watching Charli remove her chaps and jacket, laying them on the bike, then taking a pair of reflective sunglasses out of her shirt pocket, putting them on. Gabby laughed as she walked toward Charli. Gabby knew Charli was staring back at William, no doubt checking him out. All of him.

Gabby couldn't stand it any longer. She closed the distance to Charli and gave her a giant hug.

Looking over Charli's shoulder, Gabby saw the guys move as one toward them. She moved back a step and told Charli, "You're about to meet the gang. Well, part of them anyway."

Clint reached them first. He held out his hand to Charli. "Hi, I'm Clint Anderson. Gabby provided my parents a balloon ride last night. You're Gabby's friend."

Charli shook hands with Clint.

Gabby said, "She is. We're sisters from different parents, sisters from the past. Guys meet Charli Davidson."

Charli shook hands as Gabby introduced the men. "Rhett Renoux. He's a firefighter. This is Cutter Logan." To Cutter, she said, "What is it you do again?"

The guys laughed.

Cutter responded. "Right now, a fisherman. I fished that out of the lake." He thumbed the VW.

Charli looked around. "Jefferson Jackson—?"

"The most famous of us all," Cutter injected. "He's not here, right now."

"He's on Jekyll Island, with his father," Gabby said. Seeing the guys exchange puzzled looks, she added, "Clint and I saw him earlier."

"I was hoping to meet him," Charli said. "My publisher slash editor said he was from around this area."

"And, last but not least, William Stuart," Gabby said, turning Charli in William's direction, "librarian and first owner of that car."

"Not really the first," William said, sticking out his hand "Dad bought it used."

Gabby noticed both of them reacting to the touch, Charli's eyes widening and William staring.

"It's a pleasure to meet you all," Charli said.

"Your publisher/editor?" Cutter asked.

Charli answered, "I'm a travel blogger. He was

hoping I could get an interview with the Senator."

"Where's the part?" Gabby asked.

"Aren't you the eager beaver," Charli quipped.

"Only because of the next event." Gabby sneaked a peek at Clint. He had caught her saying *only*.

Gabby followed Charli to her cycle's saddlebags where she pulled out a box.

Gabby grabbed it. "Hopefully, I can get out of here tonight."

*****

About an hour and a half later with the truck repaired, packed, and parked outside, William, Clint, Gabby, and Charli sat in a booth at the diner. While the diner had been full when they had first arrived, the crowd had now thinned.

Connie had just collected their plates. "One check or four?"

"One," Gabby said quickly.

Immediately, the other three protested. Connie turned and moved away.

"No discussion," Gabby said. "Clint, I appreciate you putting me up. Otherwise, I would have had a hotel bill." She turned to Charli. "You saved me time by bringing the part to me." To William. "You helped me...well, with nothing actually, but I appreciated the company."

They all laughed.

Connie returned, handed Gabby the bill and refilled their water glasses.

"You really don't have to leave tonight," Clint said. "Stay the night and then leave first thing in the morning."

Charli replied. "Gabby doesn't like waiting. She's a night owl."

Gabby nodded. "Besides there's less traffic on the highway at night and it's cooler out."

"Where are you going this time?" William asked.

"I'm doing tarot readings at a summer festival in north Georgia tomorrow—another reason for leaving tonight, and right after, I'm heading to Nashville for a weekend balloon festival."

"So, you're not going home at all?" Clint asked.

"I would have, had I left here right after the party, but it worked out okay. Thanks for letting me wash my clothes earlier today and insisting I eat now before hitting the road. I probably wouldn't have stopped."

Clint smiled. "My pleasure, though it's not like I did anything."

Gabby smiled back. "You did more than you know." She slung her purse on her shoulder and made a move to scoot out of the booth. "I've got to hit the road."

To Gabby, Clint said, "Even though I came with William, can you drop me off at my house on your way out of town."

William started to protest.

Clint stopped him. "No sense in your driving all the way back out to my place with your condo just a couple blocks away. Nice getting to know you, Charli. Maybe you'll stick around a few days and put Laurel Ridge on someone's map."

"Okay to drop you at your driveway?" Gabby

asked.

"Sure."

"Okay, then."

Clint and Gabby said their goodbyes, and Charli gave Gabby a hug. Gabby whispered, "Stick around for a few days. Keep JoJo and William company." She pulled away, smiling, before Charli could respond.

A few minutes later, once past the city limit sign, Clint said, "I'm going to miss you. Seems like I've known you forever."

She nodded. She didn't want to leave either, but she had no choice, not with two commitments back-to-back. She couldn't explain the pull. If only she had more time to investigate the attraction.

And then suddenly, they were at his driveway. She stopped, staying in her lane since there were no cars coming or going. Easier than pulling off to the side of the road and possibly getting stuck, what with the trailer behind her.

"Take care and drive safe," he said, getting out of the truck.

"You take care, too," she said.

He shut the door and walked through the headlight beams, crossing the street, stopping at the edge of his driveway.

She waved and then said out the window, "A lot of secrets are about to be revealed."

She drove off, looking back and forth between the road in front of her and his image in her side mirror until he disappeared from view as she rounded a curve.

If only...

"No!" she said aloud. "No if only anything! We're not going there. It wasn't meant to be."

*****

Day 5

Clint had just entered the big garage early the next morning when he heard a vehicle pull up outside one of the bay doors and turn off the engine.

He opened the closest bay door, sliding it up on its rollers. He walked toward a plain white van. A woman exited.

She stuck out her hand. "You must be Clint Walker."

He shook her hand, "And you're Josephine—"

"JoJo."

"—Wheeler. Nice to meet you. I'm glad you were able to fit me in."

"Actually, I'm glad to have the opportunity to get away. The city is hot this time of year. The race track even hotter. Totally my pleasure to drive down here and see some green again."

He turned, leading them into the garage. "Here she is," he said, coming to a stop beside the VW beetle. "You might not think it's a vacation once you get into this motor."

"Can't wait," she said, walking to the back, lifting the back hood, looking over the motor. "Hard to tell how much real damage had been done just by eye-balling it. The paint job is amazing, other than a few rust spots. I'm eager to get started."

"Your reputation precedes you," Clint said.

"Must be Gabby or Charli you've been talking to."

Clint laughed. "Both actually. Plus, I called the referrals you provided, too."

"You called them?"

"I did."

"I bet they were surprised."

"They were."

"And you learned—"

"Without hesitation, they'd all hire you again."

She grinned. "Is Gabby here?"

"No, she left for her next festival last night, much to my disappointment." He paused, then said. "But, Charli should be here soon. Said she wanted to see you when you got here. I need to call William so he can tell her you're here."

"William?"

"Charli's been staying in the condo next to his." He walked the few steps to another door and raised it. "He's a good friend and the director at the local library. "Ah, here they are now."

JoJo turned. A car turned into the driveway, parking next to her truck. Charli rushed out of the passenger side and ran up to JoJo, hugging her tight.

"I've missed you!"

JoJo laughed. "You've only been gone a day!"

Charli turned and looked back, signaling for William to come closer. Her arm still around JoJo's waist, Charli introduced JoJo to William, telling JoJo, "The VW was originally William's car back in high school, and was fished out of the lake by another one of their friends, Cutter. Clint then purchased the car from William and there's a mystery surrounding a bracelet that Gabby found under the front seat, which didn't belong to William but to Jefferson Jackson's mom who was the original owner of the car."

"Wow, you really do know how to tell a story in just a few words," William said. "When you said photojournalist, I figured your job was mostly photos."

Clint explained, "Gabby was able to do a reading on the bracelet, where they discovered a possible long-ago love affair involving Jefferson's mother. William's parents bought the car for him as a graduation present. Back then, he told us he sold it, yet somehow it mysteriously ended up in the lake, with him still as its owner, and he's not talking."

William added, "My lips are sealed." He ran two fingers, tightly together across his mouth. "At least for now, he added. "Maybe one day, I'll be able to reveal the truth of the car's late-night swim."

"I know of Senator Jackson," JoJo said. "He was a big help to some friends of mine who were trying to get some country land rezoned so they could build a pee-wee race track for kids. Folks wanting to learn how race properly. Plus, it was a school of sorts for car maintenance. He did a nice job helping that project."

To JoJo, Clint said, "And now, I'm hoping you'll be able to restore this engine so I can drive the car this summer. How long will it take to fix it?"

"A few days, if all goes well."

The conversation changed when William

suggested that JoJo should go on a blind date with Joe, a former classmate and friend of theirs—a good guy. Clint knew Joe would kill William for suggesting this, but it was a great idea.

The more they talked about it, the more Clint knew Joe and JoJo would be perfect together.

Only after Charli joined in, agreeing with the suggestion, did JoJo say okay.

She asked, "Where can I stay? All the hotels are booked around here."

"With me," Charli said.

"With Charli," William said at the same time.

"Problem solved," Clint announced.

"Let me go get settled and change my clothes," JoJo said to Clint. "Then, I'll be back to start work on the car."

*****

When JoJo, Charli, and William left, Clint walked back up to the house. He stood at the slider door, looking at the garage, where Gabby's truck had sat.

He should have taken a chance. Everywhere he turned, he saw her.

You're miserable, admit it.

In so many ways. He was wildly attracted and yet, she threatened his safe, controlled world. *Sure doesn't feel controlled, right now, does it?*

He'd never felt like this before and it scared him. Hearing himself telling his students to take a leap, to make educated guesses, to be willing to be wrong, he scoffed at himself. When had he last taken his own advice?

He shook head. He needed to take the leap. Even if it meant total rejection. But, he couldn't just show up on her door. How pathetic would that look?

Sighing, he turned on his heel. Maybe a good book or watching the basketball game he had taped last night could sidetrack him.

Half an hour later, he turned off the TV. He couldn't watch it. Suddenly, he was bored.

He was never bored.

Even going to the Indian Mound didn't appeal to him. How did she do that? In another week, he'd have no choice. He'd have to return to the mound as his mandatory vacation time—which in the past he'd always resented taking—was almost over.

The department only had the rest of summer to examine the mound. He knew his assistants and the students were doing that. He'd just get in their way if he went now, but he'd be there to oversee the closing of the mound, replacing the dirt they'd taken out, and making sure everything looked just as it had when they opened it.

How could he miss someone he met just two days ago?

She wasn't gorgeously beautiful, but he found her stunning in an exotic way—a confidence that belied her size, her long dark hair, and eyes that mesmerized him. More important, he found her interesting and funny. Unlike many of the people he hung out with at school. Like him, they were serious academics, writing papers, teaching, mentoring grad students, and always focused on the next future project. Next to her, they had become boring and yet he'd always found them interesting. Right now, he couldn't focus on anything.

If he didn't know better, he could believe she had cast a spell on him. She had the power. Who was he kidding. Her power was that she was female. Unlike any female he'd ever met before. If only he could stop thinking about her.

Pouring a glass of lemonade, he took it to the shaded veranda, sat, and looked out at his expansive yard: the guest cottage, the big garage, the shed that held all the landscaping tools, the gardens that were precisely beautiful having let his mother design them.

All of a sudden, in his mind's eye, he saw kids playing, chasing a ball, with two dogs—small terriers—running around them all, barking, and the kids laughing.

What the—?

And then, just as suddenly, the mirage was gone. He blinked. *What was that?*

He listened, hearing birds, bees, and the knocking of a woodpecker on some tree deep in the woods that surrounded his back yard. He could hear the trickle of the stream that ran through the woods, too.

How had he never heard that sound before?

He frowned. What had Gabby done to him?

He couldn't stop thinking about her. This wasn't any infatuation or shallow interest. He was wildly attracted and for the first time in his life, he didn't know what to do.

That's how he saw Gabby. As a mystical creature

with long dark curls cascading down her back, a laugh that blended harmoniously with nature and a smile that engaged her eyes, giving him the impression that she had an impish secret.

He thought about what she had said about married couples not being happy. For the first time, he considered all the couples he knew. Even though his parents quibbled, making fun of each other, he knew they loved each other and would be devastated if separated.

Could she have been saying that as a defensive move, an excuse not to get close to someone, or as a way to scare them off?

He wanted her back here. With him.

But how? And what did she really want?

He had to find out. Plus, he needed some advice. He called Mason and Joe, arranging to meet with them early at the diner for breakfast.

*****

It'd been a long day for Gabby at this paranormal festival. Usually, she totally enjoyed these events where she did readings for folks—mostly women, but not today for some reason.

No, that wasn't right. She knew exactly what the problem was.

Clint.

She couldn't stop thinking about him. It didn't help that every woman who sat down across from her wanting to know one of two things: If married, would their marriage get better, or if single, when would she meet the love of her life?

Personally, Gabby believed there was no one love of anyone's life. There could be several such individuals. The goal, though was always in finding them, connecting with them. At least, she used to believe it. Was it possible that Clint was more than just a connection? A possible soul flame?

She knew without a doubt that he could be one of those few people for her. So why was she pushing him away? Or rather, trying to push him away? The fact that he was constantly in her thoughts was telling her that she wasn't doing a good job at pushing.

So what if he was an academic and she wasn't? So what if their careers were polar opposites? After a bit of research, she'd discovered there were academics that were looking into the unseen. They called it quantum entanglement, and she'd love to find proof that her skills weren't quite so mysterious after all. The question was, would Clint enjoy working alongside her? Would he be open enough to ignore the criticism he'd endure if he did, bringing the theory into his field of exploration?

Were they so opposite that over time, they'd become bored with each other?

She stopped shuffling the cards, set them down, and put an elbow on the table, cupping her chin in her hand, contemplating.

While she'd like to blame these women for misdirecting her thoughts, she knew full well they had nothing to do with her thinking.

It was all Clint.

Just then, a woman sat down in the chair opposite

her.

Gabby picked up her cards, smiled brightly, started shuffling them, and focused on the woman, already knowing what was going to be asked.

*****

Day 6

Their breakfast orders taken, Mason said, "You look like you've lost your best friend."

Joe laughed. "That would be impossible. We're his best friends."

The reminiscing started. Once they were talking about dating, that's when Clint injected, "Do you think I'm being an idiot?"

Mason and Joe both looked at him like he had two heads.

"About what?" Mason asked.

"You weren't even listening to us, were you?" Joe remarked.

"No."

"What were you thinking about?" Mason asked

Joe scoffed. "You mean who?"

Clint's gaze went back and forth between the two men, both of whom sat opposite of him.

"I repeat," Mason said. "You look like you've lost your best friend."

"I want to get to know her."

"Her who?" Joe asked.

"Gabby."

"That must have been some ride up in that basket," Joe said.

Clint said, "I was infatuated from the first

moment."

"In what way?" Mason asked.

"She handled my parents."

Both men laughed.

"And, you know my parents."

"No one handles them," Joe said.

Clint sighed. "My longest relationship has been only three months long. I don't want to screw this one up."

Mason commented, "Hard to screw something up that hasn't even begun. Call her."

"You mean chase her the way you've been chasing Shelley."

Mason replied. "I'm making progress...I think."

Joe held up his hand, shaking his head. "Don't look at me. Mason's the one with all the experience, not me."

Connie stopped at their table to collect their empty plates. "Are you boys talking about Gabby?"

All three men looked at her with surprise.

"I couldn't help myself. I heard you talking while I was cleaning the table next to you. Honestly, Clinton, what have you got to lose?"

"Everything?" he offered. He knew when Connie called him by his full name, she wasn't fooling around.

"Everything, which is nothing because right now you have nothing. Even if you can't win her, you won't be any worse off than you are right now. You boys are all macho-like, but when it comes to girls you all hang back. Why? You can't catch a fish unless you put your line into the water. And look at you—a judge, a lawyer, an archeologist. None of those things came easy. Are you just waiting for a woman to fall in your lap? Got news for you Clinton, she did. Now it's your job to keep her there."

She picked up the last plate and walked away.

All three men watched her leave, and then Mason said, "She's right, you know."

"Yeah, she's never been wrong," Clint said.

"Plus, you need to let go of all of your past dating history and change it up," Joe added.

"That's rich coming from you. The ultimate shy guy who can't commit," Clint said.

Joe replied. "I've yet to find anyone who piques my interest enough to commit."

"What about your blind date from last night?" Clint asked.

"You mean the disastrous blind date?" Joe replied. "It was over before it even began."

Mason asked Clint, "So, what are you going to do?"

Clint thought for a few seconds, then his gaze brightened with his smile. "I'm going to talk with her best friend and roommate—JoJo. She's probably working on the car right now."

Joe winked, "And, a captive audience, at that. Say hi for me."

"If I didn't know any better," Clint said, "I'd say you *are* still interested in JoJo."

Mason said, "Looks like the jury's still out. And, all three of us need to do better, be better."

Clint sighed. "Can it be any more difficult?"

*****

Clint walked into the garage, a tall glass of lemonade in each hand. "Need a break?" He held out one glass toward JoJo.

She put her tools down on the bench that sat beside the car's back hood and took the glass from him, swiping the glass across her forehead, where the condensation transferred to her forehead. "Great timing." She lifted the drink to her lips and swallowed half of the liquid.

"How's she coming?" He looked around at the table next to the car and the assortment of parts on it. A few were soaking in a cleaning solution. A couple others were waiting their turn.

"Still taking her apart, but in another hour or so, I'll be ready to clean the framework itself. It won't take much to repair the rust spots and then polish her up good."

They talked a few more minutes about the car.

Then she said, "What do you want to know about Gabby?"

Clint turned and stared at her. "You too?"

"What? Have Gabby's gifts of mind reading?" She laughed. "Not for a split second. You just have this lost puppy-dog look on your face."

"That's what she said when I was telling her about my boyhood best friend—my dog."

"A great dog, right?"

"The best."

"And Gabby?"

"I'd welcome the chance to get to know her."

"To date her?"

"Would she even be willing to give me a chance?"

"I talked with her late last night, while she was still on the road. Keeping her company."

"Did she say anything about me?"

JoJo smiled.

Immediately, Clint knew that JoJo was keeping something from him. Was it positive or negative?

"Why are we all so reluctant to take a chance?" he mumbled.

"You too?"

"She said it too?"

"Not in so many words."

"It's scary and who likes being broken-hearted?" he said.

"It happens to everyone. Boys and girls alike. Why not give her a call?" she suggested.

"Because she didn't invite me to?"

"You really need an invitation? You called her before, you know."

"For my parents' party."

"You have her number."

He stared at her for a long moment. Then, he downed the rest of his drink. He smiled at her. "You're right. I should call her." That was four people now, if he counted Connie, all saying the same thing. He'd be stupid not to listen.

*****

Day 7

Gabby finished laying out the balloon while

Franklin got the burner positioned. Strangely, she was missing Clint, which didn't make sense. She'd known him all of two days, been separated another two days, and yet, he was occupying her mind far more than she would have liked.

What was it about him that made him so attractive to her?

Without hesitation, she knew it was because of his mind, the way he thought. He focused on what she was saying, rather than barely listening and then spending much of the time talking about himself as so many of her past dates had done. One of the reasons why she had stopped dating. If a man wasn't interested enough to ask questions in the beginning, he'd never ask them later. Clint had asked lots of questions.

You should have invited him to this festival. Now, it was too late. Tomorrow was the last full day. A half day after that with just the morning flights. And, there probably wasn't a hotel room to be had, not with all the various activities taking place around the city.

Okay, after the festival was over. She'd contact him then.

*****

Day 8

By early evening, a couple hours before sunset, Clint was pulling into the parking lot of the balloon festival he'd found on Gabby's website page. She would have arrived two days ago, with the first events occurring yesterday. He had decided to surprise her rather than call. Easier to apologize than get permission had always been his motto, something his father had taught him when Clint was in hot water with his mother.

He parked the car, paid the festival fee at the gate, then walked through the gates, stunned at the colorful sight before him. He'd never seen so many balloons in one location before. Some balloons were already filled with hot air and standing up, ready for launch. The rest were in various stages of rising, being filled. Quickly, he spotted Gabby's moon & stars balloon, almost fully upright. His heart beat wildly. He smiled, eager to see how she'd react to him being there. He hoped his presence would be a good surprise. Almost upon her, she was leaning into the basket.

"Need any help?" he asked.

Gabby jerked upright and turned. Her mouth opened in surprised seeing him. Then she smiled.

Good, she was glad to see him. Genuinely glad. He couldn't help himself. He knew he was grinning.

She reached out to give him a hug. She felt good in his arms, and her hair smelled like lilacs. All too soon, they separated.

"Your timing is perfect," she said.

"How's that?"

"In this competition, we need two people and my partner just called to say he was stuck on the highway. Some crash has all traffic at a standstill and he's still three miles from the nearest exit. I've got to go up now."

"Happy to help."

"You sure? You'll have to be looking down at the ground at targets and letting go of markers. The object is to hit the bullseye."

He teased her. "I smell a prize in the works."

Gabby laughed. He'd missed hearing that lyrical sound that made him smile every time he'd hear her laugh. He could easily imagine her as a woodland creature, a fairy with laughter that was soft, yet sounding like a babbling brook.

"Yes, it's a monetary price. And, if we win, I'll take you out to dinner afterward."

"Game on," he replied. "No need to ask me twice. Though if we don't win, can I buy you dinner?"

She nodded.

As they rose up into the sky to the required height for the competition, Gabby provided him with instructions, both on the Marker Measuring Area where he'd want his marker to land and how to best determine when to drop the markers.

They were following the GPS to find the designated area.

"I never knew that these events were competitions," he said.

"You should see the rule book."

"That big?"

"Forty-nine pages, the last time I looked. And, that covered just the simplified rules, just for the scoring."

Clint whistled. "Wow, sounds more and more like an academic presentation. So, this isn't just a hobby, then."

"A serious one. Most of us have sponsors. And, yes, I'm a member of the Balloon Federation of America."

"Guess I have a lot to learn."

"You really want to?" she asked, looking at him quizzingly.

Over her shoulder and in the distance, he saw a huge plus sign on the ground. Definitely man-made. "Is that it?" he asked.

For the next half hour, they were busy calculating when to drop the marker and then finding a good location to land. He leaned over the edge of the basket, choosing to ignore his queasy stomach and let the marker go. When it landed, fairly close to where the two lines intersected, she was pulling on his arm, then clapping her hands. She grabbed his face, a hand on each cheek and pulled him down, giving him a solid kiss!

Startled at first, he reached for her, wanting to lengthen the kiss, but she quickly was out his grasp, turning her back so she could handle the controls.

He stood there, willing for her to turn, but it didn't happen. This was crazy. She kissed him because she'd been excited. Because he had nearly hit the bullseye. Nothing more.

From then on, she was busy handling the controls for the landing.

All too quickly, the moment and the event were over.

He decided to say nothing. Better to just land and

wait for a better moment.

Once they landed, they were met up with her team, who helped fold up the balloon and load everything for the return trip back to the festival arena. He listened to the conversation as they talked about other balloons and the competition.

Back at the festival, he exited the truck, wondering when they would be alone again.

He was pulled along with the crew as they went to check on the results. The entire time he kept glancing her way, often meeting her gaze. She'd quickly look away, but he couldn't help but notice the flush in her cheeks.

From the excitement of the race, he told himself. *Don't assume anything.*

They quickly learned they didn't win or even place in the top three. Other balloonists and their crews swarmed around them. It was like being at one of his own parties. He stepped back and watched her engage with the others. It was obvious she knew them and was comfortable with them as well.

And then, suddenly, everyone was gone. She was alone. She looked around, spotting him. Finally.

She smiled and walked over to him. "Sorry about that. I didn't mean to desert you like that."

"You were in your element." He looked around and could see that the festival was winding down for the evening. "You didn't win."

"No."

"You ready for that dinner if we didn't win?"

She grinned and said, "Yes."

"Gabby!"

A voice in the distance had both of them turning their heads toward the sound.

Gabby squealed, "Franklin!" and started running toward him. She pitched herself at him and he grabbed her, lifting her and laughing as he twirling her around once, then setting her down with a quick kiss.

"You made it!" she said.

"You doubted me?" Franklin said, pouting.

She laughed and punched him. "You missed tonight's event."

"I heard you got fourth place. We would have won had I been here."

"Come meet your replacement."

She grabbed his hand and pulled him toward Clint who stood watching them. He smiled at them, but something wasn't right. His eyes weren't smiling. The two men shook hands as she introduced them.

"Clint, meet Franklin, my partner in this adventure we call ballooning, and Franklin meet Clint. He's an archeologist and was my last client. You remember, for the fiftieth wedding anniversary party."

"Oh, the one down in Laurel Ridge. I've heard that part of Georgia is pretty with all its orchards. I've always wanted to go. Couldn't make it this time."

"He was attending his brother's wedding," she said.

"And, Gabby couldn't go with me because of your party," Franklin added.

"About dinner," Clint started. "How about we do it another— "

Franklin interrupted, "Oh, you two go ahead with your plans. I don't want to— "

Gabby said, "How about the three of us go together. I know Franklin hasn't had dinner being stuck on the freeway, and— "

"Sure, sounds great," Franklin said. "Let's do it. I can drive. My car's close by."

Clint knew this was a mistake, but there was no getting out of it now. He couldn't say no to spending more time with her even if they were with someone else.

"I just need to grab my purse," she said. "I'll meet you at the car." She watched the two men walk away. To anyone else it was two men walking, talking, chatting away like friends. But, Gabby frowned. The minute she had walked up to Clint with Franklin, something had changed. Clint's aura was protected, as if he'd shuttered himself away. His inner self. Was it possible that he thought that she and Franklin were partners in life, too?

*****

Day 9

Clint picked up his bag in the motel room, dropped the key on the desk, and walked out the door, shutting it behind him, making sure it locked. Still dark out, he stashed his overnight bag in the trunk.

He shouldn't have come. Now, he was committed to at least to watching the early morning ascent of the balloons in their full second day of competition. Last night, Gabby and Franklin both had made him promise that he'd come watch.

Only this time, Franklin would be in the basket. Where Franklin belonged. Where he didn't.

Gabby was right. They were total opposites: her life in the air, both as a hot-air balloonist and medium and his life as an archeologist, always searching underground. Finding commonality would be a challenge. Besides, she lived in Atlanta and he didn't.

A three-hours' drive one way didn't make for good relationships. He'd done it in the past and now a decade later, he really didn't want to do it again no matter how smitten or interested he was in her.

He was better off calling it quits before anything really developed. One kiss didn't make for a relationship. It'd been just one kiss given in excitement after all. Nothing more.

Okay, so it was kiss not easily forgotten. He'd get over it.

At last night's dinner, he could see how much in common Gabby and Franklin had. They were already a couple if they didn't know it. As he sat there in the restaurant listening to them share another story from another hot-air balloon festival, he had decided not to stay overnight at the motel he had reserved and had checked into earlier.

But then, they had extracted a promise from him that he'd attend the festival the next day.

Now morning, with his hand on the door handle, he thought about the drive home, easily a five-hour drive. Despite last night's promise, he was going home now. He didn't like that he wasn't keeping his promise. It wasn't like him. He'd only given in because Franklin had pressured him. Gabby had been relatively quiet about it. It was all Franklin's fault, he decided.

*****

By the time he crossed the Georgia state line, he realized he should have gone to the festival first and said good-bye. He could have at least done that. Was he now guilty of doing what he heard students talking about when they thought he wasn't listening? Ghosting, wasn't it? Where someone left a relationship without a word?

He grimaced. Oh, he'd left parties when he was young, never saying goodbye, but this wasn't the same thing at all. But, he and Gabby didn't have a relationship, so how could it feel so wrong, him leaving like this?

Minutes later, he looked at his watch. Gabby would be inflating the balloon by now, ignoring her phone because she was getting ready to ascend. He decided to call anyway, even if nothing more than to leave a message saying goodbye.

The phone rang once, then went immediately to voicemail, surprising him. "Ah, hi, Gabby. Clint here. I had to leave earlier than expected. Hope you and Franklin have a great time and take home a win today. It was good seeing you again. Take care."

He pushed the red *end* control button on the screen.

Done. That was that.

Better this way. Silly for him to think that an always-moving hot-air balloonist would consider dating long distance, let alone moving—

Whoa, he was getting way too far ahead of himself. They'd only just met. What was he doing thinking about her moving?

Since his moving up to Atlanta was out of the question, why could he assume it was easier for her?

He grimaced. He was overthinking, over wishing, over everything.

Yeah, he'd been bitten by the smitten bug badly. He'd gotten caught up in the fantasy of finding a companion, someone who could become a best friend, a life-long relationship. Even though his parents squabbled, he knew it was their love language because they were always laughing. Unhappy people didn't laugh.

How long would it be before he'd be that happy, too?

Maybe his mom was right, that he was just too much in his own head when it came to women. Reluctant to commit, even to just dating exclusively. By the time he'd figure it out, the girl had moved on.

Happy people. That's what he needed. A party. Next weekend. He needed a theme. August was nearly over. An End of Summer party—a prom—and maybe he could reveal the refurbished car, then.

Excited about his plans and the thought his car could be finished, he sat up straighter, glad the traffic was minimal. He'd be home by noon and could talk to

JoJo about the car. And then, he'd call everyone and finish making plans.

*****

Once home, Clint went out to the garage and talked to JoJo about restoring the rest of the car, both inside and out. Unfortunately, she couldn't. She had another job commitment the minute she finished his motor.

So much for showing off the car at the party. Oh well. It'd give him another reason for holding another party when it was finally restored.

Not wanting to think about Gabby, he decided to get hot and bothered literally. The lawn needed mowing and flower beds weeded. Normally, he hired the work done—a young married couple—but they were at his sister's wedding in Hawaii. He'd told them that this week, he'd take care of it. Meaning to make a phone call and hire it out, he hadn't done it. To find someone now at the last minute would be fruitless.

While he wasn't above doing this type of labor, he rarely did it in this heat. Today, he welcomed it. All he wanted to do was to bury his heart. If doing some physical labor would do the trick, so be it.

By late afternoon, he was exhausted and decided to finish the yard tomorrow.

In the shower, determined not to think about Gabby, he purposefully thought about the car and what was needed to finish it. Maybe he could make a few phone calls, find someone to reupholster the seats and shine it up.

The minute he thought about the car looking all shiny and new again, he saw Gabby sitting there beside him. The car's top down and their cruising through shaded country roads.

Once dressed, he was going to the sports bar in the neighboring town to have dinner. He wondered if any of the guys would be there. The way so many of them were pairing up lately, he doubted it. The usual locals would be there, though. For once, he was looking forward to the loud TV and equally loud conversation. It was better than spending a quiet evening at home, alone with his thoughts.

*****

It was late before Gabby was finally alone. The festival had ended on a high note. She and Franklin had taken first place in today's competition, and as usual, a large number of the balloonists and partners wanted to celebrate their last evening. The day had been packed with activities and people.

Only now, as she stood in the shower, washing away the dust and pollen did she have time to think.

Originally, she thought Clint had said he'd come up for the entire festival, but then suddenly, he was gone, having left just a short voicemail that gave her no idea of when they might reconnect again.

Was that his intent? To say goodbye forever?

She'd never been attracted to people outside of her own interests before. Especially an academic. She'd always thought of them as stuffy, stuck in their self-imposed ivory towers type of people. Yet, he'd been anything but. She had discovered they had more in common than many of those in her field: politics, movies, religion, cultures, plus he enjoyed engaging conversations like she did. So, what was the problem?

Honestly? She had a gypsy life-style, always on the road. His was cemented in place, to his university and digs.

Those were two tough differences to get past.

She sighed, turning off the water. Drying off and putting on her nightgown was an effort. She was exhausted, too tired to analyze his message. Crawling under the sheet, she relaxed and drifted off to sleep, her last thought being, when had she ever analyzed anything? That was his field.

*****

Day 10

Gabby awoke discovering it was almost check out time. She never slept this late.

As she finished the packing she'd started late last night, she acknowledged that her energy was different.

Granted she, JoJo, and Charli had recently talked about the day when their jobs would change. Was that because of their age or the fact they'd each been on the road for a decade. Was the shiny autonomy they each had cherished so deeply finally beginning to wear off and growing old?

Not that they were old, but if they wanted to have children...

For someone who said she didn't like routine and enjoyed the freedom the festivals had provided, Gabby realized with sudden clarity that her life was filled with routine. Gone on the weekends, on the road a couple days before and after the weekends with Wednesdays usually at home doing laundry, scheduling, paying bills, and making repairs. And, all with the pretense that she couldn't settle down, didn't want to settle down because she had no structure.

She started laughing.

It was time to change things up. Time to take chances, too. With everything, including relationships.

Later, as the Atlanta city limits sign came into view, she realized in thinking back over her life that she had avoided anything where she lacked confidence, always turning to and embracing those things where she could succeed. A few first failures at establishing a romantic relationship, she had since then avoided nurturing any potential relationship.

Decidedly, it was time to turn some of those so-called failures into successes. If she didn't try now, she'd never know and that would be a huge loss.

*****

Day 12

Clint parked his car in the garage and entered the kitchen. While he had hoped Gabby would have called him since he'd left the festival two days ago, his phone remained silent. Well, except for the early morning emergency call he got yesterday from his assistant in charge of the dig. As a result, he'd spent the day at the dig, then later that night at the university. He'd just gotten home having spent the night there.

While it wasn't unusual for him to sleep on his couch in his office from time to time, stretching out his back and shoulders, he realized he wasn't as young anymore either.

A catastrophe adverted, he'd left the dig this morning, knowing his team was shutting it down properly. The new semester was fast approaching and he'd be in full prep mode when he returned to the university next week.

Gabby wouldn't be calling. His last message to her had been pretty final.

Looking out at the back garage, he saw JoJo hard at work on the car. Already past lunch time and hotter than blazes again, a typical late summer day, he poured sweet tea into two tall glasses and walked out of the kitchen and across the yard.

As usual, the engine's hood was up. Only this time, she was standing next to it, hands on her hips and grinning.

He heard the motor running, understanding her grin. "You got it working!" he said, walking into the garage, extending his arm to her with one of the glasses in his hand. She took it and clinked it with his.

"Sure did. Sounds like a cat purring, doesn't it?"

Clint laughed. "In record time. I'm impressed." She updated him on what she'd done.

"I know I asked you before and you said no, but I have to ask again. Is there any chance you can finish restoring the rest of the car? There's no good restoration service in this part of the state. We need one badly."

"Because so many of the classic car clubs are in the northern part of the state," she stated.

He nodded. "Any chance?"

"The seats are gone. Are you getting them reupholstered?"

"Actually, they're finished. They texted me last night."

"That's great. With the inside stripped, I could easily treat and prep the inside and finish the outside myself. It wouldn't take long. It would really be about the details of a radio—"

"Ordered."

"The convertible covering—"

"Should be here later today, actually."

"—and knobs, handles, lights, trim, etc. Thankfully, cars were relatively simple back then. Few electronics. Of course, there'd be no air-conditioning."

"Don't need it. Don't want it."

"Actually, then, if you've already got everything already ordered or finished, it's just about finishing touches and installing the various pieces and parts. You've made it easy to finish."

"Any chance it could be done for a review by the weekend?"

JoJo thought for a minute. "It might be missing some details still, but the majority of it would be done. Would that be good enough for people to see it, as in kind of a review?"

"Yes, exactly. I'm planning a party for this weekend. Would you be able to stay a few more days so you could finish it and join the party?"

"You're in luck," she replied, grinning. "The job that was scheduled following this one got canceled. It'd be like a vacation staying here instead. And, having met a good number of your friends, I'd enjoy staying for the party."

"If you want, you can move into the guest cottage. It's empty."

"But won't Gabby—"

"I went up to the Tennessee balloon festival, deciding to take your advice, but it appears she has a partner, one that's a perfect fit for her."

"What are you talking—"

Clint's cell phone rang interrupted her. He pulled it from his back pocket, looked at the screen, and said, "Excuse me. I need to take this." He stepped away, stopping just inside the garage, standing in the shade, and returned a few one-syllable responses before hanging up.

Spinning back around, he said, "Is there any chance you can go to Joe's house and pick up some papers for me? They're important. I'd go but that was a student who's on his way over. I need to stay here."

"If for some reason I'm not back right away, can you move the fans around?" she asked, picking up a rag and wiping her hands.

"Sure thing. Thanks for doing this."

Once she drove out of the driveway and disappeared, Clint stepped over to the bug again. She'd done a nice job cleaning the interior and getting rid of the rust spots that were now primed and nearly dry enough for some yellow paint.

Clint readjusted one of the fans.

He wanted to feel bad for tricking her, but he didn't.

When Clint, William, and Charli had set Joe and JoJo up on that blind date that had gone horribly wrong, she and Joe had kept trying to redo the date only to fail with more disastrous dates. JoJo had finally pulled the plug. Clint could only hope that Joe was proving her wrong tonight, helping her reverse her decision.

Hearing a motor, he turned and saw a big truck coming down his driveway. He frowned. Gabby's truck?

It was.

He stepped toward the bay opening just as Gabby pulled up, turned off the engine, and jumped down out of the cab.

"This is a surprise," he said.

"JoJo didn't tell you?"

"She knew you were coming?"

Gabby nodded.

His heart was pounding out of his chest. He hoped she wasn't reading him because he didn't want her knowing how much he had missed her or how happy he was seeing her. All he wanted to do was grab her and kiss her, but he didn't dare take the chance. Instead, he stuck his hands into his pockets, trying to appear nonchalant. "Were you bringing her a part or something?"

She grinned.

He was screwed.

He sighed. Did her grin just get bigger?

Yup, she was reading him all right.

"Something. Yes, I brought something." She turned and went to the passenger door, opened it, and stood up on the running board. The door blocked his view. She was fiddling with something on the seat. With it in her arms, she stepped down, then shut the door.

She had two terriers, one dark, the other light, one in each arm. She pushed one toward him, which he took and tucked under his arm, a hand under its belly.

"What's this?" he asked.

"Cairn Terriers. They're brothers, a couple years old. A friend's parents are moving into an adult assisted community where they can have cats but no dogs. So, they need a new home."

With his other hand, he petted the dog and it wiggled, licking his hand.

"Yours?"

"No, well, at least not both of them. Which one do you want?"

He looked at her. "You'd separate them?"

"No."

"I don't understa—"

"Well, we could do long distance, but then that could be a bit hard on them—"

"I'd say," he said, petting the dog and bringing it up closer to his face, where it started licking him enthusiastically. To the dog, he said, "We can't do that, can we?" The dog barked softly at him, his whole body wagging in opposition to the tail. "This one's mine." To Gabby he said, "So, how do you propose they stay close together?"

"I move to Laurel Ridge."

He studied her. Damn the woman. Her face was non-expressive. She was doing it on purpose. He could tell by the teasing look in her eyes.

"JoJo kicked you out?"

"Not exactly."

"What exactly?"

"You really are an academic, aren't you? Always asking questions."

He laughed. She smiled.

"I'm tired of living in Atlanta. I'm tired of being on the road all the time, too. I like it here."

"Laurel Ridge does have its attractions."

"And, interesting people."

Clint lifted an eyebrow, in question. "Like?" He knew he was fishing, but he couldn't help himself.

She scrunched her mouth, then said with a teasing twinkle in her eye that he'd seen before, "There's one catch with taking the dog."

Okay, he'd play her game. There was no way he wasn't curious as to where this conversation was going. "And, that is?"

"The dog comes with a girl." She paused, then said, "Me."

He started to take the step toward her that would close the space between them, but stopped. "Wait, what about Franklin?"

"What about him?"

"Isn't he your boyfriend?"

She laughed. "Heavens, no. If he were my boyfriend, I'd have offed him by now. We were hot-balloon partners only. And, he's already found another partner to race with."

Clint closed the spaced between them and with his free arm, scooped her against him and bent down, kissing her soundly.

Both dogs started licking them, breaking them up. They laughed and set the squirming dogs down, where they began playing around their feet, chasing each other.

"Any chance I can move into the cottage until I can find a place of my own?" she asked.

"Sure, as long as JoJo doesn't mind. She's at—"

"She won't mind."

"I have a guest room or two up in the house, if you prefer."

"The cottage will do for now." She cupped his neck, stood on tip toes, pulling him down for her kiss. Quickly, his arms wrapped around her and hers around him.

When they finally drew apart, he said, "I see an uplifting bright future ahead."

She grinned. "I could dig it."

Tangled Passions #5

When Senator Jefferson Jackson first sees Madison Butler, he's immediately smitten but learns she's a lobbyist who wants his vote on a bill he opposes. Once he exposes her employer, can she ever forgive him?

Day 3

Jefferson Jackson arrived at Clint Anderson's party for his parents' fiftieth wedding anniversary just in time to see Clint and his parents go up in the hot-air balloon.

"Quite a sight, isn't it, Senator?"

Jefferson turned. An attractive redhead barely a head shorter than his own six-foot-five stood next to him, looking up at the sky as the moon-and-stars air balloon ascended. He looked down at her shoes. No heels. A rare woman who stood nearly as tall as he. He raised his gaze. And, a natural redhead at that, no artificial color here. The curves were nice, too.

He'd seen her before but couldn't place her. She'd called him Senator. If he'd seen her in the halls before, he was sure he'd have remembered her.

She turned her head. Wow. No doubt about it. He'd have remembered those eyes. Exquisitely green. And, mesmerizing. She had to have an Irish background. Would she have a temper to match that fiery hair?

Where did he know her from? They were both out of place here in Clint's backyard.

She stuck out her hand. "Hi, Madison Butler—"

"Do you know the Andersons?" he asked, shaking her hand. The name wasn't ringing any bells. Somehow, he doubted she knew Clint who was an archeology professor. She didn't look the type to mingle with academics. She looked like she belonged in night clubs, rubbing elbows with money, enjoying the spotlight. Could she be a singer? He knew he was being judgmental and hated that he was, but in his current public career, he needed to size people up quickly. Usually, his first judgments about people weren't wrong. Which made him question why here, why next to him?

She probably knew Clint's parents. They were well-traveled and well-connected with a wide circle of friends, especially in Atlanta, where they lived most of the time. They sat on various charity boards, too.

Could Clint be dating her and keeping it a secret from all of them? Not that he himself was looking to date anyone seriously, but she *was* attractive. She could be an exception to his current casual dating habits—women who would accompany him to dinners, concerts, and plays but didn't expect a commitment or a long-term relationship. They were happy being seen on the arm of one of Georgia's youngest senators, and he was happy being seen escorting beautiful women. Beautiful and extremely smart.

He hated dull women. Probably why he and Annie Martin, an area game warden and best friend through school and since got on so well. They challenged each other mentally. A philosophy teacher would be proud of their discussions.

Joe Benton, another of Jefferson's classmates and friends, who had returned to Laurel Ridge to live and practice law, walked up, and answered for her. "No, but she knows me."

The two men hugged warmly, greeting each other.

Joe continued, "I met Madison my first year up in Atlanta while at college, where we were both serving as Congressional interns for a semester and became good friends."

Jefferson wondered if they'd been more than just friends.

Madison continued the story. "Then, he went to law school, and I stayed with the firm. Became a researcher, a paralegal instead of a lawyer. Plus, Clint's assistant, Maggie, is another one of my friends."

"So, between the two of us," Joe said, "we convinced her to come to the party."

Just then, Maggie came up to Madison, grabbed her hand, and pulled her away. Jefferson frowned. How well did Maggie know her? Maggie was in middle school when they had all graduated. Cute kid, still cute as a woman, but a bit naïve. Madison looked anything but naïve.

Jefferson couldn't help himself. "Did the two of you ever date?" he asked.

"Madison?" Joe laughed. "No, she was too busy studying. Her love of learning was her constant companion. Best study partner I ever had."

Now, Jefferson was intrigued. Smart, too, apparently. As Maggie and Madison talked, Madison laughed, throwing her head back, her red hair cascading further down her back. His hands itched to feel that hair. "What does she do?"

"Madison? She's a lobbyist."

Jefferson's head jerked toward Joe. *Her?* "You're kidding me."

Joe laughed at Jefferson's shocked expression. "I'm surprised you haven't met her by now. She's not one to give up on any job."

"What do you mean?"

"She's a lobbyist for a chemical company, contacting all of the pecan growers, and with you as one of the biggest growers in the state..."

Jefferson swiveled his head back toward the crowd, his gaze latching onto Madison. Now, she was talking with an elderly couple, good friends of the Andersons. They were smiling and nodding their heads, fully engaged in conversation with her. His staff had told him there'd been a particular company's lobbyist trying to see him, but he'd been busy and knew what they wanted from him. He'd had no desire to talk to anyone connected with a company set to destroy Georgia's current organization of pecan growers—a community of private citizens who'd been generational owners for over 150 years. He couldn't believe she worked for them, if his suspicions were right.

He wanted details and hoped Joe could help provide them.

"Do you know the name of the company she works for?"

"Some big buyer. Forget the name."

"She's not associated with the Georgia Pecan Growers Association, is she?" Jefferson knew she wasn't but didn't want to give anything away. Since he was highly engaged with the Association, he knew the names. Hers wasn't one of them, but he also knew other members had been chatting about being contacted by this company in particular. No one appeared to know for what exactly. Or, they weren't saying. It wasn't unusual for an orchard to be sold to a big corporation when there were no heirs or farmer buyers, but lately, there was something else underfoot and he was determined to get to the root of it all. Maybe Madison could answer some of his questions.

"No," Joe said, "but she was asking me a lot of questions earlier about it. About you being a member."

The hairs on the back of his neck stood up. He needed to be careful. There'd been a lot of lobbying going on in the House and Senate regarding Georgia's exports lately. Was that the real reason she was here? Was she somehow connected to the two growers who were seriously talking of selling to this company?

Until now, he thought the selling of an orchard was part of a new cycle. It happened every couple of decades, but if the organization lost too many of its growers—maybe it was time he got more involved.

He watched as she laughed at something Cutter Logan was telling her. Cutter flirted with all the women. Always had, even in grade school. Couldn't help himself. Jefferson and the other guys teased him mercilessly about his womanizing, knowing how it was a facade even if Cutter couldn't or wouldn't admit it. Not all the women appreciated his bad boy behavior. Jefferson grinned. Cutter was probably embellishing on his story of how he fished a car out of Whippoorwill Lake two days ago on the first day of the contest. Madison laughed. Obviously, Cutter was entertaining her. She'd not been subjected to his endless repetitive stories, as they all had. Cutter thought of himself as a wonderful man of nature, boasting that if he was ever on any survivalist reality show, he'd come out a winner, but the guys knew from mutual camping experiences, he wasn't any better than the rest of them. There was a reason why they had nicknamed him Beta Boy back in high school. Cutter was just more enthusiastic about camping than they were. As a result, he had turned the hobby into a business.

Joe continued, watching her too. "Of course, she was asking about the peaches and onions grown around here, too."

"Not one to put work aside when away from business?" Jefferson asked.

Joe laughed and slapped Jefferson on the back. "Like you? I don't know how you do it."

"The same as you, Buddy," Jefferson responded. "The same as you."

"Meaning, we look like we're all relaxed and casual but really not?"

"Something like that," Jefferson answered. Neither of them had taken their gaze off Madison.

She was one attractive woman. Model attractive with that tall height and luxurious red hair that fell loose down her back. Interesting that she didn't have it in a more business-like style, but then again, they were at a party.

*****

As Madison moved about the party, talking with various guests, she peeked at Jefferson who continued to talk with Joe. She could see why he and Joe were good friends. They had similar behaviors and reactions. Cool as ice blocks in the summer sun and slow to react. But, she knew Joe, knew how his mind would zip around, analyzing, observing, thinking out questions and queries before speaking them. She saw that same hyper-activity going on behind Jefferson's gaze. She admired his ability to stay uninterested and uninvolved when learning who she was. By the way the two men stood next to each other, watching her, she knew Jefferson was asking questions. If nothing else, she was an astute reader of body language and had learned to do some lip reading just for the sheer fun of it. Something she had yet to reveal to anyone.

About half an hour later, from a shadowed

portion of the yard, Madison saw Jefferson alone at the outdoor bar. Most of the guests had left or were leaving. He was alone, for the first time tonight.

Time to make her move.

*****

The party was winding down. Jefferson, standing at the bar that had been set up outside, had watched Clint walk the balloonist to her truck. Now, they were driving out of the big garage in his sports car. Jefferson chuckled. Not unusual for Clint to leave his own party before it was over, but it was unusual that he was leaving with a woman.

He turned and saw Madison approaching him. She stared at him, her gaze never leaving his. The party faded away. He liked what he saw. Hips swaying, long legs outlined against the skirt's material. She dressed fashionably but subtly. It was her hair and eyes that most drew his attention. Come to think of it, he'd never dated a redhead before. In his mind's eye, he saw her on his arm, dressed for a symphony or play on opening night.

He blinked the image away.

She was in front of him.

"Any chance we could meet tomorrow?"

"So, you *are* taking advantage of my being here at the party."

She smiled. "You caught me."

He wished her wanting to meet with him was personal, but he knew deep down to the soles of her shoes that it was all business. "Breakfast at the diner downtown? It's by the—"

"I know where it is. I've been there before. Eight o'clock, okay?"

He nodded.

"Great! I'll see you there tomorrow." She turned and walked away.

It was all he could do not to follow. He raised his glass and finished his drink, still watching, and noticing that every other man still here—mostly staff—was watching, too. He set his glass down, cursing his luck. Why did she have to be a lobbyist?

Jefferson glanced around, looking for his group of friends. The yard was nearly empty, the staff hired for the night, cleaning up.

Not seeing his friends, he looked toward the house. Yup, there they were, engaged in the usual after-party-get-together in Clint's kitchen. It didn't matter that Clint wasn't here.

Walking into the kitchen, Jefferson was immediately surrounded by the kids he'd grown up with. He couldn't remember when this after-party party had started, but it was here that the best discussions occurred.

They'd talk about the event that just happened, talk about old times, or hash out a problem one of them was having. If neither of the girls—Shelley, Mason's girlfriend in high school, and Annie who Cutter had always wanted to date—weren't part of the group, they'd be talking about the girls, which is exactly what they were doing right now.

The third girl of their group had always been Edwina, Eddie as they called her, but she'd severely withdrawn when her parents died just before their senior year. It wasn't for the lack of trying, inviting her to the parties, that she wasn't here now.

Clint was still AWOL, but Cutter, Joe, Rhett, and William were here. Rhett hadn't gone to school with them but had become part of the group soon after he came to Laurel Ridge as a firefighter.

"Couldn't help but notice you talking about your catch," Jefferson said to Cutter.

"That car isn't the catch I want."

William howled. "When are you going to give up on Annie?"

"Never. Not until she says yes."

"Yes, to what?" Joe asked. "That you'll leave her alone?"

"I don't want to be just best friends," Cutter said.

"It's more than most of us have," William said.

Cutter retorted. "That's because you've still got your head in the books."

William laughed. "Hard not to do as library director. So, what's up with Clint leaving the party this time?" William asked.

"Probably the truck not starting," Rhett said. "It was problematic when I was following the balloon. While we were packing the balloon up, she mentioned it was most likely the starter."

"Why am I always surprised at how much women know these days?" Cutter asked.

"Because you're still thinking like you're the ultimate alpha?"

They all laughed, including Cutter.

"But I am, you know," Cutter replied.

More laughter. Jefferson never knew if Cutter was being serious or not but had a feeling Cutter believed his own hype. Hence the nickname, Beta Boy. Always the jokester. Thought he was keeping others off base with his humor and constant stories, never realizing how off-putting it could be sometimes. Especially for Annie, even though she and Cutter were good friends. Unless Cutter was willing to change and reveal what was really in his heart, he'd never win her.

"I've got to get going," Jefferson said. "I'm having breakfast with Madison in the morning."

Joe raised his eyebrows.

"No, it's not a date," Jefferson responded. "Pure business."

"Funny business," Cutter offered.

Joe laughed. "Not this one. She's never been one to mix business with love."

"She and me both," Jefferson said. His last girlfriend was the reason he casually dated now. She'd been a working colleague, and then he discovered she was cheating with an ex-boyfriend. Ever since, he'd sworn off relationships. Friends first was his new motto.

His friends here thought he was nuts, but he knew the damage a scandal of any kind could do to his political career.

Jefferson left the house, shutting the glass doors to their hoots of "There's always a first time," and "Don't let that stop you."

He met the clean-up crew coming up the last terrace. They always saved the kitchen for last, knowing how Clint's closest friends liked to gather there after the party. In just a few minutes, all the boys would be leaving and Clint would return to a clean back yard and kitchen.

*****

On the short drive to the motel, Madison knew her boss would be happy that she was finally meeting with the elusive Senator Jackson. Yes, she was friends with Joe and Maggie and knew when she'd contacted Maggie yesterday that this party was taking place, hoping Maggie was going and would invite her—and Maggie had.

Madison hated that she got her invitation that way, but she'd been desperate to make this contact. She was expected to not only meet Jefferson but to get him to agree to look at their product line and hopefully endorse it for other members of the growers' association. Once her boss had realized that many of the members saw Jefferson as a knowledgeable leader, especially since becoming a Senator, he'd been hammering her to get a commitment from Jefferson, no matter how small—even if only to meet with him. If she didn't, she wouldn't like the consequences. He never came out and said she'd be fired, but she knew from experience having watched how he had fired other lobbyists and salespeople, that he was ruthless.

If she hadn't been so far in debt, needing this job, she'd have quit by now. This company's pay and benefits far exceeded other companies and had allowed her to pay down her debt more quickly than she had expected. She still had a sizeable sum to pay off, but the debt was more manageable now regardless of where she could be working. When she had looked around for other jobs, she discovered there weren't any in her field. At least, not any that would pay the bills adequately. Not if she wanted to continue living in Atlanta. Even so, her expenses were minimal with everything going to pay down her debt—all accrued while she'd been going to school.

*****

Day 4

All through breakfast, Jefferson kept waiting for Madison to bring up her company, the real reason he suspected why she wanted to meet with him. Instead, he found himself answering her questions about Laurel Ridge, its politics and policies, and about other pecan growers he knew. To all of which he revealed little, keeping any information he gave as general, that anyone would know.

She was good. He'd give her that. Ultimately, because he was curious about her, he asked her questions about Atlanta, learning she'd been born and raised there, and then she quickly changed the subject back to him.

"You've been living in Atlanta for what, just a couple of years?" she asked.

He stared. How much did she know about him? Where would she have gotten her information? He knew Joe wasn't one to reveal much about his friends.

"Actually, no. Just in this last year since I took office." He had the feeling she already knew that.

Madison frowned. "Why am I thinking you were a lawyer?"

"Because my friends are?" But, she would know that already based on his senatorial website where his education was listed.

"You didn't go to school in Atlanta."

It wasn't a question, but he answered as if it was. "No, but I did visit Joe often while he was in school, visiting him and William when they roomed together. It was easy flying up there."

"How long have you been flying?" Why did he feel like he was on a witness stand and why was he answering her so easily? He couldn't explain it, but he wanted to ask more questions of his own. That's why. He knew he couldn't be shuttered if he expected her to be open.

"I got my license when I was fifteen, well before I got my driver's license. Was always flying with my grandfather. He died my senior year of high school. He's the one who taught me how to fly. I worked at the airport, earning, and saving money so I could fly, and then later, buy a car. How come I never met you if you and Joe were such good friends?"

She shrugged. "Can't answer that. Maybe he was keeping me hidden. Said you were quite the ladies' man."

Jefferson laughed. "Joe was always setting me up with dates, women who really wanted to be with him. Usually onetime dates, at that. My flying was a girl magnet. They all thought I was rich."

She laughed. "Well, aren't you? You've got the second-largest orchard in the state, and you are a Senator."

There it was. She had to have done some major research on him to know he owned the second-largest orchard in the state. That or her company did. He decided to be up front and truthful about his situation and mode of operation as a senator.

"And, maintaining two homes and paying for a lot of jet fuel. Unlike other Congressional members, I'm not a millionaire or becoming one because of the job. Owning land doesn't make one rich, especially for farmers. Usually the opposite, in fact. And, I don't take money from lobbyists."

He paused, watching her closely for a reaction. Interestingly, her expression didn't change. He continued. "The only thing I know about my campaign fund is the total. I made it clear to everyone that I didn't want to know who made donations. I became a senator to serve the people, which doesn't make me the most popular guy on the block to big pharma and other corporations," he added.

"No one ever sparked your interest?"

She didn't take the political bait he had just offered. Instead, she was staying on his personal path. Why? "I had a girlfriend in high school for a couple months. She didn't like that I spent more time in the air than with her. My first experience at being dumped. She did me a favor. Freed me up for more flying time, running errands for people. I picked up a wedding dress for one bride. Another time, I brought home a casket for a family who couldn't afford to pick up their deceased son. The airport owner paid for my gas in those instances and others, where I didn't charge anyone."

"That was nice of you."

"People had been good to me. I wanted to help where I could. Still do."

"An endearing trait. So, you've had no other sparks of interest?"

He gazed at her for what felt like a minute but was probably more like seconds. *She knew.* He'd be foolish to say nothing.

"Actually, I had a girlfriend for about a year, a few years back. Turned out she was a gold digger. Once her boyfriend came into a pile of money and discovered I was basically a farmer, or in her words, 'working a plantation' like an overseer, she left. She made sure all the tabloids made me the villain. Guess you could say, dating seriously after that turned me off. Wasn't interested." Funny how he had said, *wasn't. Did that mean he could be? Oh, heck, yes. This woman held his interest and revved up his engine like no one ever had.*

*****

Madison glanced at him. This man was hot. Good-looking hot, well-respected, and intelligent, judging by the things Joe had said about him. And, there was a possibility he might be interested in her, too. Seeing him standing in Clint's back yard last night, all she could think about was wanting to get to know him. To become a friend. Yes, she was here to do a job, but—But what? The job had to come first. She didn't have a choice. Not right now anyway.

Jefferson interrupted her thoughts. "You're an attractive woman, Madison. If you weren't a lobbyist, I'd be asking you for a date, but I don't mix business with pleasure anymore."

"And, you're an attractive man," she responded. He could easily be on the cover of GQ Magazine. She'd heard the rumors of his dating the socialites and models in Atlanta. No doubt he had broken and was still breaking a lot of hearts every time he went out with someone different. "And, you're wise not to mix business with pleasure..." Whatever else she was thinking of tacking on to the end of that sentence deserted her completely as the image of the two of them between the sheets seized her imagination.

Connie set two more sweet teas on the table. Glad for the interruption, Madison grabbed her spoon, stirring the contents. She knew darn well that he knew she knew her tea didn't need stirring. She glanced up at him and then back at the tea. He was grinning. Darn it all! This wasn't how she wanted this breakfast to go. Her goal had been to feel him out on whether he could be persuaded to sell, as her company wanted.

"So, how about you?" he asked. "Tell me about the hearts you've strewn about behind you. I can't believe with that flaming red hair and those wicked green eyes that more than a few guys haven't been enchanted with you?"

Madison laughed. "Joe was always saying that I studied too hard. That I always had my head in the books." She smiled, her gaze looking out the window, remembering. "I can't recall a time when I wasn't reading. I wanted to be Laura Ingalls, then Nancy Drew. Later, I wanted to be Kinsey Millhone—"

"Who?"

"The heroine in the Sue Grafton's ABC mystery series. But, I didn't want Kinsey's accidents or injuries." Seeing Jefferson's puzzled look, she explained. "Things happened around her, like buildings blowing up, bullets buzzing by—" Madison frowned. "Actually, Nancy Drew had mishaps like that, too, now that I think about it." She laughed. "Glad I gave up wanting to be a detective. How long have you owned the orchard?" Even to her ears, her sudden shift back to business sounded stark and hollow.

*****

Instantly, Jefferson noted the circle back to the orchard. Eventually, she'd get to the real reason for wanting to break bread with him. "When Granddad died, Dad inherited the business, but being a farmer wasn't his thing. Even with the best of managers. So, he signed it over to me."

"Just like that?"

"Nothing is ever that easy. Once I finished my bachelor's degree, I traded school for farming."

"What were you studying?"

"Political Science, but you already know that, don't you?"

This time, Madison blushed, then nodded. "Yes, I've read your bio. It's no secret, after all. Standard bio on the government website."

"But, you have a special interest in me *because* of my orchard."

"True, but that's not the only reason why I suggested breakfast."

He stared at her. Could he trust that she was telling the truth? Time would tell. Though, he did trust Joe. And, Joe was good at judging character. He wouldn't be friends with anyone who wasn't trustworthy.

"So, why did you want to have breakfast with me?"

She paused, looked down at her plate, then back up at him. She twisted her mouth a little as she contemplated her answer, pushing her food around on the plate. He found her interesting to watch as she mulled over his question.

And then, she blurted, "I find you attractive." She looked down at her plate again. "I can't believe I said it." She looked at him, putting her fork down. "I'm never one to initiate a relationship—"

"That's what this is?"

"No, but—" She ran a hand through her hair, pushing it away from her face. "I shouldn't have said anything. This was a mistake."

"No," he blurted. "It wasn't a mistake."

She frowned.

"I'm attracted to you, too."

She looked as surprised as he felt.

He picked up his fork just as she did and saw they both were just pushing the food around, not really eating. Was she considering the ramifications of what was just said as much as he was?

A minute later, he asked, "Ready to go? Would you like a tour of the orchard?"

As they left the restaurant and got into their respective cars, with her following him out to the orchard, he couldn't rationalize why he had extended the invitation. He was conflicted. While he wasn't ready to part company, each going their own way, he couldn't doubt everything she said either. He needed to stop analyzing her, but how could he if he didn't trust her completely? He questioned if she was holding anything back.

*****

Twenty minutes later, they stood about half a dozen trees into the orchard, shaded by the already scorching sun. Despite the heat and humidity, it was ten degrees cooler in the orchard.

When she pointed out spots where there were younger trees among bigger and older trees, he told her how and when trees were replaced. She appeared genuinely interested in learning about the trees and he was in his favorite area of expertise—the trees. "It's not unusual to find roots from other trees entangled within the older tree's roots. Science has proven that the trees communicate through their roots."

They both turned hearing a car turn into the orchard. The car followed the tractor path and parked behind his and Madison's car.

Clint.

Jefferson started walking toward the car. Madison followed. When she stumbled, he reached out, grabbing her arm to steady her.

"I'm okay," she said. "Should have worn more sensible shoes." With that, she reached down, lifting one foot, then another as she removed her heels. "There, that's better."

Clint and Gabby got out of the car and walked toward them.

The two men hugged, greeting each other warmly, like long-lost brothers, slapping each other on the back, despite having seen each other last night. "Missed you at the usual kitchen talk, last night."

Clint responded. "Gabby wanted some proper food, not that expensive fluff I was serving last night. You both remember Gabby?"

"Indeed, I do," Jefferson said. "I was hoping for a chance to talk with you, having witnessed your special powers."

Gabby shook Jefferson's hand. He saw her hesitate, look at his hand, and then gaze at him more directly. He'd bet his Senate seat that she sensed something. He'd seen her do this last night with a few guests.

"You've got impressive skills at reading strangers," he added.

"Not so special, really," Gabby replied. "Powers we all have, but which I've recognized and utilize."

"And, this," Jefferson said, a hand on Madison's elbow, "is Madison Butler. She's a lobbyist, here on business."

Madison glanced at him, then returned her gaze to Gabby. "Nice to see you again."

"We shouldn't be bothering you then," Clint said.

"No, no, it's quite all right," Madison said.

"No bother at all," Jefferson said at the same time.

He and Madison looked at each other. Did his face look as surprised as hers did? He didn't like how he was reacting. These reactions and feelings weren't normal for him. He felt off center, almost as if he'd lost control.

What power did Madison have over him?

He glanced at Gabby. She grinned. Inwardly, he groaned. She knew he was attracted to Madison.

Clint reached for something in his pants pocket. Thankfully, Clint was oblivious to the underlying tensions and non-verbal communications that were going on. Just like his trees, Jefferson thought, gazing at Gabby with renewed interest. While he'd learn to read and understand trees, Gabby read people.

"Good," Clint said. "We're here looking for information on this bracelet." He pulled it out of his pocket and handed it to Jefferson.

Stunned, Jefferson stared at the bracelet in the palm of this hand.

"It was your mother's," Gabby said.

He nodded. Looking at Clint, he said, "How did you get it?"

Clint responded, "We found it in the Volkswagen."

Able to hide his feelings and reactions from most

people up in the Senate halls and elsewhere in Atlanta, here in Laurel Ridge, too many people knew him well. And, Gabby? Obviously, her psychic skills were in play. She didn't know him at all, but Jefferson sensed she probably knew more about him than even his friends. She held his gaze, then put a hand on his arm.

“You’re upset,” Gabby said.

Jefferson stared at her. "Shocked, more like it."

"It triggered a memory."

Again, he nodded.

“I’m sorry for your discomfort, for your loss.”

Clint looked confused. “Loss? I didn’t know that someone died... other than your brother, that is.”

Jefferson explained to Gabby and Madison. "My only sibling, a brother, died in a diving accident. He was nine. I was twelve. Mom took it the hardest. She was there when it happened. He dove, hitting his head on a rock."

"I'm sorry for your loss of Jay-Jay."

Jefferson stared at her. "Only Mom called him Jay-Jay. And, only in private, at home." He looked at the bracelet again. "But, you're not talking about Jay. You're talking about the death of a relationship."

Gabby nodded.

He looked down, closing his fingers over the bracelet, wishing he wasn't remembering the last words his parents had shouted at each other, his father hurling the bracelet at his mother. That's when they both noticed he was in the doorway, so they had stopped. His mother had just stared at him. His father had turned his back to both of them, going to the refrigerator, inserting his glass under the ice spigot. The sound of ice clattering into his glass had filled the room, erasing the silence.

Jefferson sighed, dropped his shoulders, and looked up, staring into the trees.

"I was home. My first year of college completed. Normally, I wasn't home at that time of day. Mom and Dad had never shouted at each other, at least not that I knew of. They had always squabbled through the years about this or that. Mostly about their jewelry business, but it was more like friendly babble, disagreements. Never really fights. That one weekend was totally different. I came downstairs just in time to see Dad throwing this," he held up the bracelet, "at Mom, shouting at her—he'd never shouted like that before. It hit her and bounced, landing at my feet. I picked it up and handed it to her. I remembered her as always wearing it. She stuck it in her pocket. I never saw it again. He left that night, returning the next day to pack his belongings, moving out to California, never returning to Georgia until he retired, moving to Jekyll Island. Mom complained that he had sold her car—the Volkswagen—out from under her a week after he had left. It was in his name, I learned, but she always drove it, feeling like it was her car and that she should have gotten it in the divorce. Said at the time that he was getting back at her. I blamed Dad, and Mom would never say anything. I didn't want to ask. I could tell she hated him. She was okay with my blaming him. And then, the divorce. It all happened so fast."

He paused. Opening his palm, he picked up the bracelet with the other hand, then used both hands to spin it around so that the inside was exposed. "There's something engraved here."

"Thanks for the memories and some initials," Gabby said.

"And, hearts," Clint added. "We couldn't make the initials out. One set has been scratched. Almost as if to remove the letters. Do you recognize them? The initials?"

"Mom's are the scratched ones. I don't recognize the other set. It's not Dad's." He looked at Gabby. "What message are you getting?"

Gabby hesitated.

"It's okay," Jefferson said, resolved. "I want to know."

"That it wasn't your dad who gave it to her."

"You're suggesting an affair," Jefferson guessed. It wasn't a question.

Gabby nodded.

"Looking back at how everything went down with Dad leaving, the divorce and all, an affair makes sense."

Clint asked, "What are you going to do?"

"I doubt Mom will talk about it. She clammed up, other than complaining, when it came to Dad." Jefferson sighed. "There's no talking with her about him. I guess I'll call Dad. I want to know the truth."

Gabby nodded again. "That would be my plan if I were in your shoes."

"Excuse me, while I give him a call to set up a meeting." Jefferson turned and walked away, pulling his cell phone out of his pocket, leaving the three of them to chat without him.

Not hearing them anymore, he stopped and pushed a speed-dial button. Just a couple of rings and his dad answered.

"Hi, Dad."

"Well, this is a surprise. Not like you to call on the weekend. How was Clint's party?"

"Well attended. The senior Andersons asked about you."

"I'm sure you gave them my best."

"I did. Say, something came up this morning. Any chance I can come meet you this afternoon?"

"You're going to fly in?"

"Yes."

"Must be important."

"It is."

"Sure, I'll be here. Was having lunch with the guys, but I won't stay for the usual cribbage game. Call me when you get here, and I'll come pick you up."

Jefferson hung up and rejoined the other three. Clint and Gabby said their goodbyes, explaining they were on their way to Clint's dig.

"Showing off, again?" Jefferson teased.

"Always."

"But, I want to see it," Gabby exclaimed. "I've never been to a working dig before."

He and Madison waved as the car backed out of

the orchard, then drove away.

"Sorry about that," Jefferson said.

"No need to apologize. I can only imagine your surprise."

"That's putting it mildly. I hate to say it, but I'm flying to the coast now to see my dad."

"It makes perfect sense. We can finish our conversation later."

"No. Actually, we need to finish it now. The conversation we didn't have. I'm not going to beat around the bush. I suspect you're here for one of two reasons. Either to entice me to sell my property to your company or to get me to purchase the spray your company is promoting. You may not be aware of it, but their product is toxic to the land and to the trees. It may inhibit the bugs, but it's horrible for people and plants, eventually killing the latter, making the ground useless for farming. I don't think their intent is to grow pecans. More like to remove the trees and industrialize the land. If they can't buy it outright, then they'll destroy the crops until the farmers have no choice but to sell. I'll do everything in my power to fight them."

He'd been watching her as he spoke. First, she had paled, then her jaw had tightened ever so slightly. Yes, he was attracted to her, but he didn't like what she represented, or rather, who she represented. The bracelet, having brought up all kinds of feelings he thought he'd buried and was over with, reminded him how he had safeguarded his heart in the past. Being interested in Madison, he needed to get to know her over time and not be so infatuated with her simply because she was beautiful. And, smart.

"I don't understand," she responded. "What you're saying goes against everything the company has been telling me and showing me in their reports."

"They're lying to you. Are you telling me that you weren't supposed to offer to buy?"

"No, but—"

"That they don't want me to buy their product?"

"No, but—"

"Are you on the side of toxicity or not?" he asked.

"Of course, I'm against—"

"Then research the product you're selling. Outside research. Don't buy their sales pitch and then use it as your own. Find out what the science community has said about what they're doing."

He ran a hand through his hair. "I need to get going." He hesitated, then added, "As attracted as I am to you, I don't see this as going anywhere. I'm sorry." He knew he was being foolish breaking it off like this. He wanted to get to know her. He hated how his rational mind was getting in the way and taking over his—His what? His heart?

She stared at him, then said, "I am, too."

Jefferson was thankful that the walk back to her car was short. Neither said anything until at her car.

"Have a safe trip," she said.

"Thank you. You too."

Once she was inside, she waved and drove off.

He hated how he'd been short and interruptive, not giving her a chance to say much.

He had a reputation as an honest Senator and had been nicknamed Abe by a few of his oppositional peers. They had meant it as a dig. He took it as a compliment.

Jefferson sighed. Once upon a time, he would have let her explain. He didn't have the patience for explanations anymore. His mother had done that to him, always complaining about his father. Until the day he told her to stop, that he didn't want to hear it anymore. She had just glared at him, turned her back on him, and walked away. She didn't talk to him for several weeks. Long weeks. He had sworn then that he'd never do that again. Cut someone off like that, but now, he just had. To Madison, and it was killing him inside. Yet, he barely knew her. It was in wanting to know her that it was killing him, he admitted.

He drove to the house, locked it up, and drove out to the small airport, waving at the manager who sat on a bench under the office window, in the shade, enjoying the breeze.

*****

As Jefferson taxied the plane at the tiny Laurel Ridge airport, lining up for takeoff, he tried to steady his nerves. For the entire flight, he thought about past conversations, including the arguments his father and mother used to have before they split, then divorced. Recalling how his father, when he was leaving the house for the last time, had told him to take care of his mother, that she would need his help. At the time, Jefferson had thought his dad meant physical help. Now, he wondered if his dad had meant emotionally and psychologically, or something else entirely.

The evidence was in his pocket. He couldn't explain it away. His mother didn't have female best friends in the past, not that he remembered. Her best friends had been all men. She often said how she loathed chatting with women. How she hated their small talk about everything domestic. She enjoyed laughter. Men were funny. But when his father left, Jefferson had seen—really seen for the first time—just how lonely his mother really was. How she drank her loneliness away. It had been there all the time, her drinking, but he'd never seen it. He'd never thought anything of his mother and father's cocktails before dinner, one with dinner, and another afterward. Apparently, she covered it up with her constant conversation whenever he or his dad was in the room. He didn't recall her drinking a lot when they were all together. And, she was never drunk or tipsy. She must have been drinking secretly.

After landing on the small coastal Georgia island and before exiting the plane, Jefferson called his dad, telling him he had arrived. By the time he had the plane secured, his dad was there.

The drive to his dad's house was filled with the usual catching up. Jefferson felt guilty that he hadn't visited his dad since Christmas, yet at the same time, they didn't have the strongest of relationships. Not since the divorce, having always blamed his dad for the family's breakup. With his only sibling gone years ago, Jefferson had turned toward and depended on his friends. His mom had rarely been home. It helped that he and his friends all went off to college at the same time. And, Joe was like a brother to him. Closer than Jefferson had been with Jay.

As his dad drove into the driveway, Jefferson realized he'd been lost in his thoughts, hardly hearing what his father had just said.

Going into the house, the air-conditioning felt good.

"Can I get you something to drink?" his dad asked.

"Whatever you're having is fine."

"Two lemonades coming up. Let's talk out here in the back room. I enjoy watching the birds."

"Still have all those feeders?"

"Not like I used to but enough to be entertaining."

To Jefferson, the small yard looked like a bird's paradise. A bubbling water bath. Several feeders each holding a bounty of food. Several hummingbird feeders. His Dad was right. He didn't have near the feeders he used to have when Jefferson was growing up. Back then, half the yard belonged to the birds. His dad was an expert on them, knew when they migrated, when they returned, what they liked to eat best.

"So, what's troubling you, Son? It's not like you to just drop in like this."

Jefferson dug the bracelet out of his pocket and handed it to his dad.

"Oh." He handed it back to Jefferson. "Where'd you find it?"

"I didn't. Clint did. In what used to be Mom's car."

"Didn't William sell the Volkswagen soon after his dad gave it to him?"

"That's what we'd all been told. Turns out it's been in Whippoorwill Lake all this time."

The older man looked genuinely surprised. "So how did Clint— "

"He bought the car from William once it was pulled out of the lake. William didn't want the memories of it anymore."

"Oh."

"That doesn't explain the bracelet, though," Jefferson said. "What really happened? I remember that day I walked in on you and Mom arguing. When you threw this at her."

Jefferson waited, seeing different expressions flitter across his father's face.

His father sighed.

"You let me blame you for the divorce," Jefferson continued.

"I did."

"And, Mom let me."

The elder man nodded.

"Why?"

"Because she was ashamed. She wasn't willing to admit that she had screwed up."

"By screwing another man."

"Men."

Jefferson leaned back in his chair. He hadn't expected that.

"After your brother died, she changed. At first, she was depressed. I couldn't reach her. And then, when she became active again, it was as if she was trying to find happiness, but she was doing it in all the worst possible ways. She started drinking. Going to bars in other towns. Far enough away not to embarrass you, us, but not so far away that I didn't hear the rumors." He paused and stared out the window. "I had driven her car to the dealer that day for a tune-up and some detail work. When I went back a couple hours later, they gave me the bracelet, saying they'd found it in the backseat."

Jefferson wanted to laugh. The backseat of a Volkswagen Beetle is what teenagers did. Not a middle-aged woman. It would be funny if it weren't so sad.

"I was confronting her with it when you walked in. I'd already scratched out her initials, wanting to know whose was the other."

"And?"

"Someone from out of town. Someone who loved her, she said."

"What happened to him? I don't remember Mom dating anyone. Not long after you left, she stopped going out at all."

"He disappeared, just like the rest of them. He was married according to the rumors," he added. "She never told me directly."

Jefferson looked out the window, remembering. "She was there in the house with me physically, but you're right. She had changed. Dramatically. She rarely cooked, just sat at the table, staring out the window. It was like she was a zombie. Just work and coming home, sitting there, or sleeping. She slept a lot."

"I'm sorry I couldn't be there for you better, Son."

"Why did you let me blame you, though? All these years. Wasted."

"Not wasted. You idolized your mother. I couldn't ruin that relationship for you."

"But, she wasn't there for me either," Jefferson said. "She preferred the bottle to me. And, here I'd been thinking it was just a cocktail or two—one before dinner and one after." Now, that he thought about, he had always disappeared after dinner, leaving her alone. No telling how many drinks she'd have each night once he was gone.

"I'm sorry for that. How is she doing now?"

Jefferson shrugged. "Okay, I guess. She finally found a friend in Mrs. Miller."

"The art teacher?"

"Retired art teacher. Mom sold the business last year and the two of them are traveling like there's no tomorrow. At least, she's getting out of the house again and isn't drinking near as much. Well, at least not that I'm aware of."

"As long as she's happy again."

"I doubt she'll ever be as happy as she was when we were kids."

"Your brother's death really destroyed her."

"He always was her favorite."

Both men laughed, then began telling stories about the days when the two boys would fight, with Jay always saying, *Mom likes me best.* It was true. She couldn't have any more kids after his birth, so she had favored him.

"So, tell me, Dad. Why did you sell her car out from under her? Even though her name wasn't on the deed."

"I was angry. Did it in the heat of the moment, without thinking. It was a stupid thing to do. It doesn't pay to do anything in anger."

Jefferson nodded, thinking back through his life quickly, wondering if he'd ever been stupid like that.

After another hour of visiting, his dad drove him out to the airport. His dad circled the plane, admiring it.

"Let's take a trip down to the Keys sometime," Jefferson offered. "A fishing trip, just you and me."

"I'd like that," his father said.

Jefferson hugged him, glad he'd gotten this chance to make up with his father. "I'm sorry I blamed you all these years."

"Forgotten and forgiven."

*****

On the flight home, Jefferson reflected on the fact that his mother had lied to him, allowing him to live with that lie. For years.

He could acknowledge that his parents' lies—the unaired truths actually—and the lies told to him by the girls wanting to date him in high school because of his parents' wealthy status had contributed to his distaste for liars. And then in college, discovering a girl in the office that he'd been dating, exclusively so he thought, was actually dating another law student at the same time, hiding it from him.

That's when his first wall went up. He'd sworn off women, unwilling to be lied to ever again. But, he'd fallen a couple more times despites his wall—only to be lied to again. He knew he was painting most all females with a wide brush, but it was the only way he could protect his heart. Thank goodness for Annie who always told him the truth whether he liked hearing it or not.

This last year as Senator, he couldn't believe how many people tried to schmooze him, wanting his favor. He had wanted professionalism in politics, but instead, he felt as if he was in high school again. Today's women were just as aggressive as the men, some dogged and determined to get what they wanted, not caring whose feet they stepped on.

Which brought him back to Madison. She wasn't pushy like the rest of them. Her style was different. Softer. She had presented her facts, then listened to him as he told her what he knew. She wasn't defensive or hostile like he had expected or had continued to push. Instead, she had surprised him by backing off.

Suddenly, he envisioned her in his orchard again, remembering her laughter, and how green her eyes were against the lush shade of the pecan trees. His pulse quickened.

Seeing the landing strip up ahead, he put on his headphones. Once on the ground, he needed to call her to set up a meeting. He wanted to see her again. He was curious if she had accepted what he'd told her at face value, was ignoring it, or if she had done as he suggested—researched the product outside of the company's handouts they gave their employees. If nothing else, maybe he'd learn more about her, where she'd reveal something that would leave him less interested.

The last thing he needed as a state senator was to have a relationship or even a fling with a lobbyist. He knew senators who did; it didn't sit well with him at all. There were a lot of norms that he wanted to change, but it wasn't easy being a lone soldier in that fight.

It's why he was already thinking he wouldn't run again when his term ended. He could do more through grassroot activities here than he could as a senator. So far, he felt his time as one was insignificant. He was just another vote and a junior senator on any committee. Now that he'd seen the inner workings, he knew he didn't want to become a career politician.

Parking the plane and shutting it down, he was eager to get back to the orchard. To see a few friends. And, to talk with Madison.

*****

Day 5

When Jefferson entered the diner, he saw Madison in the corner, sipping on a soda, reading a book. She didn't look up until he sat down and lifted the book up to see what she was reading. "A Jesse Stone mystery by Robert Parker?"

"A favorite author."

"He's one of my favorites, too."

"One of?" she asked.

"James Patterson, Dan Brown, Sue Grafton, Lee Childs, Dan Brown—"

"David Baldacci, Gillian Flynn—" she added.

"Well, at least we have mysteries and thrillers in common," he said.

"Actually, more than you think."

"How, so?"

"You were right about my boss. Everything you said was true. He denied that the chemicals were harmful, but then when I showed him the report that he had tried to bury..."

"I'm sorry."

"That you were right? No, you're not. Sorry that I had been deceived—?"

"Of course, I'm sorry that this even happened to you. No one enjoys learning they've been lied to."

"I did a background check on my boss, too," she said.

"And?"

"I'd been blinded by his employment offer. I was so stupid, not doing the usual research before accepting his offer. My inner gut didn't raise any red flags at the time."

"Inner gut?"

"You don't have one?"

"Not that I've been aware of. Now you're sounding like Gabby."

"I like her. You have an inner gut instinct, too. You just don't recognize it for what it is. Mine has only ever reared up when I've been making a dangerous mistake."

"This one wasn't dangerous?"

"Not for me, not for the salary I was paid."

"Was paid? That's past tense."

"What did you find out about the bracelet?" she asked, ignoring his statement.

"It was Mom's and that she'd been having an affair. All this time, I had blamed Dad for the divorce when it was Mom who had—"

"I'm sorry."

"Thanks."

"What a sorry lot we are," she said.

"It's not the first time, and I doubt it'll be the last. As Senator, I expect people to lie. I hate that I'm becoming a cynic. More so than ever before. I want to think the best of people—"

"Until you find out differently." Madison raised her hand to someone and signaled for them to join them. Jefferson turned to see who it was.

Joe.

"Do you mind?" she asked, sliding her belongings over so Joe could join them. "I was asking for his advice after you left yesterday. He was concerned and wanted to join us."

Joe sat next to Madison, and the three of them made small talk before Connie came and took their orders.

Then, Joe turned to Madison and asked, "How'd it go?"

"Not well. My boss verified the Senator was right,

but that it wouldn't make any difference because he'd go around Jefferson. I said over my dead body."

Jefferson frowned. She was defending him? "What happened after that?"

"I quit."

"What?" Jefferson said. She had been lied to, but rather than letting it wound her, she had cut her losses and was moving on. Why had he let lies wound him to where he had built walls?

"Good girl," Joe said.

"And, I told him that if he was still going to peddle his product that I'd be going to the Pecan Growers Association myself with the report that provided the truth about his lies."

Joe responded, "And, he threatened to sue."

"Of course. I told him to go ahead, that I already had a lawyer. I hope you don't mind that I used your name."

"What was his reaction?" Jefferson asked. "Seeing how you threw a heavyweight into the ring."

"He turned green." She smiled. "I've never enjoyed a video call more. It was nice seeing him off balance. I doubt he'll move forward with his threats, but now, I need to find a job."

"Are you set on staying in Atlanta?" Joe asked.

"I—"

"Come work for me," Joe said. "I need a good paralegal now that Rebecca has decided to stay home with the baby."

"I'd love to," she replied. "When do you need me?"

"As soon as possible."

"Are they expecting you to stay for the mandatory two weeks?" Jefferson asked.

"Of course. But they're not getting it," she replied. "Since I kept nothing personal at the office, there's no reason for me to go back, but I need to pack up my apartment and give notice to the manager."

"I'll cover your expenses and any rent that's due because of the short notice," Joe said.

"But where will I—"

"Let me contact Eddie Taylor. She might know of a rental house or apartment. She's a realtor and was part of our gang in high school."

Madison frowned. "Gang?" She laughed. "Oh, you mean the mafia." She turned to Jefferson. "That's what he called you all, behind your backs."

Jefferson laughed. "Well, we were—are a family of sorts."

"Eddie was a powerful part of the group but pulled away after her parents died just before her senior year. Became more aloof, distancing herself from everything," Joe said.

"And, everyone," Jefferson added.

"Was she at Clint's party?"

"No, but if you're going to be working with me," Joe said, "You'll meet her soon enough as she uses my office for closings. Her office is too small."

"Do you need help moving?" Jefferson asked. Now that she had quit her job, he definitely wanted to get to know her better. "We could fly up tonight, where you could get a truck first thing in the morning. I can give you the names of a couple guys who are good at packing up quickly. Sons of another senator, a little-known side business they've got going. This is their slow time. I've got a meeting tomorrow afternoon, so I'll be flying to Atlanta tonight."

"I've got some friends who would help me pack. It won't take long, as I tend to be a minimalist. Between them and the boys, I could be on the road the day after tomorrow easily."

"Leave your car at my place," Joe said. "When you get back, we'll figure out how to get you unpacked."

*****

Once they left the diner, Jefferson followed her to Joe's house, where she left her car. Then, they went to his house where he picked up his bag, and then to the hotel where Madison had been staying.

She asked if he wanted to come up to her room while she packed or would he rather wait for her in the lobby.

"I'll come up." He preferred not to sit in the lobby where he'd be prey to some out-of-towner recognizing him and snapping pictures. As he walked with her to her room, he realized anyone could take a picture of them in the hall here, going to her room. He shook the image out of his head, though he did glance down the hall behind them to see if they were alone or not.

Alone.

Good.

Walking into the room ahead of him, she grabbed

her suitcase out of the closet, laid it on the bed, and zipped it open.

Jefferson walked over to the window, looking out. Whippoorwill Lake was a shining jewel in the distance. Lots of boats on the water. The fishing contest was still going on. He wondered if Cutter was on the lake and if he was catching anything beyond the car he had snagged the first day.

He turned and sat at the little round table in front of the window, watching her movements. Every time she bent over, her hair would tumble forward. She'd stand up straight, moving it back behind her ears with her fingers. Suddenly, he had an image of him doing that for her. Then kissing her.

He shifted in his seat, unable to deny that his attraction to her. He blew out the air in his lungs, wanting to blow away the image of him sweeping the suitcase off the bed, grabbing her around the waist, pulling her down onto the bed with him on top, kissing her. And more.

He jumped up and pivoted toward the window.

In the window's reflection, he saw her glancing at him, a frown on her face. She went back to her packing, turning away from him.

He breathed a silent sigh of relief. The last thing he wanted to do was lie, saying he had a cramp in his leg when the truth was about the tightening behind his zipper.

In short time, they were in the air leaving Laurel Ridge behind, mutually agreeing that there'd be no talk about business during the flight. Only topics of family, escapes while growing up, travels, favorite meals, and other favorites.

Once they landed in a small airport just a few miles outside of Atlanta and were on their way into the city, Jefferson asked if she'd like to stop somewhere for dinner.

"It's been a long day. Can I get a rain check?" she asked. "PJs and a bowl of cereal are on my immediate radar."

"A rain check it is," Jefferson responded, understanding. Even though he would have liked to continue their chat, it was time to retire. No telling how the evening would have ended had he stayed.

Parked in front of her rented townhouse, he looked through the passenger window at the building. "Nice place."

"Actually, it belongs to the company. They kept the rent decent and since it was close to the offices, I never moved."

"How long have you been with them?"

"Not long. About a year and a half." She sighed. "Long enough to know the ropes but not long enough to have learned everything."

"Sounds about right for most jobs. I'll be done with my meetings by mid-afternoon. How about I bring pizza over for dinner tomorrow and offer my services of lifting heavy boxes?"

Madison laughed, reaching for the door's handle. Opening the door, she said, "I'll take you up on that offer. Thanks for the flight and ride home, and for making my move to Laurel Ridge easier than I had expected."

"You're welcome. See you tomorrow." He watched as she walked up the walkway, her key ready to unlock the front door. Opening the door, she turned, and waved. He waved back, watching the door shut behind her, seeing her climb the stairs through the narrow window next to the door.

As he merged back onto highway traffic a few minutes later, he smiled, reflecting on yesterday and today's events, rethinking the multiple reactions he'd had when dealing with Madison. From immediate attraction, to putting on the brakes when finding she was a lobbyist, to relief that she had learned the truth about her employer, to finding himself attracted even more than he'd been initially. She was gorgeous with a killer body and had critical thinking skills that amazed even him. He could see why Joe wanted her as his paralegal.

He wanted to date her.

Immediately, he saw he'd just missed his exit.

She was going to be a distraction. He smiled, taking the next exit. *I can live with that.*

*****

Day 6

Madison opened her apartment door, having just let Jefferson in the entrance door with the buzzer. She squealed seeing the pizza box, pulling him inside quickly and shutting the door. "I'm starving!"

"Does that mean you're happy to see me?"

"Yes, but more so because of the pizza."

"I'm crestfallen."

She laughed.

He set the box on the kitchen's island, opening it while she grabbed two plates.

"Glasses?" he asked. "I brought some soda, too, remembering what you had ordered yesterday at the diner. I hope I got it right."

"You did." She was surprised he had remembered seeing her favorite brand in the two-liter bottle still in his hand. She couldn't recall a time when any man she had dated for a length of time remembered her favorite beverage. And, here she'd only known him for a day. "Behind you, to the right of the sink," she directed him.

He grabbed two tall glasses and with the soda went around the island, setting everything down before pouring.

Madison plated two slices of pizza on two plates and slid them across the countertop to where they'd be sitting.

"You sure the caffeine won't bother you?" he asked.

"No, I need the pick-me-up. It's been a hectic day." She sat down and picked up a slice, curling the long outside edges together before taking a bite. She moaned. "Oh, this is so good."

He paused, the moan capturing his attention. Absent-mindedly, he nodded, taking his first bite. He nodded again, wiping his mouth with the napkin she gave him. "The best in town. Were you able to accomplish much today?"

She nodded, swallowing. "The boys you

recommended are coming tomorrow. They're picking up the rental truck for me—one I reserved and paid for over the phone, so that made things easy. But then, I discovered my girlfriends were all busy, so I've been packing all day by myself. Got most of it done except for a few things here in the kitchen yet, and the bathroom. One of the few times I'm thankful I've not been a clotheshorse."

"What can I do to help?" He pulled the pizza box closer, grabbing another couple of slices. He offered her the box. "More?"

She took a piece, placing it next to the one still on her plate. "Thanks. If you could reach up into the closets and upper kitchen cupboards, that would save me having to get the stepstool out."

"Would be my pleasure."

*****

She glanced at him. She sensed he really meant it. Was it possible that she'd finally met a good guy?

In less than an hour later, she had boxed up all the upper-shelved dishes he had handed her, along with other belongings from the hall and bedroom closets. They were coming from the bedroom with boxes in hand when she walked into the living area and heard, "Hello, Darlin'."

She stumbled, and Jefferson bumped into her.

"What are you doing here?" she asked the man standing just inside her door.

She put her box on the kitchen island and turned to Jefferson, ignoring his frown. "I'm so sorry," she said to him. "I had no idea."

The man, who appeared to be their age and was nearly their height, walked to Jefferson, sticking out his hand. "I'm Paul Brown, and who might you be?"

"Paul Brown, the blogging art critic?" Jefferson asked, setting down the box he carried before turning toward Paul.

Madison could have sworn that the last thing Jefferson wanted to do was shake Paul's hand, but he did. She'd just witnessed Jefferson's transformation into a politician. And, if she didn't know any better, someone who'd just retreated behind a wall, as well.

"Oh, so you read my blogs?"

"No," Jefferson replied. "But, I know of them."

Madison coughed to hide her laugh. As a Southerner, even though Jefferson had spoken politely, she knew he was probably silently adding, *bless your heart.* Paul, being a Northerner and one she'd found highly ignorant of Southern traditions and history, was clueless that Jefferson wasn't paying him a compliment.

"Came down here to Atlanta from New York City just a couple of years ago, right?" Jefferson asked.

Paul's eyebrows shot up in surprise. "Few people know that. Who are you again? I like knowing my girlfriend's acquaintances."

Uh-oh. The look Jefferson shot her way was both of surprise and something else. She wanted to kill Paul.

She wasn't a bit surprised when Jefferson announced he needed to go—a forgotten meeting. Still in politician mode. He was good at it, too.

"I'll walk you out."

"No, need," he said, heading for the door.

She followed him. Grabbing the door handle, prepared to shut it after she left the apartment to keep Paul from listening, she said over her shoulder to Paul, "I'll be back in a minute."

She shut the door and followed Jefferson down the stairs and out the front door.

"Wait," she said.

Jefferson stopped and turned slightly. "For what? You didn't tell me you had a boyfriend."

"I don't. Never was, never will be."

"You dated him."

It wasn't a question.

Jefferson continued. "He walked in like he owned the place."

"Technically, he does."

"What? You were living together?"

"Remember how I told you the building was owned by the company?" When Jefferson didn't nod or say anything, she continued. "Well, they'd bought the building from him. There's only four units. He's the landlord slash manager of the place and employed by them, as well. Thankfully, in a different department," she added, talking more to herself than to him.

"And, you dated him."

"Two dates when I first moved in. A stupid mistake."

"And, he walks in like that all the time?"

"No! I always lock the door. I must not have this

time."

"He had a key in hand."

"He did? I swear, that's the first time he's done this. At least, that I know of."

Jefferson stared at her.

"It's a master key. I never gave him one." She sighed. "So glad I'll be gone by mid-morning tomorrow."

"Going to leave a forward address?"

"Only at the post office."

"Remember on the trip up here, how we talked about our past dating experiences? How come you never mentioned him?"

"He wasn't worth mentioning. I never lied to you about my dating past."

"No. Just omitted him."

"I didn't tell you *everyone* I've ever dated." She put her hands on her hips, not liking how this was becoming all her fault. "I'd daresay you left out a few girls yourself. It's called holding back information, like you've never done that in your career, Senator?"

"We're not talking about careers, here. We're talking about you and me."

"You and me, what? It's not like we're in a relationship."

In two steps, he was toe-to-toe with her, forcing her to look up.

"Do you have any idea how infuriating you are when you're fired up, those green eyes blazing?"

She opened her mouth in surprise.

*****

He couldn't stand it any longer. She'd taken him to an emotional cliff where he teetered on the backs of his heels only. One arm snaked around her waist, drawing her to him, the other around the back of her neck, supporting her as he kissed her with a sudden passion that ignited into a firestorm of longing. As her fingers wrapped around his biceps, she pulled him closer, returning his passion twofold. He groaned. Inhaling deeply, he softened his kiss, his lips lingering slightly before pulling away completely.

When she inhaled, her chest rose. He looked down. *You shouldn't have done that.* He looked up at the sky, hearing her breaths settling down with as much difficulty as his.

He stepped back. Different emotions crossed her face. He only hoped his expression was stoic, but by the way he was feeling, he doubted it.

"What was that?" she asked.

"I don't know." *Liar.* He did know. And, he couldn't stand here anymore. He hadn't fallen over the cliff like this in a long time. His emotions were spinning. Turning away from her, he took steps toward his car.

He knew he was being rude leaving abruptly like this, but he couldn't say anything right now. Not have a conversation anyway. Over his shoulder, he said, "I'll see you in Laurel Ridge."

He didn't look back. He didn't dare.

She shouted after him. "You can't hide from me forever!"

Without looking back, he waved. At least he was

acknowledging her, not ignoring her completely.

It was all he could do to get in the car and drive away. He knew if he looked back, he'd be turning the car around, racing toward her to pull her into his arms once again. He needed to get control of himself before he saw her again.

An apology was in order, but right now, he needed distance.

*****

Madison watched him escape into his car and drive off. His body language had changed drastically from when he had first arrived with pizza, to when Paul showed up, to kissing her, and then in leaving just now. He was so struggling with himself. When he wasn't in his head, he was relaxed and natural, but the minute he started thinking—and not feeling—he became more robot like. Hiding behind a wall.

She'd have to ask Joe if he'd seen that wall before, if Jefferson had been like that all his life, or was it a more recent thing?

Because of her?

Her dad always claimed that when her dander was up, she was as lethal as Sherman's armies marching through Georgia.

She recognized Jefferson's wall because she used to have one, too. Only now, whenever she put it up, she knew when it was rising and why.

She would be moving into his home turf. No way could he avoid her there. If there was one thing she knew about men, it was that they didn't like being ignored. That kiss told her exactly how he felt.

She grinned. His wall was coming down if she had anything to say about it.

And, that kiss. Wow. She wanted more.

Remembering that Paul was still in her apartment, she groaned.

No, he'd be gone in mere seconds. He was about to get a chewing out unlike anything she'd ever done before. She didn't owe him anything, especially an explanation of why she was boxing up her stuff or about Jefferson. Especially about Jefferson.

With the boys arriving first thing tomorrow, she planned on hitting the road well before noon, slipping her key and a formal note of departure under Paul's door.

*****

Back at his condo, Jefferson opened the curtains and looked out at the skyline, the high-rise buildings lighting up as darkness descended. At least here, he had distance. This home was about business, political business. He never brought dates here or held parties. He'd rent ballrooms or restaurants instead. He wanted no hint of a scandal associated with them.

He hung his head. He was miserable here. He wasn't cut out for this life. When he was in Atlanta, he missed his friends and rejoiced whenever any of them came up to visit. In fact, they were the only ones who'd stayed in his condo—when he was there or even when he wasn't. His home was theirs. Always had been. Even when they were teenagers. His parents had always welcomed the kids into their home until that weekend, when everything had fallen apart.

Standing in front of the room's expansive window, seeing his lone shadow reflected against the beautiful panorama before him, one he never tired of because of its beauty, he realized with more clarity than ever before just how alone he had become. Would it be more beautiful if he had someone to share it with?

Oh, sure, he had the gang back home. But, here? There was no one. He'd done that on purpose, and now he was wondering if that had been a mistake.

As much as he never tired of looking at this night vista, he realized he liked it because most of the city was hidden. In that second, he knew he'd hidden much of himself, as well. He didn't belong here.

He came here as a politician, wanting to make a difference. And, he had. In small ways, but none of those changes matched the dreams in his head.

He was glad to be going home tomorrow, but he wasn't looking forward to bumping into Madison. Not yet, anyway.

*****

Day 7

Madison walked out of the front door of the small house she was going to be renting for the next six months, with an option to buy. She was grateful that Joe, with Eddie's help, had found her a home in Laurel Ridge that she could move into immediately. Fortunately, the house had been empty, having just been remodeled to sell.

She needed to return the moving truck that was

now empty before the dealership closed. Maggie was picking her up there, and then, they'd go to Joe's house, so she could retrieve her car. Then, they planned to meet at the diner for supper. Afterward, she'd do a little grocery shopping, at least enough to get by for the next few days.

In the truck's cab, she inserted the key into the ignition and looked up, seeing a car driving by. Jefferson's? No, just someone who looked like him, driving a similar model.

All day, she'd been thinking about him, wondering where they stood. Now that she was living in his hometown, they'd be running into each other.

She sighed, chasing away wishful thoughts of a future relationship with him.

She had more than enough to do without complicating her life with a love interest right away. Unpacking, starting her new job tomorrow, getting to know the community and her neighbors, and finding someone who could mow her yard. The last thing she wanted to do was buy a mower and performing that chore in this heat. She was more than happy to support a local business that would take care of her lawn and yard.

*****

Day 8

Back in Laurel Ridge again and on the 18th hole of the local golf course, Jefferson slid his putter into his golf bag and stood there waiting for Joe to hole the ball with his last putt. He did and pulled the ball out with two fingers, and walked toward Jefferson and his own golf bag, grinning.

"Don't know why you're grinning," Jefferson said. "I beat you."

"Oh, I felt sorry for you. I let you win. By one stroke. Did you notice? I pretended to choke after you said you left Madison's place because of a boyfriend, one she doesn't have, I might add."

"You know that for a fact?"

"Fact."

"You choked?" Jefferson asked. "You never choke."

"Pretended to, but talk about being surprised. For such a smart guy, you sure are being stupid. Are you in love?"

Jefferson blinked, then bent down to retrieve his bag, glad he could hide his expression. Joe knew him too well. In love and in lust. Which was it? Rising, Jefferson stood the bag on its end and housed his putter, then unzipped a side pocket, sliding the ball inside.

Joe laughed. "You don't fool me. I've never known you to make assumptions like this. No, wait, yes you did, with what's her name, you know, the one who—"

"Okay, I'll admit it," Jefferson said. "I'm drawn to Madison unlike anyone I've ever known. She's gorgeous and smart. I feel stupid around her."

Joe shouldered his bag. "No doubt about it. You're in love."

Jefferson shouldered his bag, too, and they began

the walk up to the clubhouse where they'd have lunch. Joe had named it. "Okay, okay. I am. I don't know what to do. I'm over thirty, a business owner, a senator, and I'm so whipped up, I can't think straight."

"An apt description." Joe stopped and put out a hand to stop Jefferson, forcing him to look his way. "Let me offer you some free advice. Don't be your usual cynic self. Dump it. Be humble, instead."

"I am humble. I'm the humblest guy you know."

"One of, but with that wall you put up, no girl can get past it unless you're willing to be vulnerable, too. No one outside of our mafia knows how to break the wall down."

"Probably because you all know what caused it initially."

"You need it gone for good, which requires a wrecking ball."

"And, that ball's name is Madison, isn't it?"

Joe grinned, then nodded.

They both resumed their steps toward the clubhouse. Nearly there, Jefferson said, "I'm so screwed."

Joe laughed. "When it comes to women, we all are."

*****

Day 9

Jefferson entered the diner, looking for Cutter and Mason. Cutter had asked to meet with them. Seeing them in a booth, Jefferson joined them.

"How's it going?" Mason asked.

"I'm going to lose her," Cutter stated.

"You never had Annie in the first place," Jefferson said, then added, "Ever. One date isn't a relationship."

Cutter groaned, put his hands on either side of his forehead, elbows on the table, shaking his head. Then he sat up, one hand fisted, it coming down on the table. "No! We've had two dates this week. And, we kissed. It was amazing. I refuse to give up."

"Then tell her how you really feel," Mason said.

"We're honest with each other," he argued. "All the time."

"To a point," Jefferson said. "You need to be vulnerable. Expose yourself." Geesh, what was he saying? So good with the advice but unable to follow it himself. Hadn't Joe just told him the same thing yesterday?

"Not that way," Mason injected quickly.

"You can do this," Jefferson said. "You've always been helpful and protective—"

"Sometimes protective where it's not wanted—" Mason injected.

"—but that doesn't mean you stop," Jefferson continued. "It means you have to reveal your heart." He'd done it again. Saying it, but not living it. Sitting here with these two beloved friends, he finally saw in Cutter what others had been seeing in himself. His wall. His inability to express his deepest feelings, to open his heart.

Mason agreed.

Cutter nodded, acknowledging their advice.

After a few more rounds of bolstering each other

up in the ways of the heart and sharing their own struggles in the ways of love, Jefferson rose to leave with Mason.

As he stood at the counter, waiting to pay his bill, he glanced at his watch. Nine p.m. It wasn't too late. Heck, there was still daylight outside. He debated whether he should call Madison or just stop by unannounced. But, what could he tell her? They both had acknowledged they were attracted to each other. What did he want his next step to be?

His bill paid, he stepped outside and said goodnight to Mason.

His phone rang. Pulling it out of his pocket and reading the text, he groaned.

Madison would have to wait. He needed to return to Atlanta immediately. An important bill that he'd backed was coming up for debate and a vote. He'd be gone for a couple days now, for sure.

Maybe it was for the best. It'd give him time to think about his future and what he wanted for the next few years.

*****

Day 11

"You're fidgeting," Annie said, keeping her gaze on the road as she drove.

"You're right," Jefferson replied. He took a deep breath and let it out slowly. A trick he'd learned from his secretary when dealing with contrary senators and reporters. He'd been taking a lot of deep breaths in the last couple of days. "I just don't understand why Madison hasn't returned any of my calls."

Once he got to Atlanta and sat in the chamber, listening to various members debate the bill, he'd concluded that he was willing to risk everything—including his heart and was eager to get back to Laurel Ridge. He didn't want to be at odds with her anymore.

"Because maybe you weren't a priority?"

"Gee, thanks. I was prepared to search her out two days ago but got called up to Atlanta instead." He shook his head. "All the more reason for me to walk away when my term is done."

"Really? I thought you liked the job?"

"I did, at first. Could do without all these emergency meetings while we're on break, though."

Annie laughed.

"Not sure when I started losing interest in the job." No, he knew exactly when.

"Only recently, if you ask me. After you met Madison." Annie said, echoing his own thoughts.

"You been talking to Joe? Thanks for picking me up, by the way. Hope I didn't get you out of bed. Don't know why my car wouldn't start."

"Today, I happen to be in the rescuing business. First Cutter, and now you."

"What? Cutter? What happened?"

"I pulled him out of the lake. He's fine," she added, seeing he was about to interrupt her. "You two—you and Cutter—are my family. I can't stand to see you sabotaging yourself again. Madison's a wonderful woman and if you scare her off with that damn wall of yours. For such a smart man—"

Jefferson groaned. "You *have* been talking to Joe."

"You'll be seeing her tomorrow, I guess. At Joe's office. Congrats on the business you guys are starting."

"Think she'll talk to me?"

"How's that wall?"

"Gone, I hope."

"Guess you'll have to wait until tomorrow to find out," she said.

Annie pulled into his driveway. He opened the door to exit.

"Good luck with everything, tomorrow," she said. "With the signing *and* with Madison."

"Thanks. I need all the help I can get."

Inside, he made his way to the bedroom, wondering if Madison was angry with him. Would serve him right if she was. But, he had called. Several times. Each day.

*****

Day 12

Jefferson entered Joe's reception area. Maggie, on the phone, waved him into Joe's office where the door was open. He half expected to run into Madison and was glad he hadn't. At least, not yet.

Joe picked up the papers in front of him, gathering them together, standing them on end, thumping them on the desk to even the edges. "Judging by the anxiety on your face, I gather you and Madison haven't made peace yet."

"I had to go to Atlanta right after we had dinner the other day. I've tried calling several times, but she didn't pick up. Is she angry at me, do you know?"

"She lost her phone, got a new number. Thinks she lost it in the move, that it's in a box that hasn't been unpacked yet. Mad? I'm not telling."

"The longer we go without talking, the worse it feels."

"You never did like confrontations."

"Is that why I quit the debate team?"

"Probably. Could have fooled me, though, on your reasoning. I've never seen a better litigator. You helped me a lot while I was on the debate team in school, which you were determined not to rejoin. You're a natural, even if you didn't go into law. I have no doubt you could sell snow-making machines to Eskimos with no problem."

Jefferson laughed. "With today's changing weather and climate concerns, it wouldn't be that difficult."

"You know what I mean."

"I do and appreciate the support. But women—"

"A whole different approach needed?"

"Definitely."

"You, of all people, know better than to make assumptions."

"How did you kno—?"

"I overheard her talking to JoJo the other day. The three girls—JoJo, Charli, and Gabby—who are close friends have pulled her in to their circle."

Jefferson groaned. "We don't stand a chance."

"Like we ever had one to begin with?"

"How can I assume so easily with a woman, but I

don't do the same thing in the Senate?"

Joe laughed. "It's a mystery. If I had the answer and had my way, I'd be going to tonight's party knowing JoJo was going to be there—"

Rhett, Clint, and William entered Joe's office. Mason brought up the rear, joining the merriment of greetings.

Joe directed the guys into the conference room connected to his office. Papers in hand, he took an empty chair among them. "A great day for the community," he said. "With each of us having talked about Laurel Ridge going green the past couple years, our forming this solar and wind energy plant will be a godsend for the residents."

"Both in manufacturing and creating our own power plant," Clint said.

Rhett picked up a pen as Joe slid the papers toward him. "Not only for the jobs that'll be created but with the hope that we could sell power to other communities in the future." Rhett signed the papers and passed them to William.

"Have you been able to talk to Madison about the job?" William asked Joe.

"Not yet," Joe said. He turned to Jefferson. "Want the honors?"

Jefferson looked around. Lots of raised eyebrows. Obviously, they knew of the speed bump he'd crossed with Madison up in Atlanta. This would give him the opportunity he needed to start a discussion with her in a more personal manner after talking business. "Sure, why not?"

"She's going to be a cracker-jack manager," Mason said.

The energy in the room was charged with optimism and hope. For both him and their collaborative project.

The papers signed, the men stood as one, clapping each other on the back, then left.

Jefferson followed Joe back into his office.

"Something you should know," Joe said. He dropped the signed papers on his desk. "Her hide is just as thick as yours. You two are perfect for each other. If both of you can stop putting up those walls... Well, just go with what I'm telling you, not what you heard or what you think. Trust me."

Jefferson studied Joe for a second, then smiled. The joke between them was that if a lawyer ever said *trust me,* one shouldn't. But, when either of them said it to the other, it'd been code since college for rock-bottom truth that was more important than all the rhetoric and hubbub surrounding it. "Gotcha." He turned and headed for the library and assistants' offices on the other side of the building.

The minute Jefferson turned the corner, he saw Madison bent over Maggie's desk. He stopped, paused, then blew out the air he'd been holding. Stepping forward, he said, "Got a minute?"

Madison looked up, pressing a hand down her pencil skirt, surprise flittering across her face before the expression disappeared behind the business mask, now firmly in place. He'd caught her off guard. Her surprised look was so fleeting, had it not been for his experience in the Congressional halls, he would have missed it.

He followed her into her office, appreciating the view her skirt afforded. She turned around quickly, catching him in the act.

"Sorry," he said automatically. "No, actually, I'm not sorry. You and that skirt are unforgettable. You've got a killer bod and I want to get to know you better." *Chriminy, after not seeing her for days, that's the first thing out of your mouth? Who was he right now?*

She blinked, then frowned. "Are you kidding me? *That's* why you—"

He held up a hand. "No, I'm sorry. I don't know who that was. That wasn't my intention. My mouth just got away from me." He frowned. "For the first time ever. Gawd, I haven't apologized this much since I got caught putting gum in Annie's hair." He shrugged. "I used to sit behind her in grade school."

"What she'd do?"

"Beat me up. Made me apologize in front of everyone. Talk about feeling humiliated."

Madison laughed out loud.

"Any chance I get to beat you up?"

Oh, he so wanted to say yes. He grinned, but then got serious. "The reason I'm here is that a small group of us have formed a special company for projects—"

"In Laurel Ridge. Yes, I know all about it."

"What you don't know is that we want you to become the general contractor and manager of the company."

"Joe's idea?"

"Yes, but we're all in agreement."

"All of you? Even you?"

"Yes, even me. Regardless of what's going on between you and me—"

"What is going on between you and me?" Madison asked. As she spoke, she moved a few steps closer. Slowly. One step at a time.

Jefferson took in the full measure of her movements. She was coming on to him.

And, he liked it. He took a step toward her. "I think we should investigate this further by—"

"Madison," Maggie said from the doorway.

Jefferson froze. Both he and Madison turned their heads toward Maggie.

"Sorry," Maggie continued. "Paul Brown is on the phone."

"Take a message," Madison said. She looked at him, her gaze searching.

He'd already slipped his no-expression Senator face into place. He took a step back. Between the time Maggie had said *Paul Brown* and Madison turning her head back toward him, any warmth he'd been feeling vanished. His wall was in place. His internal voice was telling him to stay, but he couldn't. How many times did he have to be tested? *Until you stop giving in to your fear.*

Ignoring that internal voice, he said to Madison, "Joe will provide details about your new position. Congratulations." He turned and walked out of her office, saying bye to Maggie as he passed her.

As he walked away, he heard Maggie tell

Madison, "He said he needs to talk to you right away. It's an emergency," and then heard Madison both groan and sigh before Maggie shut Madison's door.

Even if Madison were to say she was done with Paul, he found it hard to believe. That she was going to take the call despite that groan and sigh told him everything he needed to know. He'd been a fool to think there might have been a chance. He was being an idiot in equal measure by leaving. He hated how he felt so conflicted about her.

*****

Day 13

After leaving Joe's office yesterday, Jefferson had come home, changed his clothes and was out on the tractor into the late evening hours, eating only afterward and falling into bed from pure exhaustion.

He had tried doing bookwork first thing this morning but found his heart wasn't in it. His mind either.

His only reprieve was to come out to the orchard again. There was something about the trees and lush green grass that was both soothing and healing. A place where'd he'd always been able to clear his head.

Maybe that was the problem.

He should be listening to his heart, but his head was getting in the way.

He had checked the first two trees where his manager had been experimenting with some holistic oils and spray, hoping they'd have better results against the black aphids and mites that had become problematic. Now, he moved further down the lane to check on the difference of untreated trees.

Once everything was checked, he'd go find Madison.

A car turned into the lane and stopped behind his car.

Madison.

He stood rooted in place like one of his trees, unable to move. He watched as she walked toward him. Wearing flats this time. Sensible shoes.

The reconnaissance he'd done on her while stuck at his desk in Atlanta the other day didn't reveal much.

He remembered Joe telling him that her father was a minister whose earnings were minimal, and that she had worked her way through college as a French tutor and writing coach—basically rewriting and polishing papers. Joe had added that she was a natural at keeping an author's voice, which made her so good as a paralegal. Her mother was French, and they spoke the language at home, along with Italian, which came from her grandmother. He could only imagine how interesting *that* dinner table was growing up.

If only that stupid neighbor of hers—*wait a minute, you fool! Are you really going to dig in your heels to lose your heart on that stance? Look at her, you dummy! She's gorgeous and brilliant. She's funny and everyone likes her. She could be the mother of your children! Are you really going to be that—*

"Hello, Jefferson."

"Hello."

"After you left yesterday, I decided our conversation wasn't finished."

"You're right. It wasn't. I need to apologize. Twice I've walked off, cutting you off, not responding. The other day in your office, I realized I was jealous." He was finally admitting the ugly truth.

"Jealous? Of Paul."

"Yeah, can you believe it?"

She smiled. "Actually, it's a natural response."

"Not for me."

"First time, huh?"

He nodded. "I don't like it."

"Nobody really does. You said something the first time I was in this orchard that I couldn't forget."

"I said a lot of things that day."

"Yes, but this one thing stuck."

"Had to have been something really stupid or incredibly smart."

"Neither. It was practical."

"Oh, that." *He had no idea what she was referring to.*

She grinned.

Damn, she knew he didn't know. He'd never be able to get anything past her.

"You want me to tell you what it was?" she asked.

The twinkle in her eye gave her away. She was flirting with him, teasing him. *Taunting.* All right, he'd play. He didn't answer. Just stared at her.

"Remember how you talked about the roots of these trees?" she continued.

"Of all trees."

"Yes,"

"I remember."

"About how they communicate?"

"Yes."

"How's this for communication?"

She took the two steps necessary to reach him, wrapped her arms around him, and kissed him, provoking him to participate.

Just as he started moving his arms around her, she pulled away, taking a step back.

Surprised, he said. "What was that?"

"Communication." She paused, letting that one word sink in. "Promise that you'll always come to me with any doubts, questions... or jealousies you might have. "

"Will there be many of those in the future?"

"Not from me, but I can't control what others say and do. Paul Brown *was* my landlord, nothing more."

"Anything else?"

"Not unless you've got something to confess."

"Oh, I've got something to confess, all right, but it'd be better if I showed you."

He closed the distance between them. She welcomed him with open arms, holding him as tightly as he held her, as they kissed among the tangled roots of the lush orchard that promised an equally lush relationship.

Reserved Yearnings #6

When the reserved Library Director William Stuart meets Charli Davidson, a motorcycling photojournalist, he's immediately attracted to her but something isn't right. Can Charli keep William from discovering the secret she's been hiding her entire life? Will he walk away from her once he discovers that dark secret?

12 years earlier – 2 nights after graduation, midnight

"I am in such trouble," William Stuart wailed.

His best friend, Joe Benton, pushed his outstretched hands down, "Quiet," he whispered loudly. "You want people hearing us?"

William stepped over to Joe, whispering like Joe. "There's no one around here. "Don't you think anyone seeing my car going into the lake, would have been here by now?"

Joe ran a hand through his hair but spoke softly and deliberately without excitement. "You would think. Just stop shouting. Even though it's midnight, someone could be walking around out here in the dark. Water carries sound."

William looked out at the lake, pain on his face. "What am I going to do? What a disaster."

"But not of your doing. It's not like you drove it

into the lake."

"This is so far worse than when we broke our arms. I wish this *had been* me. I'm not about to blame—"

"No, of course not, but she was responsible."

"I know, I know, but she made me promise not to tell. My parents are going to kill me."

"Don't tell them anything," Joe said.

William stared at Joe. "Not tell them? They're bloodhounds. You know how they are."

"Which is why you're going to tell them you sold it."

"They'll make me buy it back."

"They can't. It was a parking lot deal. You hated the color—"

"I did."

"A guy in a parking lot offered you money. You had the deed on you—"

"Still do. I didn't get it into the bank box on time like Dad wanted—"

"—I know," Joe said. "I was with you, remember? That's why this works."

William opened his mouth.

Joe held up his hand. "Listen for a minute. You sold it for cash. You signed the deed on the spot—"

William shook his head, dropping it down until his chin touched his chest.

"—You weren't thinking."

"They tell me that all the time."

"—You aren't defrauding anyone."

William lifted his head and stared at Joe. "Are you

nuts?"

Joe shrugged his shoulders. "You're not. Trust me. You're just not telling the truth."

"I'll be lying. The truth's going to get out somehow. I just know it."

"Give me a dollar."

"I know you don't drink, but are you drunk?"

Joe pushed William's shoulder. "Just give me a dollar. Do it."

Obediently, William dug his wallet out of his back pocket, opened it, and handed over a dollar.

Joe folded it and pushed it into his shirt pocket. "I'm your lawyer now. You just paid me a retainer and I can't say anything to anyone."

"You are drunk."

"This will work."

William laughed. "You're no lawyer."

"I'm going to be."

"You've been to college one year—"

"I'm telling you, this will work. Are you going to say anything?"

William shook his head. "You watch too much TV."

"No one else has to know what happened to—"

William finally got it. "We're protecting her."

"Yes."

William nodded his head. "Okay, I sold it. I'll take whatever punishment they dish out, but I won't tell them the truth."

"I doubt they'll buy you another car."

"They'll tell me to use the cash toward it."

"Which you can."

"What cash?"

"Oh, yeah, right. I got carried away with your story."

They both stood there thinking the plan through, looking out at the lake, lights from houses on the opposite shore a good half mile away glittering like stars on the lake's dark surface.

William looked at the ground, noticing the grass that had been crushed under the car's wheels. "Look," he said, pointing.

Joe's gaze following William's finger. "We'll have to camouflage the damage."

"How?"

"We'll drive around and make a few donut holes here."

"At least it'll be your car." He looked toward the lake. "Thank goodness she drove it in at the drop off."

"The deepest part of the lake."

"The only one who fishes in this corner is Cutter. At least according to him." William looked at Joe. "Think it's true, or do you think it's just another one of his stories?"

"Hard to tell." Joe shrugged. "Maybe we just watch for a while. Take note if anyone does fish here."

"And hope if Cutter does fish here and doesn't catch anything for a long time—if ever—we'll be old men or the lake has gone dry before anyone finds it," William said. The more he thought about their plan, the more he liked it and became more confident by the minute this would work. "How about we ask

Annie? She fishes the lake, too."

"Might as well say, *Hey, take a look over here,*" Joe said. No, let's pretend we want to start fishing—we want to try something new this summer. She wants to be a game warden like her dad. Ask them together, where's the worst place to fish and why and where's the best and why. They'll tell us."

"We aren't going to have to buy some rods now, are we?"

"Not if we can help it, but we might have to."

"No worms!" William said. "I refuse to kill worms."

"They don't get killed. They're just hooked."

"Alive!"

"Well, there is that."

William scrunched his face in disgust. "If we do have to go fishing, we just pretend. I don't want to have to touch a fish either."

"You're such a girl."

"All the girls I know bait their own hooks."

"Is that why you don't date?"

William glared at him. Joe knew how much he hated touching worms, snakes, and bugs.

Joe laughed. "Let's put down some tracks on the grass and get out of here."

"Keep your lights off."

Minutes later, they got out of Joe's car, checked to make sure that they'd kicked up enough grass by making tracks and circles. Kids being kids.

Satisfied, they left.

*****

12 Years Later - Day 1

Late morning, William rushed into Joe's office after his assistant, Maggie, said he was alone. William closed the door securely and started pacing behind the two chairs facing Joe's desk. "It's happened!" He clenched and unclenched his hands.

"Will you sit down?" Joe demanded. "What's happened?"

William sat down, but only on the edge of the seat, placing his hands on Joe's desk, leaning forward. "They found the car! This is my worst fear. Everyone's gonna know I lied. All my friends will wonder how else I've been lying. Trust is everything to me. I'm such a failure."

"You have two degrees. You're not a failure."

"It only means I did the time and my parents spent the money."

Joe shook his head. "You're not a failure. Do me a favor. Inhale deeply."

William did.

"Now let it out and sit back."

William did.

"Now tell me who *they* is. You said *they* found the car."

"Cutter. He hooked it first thing this morning. It's been hauled out of the lake. Annie called me earlier, wanted me to come look at it."

"And?"

"Clint heard about it and wants to buy it."

"Wait, back up," Joe said. "What did Annie say?"

"That they found the car. Wanted me to identify

that it was mine. I did."

Joe looked at him, like he was waiting for more.

"What?" William asked.

"No talk about getting a ticket? Officially, it polluted the lake."

William smiled. "That's the great part. No ticket, no penalty, nothing. Because it was so long ago, plus it's Annie."

Joe nodded. "Does she know the whole story? Does she consider you to be a consummate liar now?"

"Well, no. At first, I told her I had made a wrong turn, a stupid mistake. She point-blank stared at me and said, 'you don't make mistakes.'"

"She's right. You don't make mistakes."

"But, when I do—"

"You screw up royally."

"She just stared at me. Waiting. I felt so guilty."

"You told her everything, didn't you?"

William nodded. "I didn't have a choice."

"In truth, you didn't. You did the right thing."

"So, what happens now?" William asked. He waited, watching his best friend mull the problem over.

"I want to see the report. See how it got written up."

"She contacted her boss while I was there, telling him without naming names that a stupid wrong turn got made, that I told my parents I had sold it rather than it being in the lake. No ticket's being issued. He's racking it up to a boy's reckless action followed by a stupid decision. She knows who drove it in, but her boss doesn't."

"You got lucky."

"We got lucky," William added. "You were—are my lawyer, after all."

"She said at least there wasn't any insurance fraud because I had said I had sold it. I asked if she can keep the report confidential until we can get ahold of— "

"I'll start the search, so we can give her a heads up."

"Annie is giving us a week or so before the report is actually filed in public records."

"So, everything will be in the report."

William nodded.

"What's this about Clint wanting to buy it?"

William told him the figure Clint had offered.

"Do you want to sell it?"

"Heck, yes! I want to be rid of the thing. Can you—?"

"Yes, I'll make the arrangements. Draw up the Bill of Sale, contact the state for a replacement deed. Wait, do you still have the deed?"

"Are you serious? I burned it!"

Joe frowned, starring at him. "No, you didn't. You save everything. Find it."

"Okay. Get this. Clint wants to restore it. Even asked if I knew of anyone who does car restorations. I don't, do you?"

"No. You do realize people are going to be asking why you drove it into the lake, don't you?"

William looked up at the ceiling, his thoughts

scrambling over various scenarios.

"If you don't want to go with the story that you missed a turn and felt stupid having done *that*, then tell them the truth," Joe said.

"That I drove it in because I hated the color?"

"For now," Joe said.

"That sounds so stupid."

"But so like you back then. Eventually, you're going to tell them the real story, so what you tell them now doesn't really matter."

William nodded. "I want to be sure she's okay with the whole story coming out."

"Let me contact Clint. Consider the car sold."

"I do. He's already decided to get it towed. Knowing Clint, it'll be in his garage by nightfall."

*****

Day 3

William stood in Clint's backyard in a tight circle of friends, all here to help celebrate his parents' fiftieth wedding anniversary. Earlier, he'd seen Clint and his parents go up in the hot-air balloon Clint had arranged as a special gift.

Before the party, having found the deed, he and Clint had gone to the county's State of Georgia office and transferred the title from his name to Clint's.

Now Clint was telling their friends about his plans to restore the car to its former glory. William laughed with the rest of them as they ribbed William for his bad driving skills.

Looking past their circle, William saw the balloonist—a tiny attractive woman with long hair—walk their way. Behind Clint now, she touched his arm.

Clint turned and brightened seeing her. He put a hand on her back and brought her into the circle. "Guys, this is Gabriella—"

"Gabby," she interrupted.

"—Gabby King. The balloonist. A skilled aviator."

Jefferson said, "Probably the first time Clint's been up in the air since his first plane ride with me." Laughter followed.

Clint turned to her and said, "I'm not a fan of flying. That's Jefferson Jackson, one of our state senators. He's a pilot, too. Took me up for my first and last tiny plane ride."

"Seriously? You don't enjoy flying?" Gabby said. "I wouldn't have known that. You looked quite comfortable up in the balloon earlier with your parents. But you know, that wasn't flying. It was floating." Gabby shook Jefferson's hand.

William stuck out his hand. "Hi. I'm William Stuart—"

"Books. You work with books."

"Clint told you that."

"No, I didn't," Clint responded. To Gabby, he said, "He's our library director." To William, "She's a medium."

"Some would say psychic," she replied, "but I'm a medium, too."

"There's a difference?" a woman asked. "I'm Annie Martin."

"She's a game warden," Clint said.

Gabby shook Annie's hand, then tilted her head. "I'm sorry about your recent loss."

A somber silence settled over everyone. They had all supported Annie when she'd buried her parents recently.

"Thank you," Annie said. "I lost them—"

"To a tragic accident. Again, I'm so sorry." Explaining, Gabby said, "I pick up on vibrations, which include thoughts, events, and such. I'm also an intuitive. Seems less intrusive than psychic. And no, Clint didn't tell me anything about any of you. Other than I'd be taking his parents up in the balloon."

A sudden flash of inspiration struck William. "Say, the library is looking for a presenter in two days. The one I had cancelled. I'd love to hear more about your abilities. I'm sure others would, too." He hoped she'd say yes. He was always looking for new speakers, new topics. She would draw a decent crowd.

Gabby smiled. "I wish I could, but I'll be heading north. Two festivals back-to-back." She turned to Clint. "I need to hit the road. Thank you so much for your invitation. Your parents are a cute couple." To everyone else, she said, "It was nice meeting y'all."

Clint and Gabby left the group and started walking up to the main house, where he'd left her payment.

William turned to Annie. "How about you?" he asked. "Would you be open to doing a presentation?"

Annie laughed. "I must be your go-to person. I've already done one this year. How about Cutter?"

He looked over at Cutter who was in another group, holding out his hands, which meant he was telling fish stories. Tall tales, no doubt. "Don't give him any ideas," William responded.

They all laughed.

He turned to Eddie. "How about you? Your presentations about buying and selling, what to look for, and how to spruce up a home before putting it on the market are always a good topic. Maybe a way to get new clients?" he proposed. She perked up at his last remark.

"Let me check my calendar and get back to you," she said.

"Okay. I'll give you a call tomorrow. It's good seeing you again. It's been too long." He wished he could remove the sad look that still lingered on her face when she thought no one was looking. She'd had a tough life, but she'd only made it tougher by distancing herself from them for almost a decade. It *was* good seeing her here at the party.

"Blame Jefferson," she said. "He's looking to grow the orchard, wanting to buy property next to it that's for sale, and asked if I'd meet him here."

The party had been winding down while they'd been talking. Their immediate friends were headed for the party after-party in Clint's kitchen. "Come join us," William said to Eddie. "It's been a while."

Eddie shook her head. "I appreciate the invite, but I'm headed home. Tomorrow's a big day."

"Going to the auction—the Brown house?"

She nodded. "You know everything, don't you?"

William laughed. "I try." He moved closer so he could whisper. "I can't help it that all the spinsters love gossiping with me when they return their books or seek me out to help them find more." He gave her a hug and walked her to her car before joining the others in Clint's kitchen.

*****

Day 4

Past noon and glad to escape the heat outside, William slid into the diner's booth, noticing Eddie was in the next booth and facing him. While he hadn't been at the Brown auction across the street and down a couple blocks, he'd seen people walking away from the area, so the auction had obviously ended.

Eddie looked up and noticed him. She waved. He waved back. Then her attention was focused on someone moving across the diner toward them. Surprise crossed her face as Rhett sat opposite of him. She was staring at the back of Rhett's head.

He'd seen that look before. One of attraction. Rhett was a good-looking dude—he got the girls' attention wherever he went.

Even though Rhett wasn't a newcomer having been here for about five years now, William figured Rhett and Eddie didn't know each other, given they didn't acknowledge each other.

All his classmates were pairing up, and they were making him feel... What was the word he was looking for? Left behind? Mason had moved back and was chasing after Shelley. Finally. Cutter was chasing after Annie. As always. And, with Clint meeting Gabby last night, it was easy to see sparks flying between them, despite Gabby having talked about leaving.

Even reticent Jefferson was getting snagged by Madison—a good friend that he'd gotten to know through Joe. William had been hearing from Maggie, Joe's assistant, how Madison was chasing Jefferson in the senate halls up in Atlanta. He suspected Madison had wrangled an invite to the party last night with an agenda to finally meet Jefferson in home territory. Not that William didn't mind seeing Madison again. He'd always felt connected to her simply because they thought alike. Like Jefferson. William liked Madison. Jefferson would like her too, if he'd stop standing behind the walls he'd built up over the years.

Rhett was talking about Clint's car. "Clint must have figured since I restore houses as a hobby, I might know of someone."

"You don't?" William asked.

"No, do you?"

William shook his head. "But Eddie might." He indicated Eddie behind them. Together he and Rhett turned toward Eddie, asking if she might know of someone. She and Rhett talked for a couple minutes more before she said she'd check her resources, ending the conversation.

Watching Rhett and Eddie chat, William realized that sometimes that's all it took. An impromptu meeting.

Heck, he had them all the time at the library, but nothing ever turned into that spark he was looking for. The problem was he knew everyone in town, who had a library card and who didn't.

He was resigned to becoming Laurel Ridge's resident male spinster. Was there such a word? Bachelor didn't fit, never did. Spinster was a better description.

*****

Later, through his office glass windows, William saw Clint and Gabby approach his office. He waved, got up, and welcomed them in.

The two men greeted each other with familiarity and teasing, as usual.

William turned to Gabby and said, "It's nice to finally see Clint with a woman."

Gabby looked at Clint, who held up his hands as if to push William's words back.

"You've got a vindictive streak," Clint said to William.

William winked at Gabby. "And, you already know, he likes to play in the dirt, right?"

She laughed. "Yes, I know. You must think he's vulnerable since I'm someone outside your normal circle of co-workers and classmates."

"And, he's not?" he asked.

"No more than you are."

"Touché," William said.

"Nothing gets past her," Clint added. Immediately, he changed the subject. "About the car you sold me—"

"No returns," William said quickly. "Sold as is." He'd hated it from the beginning, with its color and tiny size, and wanted nothing to do with it now. No way did he want it returned.

Clint laughed. "No problem in that regard. We're trying to locate the owner of this." He pulled the bracelet out of his pocket and handed the bracelet to William. "Do you recognize it?"

William turned it around in hand, looking at it from every angle. "No. Can't say I've ever seen it."

"There was another owner before you," Gabby said. "They were the first owners."

He and Clint looked at her in surprise.

"That's amazing," William said, feeling goosebumps up and down his spine. "You've made me a believer. What other skills do you have? Can you talk to the dead?"

"Yes, or rather they talk to me."

"Regarding the previous owner..." Clint interrupted.

William dragged his gaze away from Gabby and looked at Clint with raised eyebrows. William knew Clint was asking permission to tell Gabby. They, as Jefferson's friends, had vowed not to talk about Jefferson's parents or anything to do with the family's split back then, and they still protected that information from anyone asking because of Jefferson's position and the media that had sniffed around here after Jefferson had announced he was running for a Senate seat.

William believed Gabby wouldn't talk to anyone, so knowing the bracelet's owner could be a help to her, to them.

William gave a slight nod to Clint, then said, "Dad bought the car from the Jacksons. It was Jefferson's mom who drove it the most."

"She was a pretty woman, much admired, a businesswoman?" Gabby asked.

William nodded. "She and her husband founded and owned the jewelry store in town. She was fantastic in designing one-of-a-kind pieces. He did the bookkeeping, along with taking care of the long-standing family business—the pecan orchard that Jefferson owns and manages now." William frowned then. "If memory serves me right, they got divorced not long after we all graduated. Though Jefferson and Joe had already been in college a year as they had graduated a year ahead of the rest of us. I remember Jefferson being closed-mouth when his parents divorced. He wouldn't talk about it, at all. Not even when we asked questions."

Clint nodded at William's memory. "We were all surprised. No one had any idea that there'd been trouble in the Jackson household."

William frowned. He turned to Clint. "Wasn't there talk about the store getting sold back then?"

"I remember vague rumors," Clint answered. To Gabby, he said, "But, she kept it, selling it just recently having retired early."

"Jefferson never wanted to talk about that either," William added. "I got the impression he didn't know a whole lot, and what he did know he wasn't sharing. He was furious at his father after he left."

"Think he'd be open to talking to us?" Gabby asked.

"Don't see why not," Clint answered. "It's been a decade. If not, he'll tell you no. He's a straight shooter that way."

"A characteristic most senators don't have these days," William said. "Wait a minute," he added, looking at Gabby. "I thought you were leaving last night."

"I'm waiting for a part so I can repair my truck. I'll be leaving later today. Tonight more likely."

"Maybe I'll see you later, then," William said.

Clint and Gabby left to go talk with Jefferson. William watched them leave. Clint, nearly a full head taller than Gabby, had his head turned toward her as she talked, her hands moving as she spoke. Not paying attention to where he was going, he nearly ran into a column. Clint was already in trouble. He was going to struggle when Gabby left.

William envied Clint that.

*****

Late afternoon, William left the library and headed to Clint's house.

Pulling into the driveway and toward the back of the property, the big garage bay doors were all open with cars parked in front. A strong indication that his former car was the subject of everyone's interest.

He didn't like how all the memories of owning it had been dredged up along with the car, but he wasn't here for the car but for his relationship with these men.

Clint, Rhett, and Cutter had their backs to him and were circled around the VW's back end, the hood popped open, the engine exposed.

In the middle bay sat Clint's Mustang convertible, a much beloved car and one Clint drove only in the fall and spring when the weather was cooler and the sun not so hot.

The first bay held Gabby's massive white truck with the hood open. Good, she was still here. He wanted to chat with her more.

As he parked behind her truck, she poked her head out from around the front of the truck. She must have been up on a ladder considering how high she was from the ground. Clint, Rhett, and Cutter remained circled around the VW. They must not have heard him drive up.

He got out of his car, took a step, then heard a motor at the end of the driveway. He turned to look. A motorcycle approached and parked next to his car.

A slim-figured driver dressed in a leather jacket and leather chaps, despite the heat, dismounted and took off the helmet, shaking out thick wavy hair that extended just past her shoulders.

Seeing him, she said, "I'm not sure I'm at the right place. Is Gabby King here?"

All he could do was nod. She was a vision and had the most beautiful bronze-colored eyes he'd ever seen. Was this what it felt like to be hit over the head by Cupid? To fall in love at first sight, knowing nothing about her?

He hoped so. But then, any woman who could power a big motorcycle like the one she was riding had his attention.

Immediately, she removed the chaps and jacket, laying them on the bike. And then, she took a pair of glasses out of her shirt pocket. She smiled brightly and he heard Gabby's laugh from behind him. Gabby passed him and embraced the stranger.

He heard the guys laughing, too. He turned his head their way. Elbowing each other, they walked toward him. They'd been watching him checking out the newcomer. Immediately, he knew this was going to be awkward. Joe always said everyone could easily read him. Suddenly, he wished a hole would open, where he could drop out of sight.

Gabby turned and said, "William, this is Charli. Charli, William is the library director and first owner of the car JoJo is going to repair."

"I'm not really the first owner of the car," William said, sticking out his hand. "Dad bought it used. And, I'm glad Clint was able to hire JoJo. I heard she's an excellent mechanic, along with being your friend."

The minute Charli turned her gaze on him, he was glad a hole hadn't opened up after all. He took her offered hand, his gaze never leaving hers. Her eyes widened at his touch. She'd felt it too. He could only hope no one else had noticed.

He glanced at Gabby. Internally, he groaned. Yup, she'd noticed. He doubted she ever missed a thing.

As the other three men joined their circle, Gabby told Charli, "You're about to meet the gang. Well, part of them anyway. Guys, this is Charli Davidson. We're sisters of different parents, best friends."

Clint held out his hand to Charli. "I'm Clint Anderson."

Charli said, "Gabby was here for your parents."

"Yes," Clint said. "This is Rhett Renoux, a firefighter. He's a relative newcomer having moved here five years ago. He restores houses, too. And, this is Cutter Logan." He turned to Cutter. "What is it you do again?"

The guys laughed.

Cutter ignored Clint. "I'm the one who fished that yellow creature out of the lake." He thumbed the VW.

Charli looked around. "And, Jefferson Jackson—?"

"The most famous of us all," Cutter injected. "He's not here, right now."

"He's on Jekyll Island, with his father," Gabby said. Seeing the guys exchange puzzled looks, she added for their benefit, "Clint and I saw him earlier."

"I was hoping to meet him," Charli said. "My publisher-slash-editor said he was from around this area. It's a pleasure to meet y'all."

"Are you a writer?" Cutter asked.

Charli answered, "A travel blogger. My editor wants me to interview the Senator."

"Not to cut this party short, but do you have the part?" Gabby asked Charli.

"Aren't you the eager beaver," Charli quipped.

"Only because of the next event," Gabby replied. "I'm hoping I can get out of here tonight. Not that I really *want* to leave," she injected quickly.

William saw Gabby sneak a peek at Clint, who smiled hearing her say she didn't really want to leave.

Gabby followed Charli to her cycle's saddlebags where she pulled out a box.

Gabby grabbed it. "Let's get this thing installed."

While Gabby and Charli left their circle, going to

the front of the truck and climbing up either side of the step stool to work on installing it, William went with the guys to inspect the Bug. He hadn't seen it when it came out of the lake and now, he was curious about the extent of the damage.

He found it hard to believe that after more than ten years in the water that it could be restored.

*****

When Charli had driven up, the last thing she had expected to find was a crowd. She hated crowds. Always had. Her brother, Bradley, loved them. As he should considering he was the true heir of their family's legacy of owning a baseball club and the apple of their parents' eye. For her, half a dozen people constituted a crowd.

Several vehicles were parked in front of a massive garage with several bay doors—all quite large and open.

To adjust her thoughts and acclimate herself that she'd be facing a crowd of people, she had turned slightly from a man standing there and who immediately made her nervous as she concentrated on removing her riding gear that protected her from the bugs that slammed into her when on the road. The leather provided added protection should she ever go down, especially in a skid. Normally, she'd be wearing leather leggings, but in this heat, the chaps were all she could endure.

Why had she felt like she was undressing in front of a stranger?

Originally, she had figured she'd be dropping off

the part and be back on the road right away, but Gabby had pulled her up on the footstool, stating she needed help. The only time Gabby ever needed help was loading or unloading that bulky balloon. Helpless, Gabby was not.

No, something else was afoot here.

As Gabby took the part out of the box, Charli peeked over at the men standing around the tiny car. William was half a head taller and was getting ribbed. While she couldn't hear their words, their laughter filled the garage, and even though William's expression was chagrined, he was laughing, too.

His laugh made her smile internally. Such a happy sound. William looked her way and smiled. She couldn't resist. She smiled back. Looking back at the motor, she noticed Gabby had seen the exchange.

"Don't even think it," Charli said. "I'm not looking for a partner."

"I don't need to think anything," Gabby said. "The magic has already begun on its own. I don't need to do anything either. You're staying the night. Besides, didn't you say you wanted to meet Jefferson?"

She hated when Gabby ordered her around like that. Charli scrunched her lips together. Anyone looking would think that she was puckering up for a kiss. At least, that's what Bradley always told her.

"Okay, you win. I'll stay the night because I want to meet the Senator *and* interview him."

Charli kept watching the boys and listening to Gabby's chatter. She felt less nervous but recognized she was still wearing her bubble-like plastic suit, the one that made her feel safe. With anyone around, she always felt the need to protect herself. With this many people, normally she'd be on guard, but she was tired of it all. She wanted it to stop.

Even Gabby, with her intuitive skills, still didn't know of Charli's handicap. She'd kept the truth hidden for so long, it was no wonder that she'd been living in a bubble, frequently wearing her invisible suit, her protective armor.

Of your own making.

*****

An hour and a half later, with the truck repaired, packed, and parked outside the diner, William, Clint, Gabby, and Charli sat in a booth inside. They had convinced Gabby she couldn't leave on an empty stomach.

While the diner had been full when they had first arrived, the crowd had now thinned.

Connie had just collected their plates. "One check or four?"

"One," Gabby said, quickly.

Immediately, the other three protested. Connie turned and moved away.

"No discussion," Gabby said. "Clint, I appreciate you putting me up. Otherwise, I would have had a hotel bill." She turned to Charli. "You saved me time by bringing the part to me." To William. "You helped me...well, with nothing actually, but I appreciated the company."

They all laughed.

Connie returned, handed Gabby the bill, and

refilled their water glasses.

"You really don't have to leave tonight," Clint said. "Stay the night and then leave first thing in the morning."

Charli replied. "Gabby doesn't like waiting. She's a night owl."

Gabby nodded. "Besides, there's less traffic on the highway at night and it's cooler out."

"Where are you going this time?" William asked.

"I'm doing tarot readings at a summer festival in north Georgia tomorrow—another reason for leaving tonight, and right after, I'm heading to Nashville for a weekend balloon festival."

"So, you're not going home at all?" Clint asked.

"I would have, had I left here right after the party, but it worked out okay. Thanks for letting me wash my clothes earlier today and insisting I eat now before hitting the road. I probably wouldn't have stopped."

Clint smiled. "My pleasure, though it's not like I did anything."

Gabby smiled back. "You did more than you know." She slung her purse on her shoulder and made a move to scoot out of the booth. "I've got to hit the road."

They all moved out of the booth. William knew by the looks Clint and Gabby kept exchanging that they weren't done. He knew Clint. When he wanted something, he went after it. Kind of like himself. Look at how often he did the opposite of what his parents had wanted. Not to mention owning a car for a decade that'd been resting at the bottom of a lake.

And now, he wanted to get to know Charli better, so he was happy learning she was spending the night.

To Gabby, Clint said, "Even though I came with William, can you drop me off at my house on your way out of town?"

William started to protest.

Clint stopped him. "No sense in your driving all the way back out to my place with your condo just a couple blocks away. Nice getting to know you, Charli. Maybe you'll stick around a few days and put Laurel Ridge on someone's map."

Charli laughed. Once the guys had discovered she was a photojournalist, they had regaled her with all kinds of area sights to see, to photograph for her travel blog. She had to admit that some of them sounded interesting. And, it wasn't like she was on any timetable. In fact, she knew her publisher was looking for some new features from this area of Georgia. She was enjoying the small-town comradery of the diner and the people she'd met so far. No reason why she couldn't take advantage of her time here, but it was late and she wasn't sure about accommodations.

Clint and Gabby said their goodbyes, and Charli gave Gabby a hug. Gabby whispered, "Stick around for a few days. Keep JoJo and William company." She pulled away, smiling, before Charli could respond.

As Clint and Gabby drove off, Charli turned to William. "Any chance I can find a room locally?"

"Not within a 30-mile radius. Not with the fishing contest going on."

"Oh."

"But, there's a condo next to mine that's available. You could stay there. An elderly couple who are up north for the summer live there during the winter months. They have a cottage on Lake Michigan and family up there. It wouldn't be the first time someone has used their condo while they're gone. I have their permission to rent it out or have friends—like you—stay there."

"Oh, I couldn't—"

"Yes, you could and you will. Seriously, you're not inconveniencing anyone. Besides..." He hesitated. "I... I'd like to get to know you better."

Charli looked at him. He had hesitated, almost nervously. It was kind of cute.

"I have no girlfriend. In case that was a problem or you were wondering."

Charli nodded. She'd been about to say she hadn't given it a thought whether he had a girlfriend or not, but that would have been a lie. She had wondered. Not that she could get involved, but it would be nice to have some friendly unattached company for a few days. She was tired of the many men who claimed they were interested in her when really they were more interested in her family's fortune. Little did they know her family didn't come from great wealth. "That would be nice... to stay, I mean. I was thinking about some of the historic spots mentioned, and the plantations—"

"Rhett is an expert on the plantations around here with his remodeling skills. Even though I've lived here all my life, I've never been to Pebble Hill. It was a thriving plantation built in the early 1800s and was a working plantation until the owner's death in the late 1900s. She wanted it turned into a museum. Located in Thomasville, it's a small community nearby. Everyone who visits, raves about it. You'd be my excuse to finally see it. Geesh, I sound like a tour guide."

She smiled. "I like it. That can be one trip. How far away is Plains, Jimmy Carter's hometown?"

"Just an hour or so. Any other place else in particular?"

"You pick."

William grinned. "Okay. In the meantime, let's get you into the condo. It's probably been a long day for you."

Charli rode with William the few blocks it took until he turned into the drive of an enormous building that said *Laurel Ridge Library* on the outside. He drove around to the back. She'd left her motorcycle in Clint's garage, riding with Gabby to the diner earlier.

She peered out the window at the building as they drove around it. It didn't look like a typical library. The exterior looked more like an old-time factory, just resurfaced and refreshed. Modernized.

As they circled around back, William reached up to the visor. A garage door started opening, the door sliding upward. He drove inside the garage, parked, and turned off the motor.

Next to them was an older convertible in mint

condition.

As he got out and circled around to her side, she looked at him. "Yours?"

William nodded. "My fair-weather car."

"Didn't Clint call his convertible that, too?" She grabbed her bag and exited.

"He did. We both have one."

"Same with my motorcycle."

"What do you drive during the winter?" he asked. He pushed a button on a nearby post and the garage door slid down and lights came on.

"A truck I've had since graduation," she said, following his lead to the back wall, where there were two elevators. He pushed the down button. "A hand-me-down from my brother, actually. Mom and Dad wanted to get me something new and I wouldn't hear of it. They bought me one anyway. I traded it in for the cycle I drive now. They weren't happy that I did it behind their backs."

"I can imagine. I kind of did the same thing. If you want, tomorrow we can bring your cycle over here, and you can park it here in their garage since it's empty. There's two spaces allotted for each condo."

Charli noticed he changed the subject quickly from his parents to the condo. Obviously, something he didn't want to talk about. She'd have ample opportunity to learn more about how he didn't do what his parents wanted later. She suspected there were stories to hear. She wondered how similar his stories would be to hers.

"How long has this older couple been married?"

"More than 50 years, I'm sure. Probably more like 60. High school sweethearts, married right out of school and they're in their 80s now."

"Interesting."

"How so?"

"It's rare to see a couple together for decades. Especially if they're happy. Are they?"

"I would say so."

"Do they have children?"

"No, they don't."

"Probably why they've been happy together."

"Why do you say that?"

Charli shrugged. "I've seen too many kids be a disappointment to their parents. Mine were with me at times."

"Mine, too."

The elevator door on the left opened and they got in. As the door closed, he pushed the up button. "I probably went overboard having two elevators, but they're more private this way—we each get our own—and should one break down, at least the other works."

"And the stairway?"

"Emergencies mostly. Though I do use it for exercise now and then."

Upstairs, he led her to the door to the left of the elevator.

"This is my place. I need to get the keys." He held the door open. "Come on in."

Charli went in and found an open floor plan with enormous windows ahead of her let in lots of light.

She frowned. "Wait a minute. How many floors is the library?"

"Just the one downstairs. It's enormous, about 5,000 square feet."

"So, each apartment is 2,500 square feet?"

"A little less. Plenty big. Three bedrooms, two baths, and a great room with a kitchen and dining combo. The condo across the hall duplicates this floor plan but in reverse."

William grabbed the keys and led Charli into the condo next door. Inside, he took a key off his ring and handed it to her. "While you're here, so you can come and go as you please."

She set it on the counter. Going to the refrigerator, she opened its door. "Groceries?"

"You're welcome to help yourself to whatever you find, though if you use up any of the condiments, the request is that you replace it. Anything fresh, I might have it or you can buy at the grocery store. The Piggly Wiggly is out by the highway."

"Milk?"

"I just bought a gallon. I can share it with you."

She smiled. "Great. My choice of drink at night."

Surprised, Clint said, "Really? Mine, too. How about beer?"

"Only with hot dogs and hamburgs. Grilled."

"That's where we differ." When Charli raised her eyebrows in question, he said. "Beer and pizza."

"So, I'm interested in seeing this planation you were talking about earlier. Where is it again?"

"Thomasville. South of here. I'll call ahead and see

if you can take pictures. Hearing that you're a photojournalist, I doubt it'll be a problem."

After their plans were made and learning that the sheets on all the beds were clean, Clint said goodnight and left.

Charli closed the door behind him. Coming down as a favor for Gabby, she had already planned to stop at Plains on her way home and stay in a motel somewhere along the way. So why hadn't she done that?

"Okay, okay," she said aloud. "I was curious, okay? Besides, he's cute. And kind." She shook her head. "You need to stop talking out loud to yourself, girlfriend. The neighbor next door will think you're nuts. Well, you are," she mumbled, grabbing her bag, setting it down by the hallway.

*****

At his door, William paused, looked at his neighbor's door, and cocked his head. Was she talking to herself? Opening his door, he laughed. They apparently had that in common, too. He shut his door and walked a few steps, saying, "This could get interesting."

Just then, he heard a knock at the door.

He opened it to see Charli there holding a glass. "Milk, please?"

William laughed, took her glass, and moved into the kitchen area, getting his own glass down from the cupboard, setting them both down on the counter. From the fridge, he retrieved the new gallon of milk, opened it, and poured milk into the two glasses. He slid hers toward her and she picked it up.

"Thank you." She turned and moved toward the door as he recapped the milk container and opened the fridge door.

"Oh, and interesting?" she said from the door, her face turned toward him. She grinned. "Very." The door closed behind her.

William stood there at the open fridge door, milk still in his hand. A big grin spread across his face.

*****

Day 5

Early the next morning, Charli and William pulled up next to a white van parked at Clint's garage, where only one bay door was open. The signage on the truck said *Wheeler Mechanics,* and Clint and a woman stood near the van. They turned as one, watching as William parked the car.

"JoJo's arrived!" Charli exclaimed, jumping out of the car the minute William turned off the ignition.

Charli rushed up to JoJo, hugging her tight. "I've missed you!"

JoJo laughed. "You've only been gone a day!"

Charli turned and looked back, signaling for William to come closer. Her arm still around JoJo's waist, Charli introduced JoJo to William, "JoJo, Gabby, and I are best friends." To JoJo, Charli said, "The VW was originally William's car back in high school and was fished out of the lake by another one of their friends, Cutter. Clint here then purchased the car from William and there's a mystery surrounding a bracelet that Gabby found under the front seat, which didn't belong to William but to Jefferson Jackson's mom who was the original owner of the car."

"Wow, you really know how to tell a story in just a few words," William said. "When you said photojournalist, I figured your job was mostly photos."

Clint explained further, "Gabby did a reading on the bracelet, where we—Gabby, Jefferson, and I—discovered a possible long-ago love affair involving Jefferson's mother. William's parents bought the car for him as a graduation present. Back then, he told us he sold it, yet somehow it mysteriously ended up in the lake, with him still as its owner, and he's not talking."

William added, "My lips are sealed." He ran two fingers, tightly together across his mouth. "At least for now," he added. "I'm hoping I can soon reveal the mystery behind the car's late-night swim."

"I know of Senator Jackson," JoJo said. "He was a big help to some friends of mine who were trying to get some country land rezoned so they could build a pee-wee race track for kids. Folks wanting to learn how to race properly. Plus, it was a school of sorts for car maintenance. He did a marvelous job helping with that project."

To JoJo, Clint said, "And now, I'm hoping you'll be able to restore this engine so I can drive the car this summer. How long will it take to fix it?"

"A few days, if all goes well."

William said, "Clint, I think JoJo should go on a blind date with Joe." To JoJo, he said, "He's a friend of ours, my best friend actually, plus a former classmate of ours. He's a good guy." The more he thought about it, the more he liked his idea. The minute he'd met JoJo, he was reminded of Joe. Her temperament was like his.

At first Clint looked surprised but then he grinned. "He'll kill us, "but it's a great idea!"

Charli added, "I haven't met Joe yet, but he's a lawyer.

William's lawyer, so he can't be all bad. Plus, I've seen a picture. He's kind of cute."

"As lawyers go?" JoJo asked. Clint and William both laughed.

"He's a good guy," Clint said.

Now that he thought about it, William realized how strange it was for him to match anyone up, let alone his best buddy. Chalk it up to being struck by lightning seeing Charli for the first time. He hadn't felt the same since.

The more Clint, Charli, and he talked about it, the more William knew Joe and JoJo would be a good match.

Only after Charli joined in, agreeing Joe would be a good match, did JoJo finally agree to their plan. "Okay," she said. "You've convinced me. In the meantime, where can I stay? All the hotels are booked around here."

"With me," Charli said.

"With Charli," William said at the same time.

"Problem solved," Clint announced. "Though when Charli leaves, you can stay in the cottage here. Closer to the job."

"Let me go get settled and change my clothes," JoJo said to Clint. "Then, I'll be back to start work on the car."

"William drove me over so I could take my bike over to the condo. You can follow us," Charlie said.

*****

As William unlocked his condo door, Charli and JoJo disappeared into his neighbor's condo across the hall. He could hear them laughing. He smiled. JoJo was going to be a good companion for Joe.

Going inside the condo, he grabbed the folder on his counter. Today was a working day. As he walked out of his condo, locking it, he could hear them still laughing. He smiled, enjoying the sound. Way different from the quiet he usually heard from the condo when his neighbors were home.

*****

Day 6

The next morning, Charli and William met up at the pre-arranged time, taking William's car. He had convinced her they'd appreciate the air-conditioning on the trip home. She had to agree that it would be more fun to wear shorts and leave the chaps and leather jacket behind.

Traveling south on the two-lane U.S. 319 highway, a sign by the road announced they had arrived. All Charli could see were trees and a long driveway.

"Get ready," William said.

As they drove down the tree-lined driveway, from her side, she caught a glimpse of a large house and lots of other buildings.

"It was a family-owned working plantation, with the last owner having no children. She turned the property over to the state with the provision that it become a historical museum. Everything is as she left it. All seventy-plus acres."

William parked the car, and they walked over to a small building labeled as the Visitor's Center. They were given a map and literature, which Charli tucked into a pocket. They met the manager who walked with them to the house, where she told the docents that Charli was there to take pictures for publication.

Charli discovered that because she was taking pictures, they'd be alone in the house for an hour before the usual tours, which all started on the hour.

For that first hour, she and William went through the house on their own, where she went inside the barricading ropes to take various shots. Then, once she was done, they went back to where the docent was stationed and asked for the usual tour. As they went through the house, the docent told them about the 16 bedrooms, 19 bathrooms, and 24 fireplaces, along with the history, and stories about the 1825 first house replaced in 1850, and its restoration in 1914, along with its owners through time.

"All of this information is in the literature we were given, right?" she asked William.

He nodded. "Most of it."

She noticed he frowned, so she said, "I'll look at it all more closely later when I'm writing the article." She turned, pretending genuine interest in what the docent was now saying, hoping he was accepting her explanation. She shouldn't have asked the question in the first place.

At the end of the tour, the docent said they were invited to walk the grounds and learn about the other buildings.

"How many are there?" she asked.

"More than you would think," William answered for the docent. As they walked back into the humid outdoors, William handed her the map and said, "Where do you want to start?"

She handed it right back and said, "Surprise me. "Lead the way." She'd learned early on that most men enjoyed taking charge. She was willing to give up leader control if it kept her disability hidden.

They spent several more hours touring the grounds. At one point, William suggested they play twenty questions. "A quick way to learn about each other."

"I hate small talk. Okay, I'll go first. Why did you turn an old, unused factory into a library?"

"To make a long story short, the library was going to lose their building after their long-term lease agreement ended. At the time, the library was an old house rented by the city. There was talk for several years prior to the lease expiration how the library had outgrown the space but had nowhere to go now that the city had decided to sell the building at a tremendous profit. At that time, I had graduated with a bachelor degree in architecture, was starting my master's degree with an additional master's degree in library science, much to my parents' dismay— "

"What did they want you to do?"

"Stay with architecture, get a job in the field. It was during my early studies, I realized being an architect wasn't everything I wanted in a career, and I'd have to move to a larger city, something I didn't want to do."

"So, how were you able to redo the factory if you weren't licensed?"

"Oh, I finished the degree, but I'm not a licensed architect. I made a deal with the city."

"Deal?"

"I would create the drawings for no money, which they could get approved by someone licensed."

"No money? Wasn't that a lot of work?"

"It was, but I enjoyed it. I like to draw and provide plans for friends now and then. Helping them save money and where I get to enjoy the skill."

"What did you get in return?"

"Because I bought the building cheap, thanks to Eddie's help, I gave the city a hundred-year lease with rent basically the same as before and their proportional share of the monthly expenses: maintenance, heat, water, and so forth, as do the renting couple and I. Plus I pay the bulk of the mortgage and taxes, since I own the building. Everyone wins."

"Interesting, but that doesn't explain how you became the library's director."

"That's more than one question."

"I think it was several," she said, laughing. "You let me get away with it."

"Only because you let me talk. Are you avoiding wanting to share?"

Charli felt her face warming at his having hit her bullseye, but she wasn't about to tell him that. She could only hope he didn't notice her blush. "Don't leave me in suspense!" she said, hoping to change the conversation. "How did you become the director?"

"The usual way. I applied for the job once I had my degree. My timing was perfect in that the director at the time was retiring, and there weren't many applicants. Not everyone wants to live in a small town."

"I imagine there's both advantages and

disadvantages."

"There are, but it's my turn, now," he said. "How did you become a photojournalist?"

"My brother was into photography when we were in school. He liked to take pictures of the weirdest stuff. Closeups. He made it into an art form. Mom and Dad had gotten him a small camera for a birthday. As his interest grew, he wanted a bigger camera with more bells and whistles. He got it for another birthday and he gave me his old one. I was taking pictures of kids at school and different events. A teacher saw some of them and asked if I'd be interested in becoming the yearbook photographer."

"You said yes."

"I did. During summer vacations, as we traveled as a family, I started taking photos of different vacation spots. Because of social media, a travel magazine editor contacted me, wanting to pay me for my pictures."

"And, you said yes," William said, smiling. "What a great story."

Charli laughed. "I've been with that editor ever since. Over a decade now. I don't need a computer. I dictate text into my phone and send it with the photos, and they put the articles together. I'm not burdened with all the technical stuff or the writing itself."

They entered the log cabin school, which was the property's oldest building, William read from the brochure. It consisted of two rooms: a classroom and a playroom. The last owner of the big house had it made for her children's education during the winter months.

William walked up to the chalkboard and turned around. "I enjoyed school. Probably because of all the friends I made and had. Not sure I could handle being one of two students like these kids. How about you?"

Charli went to the expanse of windows and looked out at the grounds. She shrugged. "I hated school. I preferred spending my time out in nature. Climbing trees, watching insects. The teachers were okay. Just not my thing." She didn't want to reveal her struggles and the constant fear that she'd be found out.

She'd worked hard to improve her memory. Thankfully, her brother had kept her secret and helped her communicate with the editor. Had it not been for her brother, she wouldn't have this freedom today. She owed him everything.

"Did you have many girlfriends?" he asked.

"Not really. I didn't belong. I was too different." She was. She didn't like following the ever-changing trends. She liked her clothes comfortable and with pockets. She loved nature too much, hated malls and the idea of shopping. It was always a fight with her mother to shop for school clothes every year, but Charli indulged her, simply to make her happy.

"Did you date much?" William asked.

"Not really."

"Me neither."

"Were you scared?"

"Of course. You women are intimidating!"

Charli laughed.

William smiled. "I like your laugh."

His compliment caught her off guard. She smiled back. When was the last time a man had paid her a compliment about her? Not her work, but her personally? Besides family members, that is? She couldn't remember.

She studied him while he studied the grounds' map again.

For the first time in a long time, she was looking at a man differently, not as someone to be endured or avoided.

She enjoyed being with him.

*****

By the time they returned to Laurel Ridge, it was late and they both agreed dinner at the diner sounded like a good idea. The rush was over, with just a few patrons.

Connie told them to sit where they wanted as she went to fill water glasses.

Charli led them to a nearby empty booth. Seated, William grabbed the menus from behind the napkin holder and handed her one.

She immediately slid hers back behind the napkins, saying, "Surprise me."

"Seriously?"

Connie set their water glasses down in front of them. "Ready to order?"

"What's the special tonight?" William asked.

"Meatloaf, mashed potatoes, and green beans."

"We'll take two orders." He slid his menu behind the napkins, too. "Sound okay?"

"Definitely," she replied. "It's hard to ruin meatloaf."

"Especially here."

"Is this home away from home?"

"For good quality food, it is for me."

"You don't cook?" she asked.

"As little as possible."

Charli laughed. "I'm the same way."

"I tend to not follow recipes exactly. I'd rather try a little of this and a lot of that, but it rarely works. How about you? Are you a follow-the-directions girl or do you prefer my method?"

"Neither. I just don't have time. I prefer frozen dinners."

"Ouch. No special diner in Atlanta?"

"Not really. I'm on the road more often than not." Charli sat back as Connie placed their food in front of them. Connie left and Charli picked up her fork.

William's gaze was focused on his plate as he loaded his fork, giving her a minute to study him straight on, rather than from the side as had been her view of him most of today. He had a small smattering of freckles under his eyes and across his nose. Her brother had the same kind of freckles and he used to let her count them.

Even if her brother was mad at her for something, he could never deny her the count, something she'd done while learning to count. As they grew up and there were those times when he was mad, all she had to do was ask if she could count his freckles. He'd always laugh.

Her brother was her best friend. Even their parents had no idea how close they were and how much Charli kept from them. As kids, she and Bradley had vowed to take each other's secrets to the grave.

And then, she became best friends with Gabby and JoJo. They were unlike the girls in school. Like her, they were different from other girls. The three of them had that in common, along with their unusual careers and interests, but even her two best friends didn't know this last secret she kept from them.

"You're not eating," William said. "Isn't it any good?"

She forked the meatloaf and took a bite. "Mmmm, it's good. Really, really good. Best meatloaf ever."

"So, what had you not concentrating on your food, then?"

"Something you said this afternoon. About not dating much."

"You said the same thing."

"Yes, but we're talking about you right now," she stated.

He studied her for a long fifteen seconds, looked at his plate, and then at her again. "This is something I've never shared with anyone. Why I'm sharing it with you now... I'm not sure what it is about you. You've got a vulnerability that reminds me of myself."

Charli felt goosebumps crawling on her arms, a shiver going down her spine. She couldn't look away.

For a long half minute, they just stared at each other as if reading into each other's soul. She was the first to look away, stabbing at her food.

"There was a psychology class where we learned about Maslow's Hierarchy," he said.

"I remember seeing that chart. From my brother's class, part of his homework. I asked him about it." She'd seen the chart, but her brother had to explain it to her. "The bottom level was about air, water, shelter, basic needs essentially."

"And, the second level was about safety and security, but it was the third level that interested me the most."

Charli frowned. "Because it was about love and belonging?"

William nodded. "Because of the questions the professor asked."

His gaze was intense. She couldn't look away.

"He asked the class 'What won't you do for love?'"

"And you said...?"

"I remember other kids saying things like they wouldn't stop drinking beer, or give up shopping, but then one kid said he wouldn't move out of his town because he didn't want to be separated from his family. Then, a girl said she wouldn't marry someone who couldn't share her life. She said she'd watched her mother give up her interests, taking part in all of her dad's instead. She said it was heart-breaking watching her mother give up everything she loved and her dad never even noticing." He paused. "It was a big moment. I could see everyone was thinking differently about it."

"And you said...?" she repeated.

"That I wouldn't settle, that I want to love everything about a partner, not just some things. All the things. Truthfully, I never gave anyone a chance because I didn't want my education to be interrupted. Getting my master's degree in library science was too important."

"You didn't want to settle for a career, which is why you went against your parents?"

William smiled at her. "Exactly." He cocked his head. He was analyzing, thinking.

Her brother always cocked his head, too, like that. Instead of becoming a real estate tycoon or landlord, as she called it, he got a degree in art and art history and now worked at a big art museum restoring famous paintings.

"You're the first to really get that," he said. "How is that?"

She shrugged, looking down at her plate, pushing meatloaf into the mashed potatoes. She looked up, then back at the plate again. He was studying her. Waiting. He wanted to hear her answer. That made him sexy as hell. Goosebumps traveled up and down her arms again.

She shrugged again, smiled, and gazed at him again. "I guess because I'm not about to settle either, not for my career anyway. I didn't go boy crazy like everyone else around me, and then when I started traveling after graduation, I was too focused. Never in one place for long. Never long enough to get to know anyone."

"You don't do the bar scene either?"

"No. Last thing I want to deal with is someone's drinking problem."

William laughed. "My words coming out of your mouth!"

Charli grinned and added, "I guess I was too scared to let myself fall in love. It seemed like everyone else's dream."

What she couldn't tell him was that she wouldn't be anyone else's dream either. She was too broken. Damaged goods. Incomplete.

"What did you think you wanted to do when growing up?" he asked.

"That's easy. Racing and riding bikes with big motors." She laughed. "Dad hated that I became the roadster and that my brother preferred working with art. Mom was happy. It kept her son safe."

"She doesn't worry about your safety?"

"Not really. She's seen me fall out of trees, bucked off horses, skinning my knees. She knows I can take care of myself, though in the beginning she hated that I didn't like pretty dresses and cooking, but she got over it. Bradley, my brother, loves to cook. And, he actually likes to shop. He takes his girlfriend shopping with him all the time. They're a perfect match."

"So, tell me, what won't you do for love?"

Charli's heart began to race. She couldn't look at him, so she pretended to concentrate on the last few bites of her food, but she wasn't hungry anymore. She chewed on her lip instead.

William's hand reached over and covered her left hand. "It's okay," he said, softly. "You don't have to tell me... Even though I did share something with you."

She couldn't help herself. She looked up. Damn, she wished she hadn't. His eyes were soft, his face open. He was genuinely interested. When had she ever felt that?

And then, his eyes softened more. "I've never said this out loud to anyone that I won't settle... I've seen too many people settle. It doesn't work out well." He paused. "You're not going to share?" His eyebrows went up in questioning exaggeration.

She couldn't help herself. She laughed. "That's not fair."

"Nothing's fair in love and war."

"But this isn't war..." No, no way. She looked at her food again, the plate vanishing in her gaze. This wasn't love she was feeling. That was ridiculous. They'd only known each other a couple days, not even that.

She could tell him. Speak her truth about relationships. It wasn't like she was ever going to see him again.

Nervously, she blew out a breath of air. "I've seen too many couples bickering, trying to change each other. I don't want a relationship if it means we'll always be at odds with each other. I guess that's why I've never allowed myself to get close to anyone."

That was only part of the truth. She continued,

determined to be fully honest. "Besides, I'm broken. I've always been broken. So broken that no one would want me." She pulled her hand out from under his and put both her hands in her lap, clasping them, wringing them, where he couldn't see what she was doing. She peeked a glance at him.

He slid his hand back to his side of the table, sat back, grabbed his glass, and drank until the water was gone, setting the glass back down.

He took a deep breath and let it out with a sigh. "I understand what you're saying—"

"You can't."

"Yes, I can, because I've felt the same way. There's so much of me I've kept hidden. I've got a huge secret that I've kept for over a decade. I want to tell, but the biggest part of the story isn't my tell."

Charli gazed at him. He wasn't just mouthing the words. She could see the pain in his eyes. Something was troubling him. Something deep.

"Only two people know the full truth. Me and my lawyer. Well, actually there's a third, but I can't talk about that."

For a moment, neither of them spoke.

"Yet," William finally added.

Charli didn't know what to say.

Suddenly, Connie was there, collecting their plates. "Dessert?"

"A hot fudge sundae," they both said at the same time. They looked at each other with surprise.

"Nuts?" Connie asked.

"No," they both said at the same time.

Connie's gaze went from one to the other. "Whipped cream?"

"Yes," they both said at the same time.

"One scoop or two?"

"Two," they both said.

"Okay, then. Two hot fudge sundaes with two scoops, whipped cream, and no nuts coming up. Oh, how about—?"

"Yes, I want the cherry," Charli said.

Connie looked at William, questioning him with merely her expression.

"She can have mine," he said.

"You got it." Connie spun around and walked away.

"You don't like cherries?" Charli asked.

"I love them. You deserve an extra one."

Charli felt as if her heart had just melted, just as much as the hot fudge would melt the ice cream. "Ice cream fixes everything."

William grinned. "That's what I've said, too."

"No, you haven't."

"Yes, I have. Ask any of my friends. Ask Connie."

She stared at him. Was he daring her? Chewing on the corner of her mouth, she contemplated if he was toying with her or not.

Minutes later, Connie returned, setting their sundaes in front of them. "Look good?" she asked.

"Yup," Charli said. "Ice cream fixes everything."

She handed them each another napkin. "That's what William always says, too." She started refilling their glasses with water.

Charli replied, "He told you to say that."

"How could he have?" Connie said, finished with their glasses. "He's been sitting here with you." She turned and walked away.

William picked up his long-handled sundae spoon, shaking it at her. "Told you." He laughed and dug into the sundae.

Charli sat there, stupefied. What was happening? *Nothing,* she told herself. *Just a meal where someone else likes the same things as you do. But, exactly the same? Yes. Pure coincidence.*

"Aren't you going to eat? William asked.

Charli picked up one of the cherries, put it in her mouth, bit down so the cherry sat behind her teeth, then pulled on the stem, the cherry staying behind. She did the same with the second cherry. "Yes, I am." She replied. "Thanks for the cherry."

"You're welcome."

She dug into her sundae. For a couple minutes, she just enjoyed the sweet treat, glancing at him as he glanced at her, his gaze flirty.

She was in a happy place. A rare occurrence because she wasn't on her bike or looking through her camera lens.

William finally broke the silence. "Favorite movie?"

"That's a hard one."

"Okay, favorite movie genre?"

"Sci-Fi."

"As in..."

"Outer space, like *The Martian, Avatar, Apollo 13,*

Arrival, Alien—"

"—and monsters?"

"No, aliens," she said, smiling. "Okay, monsters in space. What's your favorite genre?"

"You'll laugh."

"No, I promise, I won't."

"Chick flicks."

Charli laughed.

"You promised."

"I did. Sorry. But, seriously? Chick flicks? Like what?"

"Jane Austen's stories, the *Jane Austen Book Club, Little Women, The Age of Adaline, Sweet Home Alabama, How to Lose a Guy in 10 Days*—now that one's way too accurate—

Charli giggled.

"—Bridget Jones, The Proposal—"

"That one is classic."

"I know, right?"

"Favorite tree," she asked.

"That's easy, live oaks—"

"Me, too! I love the—"

"Hanging moss," they said together.

"Favorite book?" he asked.

She tipped her sundae glass to scoop up the last of the melted ice cream. Concentrating on the bottom of her glass, she said, "I'm on the road so much, I don't read much. Been a while since I had a favorite."

"What was it back then?"

Charli swallowed, then grabbed her napkin, wiping her mouth, pretending it was covered with hot fudge.

Connie stopped with their check, asking if they wanted anything more. Charli shook her head, still wiping her mouth. William grabbed the bill and Connie left.

"I was going to get that," Charli said, putting the napkin down. "My treat for being my guide today."

"You can treat me tomorrow as your guide."

She slid out of the seat and stood as he did, too. "Where are we going tomorrow?"

"To Plains and Andersonville."

"Deal," she said. She led the way to the register and stood aside while he paid, thankful that the conversation had changed when it did.

If they had sat there any longer, she might have spilled her guts and then he'd know exactly why she claimed to be broken. No one would want her with her handicap. She didn't know if she could be in a relationship with someone who had her flaw.

Just then, he turned, pocketed his wallet, and smiled at her. She couldn't help but smile back. She liked him. Really, really liked him. That made him dangerous. To her heart.

"Ready?"

She nodded. She didn't think she could talk right now. She turned. He reached beyond her to push on the door. Even in the simplest things, he was taking care of her. It'd been like that all day. She wasn't used to it. She had always opened her own doors.

At his car, he opened her door. She slid in and he shut it. Her gaze followed him as he walked around the front of the car.

Be careful, she told herself. T*oo late.*

There was no way she could back out now, saying she had to leave. It would be awkward and sudden. She'd just have to be more careful than usual and not let her guard down. Unfortunately, though, William was fun and it was too easy to let go.

Maybe she could call her brother later tonight. Maybe he could tell her what to do.

*****

Day 7

Up early, Charli and William stopped at the diner for a big breakfast.

"I'll have a farmer's omelet," Charli said, "But, with no tomato. I'm allergic to them."

"I'll have the same," William said. "You can put her tomatoes on mine."

Minutes later, serving their meal, Connie heard them talking of their day's plans, their trip to several locations. "Let me make a couple chicken salad sandwiches for you and put them in a small cooler, which you can return later."

When Charli said no, William told her it was something Connie enjoyed doing. "Something special but only for the people she really loves."

"And, you're one of those special people?" Charli asked.

"Along with everyone else in town," William admitted.

Two hours later, they were in Plains, walking around the one-block downtown, marveling at the quaintness of the small community.

A couple hours later, arriving at the historic Civil War town of Andersonville, William parked in the shade of a huge live oak tree. The day had turned hot with humidity as high as the temperature.

Opening the car doors, they sat inside, eating Connie's sandwiches.

Afterward, they walked into the office for a map and information. The clerk handed William a brochure and map. He handed them to Charli as he conversed with the woman behind the desk.

Charli opened the brochure, scanned it quickly and then the map. She handed them back to William.

"Don't you want to keep them?"

"I'll take them home with me, but you can be my guide for today."

William had watched her scanning the material, noticing she wasn't reading anything, just giving it all a cursory glance, lingering at the pictures. Given how this was the second day where she'd given him the job of reading the brochures and using the map, his initial curiosity was further piqued.

The clerk told them how the train depot stood in its original spot even though it had been reconstructed, and this was where Civil War prisoners disembarked and then marched the half mile to the prison.

Because of the heat, they decided to drive to the prison since they wouldn't be returning to the town.

At the prison, they moved and stood in what had been a fully double-fenced twenty-six-acre prison.

One corner displayed a sobering replica of the fencing originally built from the area's pine forest.

Charli raised the camera to her eye and started snapping. They walked around the perimeter as she took various shots.

"How many soldiers were imprisoned here?" she asked.

William opened the brochure. "Forty-five thousand in a thirteen-month period of time. Thirty thousand died."

Charli lowered her camera and stared at him, her face in anguish. "That's horrible." Her voice was nearly a whisper.

Reading further, William said, "They had no shelter from the cold in winter, the rains in the spring and fall, and from the heat in summer. It says here that a stream came through here but it was contaminated by the camp upstream where the Confederate Army kitchen was located and where they bathed."

"Anything else?"

William held out the brochure.

She shook her head. "No, you read it. I want to keep taking pictures."

"Sure," he agreed, his gaze lingered on her for a long moment. Could she be dyslexic? Is that why she preferred not to read?

He shook the brochure against the slight breeze to straighten it out so he could read. "In August 1864, thirty-three thousand prisoners were in this small area at one time." He looked up and stared at was a grassy area. "According to the picture, back then there wasn't any grass. It hardly seems possible that many people could be imprisoned here."

"And, in this heat?"

"Probably why so many died. Brochure says there wasn't adequate housing, clothing, or medical attention."

"Not to mention starvation and drinking contaminated water."

"And, all kinds of lice, rats, and other unspeakable physical conditions." While William had heard about the preserved prison through school history lessons, being here didn't do those lessons justice.

Charli lowered her camera. "Did anyone pay for this catastrophe?"

William consulted the written material again. "Captain Henry Wirz, the commander. He was tried, found guilty, and hanged in D.C. There's a cemetery here. Want to see it?"

"Yes."

They spent some time walking around the graves, noticing names, dates, and discovering far too many graves marked as *unknown US soldier*.

Despite the bright sun and slight breeze, William felt the dark shadow that had enveloped this place when it was alive with the horrors of war.

*****

It was dinner time when they started back home, stopping at a Dairy Queen for a burger and a blizzard first.

"Do you have the Heath Bar blizzard?" Charli asked the clerk.

"No, we're out of that one."

Charli looked up at the list. To William, she said, "Go ahead and order. I'm still deciding."

William ordered. The clerk looked at Charli. "Make it a double. I'll have what he's having."

William frowned. "That sandwich comes with tomato. I thought you were allergic to tomatoes."

Charli shrugged. "Easy to remove. No big deal."

William remembered how his mother always made a big deal out of an allergen food, not wanting it to touch other foods she was eating. Why wasn't it a big deal for Charli? "How long have you had this allergy?"

Charli looked surprised at the question, but then shrugged her shoulders and laughed. "Actually, I'm not allergic. I just don't like them. Telling my mother I was allergic, she stopped pestering me. She was like a dog with a bone when I was younger, at least when it came to food. Pretty much anything else, she didn't seem to care. My brother was the one who got all the attention."

"Is he younger or older?" he asked, leading them over to a booth. They slid onto the benches.

"Older. Two years. My best friend while growing up." One shoulder went up in a half shrug. "Still is, but, Gabby and JoJo are my best girlfriends. I never had any in school."

"Why not?"

She gazed past him, remembering. "I don't know."

She shrugged again.

He was starting to notice that she shrugged as if to tell herself whatever it was she was saying or about to say wasn't all that important, yet he believed it really was... or had been.

"I guess I was too different. Didn't do all the girly things that they did. You know. Proms, makeup, shopping, dresses, cheerleading."

"Doesn't sound like you liked school much."

Startled, she glanced at him quickly. Too quickly. She waited a couple seconds before answering.

"I didn't," she finally said. "I hated English, any classes where I had to read a lot."

"How come?"

"Because I'm slow."

Their number was called. William slid out of the booth and got their tray of food.

*****

Charli blew out a breath of air, watching him walk away. He was getting too close to the truth. Thank goodness they'd been interrupted. She was determined to take control of the conversation when he returned.

When William returned and placed their tray on the table, they both started unloading it. He placed the empty tray on an empty, neighboring table, sat down and asked while grabbing his fork, "I noticed you didn't like following the maps earlier."

He was fast. Too fast. Better to answer than to segue the topic because he'd only ask it again later if not tonight then tomorrow. "I'm not good at reading them," she said. "Can't say anyone ever took the time to teach me how to read them."

"Not even your brother?"

"By the time I needed help with them, he was away at college." She shrugged. "I learned to listen to directions, instead, through my GPS. How long have you and Joe been best friends?"

William smiled. "From the first time we met in kindergarten. We became inseparable. In school, out of school. Through thick and thin, good times and bad times."

"Any one memorable time?"

"When he was in the 5th grade and I in the 4th, we built a treehouse. It was great. No girls allowed, not that any tried to climb our tree. It was too deep in the forest. Stupidly, one day, instead of climbing down the ladder, we decided to jump."

Charli gasped, then laughed. "Sounds like the typical boy."

William grinned. "We each broke our dominate arm—me the right, him his left." William laughed. "At least we both couldn't go swimming. It would have been tough if one of us could and one couldn't. We bonded even more because of our breaks."

"Wait a minute," Charli interrupted. "You said you met in kindergarten. How did he end up a grade ahead?"

"I struggled in first grade. Apparently, I was dyslexic. Because it was found early, I was given some extra skills, plus repeating the material helped. How about you? Any one memorable event?"

"Not really," she lied. This would be the perfect time to tell him about her issues with school, but she couldn't. She still struggled with the shame of it all. How could she explain that no one had noticed? "I tagged after Bradley for several years, until he entered junior high. I wasn't as welcomed with his buddies, and definitely not after he entered high school, but he was still my best friend regardless if his friends were around or not."

"That had to be tough, to not feel included. Being an only child, I can't relate to having a sibling."

"And, I can't imagine going through childhood without one." Or through life, she thought. If not for her brother, she wouldn't have been able to ride let alone own a motorcycle. And, he was the one who helped her apply for this blogging job. She'd never have been capable of filling out the application. Even now, she worried what her future would be like should anything happen to him or worse, he moved away.

"What were your parents like?" he asked, scooping up the last few French fries from his basket.

"More concerned about my brother than they were about me."

William frowned.

"I was a girl. It's the boys in our families that get the attention. We girls are expected to marry and produce heirs."

"You must be a disappointment since you're not following their blueprint."

Charli shrugged. "It doesn't bother me anymore.

In fact, I prefer it."

In truth, she preferred having her parents focusing on her brother and leaving her to her own devices. If anything, they had given up on her, and frankly, she didn't blame them. She wondered if she'd been her own child if she wouldn't have given up, too. She wanted to think that she wouldn't, but—

"Did you date in high school?"

"Not really. No one ever expressed interest anyway."

"I find that hard to believe," he said.

Surprise filled her completely, and then her heart skipped a beat. Was he really seeing her for who she was as a person, rather than the person behind the name? "How's that?"

"You're beautiful. And, funny. And, curious. Do you have any idea how attractive that is?" More to himself than to her, he said, "I can't believe I just said that." To her directly, he said, "I never say things like that. I'm sorry."

Slowly, she grinned, maintaining eye contact. "I'm not."

"Done?" he asked.

She nodded.

They gathered their dishes, leaving them in the bin by the trash receptacle.

He held the door open for her as they exited the restaurant and at the car, he started to reach for the passenger door handle, then stopped.

She looked up, her gaze connecting with his. Her gaze dropped to his lips, then back to his eyes that were now hooded. His face inched toward hers.

Her heart beat fast and her mouth opened just a fraction with anticipation. Her eyes closed as his mouth captured hers. At first, his lips barely touched hers, then he fully embraced her lips with his. And then, suddenly, it was over.

She opened her eyes, surprised to see his face still close to hers.

"Good?" he asked.

She couldn't speak. Only nod.

"Good," he said, opening her door.

She slid in and he shut the door. *Oh, she was in such trouble.*

*****

As William walked around the front of the car, he thought, *What had he just done?* He couldn't help himself. He'd been drawn to her from the minute he'd first seen her. A moth to her flame. He was in love with her.

He turned his head and looked through the windshield at her. She was following his movement, watching him just as he watched her. He grinned. She grinned back. *Thank the gods.* He hadn't offended her. He knew, though, this was a foolish path to wander upon. She'd be gone in another day or so, and then what would he do? Follow her?

He couldn't. He had a job, responsibilities. Even though she had him feeling like he had none whatsoever, he couldn't just throw his life away. *Stop thinking about the future. Stay in the moment.* Easy to say—or think in this case. Hard to do.

The drive home became easy as they reflected on the day's discoveries. Tomorrow, she was going to help JoJo work on the car and catch up on girl talk. On one hand, he was disappointed that he wouldn't be spending the day with her again, but on the other, he was slightly relieved. He needed to sort out his feelings. Besides, he was scheduled to work.

About to separate for the night, William asked, "Wanna grill steaks tomorrow night? My place?"

Charli hesitated for a second, then smiled. "I'd like that. Would it be okay to invite JoJo?"

While William would have preferred it just be the two of them, he wasn't going to turn down an opportunity to see her. "Sure. Seven o'clock?"

"It's a date." She inserted the key into her door, opened it, stepped in, and turned. "Night."

"Night," he replied. Her door shut, he opened his and went straight to the freezer, getting three steaks out, putting them in the fridge to defrost. As he walked down the hall to shower before bed, he figured out the rest of the menu, making a mental note that he'd have to stop at the store after work.

He was missing her already.

*****

Day 8

At seven o'clock, Charli knocked on William's door and heard a muffled *come on in* from inside. She opened the door and went in, carrying the tub of coleslaw that she had stopped and gotten from a nearby deli.

William closed the refrigerator door, with steaks

in his hand. Unhusked sweet corn sat on the counter, along with a jar of pickles, and a store-bought chocolate cake.

"JoJo isn't with you?"

"No, she's working on the car." She set the slaw and her phone on the counter near the other food.

"What'd you bring?" he asked, while he seasoned two steaks, putting the third back into the refrigerator.

"Coleslaw."

"Fantastic. The one thing I forgot to buy."

"What can I do?"

"Not a thing." He grabbed the four ears of corn and plate of steaks and opened the slider door to the deck and electric grill. From here, she could see heat rising from the grill. Quickly and efficiently, he put the steaks and corn on the grill and was back in the kitchen. "How do you like your steak?"

"Rare."

"Seriously?"

She nodded.

"So do I."

"Rare to find—"

"—others who like their meat—"

"—Rare," they said together, laughing.

He got two plates and silverware out. "Have a preference for sitting at the table or here at the counter?"

"Counter," she answered. "I prefer casual and informal."

"Something else we have in common."

While he set out their place settings, she moved to the living room area to get a closer look at the artwork on the wall. "You like the impressionists," she said.

"Let me guess. You do, too."

She nodded and smiled. This was getting scary how much they had in common.

Then, she saw his framed degrees on the wall. She knew they were degrees, having seen her brother's, but she couldn't tell what they were exactly. She moved back into the kitchen area where he'd put two glasses of lemonade on the counter. She grabbed one and sipped.

"Okay, I know, I know," he said. "I should probably hang those somewhere else. Joe told me I hung them there just to irritate my parents."

"How so?" She was glad he was telling her stories rather than her having to deal with questions she couldn't or didn't want to answer. "Oh, wait, because you got both degrees."

"Yes, they were proud that my design was part of the renovation for this old factory, but they can now see that I love my job as the library's director."

If only her parents could be as proud of her. How could they when she told them so little? If she told them about her reality, they'd be appalled. As would be most people.

Her brother had told her not to be ashamed, but deep down, she was, despite living with the problem and finding acceptable solutions. Acceptable to her. Or had been.

She sighed.

If only William wasn't so attractive, so nice, and so much fun to be with. She'd only known him a couple days and already he felt like a best friend, like her brother, but more than that. The big difference: one knew about her handicap and didn't judge her and the other knew nothing and she feared his judgment.

Seated next to each other as they ate, they joked, laughed, and shared childhood escapes. She learned he skipped classes nearly as much as she had. His stories had her laughing and now she was choking on her food.

He jumped up and slapped her on her back, then got behind her and lifted both her arms up above her head. "That should open up your airway."

She inhaled just enough to get enough air so she could cough again. Then, several times before she could finally inhale enough air to fill her lungs and breathe properly.

"It worked." He turned her around. "Are you okay?"

She nodded. Now, she was holding her breath because he was so close. She glanced up, saw the desire in his eyes. Her gaze dropped to his mouth. He was just about to kiss her when her phone rang.

He straightened, turned, and reached for it, handing it to her, glancing at it as he did.

A picture of her brother. She swiped the screen so that the call went to voice mail, then set the phone down next to her plate.

"You're not going to answer?" William asked.

"It's my brother. I'll call him back later."

"I noticed you don't have many apps on your phone."

She shrugged her shoulders. "Don't need them." She smiled brightly, changing the subject. "Are we ready to dig into dessert?"

He stared at her for a long second, then returned her smile. "Of course."

She cleared their dishes while he cut the cake. This time, he put the plates on the dining table, where they sat catty-corner from each other.

"Tomorrow's the last day of the fishing contest and it includes a photo contest. Awards are handed out the day after that. The entire contest would be a great article for your travel blog. It might interest some fishermen for next year. Of course, that means you'd be staying a couple more days. Are you interested?"

As she forked the cake, getting a sizeable amount of frosting and taking her time doing so, thoughts about the pros for staying swirled around. She was playing a dangerous game by staying. Both with being found out and with her heart.

For the first time in a long time, she ignored what her head was telling her and went with her heart. "I'd like to take some pictures," she said. She inserted the cake into her mouth.

"Okay if I tag along with you tomorrow to the lake?"

Her mouth full, she nodded.

His hand moved toward her mouth, his thumb

brushing at her lower lip and the edge of her mouth. "Some leftover icing," he said. Then, he licked his finger, his eyes darkening.

She swallowed, unable to remove her gaze from his.

As he moved closer, she tilted her head back, providing him better access. This time, no phone call interrupted his kiss. Was that a growl? And, did she just moan?

She moved away slightly, but just enough to end the kiss. He backed up, a bit out of breath.

She scooted her chair back, getting up, and grabbing her plate and fork, taking both to the sink. He mimicked her movements.

"Thank you for dinner," she said, turning toward him. She put a hand on his chest, then kissed his cheek. "I enjoyed it all immensely."

"Tomorrow then?"

She nodded. "Tomorrow." She scooped up her phone from the counter, pocketed it, and walked to the door. He followed.

She didn't look back until she was at her door. "Goodnight," she said.

"Night."

The look on his face was of the same longing she felt. But, she had to leave, to put distance between them right now.

Inside, she rested her back against the closed door. He was safely out of reach, no longer a threat to her losing control or her heart completely. At least not tonight.

*****

William still stood in the hall, unable to move. He closed his eyes, letting the feelings of the last ten minutes wash over him again. He wanted her. As a friend, a mate, a lover. He knew so little about her, and yet, felt as if he'd known her his entire life. Longer.

Everyone would tell him was being foolish. Everyone being his parents. He and the guys had talked about falling in love a number of times, especially this past year as they all started turning thirty and none of them were in steady relationships.

Lately, he'd been watching it happen to them, and now it was happening to him. He finally got the ridiculousness, the glory of it all. That there were no words to describe it.

He turned and went into his condo, shutting the door and cleaning up the kitchen. Minutes later, he stood in front of the artwork on his wall, still thinking about Charli, and how much they had in common.

Yet, there was something off. The way she'd stared at his diplomas on the wall, saying nothing. Suddenly he realized, she hadn't said a word. Just letting him ramble on about them. And, what was up with having hardly any apps on her phone? Everyone had apps. Lots of them. Why not her?

It didn't make sense.

It wasn't as if red flags were suddenly appearing. Instead, it all was more like a puzzle—that was missing a piece or two.

*****

Day 9

Early the next morning, Charli knocked on William's door. He answered, his hair tousled, his chest bare, drawstring pjs hanging low on his hips. She swallowed, her fingers curling to keep from reaching out. If she hadn't woken him up, then he hadn't been up long.

"I'm sorry to wake you up," she said.

"No, no, I've been up. Just not dressed yet."

"I'm going to walk to the lake. I want to get some shots of town and the neighborhood between here and the lake."

"I'll see you there then, shortly?"

She nodded, then turned quickly, walking to the elevator. If he had invited her in, she knew she would have done so. Not like her at all. Usually, she could turn off any attraction she'd had in the past. Why not now?

Half an hour later, she was walking on the beach and stopped to take a photo of the posted signs. She'd send them to her brother later or better yet, to a new app he'd told her to try—one that read aloud any text in the picture or graphic. She headed for the pier and boat slips.

Starting down the pier, she heard her name being called. She stopped and turned around. William.

She waited for him to catch up.

"You're not allowed on the pier," he said.

"Says who?" she asked.

The sign did. The one you took a picture of. It's only during the fishing contest, to keep the pier free for the fishing parties and judges.

"I must have missed that," she said. She retreated, walking past him to get off the pier.

He grabbed her arm, stopping her. "Are you okay? You look flustered."

"No, no, I'm fine," she blurted. Even to her own ears, she sounded a bit panicked. "I'm starving, actually."

He was looking at her in that way she'd seen others looking at her when they suspected. Always before, she'd been able to sway them away from their suspicions.

He spoke softly, quietly. "You can't read, can you?"

She looked down at her feet. He knew. She should have guessed that he'd find out. He was smart. And, caring. Too caring. She didn't want that kind of caring. Sympathy. Feeling sorry for her.

She raised her head and stared at him, taking a deep breath. "No. I can't." She didn't wait for the look of pity that was sure to follow. Instead, she spun around and took off running. To get away as far as possible with her shame.

"Charli! Wait!"

She couldn't. Only when she knew she was safely out of his sight did she slow down.

*****

William cursed himself for asking the question that should have waited for when they were alone in private somewhere else. Not out here in the open where anyone could have walked by.

He'd hurt her, judging by the pain that crossed her face when he'd asked the question.

How stupid of him. Of course, she couldn't read. He'd seen all the signs. It wasn't like he hadn't seen them on others before this. It was his specialty, his minor in college while getting his library science degree. What was so different this time?

Because he loved her. He had felt her pain and wanted to help her exorcise it. Only trouble was, he'd just made it worse.

He had to find her.

"William!"

Hearing his name, he turned and saw Cutter coming down the pier from his boat. William groaned. There was no getting away right now. It'd be probably fifteen minutes before he'd be off the beach, what with Cutter this animated.

*****

Twenty minutes later, William pulled into his garage. Charli's bike was gone. She couldn't have left. Not yet.

Running upstairs, he knocked on her door. No answer. Not that he had expected her to be here with her bike gone, but...

He went into his apartment and got the spare set of keys for his neighbor's place. Opening the door, he walked in. Immediately, looking down the short hall and into the kitchen, he could see the key on the counter.

He checked the bedrooms. Her stuff was gone.

Back in the kitchen, he picked up the key and

pocketed it.

Where could she have gone? Could she have left town already?

No, she would say goodbye to JoJo first. But wait, she had said she was starving.

*****

He hurried into the diner and saw her, with her back to the door, in one of the corner booths.

He slid into the opposite empty bench, glad to see that he had surprised her. Had she seen him, she might have run.

Before she could say anything, he said, "Charli, I am so sorry. That was rude of me to ask you like I did, especially considering where we were."

She just stared at him, her eyes blinking faster than normal. Her jaw moved as if she was clenching her teeth or grinding them.

"Don't go," he said. "Please, don't go. Stay so we can talk this out."

"You think I've not talked this out before?"

Immediately, William wanted to say not really. He'd seen this defensive stance before. Maybe in her head, she had. Maybe even with her brother, but anyone else? No. He knew better than to be directly honest with her. At least right now. He needed to win her over, to let her believe anything that happened here on out was her idea.

He just looked at her, pleading, and appealing with his eyes.

"I need to go."

"I haven't been honest either," he said.

She frowned.

At least she appeared curious and wasn't about to bolt.

He continued. "I've got a 12-year-old secret I've been keeping from my friends. Joe knows everything, and now Annie does, but no one else knows."

"Knows what?"

"I can't—"

"That's rich. You want me to be honest and here you're telling me you can't."

"Actually, I'm going to tell everyone everything. Once, I have permission to tell the story that isn't my story to tell."

"You're talking about the car, aren't you?"

He nodded. "I wasn't the one who drove it into the lake. Joe is trying to find that person now so we can get permission to tell the truth."

Her eyes twitched. She was having trouble believing him.

He sighed. This wasn't going well. Finally, he said, "I don't want to lose you. You're the first person outside of the group who's actually been listening to me. My parents never listened. Not really. I've never enjoyed myself more with anyone. Including Joe." He paused, then said, "I'm in love with you."

Charli gasped. Then, she had the saddest expression he'd ever seen.

"My parents never listened either." Her expression softened, but the pain remained on her face. "They only heard what they wanted to hear, often ignoring the rest. Because they doted on my brother, I was invisible to them."

"I'm so sorry."

"I'm sorry for you, too. A fine pair we are."

"But we are—"

"I can't, William. I just can't. I've got to go." She slid out of her seat, went to the register, paid for her meal, and walked out without ever looking back at him.

He felt like his heart had just been ripped out of his chest. And, that she'd taken it with her.

All he could do was stare through the window as she straddled her motorcycle and headed toward the edge of town to the highway that would take her away from him.

"She's no dummy."

Startled, William looked up. Connie stood just out of his peripheral view, which is why he hadn't seen her.

"She'll be back," she continued.

"From your lips to—How do you know that?" he asked.

"Because as much as you love her, she loves you even more. Trust me."

"When did you become psychic?"

"I'm not. I just know people. I've certainly served y'all long enough. You tend to pick up on the clues. Same as you did in figuring out she couldn't read."

"You knew?"

Connie nodded. "And, you're probably the only one who could teach her how. Or be allowed to."

Since he had another hour before he needed to be

at work, William decided to go see JoJo. He hoped... actually, he wasn't sure what he hoped. He just knew that he had to see her. That this wasn't finished. That he and Charli weren't finished. They'd only begun. He wasn't ready to give up on her. Or give her up.

*****

"She's coming back," JoJo said, grabbing a rag and wiping her hands on it.

When he'd entered the garage just minutes ago, he'd foregone the usual pleasantries and asked right away if she knew whether Charli was gone for good.

JoJo smiled. "You've got it bad."

"I do. I love her."

"Oh, you're so in for a rough ride. She doesn't love easy, you know."

"I'm beginning to realize." He paused, letting that knowledge sink in. "How do you know she's coming back?"

"She wants to see the reveal. She left because she's got a photo job in Atlanta for the new few days."

"She never said."

"She rarely does," JoJo answered. "She tends to keep everything a secret. It's her nature. Can you blame her?"

"You know?"

"Sure. Gabby and I both know. Though she doesn't know that we know. We've always been waiting for her to tell us." JoJo moved so she was standing in front of William and wrapped her fingers around his upper arms. "I know this is going to sound hard, but if you really love her, you've got to let her go." She let him go to emphasize her words, almost pushing him away. "If the two of you are meant to be together, she'll come back to you."

William stared at her, troubled at the thought she might not come back.

JoJo continued. "It's like trying to love a puppy. You can't hold it for long. It'll wiggle, wanting to be free. But, it'll always come back.

William cheered slightly. "Yeah, but puppies are stupidly loyal to anyone who gives them love."

"Humans are kind of the same way. Especially when they know who really loves them and who doesn't."

"Except for the bastards who take advantage of that love."

JoJo nodded. "There is that."

William frowned. Was she speaking from experience? He looked at his watch. "I've gotta go." He gave her a quick hug. "Thanks for your help."

"I didn't do anything."

"Yeah, you did. You were her friend."

*****

Day 10

Charli sat at the counter in her brother's condo in Atlanta. He was cooking them dinner, or rather removing everything from the various takeout boxes where he'd picked up their favorite dishes at the Chinese deli a couple blocks away on his way home from work.

She'd just finished shooting for a client and would complete the work tomorrow. As much as she was in a hurry to get back to Laurel Ridge, at the same time, she was wondering if she should return.

With her elbows on the counter, she ran her hands through her hair, starting at the sides of her face and moving them back, getting the curls out of her eyes and moaning at the same time in frustration. "What should I do, Bradley?"

He stopped opening the boxes and stared at her. "Seriously, Charli? I thought you were done needing my advice."

"Never," she said, then added, "I know it's been a while since needing it—like this—but I'm not sure how I feel."

He raised one eyebrow and then the second one went up, too. "I don't believe it. You're in love."

She frowned, shaking her head. "No. No, no, no."

"Yes, you are, but you don't want to admit it. You'd rather deny it, just like you deny everything else."

Charli dropped her arms so they rested on the counter. She starred at him, then frowned. "He guessed that I can't read."

"From what little you've already told me about him, it doesn't sound like he guessed at all."

She chewed on her lip.

"So what?" he said. "So, what if he knows? You can't hide it forever. I'm surprised you've been able to hide it this long."

"Only because you were so good at setting up my phone, teaching me how to dictate my articles and send them, without my ever needing to use a computer."

"Probably a big mistake doing that. It kept you from dealing with reality." Finished opening the boxes, he pushed them toward her, grabbed two plates and a pair of forks, and walked around the counter, sitting next to her.

She scraped food from several boxes onto her plate. "I'm dealing with it now, aren't I?"

"Just be honest about how you feel. Be honest about your past, too. He probably wants to know what happened that you weren't able to learn how to read." He put some food in his mouth, chewed, then swallowed. "He isn't going to think less of you as long as you're honest."

"How do you know?"

"How can anyone not think it's cool what you've done, what you've achieved, and not think you're brave for being honest?"

*****

Day 12

Rhett, Clint, and William entered Joe's office. Mason, a classmate who had returned to Laurel Ridge and was now a circuit judge, brought up the rear, joining the merriment of greetings.

Joe directed the guys into the conference room connected to his office. Papers in hand, he took an empty chair among them. "A great day for the community," he said. "With each of us having talked about Laurel Ridge going green the past couple years, our forming this solar and wind energy plant will be a godsend for the residents."

"Both in manufacturing and creating our own power plant," Clint said.

Rhett picked up a pen as Mason slid the papers toward him. "Not only for the jobs that'll be created but with the hope that we could sell power to other communities in the future." Mason signed the papers, passed them on to Clint who signed, and then passed them to William.

He looked at the papers, realizing his dream of helping the community both as a leader and being able to use his architecture skills even more were coming true, and all while as the library's director.

If only my personal life could be as fulfilling as my professional one. He signed the documents and pushed them toward Joe who wrapped up the meeting.

Once everyone had left, William followed Joe into his office and shut the door. "Have you found her?" he asked.

As Joe sat in the chair behind his desk, he said, "I did. And, she's okay with the truth coming out but only to our small, tight circle of friends."

William sigh with relief and nodded. "What now?"

"Since Clint's reveal party is in three days, let's meet an hour before the party begins, where you can have your own reveal."

Immediately, they divided up the short list of friends, called them, and ten minutes later, congratulated themselves on their plan being set up. Suddenly, William felt nervous. He'd been keeping this secret for over a decade. This group didn't keep secrets from each other. It was one thing for his parents to be disappointed in him, but he wasn't sure he could take his friends being disappointed, too. Would they hold it against him?

Charli had to have felt the same way with him revealing her secret the way he had. If only— Nope. No looking backward anymore.

If only he could call her. If only to tell her how sorry he was.

*****

Day 14

Early evening, William pulled up to Clint's garage. JoJo saw him, waved, and started walking out to greet him.

"Thanks for coming," she said. "For saving me. For being here to sign for the part that's arriving special delivery."

"Happy to help."

"They should be here in under half an hour. They promised to be here before seven. Hopefully, you won't have to wait long. I'll probably be back before they get here, anyway."

"Don't worry about it. Don't rush on my account. I brought a novel I've been wanting to read." She thought she was going to Joe's house on an errand. Little did she know what Joe had planned.

JoJo left and William grabbed the folding sports chair that Clint kept handy in the corner. Unfolding it, he set it up just inside the open bay, out of the sun but in clear sight for anyone who pulled into the driveway.

Fifteen minutes later and deep into the third chapter, William heard a motor coming down the drive. Pulling the bookmark from the back of the book, he inserted it to mark his place and shut the book, getting up.

Charli was behind the wheel of her truck.

His heart leapt and his mouth went dry. He started to smile, lifting a hand to wave.

No, she was here only to deliver a part. She hadn't been expecting to see him. She was expecting to see JoJo. He dropped his hand and stood waiting.

He sighed deeply, steeling himself.

*****

The minute she had turned into the driveway, she'd seen him, reading. Immediately, the palms of her hands dampened.

Parking in front of him, she turned off the engine and slid her hands on her jeans. She had told JoJo, she wanted to surprise him. Now, she wondered if that had been a good idea. She couldn't tell if he was happy to see her or not.

Nervous, she exited the truck.

As she walked toward the garage, she couldn't tear her gaze away from his. His expression wasn't changing. Stoic.

What did she expect? Open arms? She'd made it perfectly clear when she'd left that she never wanted to see him again.

Now, she couldn't stop looking at him.

"Surprised?" she asked, stopping in front of him.

She could tell the moment he figured it out,

seeing that she had no part in her hands. One side of his mouth twitched and an eyebrow went up. "Should I be?"

"I asked JoJo to set this up."

"Why?"

"I had to see you."

"So, there's no part coming?"

"No."

"Well, now you've seen me."

"You're not going to make this easy, are you?"

"Should I?"

She looked down. She wanted to smile, so she sucked in her cheeks instead. She wanted her expression to be as grim as his. That's what she liked most about him. His directness. Even if it did make her uncomfortable. She met his gaze again. Then sighed heavily.

"No."

He just stared at her.

She took a deep breath. "I made a mistake."

Silence.

"I shouldn't have left the way I did."

More silence.

"Blame my stupid pride. It's the only thing I had."

"Had?"

She nodded. "It got in the way of everything. I had to let it go."

"As in forever?"

"Well... I'm not so sure about that," she drawled slowly. She could have sworn she saw the hint of a smile beginning. "I have a favor to ask."

"Go ahead."

"First, I have to explain something. When I was learning how to read, I got sick. Really sick. First pneumonia, then mono. I was out for a couple months. Then home more than I was in school. I fell behind. In the process, my reading skills... Well, they're non-existent. I struggled a lot to the point that I gave up. Will you teach me how to read?"

She saw the surprise and joy in his face before he looked down at the ground quickly so she couldn't see his face completely. "I don't know," he said, slowly. "I'm really busy these days. Plus, that would take time. Weeks and weeks." He looked up, studying her. His face serious now.

Was he playing her? "Months?" she asked.

He nodded. "Years."

Trying not to grin, she mimicked his nod. Finally, she said, "Okay."

He stepped forward and she flew into his arms, pulling his head down toward hers, letting him know with her lips just how much she'd missed him.

Minutes later, he said, "We'll have to make arrangements for you—"

"All arranged. I'm going to stay with JoJo in the cottage until I can find my own place."

"It just so happens that my neighbors are going to stay in Michigan until October. You can stay in the condo."

She grinned at him. "Close by, huh?"

"I don't want my girlfriend being too far away," he said.

Her mouth opened in surprise. "Girlfriend?"

"You will be, won't you?"

"Yes! Yes, yes—"

She squealed as he hugged her tightly, lifting her off the ground, twirling around.

"Let's wait to make an announcement at the party tomorrow," he said.

Charli laughed again and was quickly silenced with another kiss, one that told her she *was* indeed his girlfriend.

Sweet Cravings #7

Can a blind date with an attorney and an acclaimed mechanic gone wrong with multiple hilarious do-overs gone wrong ever become a relationship gone right? Can these two cynics who have given up on relationships find happiness in a long-distance relationship without sacrificing their careers?

Day 5

Shortly after the crack of dawn, Josephine Wheeler, called JoJo by her friends, slowed her large white van, lettered *Wheeler Mechanics*, at the Laurel Ridge, South Georgia mailbox with the same address as on the legal pad in her portfolio. The van served as her on-the-road shop, and she was here to do a full engine restoration.

Having had her cell phone die or having no bars at critical times, she'd learned to use her zippered portfolio as a mini office instead of her phone, ignoring the advice of others. Actually, over time, she found it saved her time as she wasn't dependent on having power. It was also easier.

She liked things easier.

She loved shortcuts, too, but not when repairing engines. That was one place she would never shortcut.

Right now, she was here to overhaul an engine that'd been in the water for over a decade. So far, there wasn't an engine she couldn't fix. She refused to give up. At least, when it came to engines.

If only relationships were as easy to fix.

She'd given up on relationships more times than she wanted, but she found she didn't like being the only one doing the work it took to keep the relationship going. Her ability to choose men was dismal, so she had stopped dating altogether. Besides, she was focused on her career, hoping to open a shop one day, though unsure when or where it would happen.

Pulling into the driveway, she passed the main house that sat on the left as instructed. The house was an old-fashioned two-story brick colonial house, looking like it had been built in the 1950s but wasn't tired looking. Either that or the owner was meticulous about its upkeep.

She continued down the drive as further instructed and saw the large garage at the back of the property. A small guest house was tucked into the corner of the yard, a short walk from the garage. She parked in front of the large building.

Just as she turned off the ignition, one of the big bay doors slid up on its rollers, exposing the man who opened it. Clint Anderson, she presumed. The man who had hired her.

He walked toward her as she stepped down from the cab. He reached her by the time she shut the door.

She shook his offered hand. "You must be Clint

Anderson."

"And you're Josephine—"

"JoJo."

"—Wheeler. Nice to meet you. I'm glad you could fit me in."

"Actually, I'm glad to get away. The city is hot this time of year. The race track even hotter. Totally my pleasure to drive down here and see some green again."

He turned, leading them into the garage, opening bay doors along the way. No doubt for air flow. "Here she is," he said, coming to a stop beside a dull yellow VW beetle. At one time, she imagined it'd been canary yellow. "You might not think it's a vacation once you get into this motor."

"Can't wait," she said, walking to the back, lifting the hood, and looking over the motor. Hard to eyeball how much actual damage had been done. She was eager to put on her coveralls, put some tools in her hands and start taking the engine apart.

"Your reputation precedes you," Clint said.

"Must be Gabby or Charli you've been talking to." She knew her two best friends had been here recently. Charli was still here, somewhere. The three of them often did video calls to stay in touch since they weren't always home at the same time. She and Gabby were roommates, too.

Clint laughed. "Both actually. Plus, I called the referrals you provided."

"You called them?"

"I did."

"I bet they were surprised."

"They were."

"And you learned—"

"Without hesitation, they'd all hire you again."

JoJo grinned. She liked knowing she had a reputation as an motor expert. One thing she was good at. "Is Gabby here?" Gabby was a balloonist and psychic and had been hired to airlift his parents for Clint's anniversary party he'd given them a couple nights ago.

"No, she left for her next festival last night, much to my disappointment."

JoJo raised an eyebrow. *Gabby, you holding out on me?* JoJo had some questions to ask her friend.

Clint continued. "But Charli should be here soon. Said she wanted to see you when you arrived. I called William when I saw you driving up." Charli was a motorcyclist travel blogger.

"William?"

"He's a good friend, the library director, and she's been staying in the condo next to his." Clint followed JoJo back out to her van. "Ah, here they are now."

JoJo turned to see a car turning into the driveway, watching it drive up next to her van. Charli rushed out of the passenger side and ran up to JoJo, hugging her tight.

"I've missed you!"

JoJo laughed. "I missed you more, but you've only been gone a day!"

Charli stepped back, examining JoJo's hair, and exclaimed, "You cut your hair!"

JoJo reached up and touched the thick curls that ended just above her shoulders all the way around. "I couldn't stand the length anymore. I did it myself last night."

"It's cute and suits you." Charli turned and looked back, signaling William to come closer. Her arm still around JoJo's waist, Charli introduced JoJo to William, "JoJo, Gabby, and I are best friends." To JoJo, Charli said, "The VW was William's car back in high school and was fished out of the lake by another one of their friends, Cutter. Clint then purchased the car from William, and there was a mystery surrounding a bracelet that Gabby found under the front seat, which didn't belong to William but to Jefferson Jackson's mom, who was the original owner of the car."

JoJo laughed at how much information Charli had packed into one sentence. As usual.

"Wow, you really know how to tell a story in just a few words," William said. "When you said photojournalist, I figured your job was mostly photos."

JoJo noticed how William's gaze was fixated on Charli. Even though Charli never noticed men looking at her like that, JoJo noticed it every time. Charli was a looker, and William's eyes revealed he was already in love with her. Poor guy. He didn't stand a chance. While JoJo couldn't seem to date the right guy, Charli just rejected them all—rarely giving any man a chance.

Clint explained further, "Gabby did a reading on the bracelet, saying there was a possible long-ago love affair. Talking with Jefferson, he confirmed that while he didn't know all the details, that bracelet was the catalyst for his parents' divorce. He went to visit his father yesterday. His father sold the car to William's parents, who had bought it for William as a graduation present. Suddenly, William didn't have the car anymore, telling us he'd sold it because he didn't like the color." Clint paused.

Everyone turned to William, who shrugged his shoulders, and said, "Well, I really didn't like the color. I hate yellow."

Clint continued, "And yet, somehow, the car mysteriously ended up in the lake, with him still as its owner, and he's not talking."

"My lips are sealed," William said, running two fingers across his mouth. "At least for now," he added. "I'm hoping I can reveal the mystery behind the car's late-night sinking soon."

"I know of Senator Jackson," JoJo said. "He was a big help to friends of mine who were trying to get some country farmland land rezoned so they could build a pee-wee race track for kids. Those wanting to learn how to race properly. Plus, it was a school of sorts for car maintenance. He did a nice job helping that project."

To JoJo, Clint said, "And now, I'm hoping you'll be able to restore this engine so I can drive the car this summer. How long will it take to fix?"

"A few days, if all goes well."

Charli said, "Clint, William, and I have been talking. Knowing you were coming, we think you should go on a blind date with Joe. I've met him."

William added, "He's a friend, my best friend actually, plus a former classmate of ours. Joe's a good guy."

"Joe? That's his name?"

"Joe Benton," William said, then brightened. "Joe and Josephine. Sounds like a match to me."

JoJo said, "I wouldn't go that far—"

"I would," Charli answered. "You know what Gabby would say."

"Serendipity. It's written in the stars," she sighed. Already she knew there was no way out of this. Charli would insist.

"He'll kill us," Clint replied, "but it's a great idea!"

It was an awful idea. JoJo wanted to kill them all for even suggesting it. She was here to work on a car, not satisfy their matchmaking inclinations. And, since when did Charli start matchmaking? That was more Gabby's thing—at least when she was doing readings.

Charli added, "He's cute."

"Uh-oh," she said.

Clint laughed. "No, he's the best. And, better looking than the rest of us."

"The rest of you?"

"It's a group of nine friends," Charli injected. "Who went to school together. Three girls and six guys—classmates. Some close like you, me, and Gabby. One couple dated in high school, another wished—"

"Cutter wished, still wishes, but Annie keeps running," William interrupted.

Charli nodded. "It sounds complicated, but it's not once you get to know them."

JoJo looked around at them. "So, what's really wrong with him?"

"Nothing!" all three emphasized together in a chorus.

Charli put a hand on JoJo's arm. "Seriously. He's nice. Really cute, just a bit shy."

"Not shy," Clint countered. "He's dated before."

"Just been working too hard, lately," William added. Clint nodded.

"A best friend and my lawyer, too," William offered.

"A lawyer?" JoJo said.

"He's all of ourses lawyer," William said. "That didn't come out right. Talk about being Southern."

"All, as in—"

"Our entire gang," Clint said.

"He's that good?"

The two men nodded.

"And, there's nothing strange about him?"

William shook his head. "No. Nothing. I was his roommate in college. He focused on his studies when the rest of us were more focused on dating and doing other fun activities. He didn't date much in high school."

"Hardly at all, and he had pimples," Clint admitted.

"Was great on the debate team," William added, "but had no self-confidence when it came to girls. In college, none of the girls he asked out were his type."

"And, I am?" JoJo asked.

Charli answered. "I think so, especially knowing the types I've seen you date. He puts other people before himself."

A man who could put her needs ahead of his own? That sounded too good to be true. And, yet, Charli wouldn't deceive her.

"Oh, come on, JoJo," Charli challenged. "Take a chance, for once in your life. Stop analyzing everything. He's not an engine. It's just a date."

JoJo sighed. "Oh, all right. It's not like I can work on this car 24/7."

"That's right. Everyone should have a little fun now and then," Clint said.

"Okay, okay," JoJo said. "In the meantime, where am I staying? I've already learned all the hotels are booked."

"With me," Charli said.

"With Charli," William said, at the same time.

"Problem solved," Clint announced. "When Charli leaves, you can stay in the cottage here."

"Let me go get settled and change my clothes," JoJo said to Clint. "Then, I'll be back to start work on the car."

"William drove me over so I could get my bike. You can follow us."

Clint said. "And, I'll contact Joe."

"No, let me," William said. "I need to drop by his office, which I'm doing before I go to work."

"One favor," JoJo said. "Make it for after dinner. I haven't had good dinner dates lately, especially as first-time dates. Something less formal. Something easy-going."

"Done." Clint said.

Something short, she thought. In the event it was a lousy match, she wouldn't have to suffer through an awkward meal.

*****

Joe looked up from the brief he was reading when William burst into his office. He knew his assistant, Maggie, okayed the interruption. She'd never let anyone, including his best friend, interrupt him if he was on the phone or was with clients.

Dropping his pencil on the desk and leaning back in his chair, he chuckled as William flew to the chair opposite his desk and dropped into it, barely sitting on the edge of its seat.

"You look like you're up to no good," Joe said.

"That's not fair."

"Totally fair," Joe said. "I *know* you. The only time you get this excited is when something's gone wrong or you've got a big plan. Which is it? You got rid of the car, so you must have a plan."

William sighed, then chuckled. "I do have a plan, and you can't say no."

"Wait—"

"Nope, the lady already said yes."

"What lady?"

"Your blind date for tonight."

"I'm beginning to regret ever becoming your lawyer for one buck back—"

"Back when you weren't officially a lawyer?"

"Yes."

"Too late."

Joe groaned. "What have you done this time?"

"Seriously, you're going to like her. Charli says she's just as cynical as you are."

"Hey, I resent that! I'm not cynical."

"And, just as reluctant as you are, too. A perfect match."

"There's no such thing as a perfect match. Not when it comes to love."

"I beg to differ. Seems like a bunch of us are finally maturing and finding our better halves."

"There's no such—"

"Okay, okay, how about matches that give back as good as we want to give and what we dish out?"

Joe cocked his head, giving him a stern look beneath hooded eyes.

"Don't give me that evil eye you save for clients about to perjure themselves. Seriously, Dude, you need to trust me on this one. She's your equal. She won't take any of your double-talk. She's already on to you."

"Without even meeting me?"

"She already knows you're a lawyer."

"That can't be good. Why would she say yes?"

"Because we told her you were one of the good guys. You're one of us."

Joe laughed. "Talk about double-talk."

"Oh, come on. Take a chance. Isn't that what our beloved Connie is always telling us?" Connie was a long-time waitress at the diner, having watched them all grow up and advised them when they most needed it but hadn't asked for it.

"All right, all right. If I'm doing this tonight, I need to get back to work. So, where are we meeting for dinner?"

"No dinner."

"What?"

"You're going to pick her up at the condo next to mine at eight. Up to you where you go from there."

"Drinks?"

"I wouldn't," William said. "But then, that's me. She's a mechanic. Be creative, be daring for once."

*****

An hour before sunset, JoJo heard a knock on the condo door. She'd gotten here an hour ago, had unpacked and gotten cleaned up, glad she'd been given a key as Charli wasn't back from her day trip on the road and William was still at work.

She opened the door. "Oh," she exhaled, embarrassed that she had spoken her surprise, even if only a syllable. He *was* handsome. And, cute at the same time, too. How was that even possible? Charli had never lied to her before, so why would she think Charli might have been stretching the truth by telling her that Joe was the best looking of the bunch.

Clint and William were both good-looking, but Joe... Wow. She couldn't wait to see the view as he walked away from her. "I'm sorry," she said, recovering. "You must be Joe."

"I am. Joe Benton." He held out his hand.

"JoJo Wheeler," she said, putting her hand in his.

What the hell was that? She'd felt electric shocks before but nothing like this! She slid her hand out of his.

The look on his face, told her he'd felt it too. "JoJo?"

"For Josephine."

"Interesting."

"That's what our matchmakers said," she replied.

Joe laughed. "I can only imagine."

"Would you like to come in?"

"If you don't mind, I'd rather get going before we miss the show."

"The show?"

"You'll see."

Minutes and a half dozen usual first-date questions later, they drove down a service road that passed a large farmhouse with a blue tarp on its roof, the first and second floor windows of one section charred. Corn fields on either side blocked her view and then suddenly the corn became wild grasses and a few wildflowers sprinkled here and there.

A large lake was in front of her. So large she couldn't see the opposite shore. The sun was about ready to set in front of them, where it would seemingly disappear into the water.

She took his offered hand after he opened her door. Once again, she felt that current of electricity. She'd been so stunned seeing the vista in front of her, she hadn't seen him walk around the car and open her door. Usually, she was out of a vehicle before any date could open her door.

Out of the car, they walked side-by-side to the

edge of the lake and stood in the shade of a huge live oak that had a couple branches thicker than her two thighs together touching the ground.

Even though it was approaching nine o'clock, it was still hot and muggy. She was thankful she'd opted for a sleeveless dress, one that had a full skirt that moved in the slight breeze. Just a pair of studs that she always wore in her ears and a pair of flat sandals completed her outfit. To her mind, less was more.

A couple of large rocks close by afforded them a place to sit while they watched the sun set. Several other large live oaks stood at the water's edge, with branches reaching out across the water. A few fish jumped up, splashing as they disappeared beneath the surface. Probably after mosquitoes or other bugs.

With the sun setting, there were no boats out on the water. Just a pontoon in the distance, which looked like it was heading to shore.

Other trees, cattails, and tall grasses dominated this of the lake, lining the shore until houses appeared about an eighth of a mile away on either side. No real beaches anywhere else nearby. This clearing appeared to be the only one until reaching the houses and even this clearing was rocky.

Just as the sun disappeared beneath the horizon, she felt something hit her head. She jumped up. "What was that?"

"What was what?"

"Something landed on the top of my head! Is it still there?" she squealed, reaching up.

Immediately, Joe stood and grabbed her wrist, stopping her movement with one hand, taking a handkerchief out of his pocket with the other. "I hate to tell you this, but a bird—"

"Pooped on my head!?!" She backed away and bent over at the waist, shaking her head. "Is it gone?"

Joe did his best not to laugh. He was equally horrified and amused that she was making it worse with every shake. Not sure about her sense of humor, he'd surely find out now. "Stop shaking your head. Here, let me." He took the handkerchief and tried to blot it, hoping it would come out of her hair. It didn't. He'd only managed to smear it around. "Um—"

"It's not coming out, is it?" She raised her torso so she was fully upright again.

He couldn't tell if she was about to laugh or cry.

"Want to try putting some water on it and rinse it out?" he suggested.

"That's a great idea."

He pointed to a large rock next to a solid branch that stretched across the water.

"How about using a rock like a pier? You could lean over and get the top of your head wet, and rinse it out."

"It's worth a try."

They walked over to the rocks.

Joe jumped up onto the biggest rock closest to the water and offered a hand, pulling her up. Her foot slid a little.

"Careful," he said. "It's slippery than it looks."

She kneeled down and bent toward the water.

She was still half a foot above the water. "How about you holding on to me, so I can lean over more? Keep me from falling in."

He kneeled down beside her, the rock hard on his knees.

"Can you hold me by my waist?"

"Sure," he said. He did, trying to do so with one hand, while holding on to the branch with the other to keep them both from falling in.

He couldn't help but notice how slender she was. No fat on this girl. A slim waist and firm hips. He swallowed. She slid forward a little.

"A little more," she said.

He inched her forward. Suddenly, his hand slipped from the branch. He slid toward her and couldn't stop. He let go of her to keep her from falling with him, but in letting her go, she fell in anyway.

As they fell forward, Joe angled himself so he wouldn't smack her with an arm, or worse, land on top of her.

As a result, he fell in sideways, on his left side. Quickly, he tried to stand, as the water was only a few feet deep, but they'd gone in completely.

She'd fallen in on her right side. She must have tried to avoid falling under or on top of him.

He helped her to her feet.

They stood there, looking at each other, neither saying a word, just looking at each other with horrified expressions.

At the same time, they started laughing.

"Are you okay?" they both asked.

He nodded.

JoJo showed him the top of her head. "Is it gone?"

"Almost. Another rinsing might do the trick."

Instantly, JoJo fell backward, going completely underwater. Her arms came out of the water, her hands ruffling her hair. She rose out of the water, looking like a goddess. From where she stood, she bent her head a little and asked, "How about now?"

"Gone."

She thrust her head back so that her hair went back and wasn't in her face anymore.

He swallowed. The sun's last rays hit her from behind, her legs clearly outlined under her dress, a golden aura framing her entire body. Then, suddenly, the sun's rays were gone.

"Good," she said. "Wouldn't be right if I went home with poo all over me."

He burst out laughing again. "But a good soaking is all right?" he choked out.

"Not quite the relief from the heat I had in mind," she chuckled.

"Should we go?" he asked.

They walked back to the car in silence.

He opened her door for her. He noticed her hesitation. "It's okay. The seats will dry."

"Not quite a memorable first date," she said, sliding in.

"Quite the contrary, I'd say." He shut the door before she could respond and walked around to his side.

When they were back on the road, she said, "I'm

sorry it turned out so badly."

"It wasn't like either of us intentionally meant to get wet," he responded. "It was the bird's fault, after all."

"It was, wasn't it?"

"Want to try again?"

"Tonight?"

"No, tomorrow. We'll have a do-over. A mulligan."

"Mulligan?"

"It's a golfing term. It's a do-over allowed on the first tee when you flub the first stroke." He noticed she didn't respond right away. Maybe a first try was all that he'd get. "Or not," he added. He wanted a do-over. He liked her contagious laugh, her sense of humor. He had liked that brief view the sun had provided, as well.

"I'm game for a mulligan. But, no water."

"Deal. How about dinner? I know a little place off the beaten path that has the best ribs anywhere. The place isn't great looking or has the best decor, but the food is fantastic, well-known, and gets lots of customers."

"Okay," she said.

*****

Day 6

JoJo was in Clint's garage, working on the car just as the sun appeared on the horizon.

A few hours later, she looked up to see Clint walking down the driveway toward the garage, holding two tall glasses jammed with ice cubes and what appeared to be lemonade.

It was.

She'd already had her allotted number of morning coffees earlier. Lemonade would hit the spot now.

Clint held one glass out. "Need a break?"

She put her tools down on the bench that sat beside the car's back end and took the glass from him, swiping it across her forehead, where the condensation transferred to her forehead. "Great timing." She lifted the drink to her lips and swallowed half of the liquid.

"How's she coming?" The table next to the car held an assortment of parts. A few were soaking in a cleaning solution. A couple others were waiting their turn.

"Still taking her apart, but in another hour or so, I'll be ready to clean the framework itself. It won't take much to repair the rust spots and then polish her up good."

They talked a few more minutes about the car. She could see that while he was interested, there was something else on his mind. "What do you want to know about Gabby?" she asked.

Clint turned and stared at her. "You too?"

"What? Have Gabby's gifts of mind reading?" She laughed. "Not for a split second. You just have this lost puppy-dog look on your face."

"That's what she said when I told her about my boyhood best friend—my dog."

"A great dog, right?"

"The best."

"And Gabby?"

"I'd like to see her again."

"To date?"

"Would she give me a chance?"

"I talked with her late last night."

"Did she say anything about me?"

JoJo laughed. The two of them would be perfect together. She couldn't tell him that Gabby had asked the exact same question.

"Why are we all so reluctant to take a chance?" he mumbled.

"You too?"

"She said it, too?"

"Not in so many words. My thoughts mostly." She thought it often enough.

"Love is scary and who likes being broken-hearted?" he said.

"Why not give her a call?" she suggested.

"Because she didn't invite me to?"

"You really need an invitation? You called her before, you know."

"For my parents' party."

"You have her number."

He stared at her for a long moment. Then, he downed the rest of his drink. He smiled at her. "You're right. I should call her. She's not going to call me, is she?" When she didn't answer, he said, "Right."

JoJo smiled, watching him disappear into the house. Knowing Gabby, he'd probably get her voicemail this time of day. She'd be in the middle of the paranormal festival she was attending, and then immediately after closing shop, she'd be on the road to Tennessee for the next balloon festival. JoJo shook her head, marveling at Gabby's schedule. How did she do it?

Actually, how do any one of us three girls maintain these schedules?

She hoped Clint wouldn't stop trying. Gabby was a one-of-a-kind woman and deserved love, even if she didn't think so. Usually, the men gave up on her, not understanding her quirkiness. Clint and Gabby were both quirky nerds. JoJo had talked with Clint enough, conversations about his dig, his studies, and interests to know he was just as nerdy as her good friend. A perfect match.

*****

Day 7

JoJo looked around as Joe parked the car in a nearly full parking lot that was nothing more than a dirt yard on two sides of the restaurant.

When Joe called her last night to cancel their dinner just as she was getting ready to leave the garage, she sensed he wasn't happy about it. Truthfully, while she'd been disappointed, at the same time, it allowed her to continue work on the engine, to where she'd made tremendous strides in getting it done.

When she had suggested tonight instead, he had sounded relieved.

Through the windshield, other than a billboard sign in the front yard and the expanse of bare earth,

JoJo would have thought the place was nothing but a huge, well-used Victorian home, but one without all the typical bric-à-brac. The house desperately needed paint. By all appearances, its color might have been a green...maybe a greenish gray. Only the parking lot, packed with cars, provided the needed clue that the food would be good.

She'd learned in her travels that often the least-attractive locations had the best food. It was the parking lot that always told the true story.

They walked up the weather-worn wooden steps and Joe opened the front screen door that creaked loudly. She stepped over the threshold into a dark room. She moved aside so Joe could enter and shut the door, keeping the flies that buzzed outside from coming in.

While there were a few windows, all with no coverings, the room was still dark, probably because the floor was an aged wooden floor. Original, no doubt. The walls were dark, too. A dark green. A popular color decades ago.

She noticed they stood in the entry of a long hall that extended to the back of the house, where she could see another screen-door.

A man with an apron once white but now featured smears of grease, barbecue sauce, and who knows what else, opened that back door, holding a huge tray of ribs. A breeze, blowing from the back door to the front, filled the hallway with a mouth-watering aroma. Her stomach growled.

A woman with a bright smile met them and led

them to a table in another room toward the back. As they walked down the hall, JoJo looked both left and right into the rooms with seated customers. Most of the tables were square, oak with oak chairs, seating four. Old tables and chairs. Probably antiques now. This place had been here a long time. In a few places, two or three tables were lined up side-by-side to accommodate large parties of hungry customers.

Everyone was eating ribs and corn on the cob. A specialty, no doubt. Her stomach growled again.

Finally, they were seated at a small table by one of windows. Looking through the window, she saw the man who had brought in the ribs earlier. He was tending several grills, all smoking and ladened with meat.

She turned her head away from the window, catching Joe's expression. He appeared pleased with himself.

"Yes, Joe, you did good. I'm starving, and the food smells wonderful."

He grinned. "Best ribs anywhere."

Looking around, the place needed some deep cleaning and repair. The old oak floors were worn. Sanding and revarnishing would do wonders. A few cobwebs sat in the ceiling corners, a few more adorned the large chandelier that hung high from the center cornice. A couple light bulbs were burned out.

The table top, though, was clean as were their dishes. She had dined in worse conditions. It amused her how such locations could have the best food.

"How often do you come here?" she asked.

"Not often enough. If it were closer to town, I'd get take out."

"If they were closer to town, they'd probably have to clean up better."

"Truthfully, from a legal standpoint, it doesn't matter where the location is. If they're registered legally with the state, they have to comply like every other restaurant. I doubt this place gets complaints," he added.

"How often are inspections made?"

"Once or twice a year?"

"Have you ever checked its grade?"

"No. And, I don't want to. Do you ever check the grades of the restaurants you frequent?"

"No. Don't want to know. I guess we have that in common."

"Does that mean we like to live on the edge?"

JoJo laughed. "Hardly."

"Not even after last night, when we fell from the edge?"

She laughed again.

Their waiter placed large oval-shaped plates, ladened with ribs and corn on the cob in front of them.

JoJo picked up her napkin.

Suddenly, a loud booming voice with the aid of a megaphone, announced: "Everyone, please exit the premises, immediately."

Joe jumped up. "I'll be right back." He left their dining room and headed toward the back. Seconds later, he returned and came to her chair. "We need to leave."

"Can we take this to go?"

"Nope. We hadn't paid for it yet." His face was grim.

He pulled her chair back as she rose. She grabbed her bag. He put a hand on her elbow as he propelled her outside. Once they were in the car, they sat watching other patrons leaving. A police car and a white state government health department car, according to the car's logo, were both parked near the front door.

"What happened?" she asked.

"Health code violation."

"Are they a client?"

"Yes, but there was nothing I could do. They hadn't fixed the issues in the time allotted, which was generous even for the state, so the health department had to shut 'em down. It happens."

"Like that, right in the middle of the dinner hour?"

"A filled-to-capacity dinner hour. They're making a point."

"Not the first time, huh?"

"Nope. I have a feeling it'll be the last time, though. Richard, the owner, can be a bit of a procrastinator. He certainly is being taught a huge financial lesson this time. He'll be open again in a few days, after he fixes what are really just minor issues that he kept ignoring."

Joe started the car, driving out of the parking lot. They were one of the last to leave.

"You know what this means, don't you?" JoJo said.

"Second-date failure. We can still rescue it, though."

"With equally great tasting ribs?"

"No, sorry. Hard for you to make that claim—that they're great tasting—since you didn't get that chance," he stated.

"But *you* can. All I have is your word. I'm starving and need food. I was planning on going back to the garage when we were done."

As he turned the car onto the road, Joe was disappointed on two levels. First because the rib dinner was a complete failure, and second because she'd planned on returning to work afterward, thus shortening their time together. As excited as he'd been earlier, his disappointment was heavy.

He was failing miserably. How could he be so good in court and so lousy on dates, especially with a woman he wanted more than half a chance with? He needed the odds better stacked in his favor. His stomach growled.

"Willing to play a game?" she asked.

"Sure, I'm up for anything at this point." He was. He knew from past experience the only way to get out of his head was to concentrate on something else.

"We both pick a number from one to ten."

"Three."

"Five."

"Do you want to subtract or add?" she asked.

"Subtract."

"Two. That means we're stopping at the second restaurant we come to. No questions asked, no discussion."

"Out here? There aren't going to be too many options."

"Whatever," she said. "That's the plan, and being a stranger to these parts—unlike you who probably knows every road and restaurant—I get to pick the direction we go anytime we come to a crossroads."

"We could end up in Macon at that rate!"

She laughed. "Not by a long shot. There has to be small burgs around here, and I know from experience that many of them have diners and drive-ins of some kind or another."

He agreed, but he didn't dare tell her that they could be worse than the one they had just left.

"And," she added. "You can't give me any hints or make any disgruntled noises."

"Me? I wouldn't do that," he laughed. He wondered who she'd been talking to who would have ratted him out. William?

"Nothing!" she emphasized. "Not a twitch of an eyebrow—"

He raised his eyebrow.

"—or the downturn of your mouth."

He frowned and grimaced.

She laughed.

"I'm not even going to look at you."

"No! Not that. Okay, okay, I promise, I'll be good."

"Turn left."

"That isn't a stop where we have to make a decision." He turned left at the road she had indicated.

"Doesn't matter. I just changed the rules."

"You get to do that?"

"All day long because you're driving and I'm directing. Turn right."

He did and groaned.

"I told you, no noises." She looked longingly at the steak house on her side of the car. "The parking lot is full."

"We probably would have waited a good forty-five minutes to get seated," he admitted.

"We can't have that then, can we? Left."

He followed her directions for the next few minutes. Approaching another road up ahead that he really didn't want her to take, he pointed out her window. "Look at that moose!"

The look she gave him could only be described as *the mom look*. "Take the next left. A moose? Here? You're funny."

He turned. A minute later, they drove past a sign announcing a township. Up ahead at the stop sign there was a gas station on one side advertising sandwiches and a hot dog stand on the other side of the road.

"Do I get to choose?" he pleaded.

"Not on your life, Counselor. We're having hot dogs."

"Dogs it is," he conceded, turning into the dirt parking lot that had space for about five cars. Theirs was the only one. He couldn't see if there was a car in the back or not. He hoped the place was closed.

She opened her door, saying, "Last one in is a rotten egg."

He got out, hoping the front door was locked. She disappeared inside. Just his dumb luck. He hated hot dogs. Okay, they weren't his favorite. Maybe there'd be another offering.

Inside, a quick look at the menu said nope. It was hot dogs or bratwursts. Brats were disgusting, in his opinion. At least he could smother a hot dog with condiments.

"Once they had their food and were seated, he asked," Do you still count this date as failure?

"Technically, yes." Just before he could say anything, she added. "And, that assessment would hold up in court because you made a date, enticing me with a specific rib, which legalese-wise would be a spoken contract. Not fulfilling that contract would be a breach of contract."

"I'm impressed."

"I was pre-law to make my parents happy, but when they saw I was making more money in restoring and repairing motors, they stopped insisting." She grinned back at him. "Failure. This is strike two."

*****

JoJo leaned back in her seat, her hunger gone. The meal was satisfactory. Not horrible, not great. Just okay. Joe wrapped his lips around his soda straw and sucked up the last of his drink. An image of his lips on hers sent goosebumps up and down her arms.

She liked how he didn't get upset or uptight at the change of their plans for these two dates. Not only handsome and cute, but smart looking, confident, and nice. A rare combination. Yet, she sensed in him a vulnerability at the same time. "Tell me about your parents."

Joe set down his drink. He looked surprised at the question.

"Surely, people ask you personal questions," she added.

"It's been a while."

"Your friends said you don't date much."

"Usually, just dinner dates with people I already know. People I've grown up with. No one special. Not that I can say some aren't hoping."

"Tough being a local bachelor?"

He laughed.

"Broken a few hearts, have you?"

"Can't break something that hasn't started."

"True. So, what about your parents, your family?" she asked.

"I'm the oldest—"

"Driven."

Joe laughed. "I suppose. I bought the family house when Mom and Dad wanted to move closer to where my sisters and their kids live. In Annapolis. Both of my brothers-in-law are in the military."

"Lifers?"

He nodded. "This way, whenever they all want to come home for a holiday, there's room enough for them."

"The house is that big."

"Too big just for me. I'd prefer something smaller." He shrugged. "But it works. It helps that someone comes in and cleans for me. I never was good with a vacuum."

"Big kitchen?"

"That's where I really live."

"You cook?"

"Love to, especially in trying out new recipes and making bread."

She raised her eyebrows in surprise. "That I would never have guessed."

"There's something peaceful and relaxing about kneading all your worries into a dough."

"You don't look like the worrying kind."

"With two younger sisters, always was." He chuckled. "I even got some of the guys—my friends—watching out for them. The girls hated it. As a result, neither dated much until they went to college. What about you? Any siblings who watched out for you?"

"A few," she laughed. "I have three older and two younger brothers. Our two sisters are the babies of the family and completely spoiled."

Joe whistled. "Eight kids and you're in the middle. Did you feel lost in the crowd?"

"Yes and no. With so many kids, I never asked for much. I guess I didn't feel comfortable ever asking for anything either. I hung out with my older brothers, always following them. It's how I learned about motors. I was their go-for girl." She noticed his frown.

"Go for the wrench. Go for a screwdriver," she explained. "As long as I was useful to them, they let me stay. I always thought it a great compliment when they said I didn't talk much."

"You don't. I bet, though, the more comfortable you get, the more you talk."

"Yeah. Actually, I haven't talked like this outside of my family and Gabby and Charli. We hang out together quite a bit. When we're all in town together, that is. Usually that's at Christmas. In between our get-togethers, we do group video chats."

As he talked, JoJo liked how his face lit up when speaking about his family. Charli, William, and Clint were right. He *was* a good man, the likes of which she hadn't dated in a long time. The last few dates she'd been on, they'd always talk about themselves—their plans, their future, their boy toys. Not one of them ever asked any questions. Second dates never happened. The warning flags were there from the beginning.

Did it really matter that so far their two dates had turned disastrous? "Is there any place to do some fishing around here?" she asked. "Away from the lake, that is? Somewhere quieter?"

"Without the skiers and pontoons?"

"Exactly."

"There's a stream that has a park with picnic tables."

"No picnic tables. That means people. No, some place where people wouldn't be disturbing the fish."

"Well, there's a place upstream—I think that

comes from a deep spring—where William and I used to fish when we were boys—"

"You've not been back since?"

"No. Haven't had time. Can't say that my interest ever really was in fishing. Just did it a couple times. Do you fish regularly?"

"No, not really. Just an idea. How about a picnic there instead?"

"I'd recommend lunch over dinner," Joe said. "Fewer mosquitos, but they'll be plentiful as it is. You'll want repellant."

"Noted."

"So, are we counting this as date three?"

She nodded. "But you know what that means, right?"

"We're going to have a good time."

She liked his positive attitude. Actually, she was going to say *three strikes and...* "We can only hope," she said, instead. Actually, despite the bird poo and the interrupted sumptuous dinner, they had rolled with the sudden changes quite well. Question was, did he think so? "But, it'll have to be the day after tomorrow. I've got parts arriving first thing tomorrow morning and I need to spend the day with the car."

"Need any help?"

"You offering?"

"Maybe."

"So, you're telling me you know what a fuel injector is?"

Joe swallowed, then grinned weakly. "Maybe."

"I don't pander to pretenders."

"If at any time I'm not performing to your tough standards, you can ask me to leave."

"You good with making or fetching ice tea?"

"They don't call me Speedy Joe for nothing!"

She threw back her head and laughed.

He grinned, picking up his ice tea.

She reached for her ice tea and held it out to him. He clinked his glass against hers.

"Tomorrow," she said.

*****

He drove home after dropping her off, glad that she wasn't giving up on him. Yet.

Tomorrow had to be perfect. Even beyond his own expectations. *You may be good in the courtroom, but you're asking for trouble on this one, Buddy.*

He blinked, mentally brushing away the naysaying voice.

No, he had to believe this could work because they both appeared able to go with the flow, to deal with whatever was handed to them.

To his way of thinking, they had similar likes despite the disasters.

*****

Day 8

JoJo stood in the shower after a long day, reflecting on how she'd never spent a day like she had today, never getting as much done either. And yet, she'd had company the entire time.

Joe, true to his word, was there first thing in the morning, with her favorite coffee—he had noticed what she ordered!— remaining the entire day being her *go guy*. She'd lost track of how many times she had him go for a part or a tool, which ultimately saved her time. Lots of time.

They spent the day laughing, telling stories, jokes, sharing likes and dislikes about books, movies, politics, and people, particularly in relationships. And, their discussion felt carefree, without strings of any kind attached. Plus, he'd kept her supplied in iced tea.

Then, late in the day, he had disappeared without saying a word. She couldn't believe he'd left without saying goodbye. But, he hadn't. He'd simply gone to the diner and came back with BLT sandwiches, chips, and peach cobbler for dessert. They'd worked another few hours, late into the evening before she called it a day.

She was not only surprised that he'd hung in there asking questions and learning as she went along, but never appeared bored or eager to leave. If anything, she bet he would have stayed longer if she had.

The biggest surprise came when they were done, and he walked her to her car. He'd taken her face in his hands and kissed her. Not long, not sensual, but strong and thorough. And then, as he pulled away, he thanked her for a wonderful day, wishing her a wonderful rest of her evening.

He turned, got into his car, waved as he backed up into the turnaround, then drove off, leaving her standing there watching him drive away. She waved a second time, just in case he was looking in his rearview mirror.

He was. He waved back.

And then, he turned onto the road and was gone.

She wanted him back.

She wanted another kiss.

Oh, you're in such trouble, she had thought then and was thinking it again as she stood under the stream of water and rinsed the soap out of her hair and off her body before turning the spigots off.

There was no way she could afford to have a long-distance relationship, compounded with being on the road more than she was at home. He'd never move away from Laurel Ridge, and she couldn't blame him. It was a lovely community. If only her business could support being three hours away from the circuits where her clients were stationed.

She stepped out of the shower, grabbing a towel. *Just enjoy the moment, the next few days. Don't think beyond that,* she told herself. *Stay in the moment.*

*****

Day 9

Even though she had accomplished nearly two days' worth of work the day before, JoJo was determined to do as much as she could this morning, before her afternoon picnic date with Joe later on.

If she got the work done here sooner than expected, she could return to Atlanta with some down time where she could run some long over-due errands and cross off some of those to-dos on her list.

Wiping and drying a part that had been soaking overnight, she heard a car pulling up to the garage.

William.

A glance at the clock told her he was probably on his way to work. Her instincts told her he was probably here to talk about Charli.

Not even giving him a chance to start a conversation, she said, "She's coming back."

He stopped in his tracks, surprised. "You mean she's not gone for good?"

She smiled. "You've got it bad."

"I do. I love her."

Her smiled widened into a grin. "She doesn't love easy, you know."

"I'm beginning to realize." He paused, then asked. "How do you know she's coming back?"

"She wants to see how the car's coming along." She stuck her hand out, indicating the car. JoJo knew Charli was coming back to see William more than the car even if she wasn't saying so explicitly. The car was an excuse. "She left because she had a photo job in Atlanta for the next few days."

"She never said."

"She rarely does," JoJo answered. "She keeps everything a secret. It's her nature. Can you blame her?"

"You know?"

"Sure, both Gabby and I know that she can't read. Though she doesn't know that we know. We've always been waiting for her to tell us." JoJo moved so she was standing in front of William and wrapped her fingers around his upper arms. "I know this is going to sound hard, but if you really love her, you've got to let her go." She let him go to emphasize her words, almost pushing him away. "If the two of you are meant to be, she'll come back to you."

William stared at her, troubled.

JoJo continued. "I know it sounds contrary, but it's like trying to love a puppy. You can't hold it for long. It'll wiggle, wanting to be free. But, it'll always come back. To love, knowing where it's free to love."

William cheered slightly. "Yeah, but puppies are stupidly loyal to anyone who gives them love."

"Humans are kind of the same way. Especially when they know who really loves them and who doesn't."

"Except for the bastards who take advantage of that love."

JoJo nodded. "There is that."

"Is there anyone anywhere who hasn't been hurt in loving someone?" He looked at his watch. "I've gotta go." He gave her a quick hug. "Thanks for your help."

"I didn't do anything."

"Yeah, you did. You were her friend."

*****

"How's this spot?" Joe asked. He'd chosen this spot carefully. The spring was close by and this was a flat area that had more sand than dirt and grass. It was as close to being on a beach without actually being on a beach.

"Too much sun," JoJo replied.

"You're the one with the big hat."

"But it's way too hot to be sitting out in the sun."

She pointed to a live oak some yards away from them, and where one huge branch stretched out over the water. "There under the tree," she pointed.

He followed her to her desired location, set the basket down, and pulled a blanket out of the basket. He shook it open, letting it float to the ground, then picked up the basket and placed it on one corner of the blanket. "I'm starving."

"Me too." Kicking off her shoes, she stepped onto the blanket, dropped to her knees, and pulled some containers out of the basket. "This looks like diner food."

He kicked off his shoes, too, joining her. "That means you've gotten takeout if you can recognize its containers."

"Guilty as charged."

With the food between them, they stretched out their legs, their feet at the edge of the blanket, conversing and eating.

"Ow!" JoJo exclaimed, slapping at her feet. Quickly, there were ants everywhere, covering their feet way too fast.

"Fire ants!" Joe jumped up, swiping at the ants, his foot stepping off the blanket and sliding under the blanket's edge. Stings of pain. He jumped, kicking the blanket corner back at the same time. Hundreds of ants swarmed the ground, moving rapidly onto the blanket.

He grabbed JoJo, pulling her up, slapping ants away from his feet and hers, as much as he could, while she was slapping them away, too.

They were losing the battle.

"The water," Joe yelled. "Get in the water."

They both ran into the water. "Don't go too far," he said. "There's a drop—"

She jumped and disappeared from sight.

He dove under, looking for her. She wasn't too far away and was okay.

He surfaced. She surfaced before him but had to turn around to see him.

She started laughing. She couldn't help it. The situation *was* funny. Their whole time together, so far, was one comical event after another.

And, a surprise. Actually, she was enjoying this. Nothing was predictable at this point. Wasn't that why she liked her job? Because each week, sometimes each day differed from the previous?

"I think I lost my hat. I had it on when I jumped in."

"It's right here." He raised a hand above the water. A soggy, droopy hat was in his hand. "I saw you jump in and it immediately starting floating away, so I grabbed it when I jumped in."

"Thank you. Though, it's probably ruined."

"Nah. Just dry it on a head form—a bowl—and it'll dry decently. If you can fix a water ruined motor, surely, I can fix a water-ruined hat."

"Deal! So, how do we get out of here?" she asked, indicating the drop off they jumped from that wasn't an option.

"Just have to move past this enormous tree."

Swimming around the limb, JoJo saw a natural

path at the water's edge. If not people, animals had formed that path.

Joe climbed out ahead of her, took a step, turned, and extended his hand as she started to climb out. She took it, appreciating that he was pulling her up and out more easily than she could under own power.

With a final tug, her hand still in his, she stood in front of him, toe to toe. She looked up, his face shadowed with the sun behind him. His eyes, though, were bright, scanning her face, his gaze settling on her lips.

She tilted her head up.

He lowered his head.

The kiss was everything she had imagined and more. Soft, yet firm. Long, but not too long. And, as he lifted his head a bit, she wanted more. She stood on tiptoes, her hands wrapped around his biceps. She met his desire with hers. This time the kiss was thorough and breath-taking.

Minutes later, back to their blanket, they discovered ants all over the food. Carefully shaking everything out and dumping the edible food on the ground for ants and any other creature that might come by, they put everything into the trunk of the car. Just in case they missed an ant or two.

Joe broke into her thoughts with, "How about a home-cooked meal at my place tomorrow?" he asked, as they turned onto the main road.

"Is this another mulligan?"

"No, the restaurant was a mulligan. Golfers are only allowed one mulligan and on the first tee."

"You could have made anything up. I wouldn't have known the difference."

"Yes, but you would have found out, and I don't want to lie to you about anything."

"Anything?"

"Ahhhhh, yes."

"Are you a good cook?"

"Fair to middlin'."

She laughed. "Okay, I'm good with that. Considering I'm not anywhere near fair to middlin'."

"Oh, dear, that doesn't bode well for our future."

"*Our* future?"

"Well, you do like me, don't you?"

"Yes."

"But? I hear a *but* in there."

"We live so far apart."

"Lots of people do long distance."

"Have you?"

"Not yet. Have you?"

"Once and it didn't go well."

"How so?"

"He expected me to do most of the traveling."

"Stupid man."

JoJo stared at him. Was he being cute? As in funny or was he being sincere? Like her, he used sarcasm frequently. "I can't do dinner tomorrow."

Disappointment flitted across his face, then was gone.

"How about the day after?" she offered.

He grinned like Alice's Cheshire cat. "You won't be disappointed."

"Promises, promises." Actually, she hoped this next date would exceed her expectations. She was good with change and events going bad, but not *every date.* After a while, this relentless string of bad dates could be—be what? Exhausting? *Not really. You're looking for excuses, Girlfriend!*

*****

Day 11

JoJo pulled up to Joe's house and got out of her truck. She smoothed down her dress. She liked wearing them when not working. Dresses were freeing compared to the coveralls she had to wear because of the grease and occasional spark. It'd been especially hot in the garage yesterday and today. Plus, this was her last clean outfit. That or rummaging through dirty clothes for the cleanest pair of shorts. She needed to do some laundry.

Smelling smoke, she looked up. Smoke billowed from behind the house where she imagined the kitchen faced the backyard.

She rounded the house, racing up the deck's steps, smoke rising from something Joe was tossing out onto the lawn.

She reached his side and looked over the rail at the large roasting pan that was still flaming and smoking badly. He grabbed the bucket of water that sat next to his unused grill, emptying its contents over the pan. It sizzled and smoked some more, but the flames were gone.

"Dinner, I take it."

They both kept staring at the pan, but a peek at

Joe revealed his disappointment.

"Yup," he replied.

"I hope that was the middlin' part."

"Not even the fair part."

She started laughing.

He put a mitted hand on his hip and stared at her.

"I'm sorry," she choked out. "It really isn't funny." She burst out laughing some more. "But, it is. You appear okay—"

"I am."

"And, the kitchen?"

"I'm dubbing the oven Smokey. Nothing a major fan can't blow out of the room."

"How about I take you out to dinner?" she asked.

"But, I had asked you."

"You're going to reject an offer from a woman?"

"No, Ma'am."

"Smart boy."

"So, where are we going?" he asked.

At the same time, they both said, "The diner."

Joe laughed. "Let me set up the fan to blow the smoke out of the kitchen and I'll be right out. No need for you to come in and inhale Smokey's wrath."

JoJo went back to her truck, started it, and turned the air-conditioning on full blast. Standing outside even that short bit had wilted her.

She looked at the house. She had been looking forward to seeing his family's home. She wondered if she'd get another chance. Probably not.

Since she had finished the engine just before coming here, she expected she'd be leaving tomorrow morning after testing it for any final small tweaks—if needed. Rarely were they. After she handed the car back over to Clint, by noon she figured, she'd be on her way out of town.

It surprised her to feel disappointed at leaving this small community. She enjoyed the people who would drop by the garage to see how she was doing—Clint's friends and neighbors. Everyone had welcomed her as if she'd been a long-lost relative.

What was amazing now that she thought about it, she knew more people here than she did in her own apartment building back in Atlanta. Born and raised in Atlanta, she never thought much about how small was her circle of friends. Here—it was so different. Warm. Fun. Lots of sharing and laughter.

If only she could spend more time here. Or live here. But, that would be impossible. Her business—even if she spent a good deal of time traveling—was based in Atlanta.

She didn't like dwelling on things that didn't have clear-cut outcomes or things she couldn't control. To worry or dwell on it was wasted effort, wasted emotion. That's where focusing on motors helped her. She knew how to plan and work ahead on them. It was easy.

Joe burst out of the front door and scampered down the steps, heading for her truck car, looking at her, and grinning ear to ear.

Her heart exploded with joy. He was the perfect man for her. How could she possibly leave tomorrow?

You just will.

When he opened his door, she pasted a smile on her face. A second later, it was genuine as he slid in next to her and started fastening his seatbelt.

She would fully enjoy their time together and not think of the days to come without him. It was the only way she was going to survive. She could have her breakdown once she got home.

*****

Their dinner served, Joe announced, "You know this date doesn't really count. We need a mulligan."

"But, I thought you said the second date, the restaurant was a mulligan."

"Yeah, I did, but it was a ruined mulligan, so it doesn't count."

She chuckled. "Do you change the rules like this in the courtroom?"

"With Mason as judge? Not a chance."

"We're really just having a string of mulligans," she reminded him

"Is that so bad?"

No! she wanted to exclaim. Instead, she cocked her head, pretending to be deep in thought.

"Seriously?" he asked.

She told him the truth. That the car was finished and that she would be gone by tomorrow night.

His face said it all. He was crestfallen. True to his nature, though, the expression was fleeting. Not meant for her to see.

While they continued to converse, the rest of the meal lacked the merriment of previous meals.

When she dropped him off later, he pulled her to him and gave her a goodnight kiss, but it lacked the depth of his previous kiss.

It was over. They were just friends now.

She saw him watching her leave via her rearview mirror. He waved and she reciprocated likewise, then dropped her hand.

Sighing, she turned onto the road. *Well, that was that.*

*****

Once JoJo drove off and he went up the deck's steps to enter through the kitchen, Joe began wondering where she was with the car. She said it was finished, but was it?

Entering the house, he turned off the big fan. The room was clear.

He tossed his keys on the center island and pulled his cell phone out of his pocket. He pushed a button. Clint picked up on the second ring.

After a few minutes of usual chitchat, Joe got to the point. "Is JoJo finished with the engine?"

"She said earlier today that she expected to be. Why?"

"Any chance you can hire her to restore the entire car? Have her get it done in time that we can show it off for the big party you're going to hold in a few days."

"What party?" Clint asked.

"The one to celebrate the car being done for one thing," Joe said.

"And the other thing?

"I can't reveal anyone's secrets."

"Since when?" Clint asked.

"Since the fact I never revealed you were the one who egged Mr. Smith's—"

"Okay, okay. Point made. Sure, I can ask her. Does that mean regardless of her response, we're still holding a party?"

"We are," Joe confirmed. "And, you're going to make sure she says yes. I don't care how you do it. Party's taking place in three days. All you're doing is providing the yard. As to JoJo, I'll pay—"

"You're not paying for my car's restoration. I can foot the bill. I was going to hire the rest done anyway."

"Good man. Just don't tell her I had anything to do with her staying. She can't know." Joe didn't want JoJo knowing that Clint's full restoration request was his idea.

"What are you up to?"

"If things go like I hope, you'll find out soon enough," Joe said. "Of course, if they go badly, you'll find that out soon enough, too." A few minutes later, with a plan in mind and Clint giving him some additional ideas without knowing it, Joe hung up the phone.

He'd never put himself out there like this. Not outside of the courtroom, that is. In court he was Superman. Outside of court, he was Clark Kent.

Until now.

*****

Day 12

JoJo was at the garage early. She had tossed and turned all night and that was after she had done laundry, plus cleaned everything thoroughly. She'd gotten up this morning determined to test the car one final time and then leave Laurel Ridge quickly.

She spent the morning fine tuning the motor, taking longer than she would have liked. As a result, she decided to do her final test after lunch, knowing if it didn't run right away, that she'd skip lunch to work on it, and as hot as it was outside, she needed an air-conditioned break along with the food.

An hour and a half later, she stood at the side of the car, grinning. It had started immediately and purred like a kitten.

Clint walked into the garage with two tall glasses of sweet tea and handed her one. "You got it working!"

She took the glass and clinked it with his. "Sure did."

Clint laughed. "In record time. I'm impressed." She updated him on what she'd done.

"I know I asked you before and you said, no," Clint said, "but I have to ask again. Is there any chance you can finish restoring the rest of the car? There's no good restoration service in this part of the state. We need one badly."

"Because so many of the classic car clubs are in the northern part of the state," she stated.

He nodded. "Any chance?"

"The seats are gone. Any chance they're getting reupholstered?"

"Actually, they're finished. They texted me last night."

"That's great. With the inside stripped, it would be easy to treat, prep, and paint, both inside and out. It wouldn't take long. It's really be about the details of a radio—"

"Ordered."

"The convertible covering—"

"Should be here later today, actually."

"—and knobs, handles, lights, trim, etc. Thankfully, cars were relatively simple back then. Few electronics. Of course, there'd be no air-conditioning."

"Don't need it. Don't want it."

"Actually, if you've already got everything already ordered or repaired, it's just about the finish and installing the various pieces and parts."

"Could it be done for a showing by the weekend?"

JoJo thought for a minute. "It might be missing some details still, but most of it would be done. Would that be good enough for people to see it?"

"Yes. I'm planning a party for this weekend, three days from now. Would you be able to stay the week? Join the party?"

"You're in luck," she replied, grinning. "The job that was scheduled following this one got canceled just minutes before you arrived. It'd be like a vacation staying here instead. And, having met a good number of your friends, I'd enjoy being here for the party." Actually, she was happy that she was staying. She could see Joe a few more times.

"If you want, you can move into the guest cottage. It's empty." JoJo had remained in the condo after Charli had left and William didn't see a problem with it, but now she'd enjoy being in the cottage. While she had enjoyed the peace and quiet at the condo compared to the constant comings and goings of people here at Clint's, she was ready for a change. His house appeared to be a gathering place for his friends. She enjoyed their company.

She and Gabby could share the cottage easily enough. "When Gabby gets here—"

"She won't be coming. I went up to the Tennessee balloon festival, deciding to take your advice, but it appears she has a partner, one that's a perfect fit for her."

What he was saying didn't make sense at all. "What—"

Clint's cell phone rang. He pulled it from his back pocket, looked at the screen, and said, "Excuse me. I need to take this." He stepped away, stopping just inside the garage, standing in the shade, and spoke a few one-syllable responses to whomever he was talking to and hung up.

Spinning around, he said, "I've got to go. Needed down at Joe's office to sign some papers. Don't hesitate to call if you need anything from town. I'll be back in a few hours."

JoJo frowned. Something wasn't right. She went to her cell phone that sat on the bench, picked it up, and speed dialed Gabby.

*****

Hours later and a long day of concentrated dirty work, she went to the condo, showered, donned a pair of capri pants and a sleeveless top that didn't cling to her, packed her belongings to move into the cottage, and went to the garage to inspect the car. She couldn't stay away now that she was nearly finished, even though she was done working for the day.

Earlier, she'd been able to sand both the inside and out and got a primer coat on both earlier once it was agreed that she'd be refinishing the entire car.

Clint had rounded up some fans for her, so she could set them around the car, enabling them to dry the primer faster in the heat.

Standing just outside the big overhead doors, she looked to the west. The sun was about an hour away from setting. The night was still young. So many choices. Should she grab a book and go to the diner and order lemonade and pie? Go to the ice cream stand nearby? Or go to one of the parks and enjoy the scenery under trees that shaded the benches by day?

Clint's slider door sounded. He was heading her way. In a hurry, too.

"JoJo! I'm so glad you're here. Can you do me a favor?"

"Sure, anything."

"Can you retrieve some papers for me? One of my grad students is on his way here for the papers and to get some help. He's almost here, in fact. I was going to go get the papers and be back before he got here, but—"

"Where are the papers?"

"Joe's house." His phone rang. He looked at it and said, "Sorry," then started walking away from her. But then, he turned around, covered the phone, and mouthed, "Can you do it?"

She nodded.

He gave her a thumbs up, smiled, and returned to his phone call.

The last place she had expected to be tonight. But wait. This gave her the excuse she needed to go see him. To tell him she'd be in town a few more days.

But seriously, she countered, as much as she wanted to see him, what's a few more days going to do? *It's not like you won't be saying goodbye in the end. Listen to you! Just go with the flow. Live in the moment.*

Isn't that what she'd always done? All of her life, in fact? Being stuck in the middle of a large family, she'd often felt invisible. It's how she learned to go with the flow and not cause any problems.

Though, she hadn't gone with the flow when it came to her career. Well, she had gone along in the beginning, but in the end, she got to make her own choices and she'd been making them ever since. At the same time, though, there hadn't been anyone else involved.

Was she willing to give up her autonomy? Her ability to make decisions without consulting anyone else? No matter how much she was attracted to Joe, he was a lawyer, someone who made decisions, giving sound advice to clients. Why was she bringing him into her pictured thoughts? It wasn't like they were a couple. She'd only met him seven days ago!

This whole scenario of them even being a couple was irrational.

Joe rattled her senses. She couldn't remember how long it'd been since being this attracted to a man. High school crushes, yes, but love?

"Fairy tales," she said aloud as she went to her truck. "Just stories. Nothing but stories." Fairy tale endings happened to other people. Not her.

But, wait a minute. Wasn't she in control of her future? Couldn't she manifest and manufacture her fairy tale ending if she wanted?

Of course she could.

She'd have to speak up, though. Did she have the courage to do it?

But, what about your business? Nothing like being on the proverbial fence.

A long time ago, she'd told herself that she would never let a relationship get in the way of her career. Was it possible to have both? If not, then sitting on a fence wasn't necessary. She'd simply enjoy their time together without any expectations, return to Atlanta, and work toward her goal of owning a shop.

*****

JoJo pulled into Joe's driveway. His car was in the garage with the door up. Her nervousness meter shot up. As she stepped out of the car, she noticed a small woods between his house and his closest neighbor. On the other side, was a service road, from all appearances. To the fields behind the houses, apparently.

Somehow, she'd failed to see any of these things

the other day. *Blame it on your nerves.*

She knocked on the door, took a deep breath in and blew it out. The door was open, but he didn't answer. She called to him through the screen door. Silence.

She turned around and went to the edge of the porch.

Joe came from around behind the garage. Seeing her, he stopped. She stepped down and walked toward him. He waited for her to reach him.

She couldn't look away. He looked so good! What was she going to say? Only ten feet away, she said, "I came for the papers that Clint wanted." She stopped in front of him.

He smiled, then grinned mischievously. "Uh, actually, there aren't any papers." She put a hand to her eyes as the last rays of the sun blocked her vision.

"What?"

And then, the rays were gone. She dropped her arm, and Joe grabbed her hand. "Come with me."

She went obediently. "I don't understand—"

They were behind the garage now, well into the yard. She was speechless. Because she'd been so focused on the smoke, fire, and Joe's disappointment that she hadn't even looked at the yard the other day.

The most beautiful flower garden she'd ever seen bordered a lush green patch of lawn. A huge shade tree resided in the back corner with lots of flowering groundcover around it.

In the middle of the shaded grass were a couple of fold-out camp chairs, with screw-top plastic cups with a straw in each of the chair's beverage holder. Had to be ice tea. And, on one side of the chairs was a small folding table and a projector. Projector? She saw a cord running from it to the garage. Light was coming out of the projector, too.

She walked a few steps into the yard, getting a bit of distance from the garage. The garage wall was a screen for the projector! "What is the world—"

"Surprise! It's my secret garden—well, my mother's, actually. She started it, but I became a garden enthusiast with her help."

JoJo looked past Joe and saw birdhouses hanging from different trees. More bird feeders hung from different shepherd hooks stationed in front of ground-floor windows. Birds were busy at the feeders, oblivious to the two of them. "You're a bird watcher?"

"Yes." He looked a bit sheepish.

"I am, too. Though I never have this kind of activity. Who made the birdhouses? They don't look manufactured."

"I did. I build them and give them away."

JoJo took that last step so she was standing toe-to-toe with him. Wrapping her arms around his torso, her hands on his back, she arched her neck, looking up at him. Surprise, then delight flittered across his face. He bent down. The kiss was warm and tender. And long. His arms wrapped around her, bringing her even closer.

She was the first to break the lip lock, but she didn't move far.

"Was that because of the birds?" he asked.

"What if I said yes?"

In answer, he kissed her again. If the first kiss was thorough, this one was even more so. His tongue teased at her lip. She groaned. She kissed him back even harder until he groaned.

This time, he was the one who disengaged. "Wow."

His expression said, *I'm mulling something over again*. What was he thinking?

"Ready for a movie?" he asked.

"A movie, too?"

"One of your favorites."

"How would—"

"Reconnaissance. I'm good at it."

"Who told on me?"

"Can't say. It's a mystery."

"*Shakespeare in Love*?!" She grinned at his clue. Then clapped when he nodded. "I like what you've done here. Setting this up for me." She bit her lip, debating.

Should she, or shouldn't she?

"Go ahead and say it," he said.

She looked at him, surprised.

"Your expression looks like how I imagine mine looks when I'm thinking."

She laughed. "You're right." She took a deep breath. Why not? The worst that could happen is that it wouldn't happen. But, if it did—"Okay, here goes. I'm toying with the idea of moving my business here to Laurel Ridge. Well, not moving actually, since I run it out of my truck—"

"How'd about a building that could house cars you're working on?"

"A dream actually, but to build my dream shop would be—"

"Easy to do." He pointed to the land behind him. A large barn with a small fenced-in pasture was immediately behind his yard. "My sisters used to have horses and would board others. Since they've been gone, the building's been empty. We could easily turn it into a restoration/repair shop."

He'd just given her the ability to have customers bring their cars to her rather than her always having to go to the cars. The barn would have to undergo a major restoration, but she was willing to do the work, to at least give it a try.

"That was too easy."

"Well, I can't guarantee every decision will be easy, but—"

"I need some cheap labor to get a car—a VW—ready for review. Wanna—?"

"For you? Always."

She grinned as he moved in for a kiss.

Who said she couldn't have her fairy tale?

*****

Day 15

Clint surveyed the yard. Lots of friends on the lawn, sharing stories, eating, and drinking. In particular, he observed his close circle of friends and Gabby.

Long ago high school sweethearts broken up,

Mason and Shelley's arms were wrapped around each other as they stood talking with firefighter Rhett and relator Eddie. Cutter, always with a story, was laughing at something either game warden Annie or psychic balloonist Gabby had just said. Clint smiled seeing Gabby laughing and enjoying herself. He wondered if he'd be able to surprise her tonight.

Joe joined him. He followed Clint's gaze, not surprised he was focused on Gabby. "Think she has any idea—?"

"Don't even think it. You know how she can pick up on our thoughts."

"You do realize that you'll never have another secret. Ever. Right?"

"I don't care. I'm an open book."

Joe laughed. "You? The cliched professor with his nose in the books."

"Not anymore."

Joe laughed again.

"Seriously," Clint said. "I'm changing. I want to change. Don't tell me that JoJo hasn't had any influence on you. I've never ever seen you in a garage getting your hands dirty until these last few days."

"She needed help."

"Uh-huh, call it what you want. We all know—"

"That we've all been getting whipped these last couple weeks. Every single one of us: Cutter, Rhett, Mason, Jefferson, William, you, me—"

"Hard to believe," Clint said, "how we started as nine classmates, ten best friends with Rhett added—single best friends—and over the last fifteen days, we're now seven couples with four more added to our group."

"Think William's reveal of how the car disappeared and your surprise are going to be the only ones?" Joe asked.

Clint winked at him. "Knowing these guys—?"

"Affirmative," Joe injected.

"Not to mention I suspect you have something to announce, too."

"Who? Me?" Joe laughed. He raised his glass to Clint, who clinked it with his. Together they drank.

JoJo came out of the closed-up garage, giving Clint a thumbs up.

"It's time," Clint said.

Joe clapped him on the back and walked back toward the crowd.

Clint watched as the girls—Charli and Gabby—grabbed JoJo and pulled her into the crowd.

Clint escaped into the garage, raised one door, got into the Bug, turned the ignition, and backed the restored VW out of the garage. Turning it toward the party, he drove it on the lawn so that it was on full display. A cheer arose.

By the time he was out of the car, they had surrounded it. He grinned and held up his hands to quiet the crowd.

"I know y'all have questions," he announced. "And, we'll answer them, but first I want to thank JoJo Wheeler for the remarkable job she did in restoring this little beauty. William, where are you?"

From the back of the crowd, a hand shot up.

Clint stretched his neck looking for him. "Sure you don't want this beauty back now?"

"Never!" William shouted. "Besides, you'd charge me an arm and a leg for it."

Everyone laughed.

"I understand there are a lot of announcements," Clint said. "Joe, I'm turning it over to you."

Joe faced his friends. "Mason, you're first!"

Mason grabbed Shelley's hand, raising their arms, fingers intertwined. "We got married this morning!"

"About time," someone cheered.

"Where'd you get hitched?" Cutter asked.

Shelley replied, "Why at the courthouse, of course!"

"And, we leave for Hawaii later tonight," Mason added. "You're all invited to our wedding party when we get back."

Clint asked, "Who stood up for you?"

"Joe for me and Connie for Shelley," Mason replied.

After the hugs and congratulations were over, Joe asked, "Who's next?"

Eddie spoke up. "I eloped yesterday."

What? and *Who*? were asked by many, and everyone had surprised looks on their face.

Mason said, "I married them yesterday. Another courthouse wedding. May I introduce Mr. & Mrs. Aaron Rhett Sinclair Renoux." Rhett joined Eddie, gave her a kiss, then held their clasped hands up in the air.

Repeated gasps of surprise and delight arose.

Eddie grinned. "As Rhett helped me repair Grandma's house after the fire, we decided we wanted to flip houses together—"

Rhett added, "And, we're going to the east coast for a tour of homes tomorrow."

"Just for some ideas, right?" asked Shelley.

Rhett winked. "Exactly."

Everyone laughed.

"Speaking of new businesses," Cutter said. "Annie and I want to invite you to our week-long open house at our bait shop. We renovated the old store by Whippoorwill Lake."

"Thanks for making that sale happen, Eddie," Annie said.

Cutter reached for Annie, pulling her so she stood in front of him, pulled something from his back pocket, and got down on one knee.

"About time!" someone yelled.

Someone else said, "Go, Cutter."

Annie's hands flew to her face, her fingers covering her opened mouth of surprise, her eyes wide.

"You know you have my heart. Always have," Cutter said, opening a ring box. "Will you marry me, Annie?"

With tears in her eyes, she nodded.

Everyone roared with approval.

Cutter rose, took hold of Annie's left hand, and slid the ring on her finger. She wrapped both arms around his neck and they kissed.

When they broke apart, Eddie and Shelley

grabbed Annie, hugging their friend.

Cutter said, "Anyone dare to follow that?"

"Me!" Gabby said.

Clint looked at her, along with everyone else. "Do you know something I don't?" he asked. Everyone laughed.

Gabby nodded. "I see a wedding in your future." She closed the distance between them.

"Well, naturally," he replied with a grin on his face. "Now, that Cutter has finally obtained his dream girl and proposed to Annie—"

She stopped in front of him, looking up. "No, Silly. Yours." Before he could say anything, she kissed him, wrapping her arms around his neck.

William, who stood next to Clint, clapped him on the back. "About time you got your head out of the ground!"

Gabby and Clint parted.

"But, I wanted to be the one to propose," Clint said.

Everyone laughed again.

Gabby nodded her head. "When you're ready. But, you know you'll never be able to surprise me."

"I'll give it a try," he said, getting down on one knee. "Does now work?"

Gabby laughed. "I didn't see *that* happening tonight."

"That's because I don't have a ring. I knew buying one, you'd pick up on it."

"We can fix that later," she said, welcoming his kiss and hug.

Jefferson spoke up. "Well, I know some of you are aware of the corporation that Joe, Rhett, William, Clint, and I formed. We're building a manufacturing plant for solar panels and we're going to create a solar and wind power station. Laurel Ridge is going green."

A cheer arose.

Jefferson pulled Madison toward him, tuckering her under his arm. "And, Madison here is going to be the plant's contractor, then manager, *and* she's going to manage the corporation's operation."

Another cheer.

Madison said, "And, we're engaged!" She lifted her left hand, revealing her ring. "It's going to be a fall wedding."

The couple received lots of hugs and congratulations.

"What about you, William?" Cutter asked.

"I can answer for him," Charli announced. "What most of you don't know is that I can't read."

Silence. Surprised looks.

She smiled. "This man," she said, giving him a kiss on the cheek, "is going to me help me change that. We're dating!"

Cheers.

He looked down at her, surprised. "We are?"

Laughter from the others.

She grabbed his hand, entwining her fingers with his. "We are. I'm here to stay."

Gabby exclaimed. "I knew it! But, I couldn't figure why I wasn't get a reading."

William laughed, "And let's keep it that way. I'm

not sure I like y'all knowing everything before I do!"

Joe said, "That makes up for the secrecy of this car that you kept all these years."

"That you kept with me," William added.

Surprised expressions all around.

"I guess it's time to tell the truth about this car," William said, glancing at it. "I really did hate the color."

Laughter.

William continued. "I hadn't sold it like I said, nor did I drive it into the lake."

"Who did?" someone asked.

"Remember Barb from our class—" William started.

"The cute little blond—"

"Cheerleader—"

"Yes, her." William paused. He had everyone's attention. "The night of our graduation party, someone assaulted her—"

Gasps and mutterings of *scumbag, who was it,* and *was she okay*?

William held up his hand. They quieted. "She was okay, though terribly upset. She got away by kneeing him—"

"Good for her—"

"And, I offered to drive her home," he continued. "She wouldn't let me, but she let me give her the keys to the car, which I was to pick up the next morning."

"She lived down that road."

"She drove it into the lake?"

William nodded. "It was an accident, and she

called me right away. We—Joe and I told her to go home when we learned she didn't have her license with her. Plus, we'd all been drinking and being underage... well, that's how Joe became my lawyer that night. He was advising me."

Laughter and mutterings of Joe's take-charge action.

Joe told the story from there, providing lots of details, ending with, "And, that's how Clint became the new owner."

Everyone applauded, chattering at once.

JoJo held up her hands. Everyone quieted. "I have one last announcement. I'm bringing my business to Laurel Ridge. We're going to renovate Joe's barn from housing horses to housing cars—"

"And until it's ready, you can use my garage," Clint offered.

"I'll take you up on it!" she said to Clint, and then to the group. "But, my real announcement is this—" She turned to Joe, the noise fading around her as she concentrated on him. "I want the fairy tale. You're my person—"

"As you are mine," he said, grabbing her left hand. "Will you continue to go on bad dates with me for the rest of your life?"

She nodded, and he placed a stainless-steel spring washer on her ring finger.

"I love you," he said.

"I love you more," she replied.

Cast of Characters

12 years after high school graduation

LEGEND
(N) - Native to Laurel Ridge
(T) - Transplant, living here from somewhere else
(V) - Visitor, here for a specific event or activity
(BF/name) - Best friends with
(F) - Friends with

Shattered Dreams #1 (SD#1) – High school sweethearts – reunion story

- Mason Baylock (N)– lawyer, now judge
- Shelley Willis (N) – waitress

Burning Desire #2 (BD#2) – A new love

- Aaron Rhett Sinclair Renoux (T) – firefighter, restores & flips houses on the side
- Edwina (Eddie) Taylor (N) – a realtor

Arrested Pleasures #3 (AP#3) – Dated once in high school; once was enough for Annie

- Cutter Logan (N) – sportsman
- Annie Martin (N, BF/Jefferson) –game warden

Buried Hearts #4 (BH#4) – A new love

- Clint Anderson (N) – archeology professor
- Gabriella (Gabby) King (V, BF/JoJo & Charli) – balloonist & psychic

Tangled Passions #5 (TP#5) – A new love

- Jefferson Jackson (N, BF/Annie) – state senator,

pecan orchard owner
- Madison Butler (V) – lobbyist

Reserved Yearnings #6 (RY#6) – A new love
- William Stuart (N, BF/Joe) – library director
- Charli Davidson (V, BF/Gabby & JoJo) – photo journalist

Sweet Cravings #7 (SC#7) – blind date disaster
- Joe Benton (N, BF/Wm) – lawyer
- Josephine (JoJo) Wheeler (V) – car restorer

The Car – a classic yellow Volkswagen Beetle

Minor Characters
- Connie (N) – waitress at the diner, all-knowing mother & friend to everyone
- Daryl (N) – (6'8") Annie Martin's boss, Director for the Dept. of Natural Resources, currently covering several counties; Daryl was a good friend to Annie's father who worked as a game warden, too.
- Grandpa (N) – Shelley's grandfather, Henry
- Hank Thompson (N) – school teacher, volunteer fireman
- Karen (N) – younger assistant, covers the phones and helps Sarah
- Maggie (N) – Joe's assistant, friends with Madison
- Reggie (N) – Fire House Captain
- Sarah (N) – assistant for 40 years at the Dept. of Natural Resources, soon to retire

Additional helpful relationship info

Classmates – 12 years ago

- All in one class - Mason, Dan, Clint, William, Shelley, Annie
- Class ahead of them - Jefferson & Joe

Love Interests in School

- Mason & Shelley
- Dan dated Annie once in high school (a disaster), has been in love with her ever since.

Good Friends

- Mason, Dan, Clint, Joe, William, Jefferson
- Joe and Mason (roommates in law school)
- Joe and Madison (after Mason left law school, no longer Joe's roommate)
- Madison and Maggie (friends in college)

Best Friends

- William & Joe (roomed together in college 2 years)
- Annie & Jefferson (grew up as neighbors)
- Gabby, Charli, & JoJo (live in Atlanta; Gabby & Jo are roommates)
- Shelley & Eddie (in junior high, then had a falling out just before high school)

Restoration Corporation Partners

- Mason
- Rhett
- Clint
- William
- Joe

ABOUT THE AUTHOR

Diana Stout, MFA, Ph.D. is an award-winning screenwriter, author, and former English professor whose writing led her into academic teaching. Her students would say, "She smiles when she talks about writing." Published in multiple genres, she enjoys helping other writers learn the craft.

When not writing, she enjoys reading, rainy days, movies, watching birds at her feeders, gardening, jigsaw puzzles, and visiting with family and friends.

To learn more about Diana

Website: sharpenedpencilsproductions.com
Facebook: facebook.com/drdianastout
Twitter: twitter.com/ScreenWryter13
Pinterest: pinterest.com/drdianastout
Instagram: instagram.com/authordianastout
BookBub: bookbub.com/authors/diana-stout
Goodreads: goodreads.com/user/show/43124185-diana-stout

Blogs

Behind the Scenes – life as a writer
dianastout.net
Into the Core – life as an intuitive
dianastout.com
Behind the Scenes with Diana Stout & Featured Guests
dianastout.org

Can You Help?

Are you able to leave a quick review?
Providing a review is the best way for a reader to thank the author.

Reviews can be short!

- I loved this book!
- I like this book!
- I couldn't put this book down!

It's not the length of a review that counts; it's the number of reviews that a book gets that counts.

THANK YOU!

Want to be informed and notified of new releases, classes, freebies, and other announcements? Click on the SUBSCRIBE button on her website at sharpenedpencilsproductions.com.

SUBSCRIBE NOW!

I promise your mailbox will love me.